S0-BOL-675

## *"If you spread any rumors to harm him—"*

"What?" Sanburne braced his arms at either side of her head. He was tall and surprisingly muscled; he had her pinned like a hare. "You will do what?"

"I will do something," she said unsteadily, "that you won't like much."

"Oh, yes?" His finger touched her cheek. "Will you look away very coldly when we meet?" His voice dropped. "Will you badmouth me, darling?" He drew his finger down to her mouth, tugging lightly at the seam. To her mortification, she tasted him—the tip of his finger, the salt of his skin.

Holding her eyes, he lifted his finger to his own tongue. "Lovely," he murmured. "Doesn't taste at all like a deceitful little spinster. Why, with a little coaxing, I might let you kiss me into forgiveness."

### Praise for *The Duke of Shadows*

"Fascinating, emotionally intense. . . . "
—*Romantic Times* (4 ½ stars)

"A riveting novel. . . . With its combination of engrossing story and emotion-packed romance, this is a guaranteed page-turner and a book to savor."
—*The Romance Reader* (4 stars)

"This is without a doubt the best historical romance I have read this year."
—*Romance Reviews Today*

**Bound by Your Touch is also available as an eBook**

ALSO BY MEREDITH DURAN

*The Duke of Shadows*

# MEREDITH DURAN

## Bound by Your Touch

Pocket Books
New York London Toronto Sydney

The sale of this book without its cover is unauthorized. If you purchased this book without a cover, you should be aware that it was reported to the publisher as "unsold and destroyed." Neither the author nor the publisher has received payment for the sale of this "stripped book."

Pocket Books
A Division of Simon & Schuster, Inc.
1230 Avenue of the Americas
New York, NY 10020

This book is a work of fiction. Names, characters, places, and incidents either are products of the author's imagination or are used fictitiously. Any resemblance to actual events or locales or persons, living or dead, is entirely coincidental.

Copyright © 2009 by Meredith McGuire

All rights reserved, including the right to reproduce this book or portions thereof in any form whatsoever. For information address Pocket Books Subsidiary Rights Department, 1230 Avenue of the Americas, New York, NY 10020

First Pocket Books paperback edition July 2009

POCKET and colophon are registered trademarks of Simon & Schuster, Inc.

For information about special discounts for bulk purchases, please contact Simon & Schuster Special Sales at 1-866-506-1949 or business@simonandschuster.com.

The Simon & Schuster Speakers Bureau can bring authors to your live event. For more information or to book an event contact the Simon & Schuster Speakers Bureau at 1-866-248-3049 or visit our website at www.simonspeakers.com.

Illustration by Jon Paul.
Hand lettering by Dave Gatti.

Manufactured in the United States of America

10  9  8  7  6  5  4  3  2  1

ISBN 978-1-4165-9263-1
ISBN 978-1-4391-0093-6 (ebook)

*For my mother and father,*
*whose encouragement*
*is my greatest strength.*

# Acknowledgments

During the writing of this book, my gratitude accumulated in direct proportion to word count. 96,000 thanks, then, to the following: Steve, for caves, pet parades, encouragement when I most needed it, and the main miracle; Janine, my extraordinary crit partner, whose thoughtful insights clarified my view at a crucial moment; BFF Ronroe, for, among numberless other things, admiring my tissue box; Lauren McKenna, editor non pareil, whose every critique further enlivens my engagement with the story; Nancy Yost, my winning and winsome agent; and Megan McKeever, patient shepherd of the puzzled author. Finally, I'm incredibly lucky for family and friends who understood why I vanished, generously replenished the fortress when supplies ran low, and were waiting when I reemerged: Shelley, Rob, Betsey, Maureen, Maddie, Elizabeth, Royal, Mom, and Dad—I missed you!

# Prologue

In the garden beyond the window, afternoon sunlight spilled like honey over the graveled path and the lilac blossoms trembled in the breeze. Inside the drawing room, her own limbs felt not much steadier. Only the sight of George's reflection in the glass gave her courage. This urbane, dignified man had forgotten to leave his hat with the butler. Now he clutched it before him, like a shield against his nerves. No doubt his anxiety appalled him. He often said that a politician was nothing without his composure. But she would also be an asset: when his voice failed, she would speak for them both. "I love you," she said.

Her first reply was the faint creak of shoe leather as he stepped immediately forward. "I beg your pardon?"

The window reflected her growing smile. As a small girl, she had dreamed of this moment. Later, when the mirror had proved that she would not grow into her mother's beauty, she'd begun to wonder. Perhaps she would never find a husband. Her bookishness, her eccentric interests, would not recommend her.

But then she'd met George. Awkward with trivial conversation, embarrassed to debut at such a late age, she had dreaded the Hartleys' ball. In his arms, though, dancing felt easy. *So this is why girls like to waltz,* she'd thought. They'd talked through supper, and George's questions were thoughtful, substantial. *Your wit is an education for me, Miss Boyce. I'd not realized that cleverness could coincide with such feminine graces.*

She turned now, feeling weightless with the premonition of joy. He stood next to a bouquet of yellow roses that he'd sent only yesterday. Against the rich mahogany of the chiffonier, they glowed like pieces of sunlight. Indeed, everything in the small, airy salon seemed gilded to her—the pale walls and chintz upholstery brightening and clarifying before her eyes, the cool air sparkling, perfumed with the roses' scent. Here was the moment she would always remember. "I said that I love you."

He took a sharp breath that sounded like a gasp.

In the hallway outside, the grandfather clock began to gong. It was an old piece, and she'd always detected a note of boredom in its low, slow chimes, as if it were tired of its duties, fed up with their curiosity about the time. She had confided as much to George last month, and he had laughingly called her his clockwork philosopher. Her smile wanted to widen now in reference to the joke. But the muscles in her cheeks disagreed, and her eyes were telling her something. They noted the heightening color on his cheeks. The tightening of his brow. What was this? Would he not speak? Would he only stare?

A dray rumbled through the back street. It set the tea tray to rattling, and this seemed to startle him. His lips twitched, convulsively. Then his shoulders squared. "Miss Boyce," he said. Five minutes ago, he had called her Lydia. Running a hand over his moustache, he shook his head. "My dear lady. I am so sorry. If I have misled you in some manner . . . believe me, it was not my intention!"

She put a hand on the back of the chair she'd been sitting in earlier. She had served him Earl Grey; their cups still sat on the center table, her spoon slumping at an indecorous angle from the saucer. *I have a question of great import to discuss with you,* he'd announced, and she'd leaped to her feet like a jack-in-the-box, at once so elated and overwhelmed that tears pricked her eyes. *Misled* her?

"I—" No, her voice would not work properly. She swallowed. "I do not . . . understand."

"I am mortified." He extracted a handkerchief to blot his forehead. "Please, Miss Boyce. I am—*abjectly* apologetic."

A strangled sound escaped her. He was— *Why was he here, then?* Dear God! *Misled her?* This was impossible. What of all his tokens of regard? The roses. Yellow, yes, but one could not read so much into flowers. Their drives through the park? Every Thursday he had driven her through Rotten Row for six weeks now! And only yesterday, as he'd helped her from the barouche onto the gravel, he had pressed her hand and smiled into her face very intimately, as if his thoughts were as warmed by their touch as hers were. She had not *misread* him!

"You must speak plainly with me," she said haltingly. "We have become . . . close, these last weeks—"

"Indeed." His hands worked convulsively on the brim of his hat; it would never recover from this crushing. "I have formulated the highest regard for you, Miss Boyce. So much so, that—" The color in his cheeks now faded entirely. "My fondest desire is to have the honor of calling you my sister-in-law."

A muted gasp. Sophie. That would be Sophie watching through the keyhole. "Your sister-in-law," she whispered.

"My sister-in-law," he confirmed.

Her body prickled with cold, as if thrust into a winter lake. Sophie. *Sophie,* of course. Sophie had always accompanied them on these drives through the park, on their sunny strolls. But no one had ever guessed—he'd never hinted—his eyes had only been for her! It had not been Sophie whom George asked to dance that first time! It had not been *Sophie* who received his flowers after that ball!

But it had been Sophie who insisted on coming with them during their outings. Sophie who had touched his elbow when Lydia felt too shy to do it. Sophie who had leaned past her to laugh at his every joke.

God in heaven. Sophie would not refuse.

She let go of the chair and stepped back. "It is not quite the done thing, is it?" Her voice sounded terribly dry; she did not recognize it. "To propose to the younger sister, when the elder is yet unwed?"

And there came the color again—a flush, she thought now, of offense. "It has troubled me. But with your father in Egypt, I did not know to whom I should apply. I wired him two weeks ago, but haven't received a response."

"Two weeks?" He had been nursing designs for Sophie for two weeks? When he had come to the charity bazaar to buy the shawl she'd embroidered *(the perfect gift for my mother's birthday; I believe that I have told you how much she admires you)* he'd been thinking to marry *Sophie*?

"Indeed," he was saying. "That's why I wished to

speak with you today. Your sister informs me you are something of the . . . the *manager* in familial matters. Not," he added quickly, "that I find it anything but admirable, the competence with which you have assumed this most strenuous role, at your tender age and experience. Why, I cannot imagine what a toll it must take on you, managing your father's affairs—"

But a fresh and dreadful thought had occurred. Sophie had told him? "My sister—she *knew* that you hoped for this conversation?"

A brief silence. His eyes dropped. He was seeing the illness of it, himself. "Yes."

So there was the root of her premonition: a premonition of shame, and hurt, and rage. For she could not deny Sophie this match. It was brilliant. George—*my George*—was the heir to a barony, to a fortune. No one could hope for better. But to think—to think that her sister had *betrayed* her this way! Sophie had known exactly what she believed and hoped with regard to George. Sophie had listened in smiling silence to her confidences, had all but encouraged her to flirt, all the while *knowing* where his true affections lay! *Not with me. Not anymore.*

The truth spun around and around in Lydia's mind, like a riddle whose key eluded her, although, by all appearances, everyone else had solved it two weeks ago.

*Dear God. I am a fool.*

Lydia looked to the door. Why was Sophie at the keyhole? To watch her sister make a terrible idiot of herself? For that was what she had done. He'd begun to make his declaration—his declaration of feelings for *Sophie*!—and she had jumped in with her own *I love you!*

Stars above. If only Persephone would share the joys of the earth swallowing her! She had never misjudged anyone so badly. She, who prided herself on her powers of observation!

Alas, the earth did not open. Only silence filled the space of the parlor. With each passing second, it seemed to gather weight and density. Soon it would become unbreakable. But her mind felt limp. Papa was so far away. To whom would she turn when she left this room? Papa would not be waiting to hug her, to tease her, to remind her of the many reasons a gentleman of sense would be glad to have her to wife. *You are my pearl, Lydia. Promise me that you will never waste your time mooning over swine.*

She must speak. For in a few moments she would begin to cry, and she could not bear George to witness that. *That* mortification was beyond her power to endure.

She drew a breath. Even in the depths of her horror, she knew exactly what she must say—those powerful, meaningless words that would bring this misery to an end. There was always a script. She knew how to read the lines well enough. And George was waiting for them. He expected them.

No doubt, she thought with a sudden and foreign contempt, he believed they *meant* something.

Lydia lifted her chin. "Let me be the first to offer you congratulations." Her voice would not break. She dug her fingernails into her palms. "I know that you will be *very* happy, indeed."

# One

*Four years later.*

On this new electric light, the white marble blinded. James Durham propped his elbows on the balcony, laced his hands together, and stared down into his foyer. It had been a bit dramatic, he supposed, a bit too *Grecian*, paving the foyer with flagstones. At the time, he'd considered it the epitome of pure aesthetics. Now it nauseated him. Too much white: a funeral shroud of a foyer. Silent but for the buzzing of the lights, like vultures in the distance. He felt dizzy. His mouth was dry. It would be so easy to trip over this rail. One careless movement, a sweet swan's dive downward, and the floor would not be so white anymore.

His breath left him in a shudder. He stepped back, and his head seemed to soar from his shoulders. Good God. He was never trying another of Phin's little concoctions.

Hmm. That resolution felt . . . familiar. As if he'd made it before. Several times, in fact. How hopeless he was. He laughed softly. Yes, how predictably, tediously hopeless.

"Sanburne!"

The word came spearing through his consciousness,

scattering the fog. With a start, he realized it had never been silent. Music, laughter, high-pitched squeals were spilling down the stairs. Yes—*that* was right! He had twenty-odd guests above; there'd been a party afoot since last evening, and he was the host. "Bloody hell," he said, and the astonishment in his voice sounded so queer and overdone that he had to laugh again.

*"Sanburne!"* It sounded very close now, this shrill cry, which might or might not belong to Elizabeth; he could never be sure without looking, not in this state. *Then look up, you idiot.* Yes, excellent idea. In one moment, he would.

"Sanburne, have you gone *deaf*?"

With an effort he raised his head. It was indeed Lizzie; she appeared to be floating down the staircase. Magic? But no; if there were any magic in the world, it would not reside in Elizabeth, no matter how she might need it. Poor, luckless darling. He walked toward her with sympathetic intentions, intending to take her hands, for she looked distraught, her once-rakish coiffure now slipping over a tear-filled eye.

But walking proved beyond him. He tripped over the first stair and sat down. The impact astonished him. What *had* he been thinking, not to carpet the place?

He shook his head and reached for the banister. Before he could pull himself up, Lizzie was at his side, her skirts—stained by something; wine, smelled like—bunching around her calves. "Sanburne, he—he's got a w-w-woman—" She sobbed a breath that brought her décolletage into his nose. A bit of caviar had gotten lodged in her neckline. He brushed it away. Most mysterious. What the hell were they doing up there?

"He's got a woman on his lap! One of your maids! Fondling her right in front of me!" Elizabeth's fingers fastened onto his upper arm, digging for attention. "Do you *hear* me? Are you awake?"

He was curious about that, too. "Are my eyes open?"

She made a noise of exasperation, then took his chin in her grip, yanking it up so their eyes met. "They are open," she said. "Behold: it is I."

"It is you," he agreed. "Your eyes are particularly lovely when you've been crying, my dear. So green. *So* much lovelier than white."

The corners of her mouth began to tremble. "Nello's got one of the maids," she said.

Something . . . insistent there. He did not like her look, suddenly, but he could not break from it. It made the world around him take on weight. Stairs, his house, a party. For one last second, the giddiness remained. And then his mind clicked, gears grinding. "One of the *maids,* did you say?" He pulled himself up by way of a baluster. The first step was the hardest. Damn Nello for a tosser; he always made a scene.

"Wait!" Elizabeth came scrambling up behind him. "James, you won't . . . *hurt* him, will you? He's just a bit drunk, is all. Or whatever it is that Ashmore gave him. I didn't mean to start a fight!"

"Of course you bloody did." He said it without rancor as he mounted the staircase. The drug was still coursing within him; he felt incapable of dividing his attention. Nello! Chap knew the rules. One couldn't break host's rules. Deuced poor taste!

He crested the stairs to discover the party had spilled out of the salon. Elise Strathern was weaving her way down the corridor, Christian Tilney nipping at her heels. Colin Muir, scoundrel Scot, was trying to feed liquor to the stone bust of one of James's forebears, while his audience—the Cholomondley twins, who else?—giggled appreciatively.

Inside the yellow room, things were no more civilized. Glass crunched beneath his feet and the air held a stinking miasma of opium and cigar smoke. Someone had broken the palm fronds that screened the musicians from the gathering, and damn if the violinist did not have a cummerbund tied around his head as he manfully sawed out the latest music hall ditty. The flutist had given up, and was watching with avid amazement as Mrs. Sawyer turned a jig atop the banquet table—beneath which the cellist, and his instrument, were sleeping in a pool of punch.

And there was Nello, arguing in the far corner with Dalton. Elizabeth was right (but she was always attentive to detail in this one regard: namely, the idiotic regard she felt for Nello). He'd lodged one of the parlormaids beneath his arm, and she was thin-lipped, squirming. James picked his way through the debris and came up just as Nello lifted his fist for the first punch.

James caught him by the wrist. "Now, now, children."

"Damn his eyes, Sanburne! I'll have at him! A cheating swot, am I?"

"Just about," said Dalton, grinning drunkenly. "Why, you swived that Egyptian wench so hard that Sanburne just about puked to death from the boat rocking."

"You little—"

James wrapped his forearm around Nello's neck and hauled backward. The parlormaid shrieked and fell to her bum, from which position, James ascertained with a glance, she crawled toward safer quarters. "As for that," he said into Nello's ear, "you *are* a cheat, and if you don't believe me, Lizzie will set you straight."

Nello abruptly ceased struggling. "Lizzie . . . ?"

"Indeed," Elizabeth said, coming round to confront him. "You pig!"

James loosened his hold. "Just full of snap, ain't she?"

Indeed, her face was pinched with rage. She stepped forward, her hands raised over her head—and in them, James spotted something he'd been meant to deliver this morning. *His Egyptian funerary stela!*

"Lizzie, no!"

The rock slab smashed down on Nello's shoulder. The awful cracking sound caused even the violinist to falter. With a cry of agony, Nello dropped to his knees. "My shoulder!"

"Broken it," Dalton predicted, and slid down the wall to nap.

"Dear God!" James pried the stela from Elizabeth's fingers. He turned it over, searching anxiously for damage. He'd been coddling the thing for days, toasting it with evening brandy, gloating over the bitter envy his father was sure to feel at the sight of it. And Lizzie used it to *bludgeon* someone!

"Have I broken it?" she asked. She was looking down at Nello, a curiously blank expression on her face.

"No," he decided, on a long breath of relief. "It looks intact."

"His shoulder, you buffoon, not your precious rock."

"My precious—? *Priorities,* Elizabeth!"

She snorted. "Oh, stuff. My priorities do not include your foolish antics with your father."

James grinned. His father, indeed. Moreland would be at the lecture by now, blissfully ignorant of what was in store for him. There was no way he'd be able to resist this piece. "Lizzie, love, your priorities have nothing to do with me. Now look here," he said more briskly, "be a dear and send round for the doctor. Also, tell Gudge he may set up Nello in the blue bedroom." Nello moaned again, and James bent to eye him. "Perhaps with a very large bucket," he added. Old boy was looking rather green.

"Don't go," Nello managed. "I need . . . help."

Lizzie was more shrill. "You're *leaving me*? With Nello nearly *dead*?"

With a reassuring pat to the stela, James rose. "Never. Friendship is eternal, etcetera. But I have an appointment at the Archaeological Institute, you might recall." A month in Egypt, spent suffering seasickness off the edge of a houseboat that—Dalton was correct—rocked like a pendulum. Countless letters to and from Port Said. A fortune spent on various, ultimately second-rate antiques. Thousands of pounds to finally secure the right one. Six months of work leading to this moment, and he'd almost forgotten! Phineas certainly had a way with the toxins.

"Oh, of course," Lizzie said, "the *Archaeological Institute*. If Nello were dead, I doubt you should miss your appointment!"

For Nello? "You might be right." He gave Lizzie a quick kiss on the cheek, then picked his way out of the salon, eager to depart before she started crying again.

Lydia had managed to keep her voice from shaking. Nor had anyone yet stood to decry her as a lunatic.

Sophie was falling asleep—her hat tipped, abruptly righted when Antonia poked her, then began tipping again—but that was not unusual. Most importantly, Lord Ayresbury, in the front row, was listening with every sign of interest. All in all, she thought cautiously, it was going very . . . well.

The hope she'd been repressing for days swelled and burst free. It washed through her at such dizzying speed that she actually stuttered from the impact. "If—ah, if my father's findings are correct, then this strongly suggests . . ."

A door slammed open at the back of the hall, admitting a much-rumpled gentleman. The sight startled her into a pause. It was coming on noon, and he was wearing evening attire, black tailcoat and bow tie.

Some of the audience turned to mark his advance. He was trailed by a footman in garish crimson livery, who cradled a greatcoat in one arm, and some sort of slab in the other.

An eccentric latecomer, no doubt. No need to feel uneasy. Lydia adjusted her spectacles and focused again on the text. "This strongly suggests that Tel-el-Maskhuta was *not* the location of the first stop in the Exodus."

A snort issued from the fat, ginger-haired man seated next to Lord Ayresbury. Lydia did not look up; it would only rattle her. For the last hour, he had been making these contemptuous noises. The part of her mind not occupied with her lecture had already prepared the condolences she would offer for his poor health. They would be introduced later, she assumed. Papa had written a long letter about what to expect: "*Hospitality, tempered with suspicion and random pockets of hostility, to which the director will steer you directly at the conclusion of your speech. Mold your spine in steel, and give them what-for!"*

Sweat beaded her nape as she fumbled for the last page. She had wrestled with this conclusion for days, determined to phrase Papa's findings in the most diplomatic manner possible. His data was sound, but it required them to take a *very* strong line against scholars who claimed to have located Pithom and Succoth. Some of those men were in the audience today, and if they decided to jeer, it would not help Papa's bid for funding.

*Steel,* she reminded herself. Lord Ayresbury was tremendously influential with the Egypt Exploration Fund, and rumor held him to be a man who appreciated innovation. With his endorsement, they would certainly secure EEF funding. Papa needed only two more seasons to prove beyond all doubt that he had located the *true* site of the first stop on the Exodus. And then, why, all his worries would be over. There'd be no need for him to continue in the antiquities trade. So many funds would pour in for his projects, they'd have to turn *down* offers of support.

The thought bolstered her. He had wanted this for so long, now. And she would be the one to achieve it for him. She licked her dry lips. "Now, if I may—"

"Aha! *There* you are!"

The recent arrival had drawn up halfway down the aisle. He was addressing someone seated in one of the rows. A murmur ran through the theater.

"Stand up, then," the interloper said. "No use skulking."

Lydia's stomach sank. It had all been going *too* well, hadn't it? She should have known not to count her chickens beforehand.

Of course, her wise father had foreseen this. *"And if, my dear, some ill-bred ruffian should take the room from you—why then, you must simply take it back."*

She drew a breath and flattened her hands on the lectern to brace herself. "If I may," she called.

He glanced up, looking startled. As though he could possibly have missed that there was a *meeting* in session! He stared at her as if trying to place her. Her heart drumming (for she had no practice in "taking back" a room; as an activity, it sounded alarmingly martial), she returned his regard. He was an extraordinarily tawny creature, with a firm jaw and a long nose. No doubt he was considered very handsome by those who liked exhaustion: the shadows beneath his eyes suggested sleepless nights. "Not right now," he said to her, starting to turn away. Then, looking back, he ran an eye down her and added thoughtfully, "But later, by all means."

Strangely, his impertinence calmed her. An Adonis might be rare and baffling, but she knew how to handle the commonplace blackguard. "Perhaps, sir, you might allow me to finish my lecture first!"

But she was addressing the backs of heads now; his attention had moved on, and he had taken her audience with him. *Papa's audience!*

She watched in disbelief as he said, "All right, then," to an elderly gentleman sitting at the edge of the row. "The mountain will come to Mohammed." He beckoned to the footman, who stepped forward, holding out a slab that had been tucked beneath his arm.

Several members of the society stood to have a look, Lord Ayresbury among them.

The elderly man rose to his feet. "What is the meaning of this, you devil?"

"That, sir, you will have to tell *me.*" The interloper's nod prompted the footman to deposit the rock at the older man's feet. "My stela. Not to be confused with *Stella,* whom you have permanently sequestered from view. Anyway, I have no idea what it is, but I'm assured it's quite valuable. And *very* rare."

There was a moment of rapt silence from the onlookers as the footman arranged the piece to his master's satisfaction. Her lecture had turned into a carnival show. Lydia found herself looking through a curious, filmy haze, which she realized with horror must be tears. Dear God, to cry like a babe, in *public*! Suddenly grateful for the crowd's distraction, she dashed a wrist across her eyes. This was too silly of her; she must behave with dignity.

Oh, but hope died far less pleasantly than it was born. It loosed a terrible death rattle, just above one's heart.

"I say," cried a man in the far corner. He pushed his way into the aisle, occasioning a chorus of grunts and protests from those seated in his row. "Is that *Nefertiti*?"

The interloper considered the slab. "Might be," he said. Didn't he even know? These pretty men were always the worst sort of dilettante. "You mean the one snuggling up to the chap in the . . . ?" He sketched some mysterious shape in the air above his head.

*Ah.* A conical hat of the pharaonic type. Lydia braced herself.

Indeed: direct chaos. Chairs toppled, programs went

skidding, and exclamations and speculation rent the air as three quarters of her erstwhile listeners swarmed forth to view the object.

A couple of those who remained in their seats spared her a sympathetic look. She managed a polite smile in return. The redheaded gentleman smirked, and she turned her face away, giving him a cut that even his beady eyes would remark. Out of the corner of her eye, she saw him whisper something to his female companion, an immaculately turned-out blond about Lydia's age. In reply, her thin, patrician lips curved slightly.

Lydia fought the urge to roll her eyes. She was very familiar with the meaning of such looks. At twelve years old, it signified that your bookishness was boring and your short skirts outmoded. At seventeen, that your interest in heathen civilizations made you mannish. At twenty-two, that you'd said something odd and no wonder your brother-in-law had jilted you for your sister. And at twenty-six . . . ? At twenty-six, Lydia was too mature to care for its significance. She toed the line of acceptable behavior, and that was all she owed to polite society. Certainly she asked nothing of it in return.

Silently she began to stack the pages of her speech. Her fingers were trembling. Pathetic. *Orientalists!* She had seen it all her life: one mention of Pharaohs, and men reverted to the schoolroom. Even Papa, the most doting husband in history, had broken vigil at Mama's sickbed when news came of some block statue arriving from Cairo. Lydia had sat in the darkened bedroom— one hand on her mother's forehead, the other switching between Sophie's shoulder and Antonia's small, trembling fingers—and listened to the rumble of his carriage, receding down the drive. She'd only been sixteen, and certainly no one had realized that Mama's fever would be fatal. Nevertheless, the future had suddenly seemed obvious. Papa might support her studies, but she could not count on his undivided attention. Not unless she, too, courted his mistress, Lady Egypt.

Well, at least Papa's passion was grounded in science. As far as she could tell, most other Egyptologists used archaeology as a ruse to disguise an unmanly fascination with shiny baubles. She eyed the interloper again. He had stepped out of the crowd and was watching, with a pleased smile only partially concealed by the finger tapping at his upper lip, the skirmish he'd caused. She could see how gewgaws might appeal to this one. His fingers were layered in a surplus of jeweled rings. Pinned at his lapel was a gaudy turquoise and silver watch. And surely he'd had to sit for *hours* before his valet managed to coax that wave of sun-striped hair to fall *just* so over his brow. A peacock. A washed-out peacock had ruined her lecture! Worse than that—had ruined, in one fell swoop, the basis of every plan she and Papa had hatched!

The redheaded man was now gloating. She caught the rhythm, if not the precise words, that he cackled into Ayresbury's ear. Mockery. There went any chance at the funding, then. When word of this fiasco reached Cairo, Papa would feel terribly disappointed. He had counted on Ayresbury's endorsement. For that matter, she had counted on securing it. She *owed* him this.

With sudden fury, she gathered her skirts and marched forward. The ginger critic harrumphed as she passed, but she paid him no heed. Elbowing through the melee, ignoring all manner of complaint, she drew up at the stela, so her skirts almost brushed the edge of the slab.

One glance decided her. "It's fake," she said.

No one appeared to hear.

"It's *fake!*"

Her vehemence startled even her. In the brief, ensuing silence, as her temper began to cool, she wondered what she had done. She opened her mouth to soften her condemnation, to qualify it, but someone beat her.

"Never," exclaimed a gentleman who, disregarding all propriety, had fallen to his hands and knees for a closer look. "On the contrary, it has every mark of authenticity!"

*That* was a bit much, she thought.

"Such a rarity," another man cooed. "Why, Lord Sanburne has unearthed a miracle! Just look at—"

"Enough of you," snapped the older gentleman to whom the stela had been presented. His watery blue eyes focused on Lydia. As he stepped forward, the crowd of people around them stepped back. "Have you some knowledge of this artifact, Miss Boyce?"

"Naturally she does." This from Antonia, who came up in a cloud of perfume—Sophie's special blend from Paris; a sniff confirmed it—to slip her arm through Lydia's. Lydia had told her time and again that debutantes did not wear such heavy scents, but Sophie *would* encourage her. "Indeed," Ana continued in merry tones, "how could she not? Why, she was reading cuneiforms while still on Papa's knee. And she spends every afternoon studying Arabic at the British Library!"

The old man looked more than gratified by this

exaggeration. "Of course. I am a great admirer of Mr. Boyce's work." He held out his hand to Antonia. "Forgive the informality. I am Moreland, Earl of Moreland."

Antonia took his hand and sank into as best a curtsy as she could manage, given her trailing skirts and the onlookers not a foot away. "How fortunate that you are not the Earl of *Less*land; I fear that would be most distressing to your well-wishers."

The earl laughed, and Lydia forced a polite smile. She was distracted by a glimpse of the interloper, Sanburne. He was working his way toward them, and proximity revealed the full extent of his disarray. His cuffs were flapping open. A wine-colored stain covered his periwinkle waistcoat.

The smile he sent her suggested imminent bloodshed.

"I am sure you have never heard that one before," Ana was saying. A saucy little smile rode her lips.

"True wit bears endless repetition," the earl said gallantly. He turned to Lydia, who, jolted from premonition, made a curtsy. He gestured to the stone at their feet. "Truly, is it a forgery?"

Oh, she was in it now. *Mold your spine of steel.* "Without a doubt," she said. She did not glance down. She felt it unwise to remove her eyes from Sanburne, who had now joined them in the inner circle.

"Well?" Sanburne said. His eyes were horribly bloodshot.

"Not well at all," she said. "Quite poor, in fact."

"Explain yourself."

She drew a breath. He really did have the most formidable glare. "I—"

"You will have to pardon my son his manners," the earl interrupted. He cast a fierce look at the man, who arched a brow, as unrepentant as Lucifer.

Digesting this unexpected news of their relationship, Lydia felt a sharper prickle of unease. The Durham family was notorious: the sister a murderess, stashed in some insane asylum in the country; and the son, she recalled now, a wild socialite who entertained the beau monde by outwitting his father in various public locales.

Dear heavens. It seemed she had stepped into some nasty familial tangle. Her every word would only implicate her further. "Perhaps you should consult one of the other gentlemen." Her spine wasn't really made of steel, after all. That was a silly saying, made up by someone who had never felt what it meant to be broken. "This is not my area of specialty. And in a room with so many distinguished scholars—"

"Precisely," said the earl's son.

"Nonsense," said the earl. "As far as I reckon, you're the only one with the good sense to take a second look before bursting into this—this *chorus* of hallelujahs. Out with it, girl; whence your verdict?"

Antonia laughed softly, squeezing her arm. "Oh, *do* tell them, Lydia." To Lydia's unease, her gaze rested on the thunderous face of the prodigal son.

Well, it seemed that the quickest way out of this was to bumble her way through it. She laid her hand atop Ana's, taking comfort from her sister's touch. "Numerous reasons lead me to suspect the authenticity of this item," she said slowly. Now she did give it a longer look, and to her relief, her intuition seemed well-founded.

"Yes. It attempts to approximate a funerary stela of the Intermediate Period, but in such a tableau, one would expect to see jars of beer. Instead we have what look to be pots of ointment. And that is not . . ." Her gaze flicked to Sanburne's, then quickly away. The scar dividing one of his brows was flushed crimson with the force of his irritation. "That is not Nefertiti, and she is not *snuggling*. She is kneeling, which is all wrong. One only kneels to divinity. I suspect, if you examine the chisel marks on the back, you will also discover that this was not fashioned with an adze. In all ways, it simply doesn't . . . look right."

Lord Sanburne snorted. "Perhaps someone with better vision should have a *look,* then."

She tightened her grip on Antonia. "I see perfectly well. That is the purpose of spectacles, after all."

"By the deuces," someone behind her called. "She's right."

The earl smiled. "My dear! Such a keen eye. We're fortunate that you've chosen to follow in your father's footsteps."

That was not her intention, but now did not seem to be the time to announce it. "Thank you, sir." She gathered herself to look once more at the earl's son. This time, she did not let his glare deter her. "I believe the field requires fresh perspectives. So often I find Egyptology to serve as an excuse, allowing men of a certain disposition to collect pretty trinkets in the name of science." Her gaze flicked down to the rings on the man's fingers, then back up.

Whatever reaction she had expected—an angry flush, a protest, perhaps even a violent assault (she did not think him beyond it)—she was not prepared for him to smile at her. And such a smile! Slow at first, as if considering whether or not to widen; and then, suddenly, shifting into laughter. It transformed his face. He was, all at once, breathtaking.

But then something went wrong. His laugh started out softly, but he did not seem able to stop it. As his mirth rose in volume, it assumed a lunatic quality. Lydia dimly sensed people scattering back to their seats, but she could not look away from the young lord's face. It was more than morbid curiosity that arrested her. She'd never seen someone lose his mind before, but Sanburne managed it beautifully. The sight tightened her throat, and only this prevented her impulse to—

To do what? Great ghosts, what could she possibly think to say to such a creature? His beauty was meaningless, as random and unmerited as the pattern on butterflies' wings. She should know better than to let it affect her.

For the earl's part, he seemed more irritated than concerned. "Snap out of it, boy! By God, what have you been smoking?"

The earl's son choked to a stop. "Got me," he said to Lydia. Then, on another burble of laughter, he snapped his fingers toward the footman, who promptly produced a coat. As he flung it on, he addressed the earl. "Maybe you should hire her to vet your collection. After all, you do seem to share a certain, ah, *rapport*."

Lydia stiffened. He'd made the word sound sordid.

"*My* collection? I am not such a fool to invest my money in untested frauds!"

"Perhaps *you* should hire her," Ana said to Sanburne.

"Evidently you require greater powers of discernment than are at your disposal."

"Indeed," Sanburne said, eyeing her.

The speculative quality of his look alarmed Lydia. "I am sure the blame lies elsewhere. Whomever you deal with in purchasing these antiquities—"

"Yes, yes," he said impatiently. "So much for him. Father, a word with you."

He started off, then paused and turned back when the earl did not immediately accompany him.

"Don't you want your rock?" Lord Moreland inquired sweetly.

"Indeed," Sanburne said. "I shall save it to use for your tombstone. Wouldn't *that* be fitting?"

This uncanny remark made Lydia's head feel light. "Let's go find Sophie," she murmured to Ana. "There's nothing more to be done here."

She was turning away when the earl called her name. "Look for a note," he said. "I am most grateful for your advice today."

"Oh, indeed, and a note from *me*," Sanburne said smoothly. "We *can* share you, can we not? I have many antiquities you might like to devalue."

She paused, counting to ten. But there was no way to answer him without further straining the bounds of propriety. With a mute curtsy to the earl, she turned her back on them both, and dragged her sister to safety.

# Two

The last caller departed, Lydia returned to her chair. How exhausting these seasonal events could be. A whole lot of fluttering nonsense, lent the illusion of substance by the vast number of rituals surrounding them. Sophie had held court today for what seemed like half the city. It would have been a real triumph, had most not come to gawk at Lydia. All the social columns had carried mention of the debacle at the Institute.

As she leaned over to retrieve her teacup, George's voice came from the hallway. Impossible not to stiffen as she sat back again. Ana's debut had forced them under the same roof until August, and the proximity had started to wear on her nerves. Only last night, Sophie had drawn her aside to mention his *immense* distress over the lecture. "He thinks you should have kept silent, and let someone else point out that the stela was a fake," she'd said.

The hypocrisy had astonished Lydia into silence. Generally George knew better than to criticize her conduct in any respect. After all, the most shocking wrong she'd ever committed had unfolded in this very room, at *his* behest.

The memory unsettled her sufficiently to make her consider saying something rash. But when the door opened, only Ana stepped into the room. She was flipping through the *cartes de visite* left by their guests. "So many people," she murmured. "Have we ever had so many?" With a smile, she looked up. "Did you hear Miss Marshall when she walked in? She mistook it for a kettledrum!"

Her nerves settling, Lydia smiled back. Ana's smiles were contagious; Mr. Pagett, third son of the Earl of Farlow, certainly seemed charmed by them. All three sisters had agreed: if he made an offer in the next fortnight, they would push for a September wedding. Ana wanted a honeymoon in northern Italy, where the autumn was said to be splendid. Sophie wanted to be rid of her chaperonage duties before her October trip to the Riviera. And the sooner Ana was settled, the sooner Lydia could continue her campaign to secure funds for Papa's project. The lecture had only been the beginning. Next she intended to travel the country, personally soliciting every over-moneyed, amateur Egyptologist who had ever bought so much as a papyrus. Certainly she could not continue to depend on the antiquities trade to finance Papa's project. It distracted him from his real work, and kept *her* in London when she would much rather be in Egypt, helping to coordinate the excavations and also to do research of her own.

Ana tossed the cards onto the center table and settled into a nearby chair. She was wearing a pretty white tulle dress, as befit a girl in her first season. Not so appropriately, her ankles were showing. "You were very popular today, Lyd."

There was a note of puzzlement in her voice that caused Lydia to hide a smile. Neither of her sisters was accustomed to being overshadowed by her. All three of them had inherited Mama's hazel eyes and waving black hair, but Sophie and Ana were built on smaller, more winsome lines, with rosebud lips and eyes that tilted like a cat's. As a girl, Lydia had studied the mirror often enough to know that it was the mouth which made them pretty, and the tilt which lifted them to beautiful. Lacking either, she had decided to surrender all vanity. "If I was popular, you must thank the viscount. His shenanigans received a great deal of notice."

"Oh, that's right. I wonder if he'll be at the Durhams' dinner tomorrow?"

She shrugged and reached again for her tea. "I doubt it. They do not get on, you know."

"How sad."

"It's by his own doing. Don't waste your pity on that scalawag." And then, because she did not like Ana's continuing fixation on the viscount, she changed the subject. "Did you enjoy your chat with Mr. Pagett?"

Ana blushed. "He is very kind. He said he would pay a call tomorrow."

"Lovely." Things were moving right along. "But you *will* take Sophie with you. If he arrives in a two-seater, you will insist on our barouche." He had pulled this trick before, and Ana had gladly conspired with him. She did not yet grasp how vulnerable a young woman was to missteps—or, for that matter, how easily a gentleman might lose interest thanks to an error of judgment which *he* had encouraged.

"I have promised it already," Ana said testily. "Sophie says a letter came from Papa?"

"Yes. He's preparing a shipment, and wanted me to contact his clients."

"Did he send any word for me?"

"I'm sorry, dearest. It was all business."

Ana wrinkled her nose. "It's always business with him!"

As it must be for the rare scholar who had not inherited a fortune to support his interests. "He's very busy, dear. If he doesn't finish the excavation before the rains begin, the whole season will have gone to waste."

A little sigh was the only acknowledgment Ana paid to this logic. She used to show more sympathy, but lately, Sophie's attitude was coloring her view. "George was saying yesterday that it's a shame Papa never visits us."

Offense brought Lydia upright. "Would he foot the bill for Papa's project? That would certainly make it possible for him to visit. But George never offered."

"Maybe he would." Ana shrugged and wound her fingers together in her lap. "He says the antiquities trade is very lowering for a gentleman. It isn't right, of course, but some people might say that Papa digs in graves for things to sell."

She sucked in a breath. How dare he give voice to such rumors! "Ana, I cannot *believe* you did not object to this!" Oh, she would not rest until she secured enough money to abandon this trading business! The Egyptian government vetted every piece that Papa exported, but it still opened him to the most *intolerable* remarks. "Really, have a little loyalty! You live under George's roof, but he is not your father!"

"Of course he isn't." Ana hesitated. "Lyd, why do you and George dislike each other?"

Was she that obvious? "Don't be silly. I simply object to his criticisms of Papa." As Ana's frown deepened, she said more sharply, "He has no right to say such things."

"I know." Ana reached out for her hand. "It's all

right. Once I'm married, you can come along with me. I promise it. Why, I shan't marry anyone unless he agrees to let you come!"

The offer might have soothed her, had she not heard Ana make a similar declaration last week about her puppy—who, despite their best efforts, continued to piddle on the carpet and chew up slippers. "How kind," she said dryly. "But when you find this paragon, do have a care." She reached down and gave Ana's hem a yank. "He may feel that only actresses flash their ankles."

"How rude!" Ana sprang off the chair. "And I was only trying to be nice!" Stalking over to the sideboard, she made an officious show of rearranging a bouquet.

Embarrassed of herself, Lydia began to apologize—and then Ana bent over, showcasing her newfangled bustle in all its glory. Lydia's mouth snapped shut. She had objected to it at the milliner's, but Sophie had overruled her. As a result, Ana's backside now occupied three times the space that nature had intended for it, and quivered so violently that one might assume a small animal lurked beneath her skirts. Horrible thing! It was obviously intended for one purpose only: to draw a gentleman's notice to areas it should not stray.

A sigh announced Sophie's return to the room. She was on the outs with the housekeeper, whom she blamed for the soggy biscuits the guests had received. "Incompetence," she muttered as she sank onto the chair beside Lydia. "Most unfortunate."

Lydia nodded grimly toward the sideboard. Ana had moved on to the newest bouquet, an eruption of luridly pink tea roses, threaded with bushy sprigs of colchicum, columbine, and geranium. The note had included no signature, but the language of the flowers, joined together, clearly admitted their origins. *I shall ever remember; my best days fled; I am resolved to win; I expect a meeting.* "Entirely unfortunate," she said.

Sophie lifted a brow. "You're certain it's from Sanburne? It's such an awful arrangement, and he's rumored to have very good taste."

"Ha! That's not the only rumor I heard today." They went on for hours. Sanburne was a rascal, a ruffian. A veritable Adonis, and an excellent sportsman. He drank heavily—but with style. He was a most modern sort of heathen: his maternal uncle had left him a great deal of land, which he'd sold to purchase some filthy factories in Yorkshire. Now he made a fortune bilking laborers of their life's blood, and delighted at every opportunity to rub his father's nose in his commercial talents. "The flowers are definitely from him," Lydia muttered. Remembering the profusion of gemstones that sprouted from his fingers, she added, "I find them quite in character. He's as gaudy as his bouquet."

"*Glamorous,* Lydia. He's very popular, you know."

"Popular! With a whole lot of drunkards and South Africans, no doubt. Mrs. Bryson was telling me all about it. She says that his parties are famous for all manner of ill-bred mashers."

Sophie snorted. "Any man without whiskers is a masher in her book. And his circle's very smart—about as smart as the Marlborough House Set, I'd reckon, but even harder to crack, because they've all been friends for ages." Her sudden sigh reeked of envy. "Do you remember when George used to take an interest in society? *He* might have known Sanburne. Why, when we first married, there wasn't a party he didn't attend. Now look: all he wants to do is sit around with his clubmen discussing politics. Even the wives talk of nothing else."

*What did you expect? They are politicians.* Lydia knew better than to say it, though. Address one complaint, and Sophie would only find another; she was constantly discovering new reasons to be disappointed in George. No doubt a kind and noble sister would help Sophie to see his strengths. *Good luck to you, Ana.*

"Not that Sanburne wouldn't make a brilliant catch." Sophie pulled out her little book. "Do you have a pen?"

Lydia let out an astonished laugh. As the only matron amongst them, it had fallen to Sophie to play Ana's chaperone. She carried a little diary she called her "campaign journal," in which she kept a list of well-born bachelors, adding relevant details as they became available. But this was too much. "You can't think to add him—he's already contracted to Gatwick's daughter!"

"Is he? I can't get a straight answer for it. Besides, they say she is in love with someone else."

"Oh, that's just what we want for Ana: a man who antagonizes his father for fun, and keeps a fiancée who doesn't care for him." Lord, what a tangle. Lydia could not understand these high-flyers. They had nothing better to do than make hashes of their lives, while the rest of the world cheered them on for it. Never mind that lesser mortals would be tossed out on their ears for such tomfoolery.

"Well, I wouldn't *push* her at him. But if he showed an interest . . ."

Here was *exactly* why Papa had asked her to keep an eye on Sophie's matchmaking. "Absolutely not. And what of Mr. Pagett? I thought you'd vowed to have a proposal within the fortnight."

Sophie sat forward, her lip jutting mutinously. "And so I will, but you mustn't get pushy. Preach all you like about old rocks and foreigners, but when it comes to *gentlemen,* you don't know a thing."

Lydia's mouth dropped open on a silent syllable. If only these walls could speak, they would make a rebuttal for her! "Indeed? I know *nothing*? When Gladstone joined us for supper last week, and you nearly fell asleep in the soup, who rescued the discussion?"

"You droned on about Home Rule for half an hour," Sophie snapped. "I am surprised *he* did not fall asleep. George was mortified."

"George was grateful for my intercession," Lydia said sharply. He had even given her a weak smile of thanks.

Sophie gave a one-shouldered shrug. "He felt too embarrassed for you to say anything, I suppose."

Embarrassed for her, was he? *George was not mortified three years ago,* she thought. *When he assaulted me in this room, when he grabbed me and groped me and kissed me, he did not find me wanting* then. "Mr. Gladstone asked my opinion of the subject," she said between her teeth. "So I responded. And what *were* we meant to talk about, then? Your décolletage? Ana's newly abundant posterior? Really, Sophie, what are you teaching *her* with this behavior? Pretty eyes aren't the only asset a woman might possess—and little good they serve when a man has nobler interests than flirtation!"

Sophie smiled at her. "There's your mistake," she said sweetly. "You mistake disinterest for nobility. Dear Lydia, just because a man doesn't find *you* attractive doesn't mean he has no interest in flirting with other, prettier women. So you see, there is no need to set your example for Ana: she will never need the skills that *you* so much require."

"How clever you are with cruelty," Lydia said flatly. "Are you very proud of it?"

"I only speak the truth. Surely a great scholar like yourself should admire that."

Never had the temptation to confess been stronger. The words were so close to emerging that she could feel their weight and shape on her tongue.

But she would not say it. It had been so long ago. And the tale would flatter her as little as it did George. After all, he'd had liquor to blame for his behavior. But what reason could she give for the way her arms had twined around him? For a few brief seconds before she'd ripped herself away, his treachery had . . . gratified her. *You made the wrong choice,* she'd thought. *You know it now.*

As always, the memory made her gorge rise. Amid the self-contempt and anger, only one thing was clear to her. She had wanted to know what it was like to be kissed; she had found out, to her own shame. She took a deep breath. "I won't bother to argue with you," she said, and cleared her throat. "It comes down to this: Papa left the task to *both* of us. We will *both* find Ana a husband."

Sophie yawned. "Papa is in Egypt. And I doubt he would turn up his nose at a future earl."

"Papa would not give a fig for a title if it meant marrying Ana to a drunkard."

A smirk curved her sister's mouth. "That is not what he told *me*."

"What? When?"

"Oh, didn't I tell you? He wrote me a letter."

Lydia knew a moment of shock. "He didn't."

"No?" Sophie smiled. "You're not his only daughter, you know."

Common sense reasserted itself. Papa always routed the family correspondence through her. "True enough," she said with a shrug. "Let me see the letter, then."

"Why should I? It wasn't meant for you."

There was no letter, of course. Sophie was only trying to annoy her. What had started this whole argument? Ah, yes. "Well, none of it matters anyway. Sanburne is already linked with Mrs. Chudderley."

"Mrs. Chudderley?" Ana had left off with the bouquets and come to join them. Her bright tone was deliberate: she did not mind quarreling when she was instrumental to it, but when it cropped up among others, it made her uneasy. "The professional beauty?"

Lydia stepped in before Sophie could. "Yes, Lord Sanburne's fiancée."

"Oh! Is he engaged to her? I'm not surprised. You see her pictures in all the shop windows. She's very beautiful."

Lydia did not like the admiration in her voice. "You should pity her. Contracted to a man who appears in public whilst intoxicated! We'll certainly do better for you."

"*I* shall certainly do so," said Sophie.

Ana divided an uneasy glance between them. She had no basis for understanding the anger that lived between her elder sisters. By tacit agreement, they would never tell her. "I should hope so," she said, and dropped into an easy chair.

"Gracefully," Lydia murmured. "Do not—plummet, so."

"Let her be," Sophie snapped.

"I'm sure they make a splendid looking couple," said Ana. "What dash he has!"

"Handsome is as handsome does." She realized how prudish and stiff her tone sounded a moment before Sophie laughed.

"And it does a great deal, in my experience." When Lydia looked up, Sophie's eyes were on her. "I am sure you would not disagree with *that,* Lydia."

Lydia stared right back at her. "No, indeed not. I've found that beauty covers any manner of deeper ugliness."

Seated atop his carriage, James had a nice view of the moment when pandemonium swept Epsom Downs. All of London had turned out for the race. Citizens of every stripe drank and ate and brawled together—gawking at fire-breathers, cheering the acrobats, tossing coins to wandering accordionists. The air was sharp with sweat and spilled cider, choked with smoke from grilling sausages and fried clams. The carnival atmosphere might have overshadowed the Derby itself, had the race not ended in a dead heat.

This shocking news did not travel instantly; after all, the crowd ranged, in some places, a half-mile deep. From his perch on the carriage roof—a makeshift island in a sea of heads—James snacked on dressed crab and champagne and watched the oncoming wave of chaos. An astonished bettor, backing away from the news, bumped into a stilt walker, who toppled with a shout onto the blanket of a family who'd been picnicking in the shade cast by James's coach. "This is why I don't gamble," Phin said at his side. "Leave it to chance, lose it to chance."

James was mildly surprised to find him awake. For the last four hours, as James had leaped back and forth from Dalton's carriage (now moved out of range, along with Dalton and Tilney themselves, by the jostling crowd), Phin had been sitting here, stock-still, eyes shut, sunning himself like some rangy alley cat. Or perhaps Buddha was the better comparison, for his appetites seemed null: offers of ale, wine, pressed beef, and boiled eggs had been rejected in turn.

If Phin's aim was merely to be ornamental, he succeeded. Burnt dark by a foreign sun, whittled to lean muscle from his mountaineering, he cut a striking figure. When James had come back from the grand stand earlier, he'd found a gang of shop girls loitering about, ogling everything from Phin's *wide as the Channel* shoulders to the *exotic* length of his brown hair to his *coo, so manly* jaw. As for James, he had *divine* eyes and the face of a *god,* but his amusement had not suited them. Accordingly, they'd moved on, making a dead set at Dalton.

Now, Dalton was a trump, and would guard a friend's back even if his own broke in the process. But with his carrot-orange hair, invisible eyebrows, and weak chin, he was no one's notion of Romeo come to life. No one knew this better than Dalton himself, who'd invited the girls up top by asking them to "lie directly into my ear." When Tilney had mocked him for it, the ladies had retaliated, forcing Tilney, through subtle adjustments, to the edge of the roof. He now slugged drams and sulked. Prettier than a girl, he was not accustomed to being ignored.

"Poor Tilney," James said, as one of the girls threw her arms wide, knocking him sideways and causing him to make a desperate clutch for balance. "We should rescue him before his vanity collapses."

Phin grunted. "True. Wouldn't be much left of him without it." After a brief pause, he added, "Except his debts. I believe his pick came in last, just as it did yesterday and the week before."

Here was truth: Tilney had bad luck with horses. James had bailed him out more times, and to greater sums, than he could count. But another habit was also in play here—Phin's reflexive suspicion of blue bloods. The fact that he was one made no difference. And to be fair, back when they'd all been at Eton, it had made no difference to Tilney, either. There'd been no intimation, yet, that Phin would inherit an earldom. Most of his peers had dismissed him as a charity case—a suspiciously Irish one, at that.

Phin had fought back with contempt. *Eggheaded dolts spoiled into uselessness:* thus, at the tender age of ten, had he dismissed the majority of Britain's future leaders. Eyeing James, he'd added, *Really, I have no idea how you turned out so interesting. I do hope you manage to keep it up.*

James had tried. For years afterward, whenever he found himself in a situation where his position gave him advantages, he tested himself with Phin's rule: *Is this interesting?*—which soon came to mean, *Is this original?* It turned out, far too often, that the answer was *No.* Buying presents with one's allowance and using them to seduce village girls: unoriginal. Likewise for abusing the staff, badmouthing foreigners, bribing his tutors, and passing tedious judgments on people for behavior that did not concern him—much as Phin was doing now. "So he's a poor gambler," James said with a shrug. "Otherwise he's turned out half-decent. Come along tonight and you'll see."

"Can't," Phin said. "Duty calls, and the whatnot."

This was news. "You've been back for five months now. I thought you were well out of it."

"Almost." Phin seemed to be staring at the track, but James (who did have a talent for gambling, though regrettably no taste for it) would have wagered that he saw something else entirely. "I'm to put a few lingering concerns to rest," Phin added. "Then I'm done."

The silence that ensued felt familiar. And rather boring. Before Phin had gone abroad, they had spoken honestly with each other about anything they pleased. But over the years, these evasions and ambiguities had increasingly muddied their dialogues. Phin was not merely a "cartographer"; James had eventually gathered that much. But whatever he had done for the army remained opaque. This new remoteness to his manner was equally puzzling. What might cause a man who'd once been intent on mapping the world to now try only to look through it? "If I can help," James said, "you'll let me know."

Phin glanced over. "Thank you." It was a mark of how distant he'd become that James felt surprise at the sight of his gratitude, so transparently displayed. "And don't mistake me. It is good to be home. Although—" He drew a breath. "It does seem a bit . . . surreal, occasionally." He gave a dismissive shrug. "Wonder when that will wear off."

"Never, if you keep producing those bizarre concoctions. The last one nearly did me in."

Phin laughed. "Yes. Strong coffee might be a better idea. Ah—here comes Elizabeth." In one smooth move, he rose and leaped off the roof. Too quickly: he wanted to get away. Any conversation that bordered on personal matters sent him haring off like a rabbit from foxes. James's first response was to count it very convenient, which bothered him mildly.

He did not want to be bothered, not on such a sunny, reckless sort of day, and so he focused instead on the slight bobble marring Phin's landing. It was a considerable distance to the ground; most people would have discounted the misstep. But Phin had always been peculiarly graceful, equipped with a physical self-possession so complete that he could make a ballerina look clumsy. "Old war wound," Phin had said this morning, as he'd similarly stumbled on the step into the carriage. But the scent on his clothes had suggested otherwise. Among other things, it seemed he'd acquired a taste for opium. James had actually found himself holding his tongue. He had no objection to experimentation, of course, but as an overture to breakfast, it seemed dodgy.

On the ground, Phin's chivalry went unappreciated; Lizzie brushed past him, hopped a drowsing dog, neatly skirted three gamboling children, and scowled down two drunkards, all the while aiming the tip of her lavender parasol upward at James's head. A footman trailed closely behind, his powdered wig—only Lizzie would require her staff to go powdered at the Derby— wilting in the heat. "Ho, villain!" she called up. "You will abandon me in the grand stand so you can hoard the champagne?"

"Anything to avoid Nello," he said honestly.

"That swot?" She laughed. "To hell with him. You really must read your mail, Sanburne: I broke it off two days ago, and have been singing ever since." With a snap, she directed the footman to kneel on the grass. Then, one hand braced on the carriage, she stepped onto the man's knee, so her head popped over the edge of the roof. "Much better. Now tell me the real reason you're skulking over here."

"Am I not allowed a bit of whimsy?"

"Absolutely not. Your job is to be amusing."

"And if I don't feel amused?"

"Then you're in a great deal of trouble," she said smartly, "for I certainly don't see you as a banker."

He tilted his head, curious now. "Are there no other options, then?"

She laughed. "Well, there's always politics, but I'm quite sure neither party would have you." She glanced off to one side, then swiveled suddenly—James had to reach out and grab her arm to prevent her from falling. "Stop right there," she called after Phin, who was beating a stealthy retreat toward Dalton's coach. "You snuck away from James's fete last week before we had a chance to talk. You *will* come back here now and atone for it—preferably by showing more charm than a piece of wallpaper." As Phin shrugged and began to amble back toward them, she returned her stern frown to James. "Surely you aren't hiding from the gossip? Rumor has it you were nearly pecked to death by a bluestocking."

Phin drew up at her side. "I heard about this," he

said. From inscrutable Sphinx to grinning Cheshire in under three minutes: he always liked to be amusing for Lizzie. She had grown up on the estate next to James's, and in their youth, when Phin had come home with him for the holidays, she and Stella had taught him to flirt. In the years since, he'd made sure they realized the excellence of their instruction. "Be gentle with him, dear. Rumor has it that she was skinny, sallow, and went directly for his eyes."

"Not at all skinny," James said equably. The footman was growing red beneath Lizzie's weight. Choosing discretion over valor, he slid to the edge of the roof and dropped to the ground. "Not even sallow," he continued as he brushed off his trousers, then offered Lizzie a hand down from her servant's straining knee. "You see the use of gossiping with dowagers. In fact, Miss Boyce turned a very pretty pink as she dressed me down."

"Pretty?" Elizabeth set her parasol against her shoulder for a thoughtful twirl, her raised brow lending this movement a skeptical flavor. "This is Lady Southerton's sister, yes? She seems a very . . . *formidable* creature."

By this disdainfully intoned word, Lizzie, whose head barely topped his shoulder, meant *tall*. "Yes, I suppose she was formidable." Also somewhat magnificent, but this word seemed a curious choice, so he did not voice it. Miss Boyce's face would never stop a wandering eye. It was her manner, he supposed. To hell with courtesy; she'd swept down the hall like a Valkyrie, determined to smite the foolish mortal who interrupted her. He'd known a governess or two with that sort of presence, but he'd been seven at the time, and they'd had the advantage of a wooden paddle and sixty pounds. As an adult, he was better able to appreciate women who didn't shrink to the wall.

"And I hear Moreland was there," Lizzie prompted, as she batted away a fly.

He had not realized he was smiling until he felt the smile grow lopsided. "Alas."

"Interesting," said Phin. "Wonder if he put her up to it."

The idea startled him. "Any reason?"

Phin blinked, as if he'd surprised himself. "None, in fact." He glanced toward Lizzie, and his tone became teasing. "Bad habit of mine—seeing conspiracies in every coincidence. Have you a remedy for it, Mrs. Chudderley?"

Her lashes batted. "Don't turn to me, Ashmore. Why, I think my milliner is out to break my back."

As they nattered on, James found himself looking across the field, to the private boxes lining the grand stand lawn. Their windows glinted like blind eyes in the sun. Behind one of them sat his father, no doubt still smirking over the event at the Institute. It wasn't Moreland's style to arrange public spectacles, but he'd certainly been pleased to witness his son's comeuppance. What chance he'd had a hand in it?

Lizzie, laughing, poked him in the arm. "I know that look. You've started a witch hunt, Ashmore!"

"Wouldn't be the first time," Phin said. He did not sound as if he were joking.


Carnelly had a warehouse near St. Katharine Docks, a ratty, run-down sort of place that from the outside looked like a workhouse. James was never sure of the attraction that lured such a variety of characters to its entrance, but there was always some antic underway. Today, a vendor was selling chestnuts off a glowing-red brazier while a small boy jumped through hoops for pennies from passersby. A woman lurked by the entrance, swilling gin and flirting with a suitor—the paying kind, James suspected.

It was not the cheeriest of neighborhoods. But then, Carnelly was not the cheeriest of men. Inside, the cavernous gloom conspired with the smell of ancient artifacts (mildew, papyrus, brass polish: the smell, James thought, of upper-class theft) to create an atmosphere stifling to one's enthusiasm. James tugged discreetly at his necktie as he settled onto a bench by the door to wait. No telling where Carnelly might be. Experience had proved that it was useless to go looking; the aisles in this place were narrow, impossibly dark, and given to disappearing beneath sudden avalanches of crates. Besides, the forged stela made an excellent footrest.

He yawned as he waited. He was tired. There had been a break-in at his house last night—some silver candlesticks and a couple of vases had gone missing—and the staff was shaken. He'd spent a tedious morning interviewing them and calming their fears. What a dutiful lord and master he was. How nobly, how tall he stood beneath his great, great burdens. He made a face at the wall. Had Phin's potions been about, the wall probably would have made a face back at him. He found himself somewhat disappointed by its stolidity.

After a few minutes, a scuffling came from the darkness. A loud sniffing followed. Thanks to all the dust, the man had a perpetual cold. "Carnelly," James called. "For God's sake, man. Wipe your nose."

"Eh?" Now came a thump, followed by the splintering of wood. Carnelly's head popped out from a stack of crates. "Guv! Right lovely to see you."

"Stuff it," James said. "I know you've seen the papers."

Carnelly stepped out. He was wearing a butcher's apron and had a dirty rag in one hand. Built like an ogre, with shoulders and thighs twice the breadth of an average man's, he was nevertheless the last thing from formidable. It came down to his hair, James thought. One simply could not take seriously any man who had brick-red ringlets growing from his head. "Can't say as I was ever a reading man, sir."

James directed a speaking look to the archaeological journals stacked in the corner.

"Oh, those are just for show."

He came to his feet. "Your illiteracy, suspect as it is, fails to concern me. In fact, there's only one matter that does keep my interest. Can you guess it?" A moment of silence ensued. "That was not a rhetorical question, sir."

The other man swallowed audibly. "Taxes?"

"Try again."

"Virgins."

"Troublesome, I grant you. But fixable."

Carnelly's head ducked, but not quickly enough to hide a smile. He shuffled his feet. "Moreland," he said grudgingly.

"Bang on," said James. "Now, I have asked myself: knowing this about me—knowing my motive for seeking a truly remarkable specimen from Egypt, one that would make my father green with envy—why, then, would you risk my patronage and my *immense* displeasure by selling me a second-rate fraud?"

Carnelly gasped and tossed the rag onto the counter. "My lord! I would never!"

James sighed. "How long have we known each other?"

"Two beautiful years," Carnelly said earnestly, "and never was there a happier day than when you first walked into my shop—"

"I believe I came in to retrieve my billfold, but we will leave aside your nephew's thieving tendencies."

"Bless his wee heart. He takes after his father's side. No Carnelly would never unload a fake on you."

"I would hardly expect one to. So what in bloody hell is *this*?" James thumped a heel onto the rock.

Carnelly pulled his apron over his head and came around the counter to squat down next to it. "Well, well." His fingers brushed lightly over the stela's chiseled surface. "Oh, yes. It's fake, all right. But it's not mine."

"It most certainly is. It came over in the same crate as the urn and Amenemhat's papyrus."

"What?" Carnelly came to his feet with a bounce. "I sent you that? That wasn't part of Colby's haul. Hold on a minute. I've got the packing list for that shipment." He crossed behind the counter and proceeded to ransack a hidden area beneath it, causing an enormous cloud of dust to be raised. "Here," he said, coughing as he produced a ledger. His fingers flipped to a page near the back. "All the items what were acquired in Cairo. My man does a final inventory before they're transported to Port Said for shipping."

James came forward to browse over his shoulder.

A necklace with scarab amulet. Sculpture of goddess Bastet, with cat head. Papyrus from nineteenth dynasty. On and on it went, a remarkably diligent chronicle. "You'll leave nothing for Egypt, man."

"But you'll see, the stela's not listed in Colby's shipment."

James turned the page. "No," he said after a moment. "Did your man slip it in?"

"There's no reason for him to risk his job over a worthless piece of rock. Don't mistake me," Carnelly added hastily. "I believe you, gov. It's only—ah!" He snapped and reached down, producing another account book. Licking his thumb, he flipped through the pages. "Yes," he said. "Here. It was from the wrong crate, see. This was meant to go to another gentleman. Bloody Wilkins! I'll have his head. This is the third shipment he's sent astray."

James was beginning to feel amused. "So you keep a different ledger for the fakes? An admirable system of bookkeeping."

Carnelly frowned. "No, sir. I meant what I said—I don't knowingly trade in fakes. Too much risk for the profit. I have my good name to think of. It's a great disappointment, this." He tapped his finger against the sheet. "Our man Boyce is usually very reliable."

James straightened. By God, and a point to Phin! "Did you say *Boyce*?"

Carnelly looked aggrieved. "Yes, and he's a reputable sort. Official, I mean, not a tomb raider like Colby or Overton. Publishes in all the major journals, he does. Since Mariette died and the trade started up again, he's sent some good pieces. Not flashy, mind you, but nice and legal, like. I can't think what happened here. That piece of rock wouldn't fool a ten-year-old!"

James let this unflattering assessment of his own perspicacity go unremarked. "Does his *daughter* see the pieces he sends?"

"Miss Lydia, you mean?" Carnelly hummed a little tune. "A looker, ain't she?"

It was not the first phrase James would have chosen to describe her. The term seemed too commonplace to capture her appeal—or her rash and ill-fated bravado, if she thought to conspire with his father against him. "That's the one. I take it she does come here for a look."

"Well, she sees most of the pieces, sure enough. She's arranged most of his sales, these last three years."

"Did she see this one?"

"I expect not. It was meant for Hartnett. He's one of Boyce's special clients."

"You expect not, or you *know* not?"

Carnelly hesitated. "Well, I can't recall. I don't keep track of it. I'd have to check my files for the instructions from Boyce."

James cast a glance into the disordered gloom of the warehouse. "Your files," he said skeptically.

"It'll take an hour or so," Carnelly said. "But I'll find it."

"Please do." It was one thing to be upstaged by a forthright bluestocking who knew her antiquities better than he did. But it was another thing *entirely* to be upstaged by a conniving spinster who'd plotted with his father to arrange the whole scene. If the little minx had conspired with Moreland, she was about to regret it extremely.

# Three

"What preoccupies you, Miss Boyce?"

Lydia glanced up, startled. Mr. Romney had borne her lackluster conversation through four courses, choosing instead to gossip with the lady to his left. But now the lady was snoring lightly in her chair. Whether this bore greater testament to the immense heat from the fireplace, the free-flowing wine, or Mr. Romney's stentorian manner, she could not guess. She supposed Mrs. Fillmore had been doomed from the outset.

Clearing her throat, she said, "I was contemplating the lovely spread our hostess has laid." She gestured toward the excess of silver vases and candelabra weighing down the table. Through all of it, Lady Moreland had twined a cunning assortment of ivies and flower vines. Such Grecian beauty had proved unkind to at least one guest, the poor Lord Stratton, who had barely taken his seat before a sneezing fit compelled him to excuse himself.

"Nothing unusual there." Mr. Romney's humor was high; he broke with habit and did not seize the opportunity to lecture her on the seasonal dangers of gluttony and intemperance. "Tell me, now, what do the ladies say of the developments in the recent bombing?"

Lydia repressed a sigh. He had been greeted earlier

with great fanfare; some police victory to do with the Irish plot targeting Scotland Yard and the Junior Carlton Club. Mr. Romney would not, of course, have been involved in this victory. Nevertheless, by virtue of his editorship at one of London's largest dailies, he had the peculiar gift of appearing to facilitate all good news, since most often he was the one to break it. "I confess, we talk little of it." As he frowned, she added, "The season, you see . . . it is taxing."

"Yes, yes, this dratted custom," Mr. Romney agreed. "Long nights and heavy meals! No good can come of such indulgences, I assure you."

The doors to the dining room burst open.

A gasp went up. Lydia nearly dropped her glass. Sanburne stood on the threshold, dressed in full evening wear. He looked up from straightening his glove to cast a cordial smile in the direction of the table. Had he *kicked* the doors open? "Good evening, everyone." His eyes flicked down the chairs. "*Ma mère.* And Father! You look jolly well."

Moreland, caught without his cane, slapped his hands on the table to push himself up. For a moment it seemed he wouldn't manage it; a footman stepped forward to assist. With an angry grunt, the earl elbowed away the help and came to his feet. "What is the meaning of this?"

"I'm hungry," said Sanburne. "Countess, is that Egyptian quail I spot? How apropos."

Lady Moreland, a petite, fragile-looking woman with a head of graying blond hair, craned to look calmly toward the game platter in the hand of the footman behind her. "Why, so it is. Would you like some?"

"Ellen," Moreland said beneath his breath, but the countess's benign smile silenced him.

Lady Moreland glanced across the table to the footman whose help her husband had rebuffed. "Please have another place set for our son."

Total silence reigned during the minutes it took for the servants to arrange another place setting. The project required a great deal of shuffling; each of the guests rose in turn to allow for the rearrangement of the chairs. Throughout it all, Sanburne lounged in the doorway, insouciant as a street arab. At one point he gave a great, cracking yawn, exposing his tonsils to the assembly. He acknowledged the scattered flinches with a lazy smile, then scrubbed a hand over his head, leaving his sun-streaked hair in disorder.

All in all, Lydia thought, he looked more likely to fall asleep than make trouble. But when it became clear that the servants intended to lay the new setting at the far end of the table, he straightened and came forward. "I should like to sit *here,*" he said, and planted his fingertip on the tablecloth precisely opposite Lydia.

A premonition stirred in her gut. Ana, who had been disguising a laugh, dropped her hand and shot Lydia an anxious look. Lydia shook her head. It was a coincidence, surely. Over a week had passed since her ruined lecture; had he wished to act on it, he would have done so earlier.

In another minute, the table was prepared. The countess gave a nod, and the guests resumed their seats. Thank goodness they had not been dining *en famille.* It would have taken half an hour to remove and then replace the dishes.

The interruption cast a pall over the gathering. As dining resumed, the only sound was the clink of silverware and crystal. Lydia peeked at the earl. His color was very high and he had not retrieved his fork. His glower fixed firmly on his son.

The son took no note of it. With overstated enthusiasm, he'd begun to consume a quail. "Very tasty," he said. And then, after the next bite: "My, my. As delicious as irony."

These comments did not reinvigorate the conversation.

Lydia noticed that Ana was ogling him. She repressed a sigh. Formal blacks suited the viscount's tall, lean build. The severe knot of his tie accentuated the planes of his face—the high cheekbones and firm lips, the precise line of his jaw. The light from the chandeliers picked out the gold highlights in his light brown hair; his long eyelashes threw shadows as he looked to his plate. But his form was not a painting, to be admired for its appearance. There was a man behind that face— one who probably used his beauty to achieve all manner of disreputable ends. Indeed, the only meaning to be drawn from his looks was that the world knew no justice, or else the philosophers had it wrong, and beauty evidenced a black heart. For Lydia feared that the Devil himself would not outshine James Durham.

Perhaps her resentment was tangible, for his gaze lifted briefly to her. His eyes were a striking light gray; she could not imagine how she had failed to notice them at the Institute. As she stared into them, his lips curved and his brow rose. *Mocking me.* She looked down, flushing. The vain knave probably thought her enamored.

Just as the silence grew intolerable, the countess recalled herself to duty. Clearing her throat, she said, "How goes your father's work, Lady Southerton?"

"It goes well, I think," said Sophie. "But you will have to ask my sister for the details. I confess I have no head for such things."

"It goes very well," Lydia said immediately. Why she hadn't been the first person asked, she couldn't understand. "He is on the edge of a tremendous breakthrough. Further excavations are required, of course, but we believe he has located the true site of the first stop in the Exodus!"

Sanburne's fork crashed onto his plate. "How exciting!"

Lydia did not dare look at him. The rube! Thankfully, the countess tried again. "How marvelous, Miss Boyce. What an historic moment that would be."

Gratitude warmed her. "Yes, wouldn't it?" Papa would finally get all the recognition he deserved. Even George would be forced to acknowledge the greatness of his work. "It would be . . . beyond anything, really."

"But I recall that you dabble in science yourself. Lord Moreland attended one of your lectures at the Anthropological Society. Also, of course, your recent appearance at the Archaeological Institute."

Sanburne snorted. Lydia ignored this, giving a look of grateful acknowledgment to the earl. "Thank you for remembering, sir." He managed a small smile in return. "I've done no original research, yet, but I've had occasion to publish articles that synthesize the findings of other scholars. Recently, for instance, I wrote a piece on Mr. Tylor's study of the indigenous cultures of Mexico.

In conjunction with the work of Mr. Morgan, I find his theories tremendously inspirational."

"Oh, yes?" This from Lady Stratton, who sat across the table and a few seats down. It seemed that Sanburne's interruption had freed the other guests from the usual constraints. "But not as exciting as ancient Egypt, I expect." Here the lady cast a sly glance toward the viscount. Like everyone else, Lydia could not prevent herself from following it.

Heedless of the table's attention, Sanburne tipped his head to swill the entirety of his Madeira. As he swallowed, the golden line of his throat made her breath catch. A purely animalistic reaction, nothing to be upset by, but—*oh!* How ridiculous that such beauty should be squandered on a man. What did a man need to be admired, but good family, a good seat, and a bit of money?

With a start, she realized Lady Stratton was awaiting her reply. "On the contrary." Her calm tone did her proud: she would not allow the lady to needle her. "My father's interest lies in antiquity, but for myself, I find studies of contemporary culture to be more stimulating."

Mr. Romney spoke up. "Tylor is the chap that argues we're no different from savages. Won him a place at Oxford, no less."

Lydia smiled. "Yes, I suppose you could summarize it thusly." To Lady Stratton, she continued, "He believes that all human races come from the same stock, but that cultures evolve at different rates. His conclusion, of course, is that research on primitive cultures proves very helpful to understanding the origins of our own society."

Mr. Fillmore frowned. "I can't expect that pagans and pygmies have anything to do with where *we* came from."

The conversation had caught Sophie's attention. "Well, I for one quite agree with Mr. Tylor! One need only visit St. Pancras at six o'clock to conclude there are savages in our midst. Have you seen the way those bankers trample over each other to make their trains?" She made a mock shudder. "It quite terrifies me!"

Laughter passed down the table. Sophie had missed the point, of course, but she had reinstated the mood very cleverly. She had a knack for such things that Lydia feared she would never master.

Alas, Ana now spotted an opportunity to draw approval in her own direction. She leaned forward and said, "But those aren't the sort of savages my sister wishes to study. She dreams of going to Canada to observe Indian tribes. Can you imagine?"

"Indians!" The countess set down her wineglass, clearly appalled.

"It was only a passing fancy," Lydia said hastily. Mentioned once, casually and on a rainy afternoon, to her dratted, loose-lipped sister! "It would not be so unusual," she added, when the countess's frown deepened. "Many scholars have taken to studying Indian rituals. For instance, did you know that certain tribes practice a ritual called potlatch, in which they deliberately give away the most valuable items they own? Think of it—what a grand riddle! To treat one's treasures like rubbish."

Sanburne laughed.

*I should ignore him,* she thought, and looked around the table for the next remark.

But all eyes fixed on her—except Sophie's. Sophie was smiling down at her plate.

Lydia shifted uncomfortably. Had she said something outré? She did not think so. The lace at her neckline was scratching her; she felt the intense urge to pull at it.

The hush lengthened. Her fellow guests would give her no quarter, then; they wanted a show. "Very well," she said on a breath. "You find the idea amusing, Viscount?"

His face lifted. A three-year-old caught playing in the mud could look no less cherubic. "Oh no, Miss Boyce. I was only thinking that you've already made your point about primitive rubbish—and in a more public setting than this one. I simply wonder that you find the subject fascinating enough to dwell on."

She gave him a cool smile. "But of course. Rubbish is an important part of daily life, is it not? It thus provides a key to unlocking the patterns of our mundane existence. Although . . ." She arched a brow. "I admit, it is more illuminating in regard to some people than others."

"Really?" Sanburne opened his eyes very wide, aping confusion. "But I don't follow. *Patterns,* you say?"

He was leading her, of course. Pity for him. "Why, take yourself, Viscount." Conscious of the eyes focused on her, she produced another smile. "You are famed for these antics of yours. But even they might be said to follow a pattern—some mysterious map not of your own devising, but of society's. I do not say this pattern is based on *reason,* oh no. But it certainly possesses its own logic. Why is it that you get away with such japes, when others would be cut for them? How have you come to occupy a position in which no real consequences attach to your actions? The study of various cultures might help us deduce the basis of this privilege—a sort of map, leading to a better understanding of how *our* society evolved to this state."

All attention swung to Sanburne. He raised his glass to her. "Rubbish," he said mildly.

Too late, she realized the significance of his tone: it left doubt as to whether he was confirming her ideas, or commenting on their quality. He saw the moment she realized it—her dratted blush betrayed her—and taunted her with a wink.

Mrs. Fillmore stirred in her seat. "Surely you do not mean *society's* devising, Miss Boyce, but our Heavenly Father's. Society has no mind, no spirit, with which to design our actions!"

Lydia pulled her eyes away from Sanburne's. Her heart was beating rather more rapidly than necessary. The rogue—pulling faces, as though they were flirting! "Of course not," she said. "I did not mean to call it an architect; only to say it consists of a sort of pattern, which shapes everything—including those choices that we believe we possess."

The lady huffed. "You sound like a heretic!"

"Then I apologize, Mrs. Fillmore. But surely faith in science need not negate faith in divinity. If society has a pattern, then can't we believe God created that pattern, and had some reason for doing so?"

"Here, here," said the earl. "Let us not forget, Mr. Darwin himself believed in a higher power."

"I appreciate the heretical element," Sanburne drawled. "It is the only remotely interesting aspect to this argument. There is nothing sensible in what I do, Miss Boyce; I act on whim, as the spirit takes me. Indeed, I pride myself on it."

"Regrettably," Moreland snapped.

"Obviously you do." Lydia grinned into his overly handsome face. *Got you.* "Although I would not have thought you'd admit to it. Since it evidently means so much to you, I will say no more. A fool's paradise is too easily disrupted."

A hush fell over the table—broken only by Moreland's guffaw. She became aware, suddenly, that Sophie was glaring at her. Why, she had gone too far. She had openly insulted him, called him a fool. But oh, what a scalawag he was! His mouth was still smiling, but it did not match the intensity of his look: she had surprised him; that much was clear. It looked now as if he were trying to see into her brain.

Well, stuff his curiosity! All he would uncover in her was disdain. It was amazing what an heir might get away with, when the rest of them labored so onerously beneath the weight of a million stupid expectations.

"Lovely weather," Ana murmured. "I hope it will hold."

"Indeed," said the countess. "Although I thought yesterday's lightning storm to be rather unusual."

"May I say," the viscount murmured, "I do like a woman of impassioned opinion. It always bodes well for other matters."

Mrs. Fillmore gasped.

He was trying to force her retreat, and in the most impertinent manner imaginable. Lydia refused to look away. She could feel shocked stares pressing on her from every direction, but she did not care now. "Very well, Viscount. You have misunderstood me, so I will explain it more simply. Even when you are piqued—"

All heads swung toward his laughter. "Piqued? Do you call this *piqued*?"

"—you act in keeping with your character," she said more loudly. "Did you ever ask yourself why you would act so consistently, if there were not some pattern ready-made for you to follow? You are an actor who plays his role very well, but *you* did not make the role possible. Society did! Given the opportunity, science could deduce the pattern that guides your actions, and account for every one of them!"

"Ha!" Moreland pounded the table, making the crystal rattle. "This is capital! Not feeling so original now, are we, James?"

At her side, Mr. Romney straightened. "A flaw! I spot a flaw, Miss Boyce! One might exercise this science to good effect where heathen communities are concerned, but you are speaking of *civilized* society— that is, Christian society, premised on God's own laws. To claim the power to divine *that* pattern is heresy indeed . . . as Mrs. Fillmore has noted," he realized, and sat back with a nod to the lady in question. She nodded back stiffly.

"And yet, could we not view it as a pursuit that may lead us to a better understanding of God's laws?" Lydia looked around the table, seeing only bafflement and titillation—and, on the countess's face, an odd little smile. "An exercise in faith, a pursuit to better divine the Lord's intent. Either way," she added, a sideways glance at Sanburne's bored expression prompting her to malice, "the viscount has declared himself unafraid of heresy. He finds it *exciting.*"

Her taunt elicited a grin from him. "As, apparently, I must! I have no say whatsoever in my actions, and am a perfect mannequin. How relieving. I had long suspected that guilt was a useless pastime!"

"Oh, don't mistake me, sir. There are other roles available to you; you only choose to play this *particular* role."

"Lydia," Sophie said sharply.

"And what is *this role,* Miss Boyce?" Sanburne leaned forward. "Come, let's not dance around the matter: what *is* my act? Am I a wicked man? Recount my sins for me, darling—describing them at length, please. You know me so well, after all; and scientists, I hear, prize accuracy of detail above *all* things."

"Sanburne," Lady Moreland said reprovingly.

Lydia held up a hand. She did not need to be defended. "It's true, I do not know you well enough to begin," she said calmly. "And to invest your acts with the proper significance, I should require a period of observation, in which to situate your behavior in its natural element. Which I suspect"—here she slid a meaningful glance over the fine spread of silverware and china, the civilized décor and elegant furnishings—"is something else entirely."

"A period of observation." Sanburne sounded speculative. "Yet it took you less than a minute to decide the stela was a fraud." The smile that curved his lips boded no good for her: it was dark, considering, a little malicious. "Why is that, I wonder?"

Moreland chortled. "Still sulking over your humiliation at the Institute, James?"

The countess rose. "I believe we will withdraw now."

The gentlemen stood along with the ladies, no doubt bound for the smoking room. Mr. Romney was already patting his jacket to locate his cigarettes. Sanburne, however, remained in his seat; thanks to his impromptu appearance, he had no partner. Lydia felt his regard like a blunt nudge between her shoulder-blades as she recessed on Mr. Romney's arm through the door.

In the hall, Sophie caught her by the elbow. "What on *earth*?"

"Go on ahead with Ana. I must visit the powder room."

In the water closet, candles scented with jasmine cast a flickering light across the marble washbasin and maroon wallpaper. She splashed cold water onto her throat and wrists, and then pressed her face into a soft towel. Heavens, but she knew better than this. It was one thing to defend herself against the rascal, and quite another to make a spectacle of herself while doing it. She had fulfilled all of George's worst expectations. Why hadn't she simply ignored him? She could have smiled and let the provocation go unanswered. It was the countess's responsibility to keep talk flowing, not Lydia's. This was a terribly poor example for Ana.

She drew a breath and lowered the towel. Sanburne's arrival had been spectacular, outrageous; that would be the first story the other guests told. In comparison to his shenanigans, her remarks must seem very tame— barely worth mentioning, really. Who was she, after all? Nobody. An aging spinster who *dabbled* in science, who'd been invited as a courtesy to her brother-in-law. She knew where she stood in polite society: the only females more irrelevant than poor spinsters were the maids. Besides, it would not surprise anyone that she nursed strong opinions. They would expect it from a so-called bluestocking.

She pushed off the counter. Too many minutes had passed now. The best way to crush talk was to proceed to the drawing room as though nothing remarkable had occurred. Giving a tug to her lace gloves, she opened the door and stepped out.

Sanburne leaned against the wall a few paces away. "I hope you will forgive my manner at the table," he said. "I am simply agog at your powers of classification. Why, you spotted that forgery so easily, one might think your own father had made it."

Her jaw dropped. This was slander, and the worst kind: it was phrased in such a way that she could not respond without suggesting that she considered him serious. *Do not give him the satisfaction,* she told herself, and forced out a laugh. "What rubbish, sir. You were the one to buy the forgery. I wish you will not punish *me* for it."

He shrugged. "I confess, the idea of punishment generally leaves me cold. But I do find it remarkable, in this case, that a man so admired, so *respected,* would risk his good name and career by trading in fraudulent pieces."

A chill moved through her. "You cannot mean that."

"But I do."

Horrified, she darted a glance down the hall. This man was a loose cannon. It was dangerous to linger here and risk being spotted, but she could not walk away from his accusation. He might repeat it elsewhere, and suspicion was the worst sort of weed: it grew in any soil, no matter how pure. "I beg your pardon," she said icily. "You've cast a very serious slur on my father's name. I will ask you to explain yourself, or to apologize at once."

"Oh," he murmured. "What a wicked tone you take with me. Quite a fierce little tigress, when it looks like your game is up."

"What game?"

"I think you know it."

"I certainly do *not* know it." Her voice was rising; she could not help it. "You are raving!"

His soft laugh disconcerted her. "Yes, of course I am, darling. Madness runs in the family—or didn't you know?"

The remark effectively robbed her of speech. Of course everyone *knew* about it. The papers had talked of nothing else, four years ago. His sister had stabbed her husband to death, and been sent to the madhouse for it. The Durhams generally had been counted lucky: had she been born to some other man, a man of humbler station, she would have hanged. But for him to allude to the matter!

He pushed off the wall and strolled toward her, hands in pockets, all tall, smiling good cheer, as if they were old friends sharing a joke. "Tell the truth," he said, his manner playful, disarming. "Did he put you up to it?"

She shook her head dumbly. "*Who?* Who put me up to *what*?"

"Why, my father. Did he put you up to decrying the stela? I will give you the benefit of the doubt as to how it came into my possession, but surely he must have known you'd recognize your father's work."

Shock prickled across her body. He thought her to be in some conspiracy with the Earl of Moreland? "My father has nothing to do with forgeries." He was still coming toward her; she found herself backing up against the door. "He is a scholar, a revered one. If you spread any rumors to harm him—"

"What?" He simply kept coming. He was going to walk right into her. She caught her breath as he braced his arms at either side of her head. He leaned in so closely that his breath ghosted across her lips. His gaze roamed over her face for a moment, and then lifted to her eyes. Very softly, he said, "You will do *what*, Miss Boyce?"

She held herself perfectly still. Her heart was stuttering within her chest. She could not comprehend this. His breath smelled like mint, and his body was warm where it pressed against hers. He was tall, and surprisingly muscled; he had her pinned like a hare. "I will do something," she said unsteadily, "that you won't like at all."

"Oh, yes?" He reached up and laid a finger to her cheek. "Will you look away very coldly when we encounter one another? Will you tell your friends I'm a bad, bad man?" His voice dropped. "Will you badmouth me, darling?" He drew his finger down slowly, until it touched the edge of her mouth. Some horrible, nervous impulse made her lick her lips, and to her mortification, she accidentally tasted him—the tip of his finger, the salt of his skin.

Holding her eyes, he lifted away his finger and very deliberately put it to his own lips. He was tasting the spot her tongue had touched, as his gray eyes held hers, mocking, teasing. A flush of heat moved through her. Anger, she told herself. That was all. It was *rage*.

His mouth made a little sucking noise as he released his finger. "Lovely," he murmured. "Doesn't taste at all like a flustered, prickly, deceitful little spinster. Why, with a little coaxing, I might let you kiss me into forgiveness."

Her breath stopped. It was the cheapest form of ridicule, twitting her for her unmarried state. Ridiculous to feel hurt by it. She should not care. It should not bother her! But the events of this evening left her unbalanced. She had not put herself forward to be judged by *him*. She struck her fists against his chest and *shoved*.

He stumbled backward a pace—graceful, even in his surprise. Of course he would be. It infuriated her. "You low-down brigand." Her voice was low and hoarse. She felt very capable of hurting him. "I don't know what rotten part of your brain has produced this paranoid story, but you will hear the truth: my father is everything kind and decent and upstanding, and his name will *not* be blackened by the likes of *you*. You could tell everyone in the world this sick little lie, and they would only laugh at you. But perhaps that's what you want. You go to such lengths to make a buffoon of yourself, I shouldn't be surprised!"

"Oh," he said, and brought his hands together—once, and then again. Applauding her in slow, hard strikes. "This is a splendid show. Sarah Bernhardt has nothing on you."

"Your insults—"

"Insults? Darling, no! I'm tremendously entertained."

She paused to catch her breath. Her heart was still racing. "Is that what this is about? You want to have a little fun at my expense? Have a bit of revenge for being shown up as a fool in public—*twice* now, I might add? So you will fluster the ape-leader." Contempt weighted her voice, brought it back to a lower register. "How unimaginative, Sanburne! Go to the zoo if you wish to poke at your fellow creatures."

"True, it's not up to my usual standards. But have pity. This house tends to stifle my genius."

A scoff escaped her. "I take it back: you belong in the zoo yourself. You are a beast. The most uncivilized creature—"

He laughed. "And now you're back to lecturing, and the urge comes over me to stop your mouth by kissing it." As she gaped at him, he went on. "I never imagined I had so much in common with Carnelly, but there you have it: we are both quite perverse."

The name brought her up short. Carnelly was the importer who handled her father's antiquities shipments. Good Lord. "Did *Carnelly* tell you these lies?" It didn't square. Carnelly was rough-kempt and poorly spoken, but he was not dishonest.

"No," he said. "Carnelly showed me the packing lists for your father's shipments, and kindly pointed out where my fraudulent stela had been entered."

Dear God. "Excuse me," she said, and darted past him, down the hall.

The next morning dawned cold and wet. In the carriage, Lydia pulled her shawl over her mouth to dull the bite in her lungs. No matter the season, the air in the dingy, narrow lanes around Carnelly's warehouse tasted acrid and thick, a mix of coal smoke and urine, rotting fish and open sewage. As the vehicle slowed to negotiate a narrow passage, stray dogs leaped from the gutter to yip, their hair hanging in dirty, matted ropes over the visible architecture of their ribs. The footman who rode across from her tightened his hand around the gun in his lap. It occurred to her that the denizens of the East End posed less of a threat than the chance of the pistol misfiring. When they finally drew up at the warehouse, she exited with a sigh of relief.

But inside, her spirits sank abruptly. "It's true enough, miss," Carnelly told her, and handed over a sheet of paper. "The forgery's listed in your father's shipment, I'm sorry to say."

Her throat tightened. It was her fault, then. She had overlooked a conspicuous fake. How would she ever explain this to Papa? "How did it get in there? My father would not overlook such a thing."

He shrugged. "Perhaps someone broke into the shipment in Port Said—or Malta, even. Switched out the real piece for that shoddy number."

"Yes," she murmured. That was the only viable theory. She set it aside for the moment to consider her immediate course of action. The viscount would have to be dealt with. "I did not know Lord Sanburne was one of my father's clients." This, too, bespoke an embarrassing carelessness on her part. "Who is his agent?"

Carnelly had been sucking on his teeth; now he released them with a wet, popping sound. "Well, that's the thing, miss. None of that shipment was ever intended for his lordship. I generally sell him Colby's stuff. He's not very interested in the cheaper pieces." At her look, he flushed and shrugged. "I mean the less expensive pieces, miss, which your father usually trades in."

"He trades in the pieces that the Egyptian government *permits* him to sell," she said. "He is not a looter, sir; he is a legitimate scholar. You know this."

Carnelly cleared his throat. "Yes, miss. Point is, there was a mix-up. The stela was never meant for him." Sheepishly he nodded toward the paper in her hand.

The script on the packing list was familiar to her—the backward-slanting hand of her father's secretary in Cairo. But the descriptions did not ring a bell. "This is a shipment for Mr. Hartnett," she realized. He was an old friend of Papa's from university, and purchased pieces sight unseen.

"Aye, that's right."

Relief flooded her. The forgery had not slipped by her, then. Thanks to Mr. Hartnett's arrangement with Papa, she was not required to examine his items. "But why were these pieces in circulation? I told you to hold them—the gentleman passed away two weeks ago."

He sighed. "Aye. It was Wilkins that did it. He messed the whole thing up. And your father's pieces weren't the only things he got muddled, miss. Overton's stuff went to Colby's buyers."

Overton was a pig, still sulking over the defection of his best client to Papa's services. "Do not expect sympathy on *his* account."

"Well, I wouldn't. It's Colby I'm worried about. He's furious, he is. Threatens to pull his business over it. I'm like to give Wilkins a paddling."

Mr. Carnelly's nephew was a terrible trial to him, and the boy's blunders had become something of a long-running joke. But she could muster no amusement today. His incompetence endangered Papa. Mr. Hartnett would have realized that the forgery was not deliberately passed to him, but Sanburne had no cause for such confidence. If he made the news public, Papa's clients would abandon him. Worse yet, Papa's colleagues might begin to look on him with suspicion. Farewell, hopes of funding! His project could be delayed indefinitely. Not to mention, of course, the threat to Ana. A debutante's reputation was so fragile. What would Mr. Pagett's family say, if it were suggested that her father engaged in criminal activities?

Her fingers had set up a nervous tattoo on the counter. She flattened them. "You will send the rest of Hartnett's shipment to me at once, I'm afraid I no longer feel confident of their safety here. And in the future, you alone will handle our shipments—provided, of course, that my father decides to retain your services."

He sighed heavily. "Aye, miss. It hurts me to hear it, but I reckon I understand."

"I should hope so. And now I will wire my father about this matter." The prospect afforded her a measure of calm. "No doubt one of his workers, or perhaps a dockworker in Cairo, is responsible for this switch. Which means the real stela is on sale in some bazaar right now—at a horrible discount, I might add!"

"As you say."

She looked narrowly at him. "You sound doubtful, sir."

Carnelly shrugged. "I know your father as an honest

man. But this is a bad business, Miss Boyce. Doesn't reflect well on me, either."

Her hand slapped against the counter. "I certainly hope you're not implying that my *father* had a role in it!"

"Of course not," he said hastily.

"Because to think he would risk his reputation by trafficking in—in *fraudulent material* is beyond outrageous!"

"I expect so," Carnelly muttered. "I humbly apologize, miss. I intended no offense."

"I can't imagine what else you might have meant by it, then. Recall that this is my *father* you speak of, not some tomb raider like Overton or Colby. Henry Boyce is a *scholar*. He trades to support his work, not his bank account—and that work means everything to him! If you will only consider the separation he must endure from his own family, sometimes for years at a stretch—" She caught herself; she had started to raise her voice. "Well," she said, flustered. "I apologize for my . . . vigor. But it must be clear to you that he would *never* risk his reputation or his legacy—or the happiness of his *family*, for that matter—on such criminal shenanigans."

"No, miss." Carnelly pulled at a ginger ringlet. "I'm right chastened. Mr. Boyce is a fine man, and don't I know it." But his face twisted in some unhappy thought.

"Then what disturbs you? Be frank with me, please."

"Nothing, only . . . there's still the matter of his lordship. I can't rightly figure what happened to the pieces *he* was owed. No doubt one of Colby's clients is sitting on them, having a good laugh at my expense. Oh, damn Wilkins! Begging your pardon, miss."

She waved away his language. Here was an opportunity to put things right with Sanburne and hush his evil mouth up. "Give me the viscount's direction. I will see his lordship recompensed for the stela."

Carnelly brightened. "Why, thankee, miss, that's right kind of you. I expect he will be a bit more cheerful at the sight of a pretty girl on his doorstep."

She scowled to disguise the flutter of pleasure that this praise occasioned. Oh, vanity! She could not help it. She did not receive many compliments, but Carnelly always had a kind word for her. No doubt he thought it good business practice to flatter her; she mustn't take him seriously. "Thank you," she said, and pretended she meant the remark in response to the scribbled address he handed her. "I will send a note when I have dealt with the viscount."

# Four

James rose four hours after he'd fallen into bed. Displeased to discover that the body was not, at present, as willing as the mind, he dismissed his valet and crossed into the dressing room, taking a seat at the window as he struggled to wake.

He had been out too late. First the Novelty, where Dalton had found a brace of underdressed beauties— a couple of dancers and a receiving-house clerk, who spoke as elliptically as the telegrams she handled. Tilney had proposed taking them to the Cholomondleys' for a lark. It turned out that Michael and Melisande were entertaining, but their guests were Parisian, and easily amused. Champagne was opened. The opera dancers did a can-can on the dining room table, to great response. The clerk, not to be outdone, clambered onto the piano to belt out a rousing version of "The Boy I Love Is Up in the Gallery." But the liquor had toyed with her balance. In the final verse, she'd fallen onto and shattered a very nice vase. The Parisians had applauded, but the Cholomondleys proved less tolerant. James couldn't much blame them. The clerk had an awful voice, like a cat being tortured.

Expelled into the night, the party had transferred to Barnes's, where James had slouched on a plush red bench, comfortably drunk, and listened to the girls giggle as they drank Moët and Chandon from the bottle. Easy enough. One more night marked off the calendar. But tedious, all the same. "Do you have another suggestion, then?" Dalton had asked. Indeed, he didn't. And afterward, he'd slept well—a deep, dreamless sleep. But not for long. His head still ached.

The sun slid over his face, making him wince and scrub a hand across his eyes. He reached for a stack of correspondence on the escritoire. The most recent accounts from his factories in Manchester. A letter from Elizabeth, barely decipherable. Written while drunk, no doubt, for Nello had been with her; he'd added his regards in a postscript. The last envelope bore no return address. The script, at least, was clear. *Return the Tears, or face their Curse.*

Right-o. The third he'd received this week. It was amazing, the number of lunatics drawn from the woodwork whenever his name made the papers. He balled it up and shot it into the rubbish, then turned back to the window.

Belgravia's lanes were empty. Unfashionable hour to stir. In two hours, though, the road would be choked with phaetons. Adventurous ladies would take the reins in hand, leaving their nervous grooms to clutch for dear life in the tiger seat. Five hours hence, these same women would not be caught dead driving themselves. For their second trip to the park, only carriages or open barouches would do. God, but he was sick of Mayfair. It operated like a tedious piece of Swiss clockwork, and its thousands-strong flock of cuckoo birds moved so predictably to its beat that he could call their actions to the second. His understanding did not please him. If only he could scrub his brain clean of such trivia. Surely there were better uses for it than remembering a massive lot of nonsense.

But there lay the rub. Unlike a clock, this little world could not be smashed, and these idiotic trivia were not, in fact, so trivial. Much like the bars in a prison cell, they laid the outlines for the rest of his whole damned life. Phin's too, though he hadn't realized it yet. He thought inheriting the title had freed him, when in fact this storybook ending only marked his enclosure in another sort of cage.

"They are only customs," Stella had said once. "They don't have to be logical. They do no one any harm."

"Tell that to the Americans and South Africans," James had replied. "They feel the harm when they appear in a tim-whisky at three o'clock, and are sneered at by all of your friends."

She had smiled and patted his cheek. She was younger by a year, but liked to behave as if he were a child. "That's the point, silly. If they didn't give themselves away as foreigners, how would we know whom to cut?"

The image of her was so clear in his mind. She took after Moreland; bright blue eyes, hair of wheaten gold. But her face never appeared to him, now, without the bruises. God, how small and forsaken she had looked on the other side of those bars. The air rotten, reeking of vomit and shit, pierced with shrieks; and the other woman in the cell had been scratching her arms, silent, focused on her own mortification, raking long, deliberate furrows into her own bloodied flesh. Stella had curled into a ball in the corner and looked at him. She had not been able to speak, yet. But her eyes had pled for help. He could do *nothing*. They had dumped her in that pit and they had called it justice. He'd known she would die there. No question of it.

But somehow she'd survived. And after he'd raised holy hell, they'd transferred her to Kenhurst, where they said she had rooms to herself, and daily walks, and every comfort she might desire. He would have welcomed a demonstration of this paradise, but they wouldn't let him see her. At his first visit, he'd not made it past the asylum gates. On his second try, Dwyer, the asylum keeper, had called the police. They'd arrived soon enough, but not before he'd gotten the man's throat in his hands. Another minute, and Dwyer would not have been so smug. Dwyer would have been dead.

His father had sprung him from jail overnight. Indeed, Moreland had pulled strings so fast and forcibly that he'd snapped several puppets' necks. The magistrate had retired. The jailkeeper had been transferred. The policemen demoted. Dwyer alone emerged intact. Nothing would turn Moreland from his unswerving adoration of his daughter's jailer.

Christ, why would they not let him see her? All he wanted was one glimpse—enough to replace this last memory he had. The look on her face, that last time, almost made him wish he hadn't seen her at all.

A little laugh escaped him. There were a million ways to betray someone, weren't there? A simple thought could do it. Who was he to judge Lizzie if she drowned her guilt in wine, or abased herself in mislabeled lust for a tosser? As the bluestocking would remind him, they were only products of their society. And the beau monde had long since perfected the fine custom of shutting away anything ugly or troublesome—or of smothering it in a haze of debauchery. He was hardly innocent, on that count.

Oh, he did not wish to forget Stella. But sometimes he did feel a morbid fascination with her situation, at least as Dwyer had described it. Giving in would be so easy, in such circumstances. A schedule laid out, all the decisions made. An entire staff willing to force one through it if one could not work up the energy to do so oneself. No need to justify rising, dressing, cleaning one's face. Hers was a thoughtless progression through the allotted days, with nothing to oppose, nothing to choose. She did not deserve or need such treatment, but he could picture it well enough for himself.

Of course, the appeal was purely profane. It hurt to reflect upon, a pleasurable sort of agony, like tipping poison down one's throat for the sweetness of its taste. And the bile that rose in his throat as he sat here—well, that was the taste of contempt, aimed purely at himself.

A knock came at the door. His valet had returned; the butler stood at his shoulder. James sat up, mildly surprised to see them together. They nursed a sharp rivalry, which he was not, of course, supposed to know about.

"Sir," Gudge said. His unflappable butler was flushed. "Pardon the interruption, but you have a . . . visitor."

"At this hour?" Apparently he was not the only one who tired of convention.

"A most peculiar woman. I tried to turn her away, but she insists she must see you. Sir, her manner—well, before I had the footmen expel her, I thought it best to inform you."

Which meant that she spoke and dressed like a wellborn woman, and Gudge feared to manhandle her. "Did she give a name?"

"She is veiled," Norton said excitedly. "Head to toe, sir!"

Gudge shot the valet a stern look. "She would not reveal her name. I expect she feared the servants might talk." The assumption clearly aggrieved him. Gudge prided himself on his zealous campaign against household gossip.

Well, James thought. And here he'd been braced for a boring morning.


The lady perched on a chair inside his study was swathed more comprehensively than an Ottoman widow. Her outfit looked to be an odd juxtaposition of mourning gear and slate-gray walking costume. No wonder she hadn't wanted to give her name. The servants would have dined out on this story for a month.

He closed the door with rather more force than required. The black crepe veil bobbed upright. "Sanburne?"

He leaned back against the door, fighting a laugh. "Can't you see through that thing?"

Black-gloved hands emerged to lift the veil. Up and up they clawed, revealing a slim white neck and pointy chin, then long, pink lips, pressed—as he was coming to believe was her habit—into a grim line. Next emerged the long, straight nose. Finally a wide-set pair of hazel eyes appeared. They narrowed on him. He'd yet to move an inch, but already she looked at him as though he'd committed treason. She would be far prettier if she managed to relax.

He gave her a moment to speak, but it seemed her audacity had overwhelmed her. Her deep, rapid breathing was audible from across the room. A pin came loose, and the veil sagged to one side; as she reached back to straighten it, she knocked her own nose.

A smile twitched his lips. She was not clumsy, precisely. He doubted Miss Boyce would ever do anything so disorderly as stumble. But even at their first meeting, he had been struck by the careless aggression of her movements. She inhabited her body as thoughtlessly as a coat. It was strangely charming, this disconnection between brain and flesh. Rather like a dare. It made a man wonder what it would take to lure her awareness out from the disciplined confines of her brain to the soft, expansive surface of her skin.

He pushed off the door. "Come to give another performance?"

"I do not seek to entertain you," she said.

Yes, that much he'd guessed. He ran an eye down her figure. That spine of hers held her more rigidly upright than a backboard. What a queer, fierce duck she was! Her black hair was escaping its chignon; her gray skirts were muddied at the hem. Another woman might have armed herself before entering the lion's den—applied a bit of blush, or at least had a footman brush down her skirts. Then again, from what he'd seen of Miss Boyce, she did not stand in need of such commonplace armor. He took the seat opposite her. "Come to seduce me, then? I confess I'm hardly prepared for it. Barely combed my hair this morning."

She eyed him with dispassionate thoroughness. "You look well enough."

He was startled into a grin. "Do not flirt with me, Miss Boyce. I can't bear it."

Her brows rose. He gathered that she was intent upon delivering a repressive look. Alas, nature conspired against her. Her eyes turned down at the corners; it felt as though he were being taken to task by a puppy. "A springer spaniel," he said.

"I beg your pardon?"

"That's the sort of puppy I'd peg you for."

She had a nice color to her cheeks, when provoked. Classic roses-and-cream complexion, not a freckle or blemish to be seen—save the one at the edge of her mouth, poised precisely in the hollow of her upper lip. He'd spotted it the other night, and for some reason, felt compelled to put his finger by it. *The freckle marks the spot.* As he'd done so, her tongue—small, pink, wet—had peeked out to lick it. As though it tasted pleasant. He'd been badly tempted to have a taste himself. Amazing, after thirty long years, how one continued to surprise oneself.

"You are likening me to a *dog*?" she asked.

"I rather like dogs. And as dogs go, it's certainly a charming breed."

Her jaw flexed. She was grinding her teeth. Bad habit, that. Good to know she had one. "Very well, tease me if you like. I know my behavior robs me of the high ground. But I will beg your indulgence, and ask you to behave yourself anyway."

Hard not to be impressed by such gall. "Bravo, Miss Boyce. You enter a man's home uninvited, then tell him to behave himself. Thackeray could not have scripted it better."

Her throat moved in a swallow. "All right, I suppose that was outrageous. But—I confess, my nerves are unsettled. You would not believe the morning I've had. My sisters required the brougham, and I could hardly tell them that I needed it to visit you. But there were no cabs about, so I was forced to catch an omnibus. And it turned out to be fake!"

He laughed. "There's irony, for you."

Her amber eyes opened wide. "Irony? It was astonishing! Unlicensed vehicles, masquerading as London Generals! There was a lady in the garden seats, very neatly dressed, whom I can only surmise was placed there to lure innocents. For a five-pence ride, they demanded a shilling! What *is* the world coming to?"

"Oh, indeed. The effrontery of the grasping peasant. Grows daily, I fear."

She scowled at him. "I am not a snob, sir. I think one can take a stand against theft without indulging in class politics."

"You're sharper than your average snob," he acknowledged. "I'm not sure whether to laud a female education, or suggest it be outlawed."

Her chin lifted. It had a provocative little point to it. He wondered if anyone had ever bitten her there. She'd gasped when he touched her, and the sound of it—so inadvertently, unwillingly sexual—had lingered with him since. Only a small, brief noise, but it had quite overshadowed the appeal of the dancers last night. As the realization came to him, he realized, with a stirring of interest, that he was not quite comfortable with the knowledge.

"I have always been smarter," she said. "My education had nothing to do with it." Noticing the twist to his lips, she added, "That amuses you?"

"It relieves me. I had been wondering if you possessed any official faults."

The war between her wills played out on her face. It took her a full minute to give in to temptation, but that was no surprise. He had already gathered she was bloody-minded. "What do you mean?" she asked. "What fault?"

"Why, what but pride, Miss Boyce. You think a great deal of your intelligence."

She pursed her lips. The movement exposed a hint of dimple. In conjunction with her starchy manner, it seemed wholly incongruous. A mere anatomical fluke, he told himself, just a trick of her tightened lips. Nevertheless, he found himself staring at it, wondering what he might do to make it deepen. Breathy gasps, flashing dimples: the idea came to him that Miss Boyce's body liked to sabotage her.

"Of course I do. I'm a woman. If I don't think highly of my intellect, who will?"

He wrested his eyes from the dimple. Such a peculiar mix of affront and bravado. Her sisters were the acknowledged beauties, but Miss Boyce had her own charms—made particularly visible now, in the context of her improvisational honesty. Her eyes were alert with intelligence. The other night, he had looked into them and discovered they were heavy-lidded. This gave her a perpetually sleepy appearance, so she looked always as if she had just risen from bed. He smiled, suddenly won over. She had risked her own comfort to come here. Let her have her victory. "Touché, darling."

She did not like the endearment. Her face, so bright when she defended her learning, went as dark as a shuttered window. "But let me come to the point. You must wonder why I'm here."

"To beg forgiveness for your father's foul deeds, I suppose."

Her mouth tightened further. Christ, but that dimple conspired against her. It drew attention to her mouth, which was overly wide and completely unfashionable, and suggested prospects that were not appropriate to the moment. Or, for that matter, precisely legal.

Amusement stirred in him. Odd, unexpected, and undeniable: he was wholly attracted to her. At some primal level, his body took note of hers. The imperative it issued was blunt and unpolished: five thousand years ago, he would have dragged her off to a cave somewhere. And no doubt Miss Boyce of the Stone Age, bereft of an education to sharpen her tongue, would have sharpened a rock instead, and neatly gutted him.

He realized that she was nearing some conclusion. "Sorry, I missed that. Can you start over?"

Her gaze leveled on him. She had resolved not to be provoked: it was clear in the set of her jaw. "I will repeat it very slowly," she said, in the manner that mothers used with recalcitrant three-year-olds. "I know that my coming here is beyond the bounds—"

"Even when you break the rules, you insist on reminding me of them? Really, Miss Boyce, have mercy."

Her voice sharpened. "But I wanted to appeal to you in person."

"Oh, you do."

Her eyes widened briefly. She started to say something, then thought better of it. No doubt she had interpreted his statement correctly, but did not want to believe it. Poor Miss Boyce. This sober, tight-laced scholar, trapped against her will in a figure that smelled like flowers and communicated with his body in a secret language that perhaps even she did not recognize. No wonder she swaddled herself. The thought of inadvertently soliciting male attentions must no doubt appall her.

"Listen," she said, and came to her feet. "I paid a visit to Mr. Carnelly."

"Did you?" It did not surprise him, for some reason, that she would feel entitled to bowl into the East End. "How was it? Did you sample the chestnuts? They're very tasty."

She rolled her eyes. Pretty eyes, the exact shade of a harvest moon. Her best feature, he thought. And then, as she began to pace the perimeter of his carpet, he revised his opinion. When Miss Boyce moved, she . . . bounced. He turned to follow her progress. Oh, yes. While the lady did not seem desirous of providing entertainment, she also seemed unable to prevent herself. She walked as though there were springs in her feet. Some forgotten governess had no doubt despaired over these long, bouncy strides.

He realized he was smirking like a schoolboy. Embarrassing, really. The woman took less note of him that she would of Canadian rubbish. Still, he could not resist his curiosity. "Do you hunt?" He could see her as a horsewoman; she was what his Scottish nanny might have termed a strapping lass. Since it produced such serendipitous effects, top to bottom, he could not mind it.

She pivoted. The violence of her movement suggested some strong emotion, and her fingers were twined together before her, pressed into her skirts like a secret prayer. But her face and voice remained composed. "No, I dislike horses. And please let us stick to the point, Viscount. I regret to tell you that your conjecture was correct. The forgery did originate from my father's shipment."

He smiled. "How kind of you to confirm what I already know. Perhaps next you'll introduce me to myself. I hear I'm very popular."

The dimple peeked out. He silently congratulated himself. "However," she said with emphasis, "the forgery's inclusion does not mean my father had knowledge of it. I believe the shipment was sabotaged—the correct piece switched for the false one. At any rate, I have wired to Egypt. I'll let you know when I learn more."

"I see," said James. "So, you've come to tell me that while my facts are correct, your conjectures should sway me to disavow them?"

She blinked. His vocabulary had startled her. Oh, she was too easy. She fell into her preconceptions of him as easily as a fish into water. "No," she said, but her denial sounded uncertain. "Only that I wish to—oh, to apologize, I suppose, for the horrendous mix-up. It could never have occurred to me that your accusations were sound—although misdirected, of course."

She spoke all the right words, Miss Boyce did. But the stiff set of her shoulders, and the fisting of her hands, suggested that apologizing felt about as pleasant as a sword through the stomach. "Manners," he said sympathetically. "Very tedious. I suggest you shelve them. I don't miss them at all."

"Yes, I can see how they proved inconvenient for you." Her manner was so dry that it took a moment to recognize he was being mocked. He gave her an encouraging laugh. She had a great deal of potential, really. A little less starch and she would be as interesting as her dimple.

"Tell me," he said. "Why should I believe that it was a mix-up at all? How do I know your father isn't deliberately importing forgeries, and passing them off on the strength of his reputation?"

"He would never do such a thing," she said immediately.

"Oh? How do *you* know?"

Her response gave him a brief insight into the life of a carnival freak. She looked wholly taken aback by him—and then, all at once, very pitying. "He is my *father*," she said, in a tone that suggested he might be unfamiliar with the concept. "I know him better than anyone, sir—and so I know that this crime is so far beneath him that the very idea is laughable. However, I understand that you are unacquainted. I will ask you to take it on faith."

"A fine idea," he said. "I'll be glad to take it on faith, if you can explain to me why so many people count it as a virtue. By definition, after all, faith is rooted in ignorance."

She made a sound beneath her breath, a wordless *hmph*: clearly, with this remark, he had exceeded her lowest expectations. "Of course, I also intend to compensate you for the mistake. I will purchase the forgery for the same price you paid in expectation of a legitimate antiquity. I hope you don't mind that Mr. Carnelly gave me the figure for it?" She opened her reticule and began to fumble about. "This will put an end to the matter, I expect."

She had it all sorted, didn't she? A proper little businesswoman. Alas for her, he was not terribly in need of money. "I will give you the stela," he said.

She looked up from her purse. "For free?"

The surprised pleasure in her voice had him grinning. He could admire an honest greed. "Not precisely. I do want something in exchange."

She looked wary now. Smart girl. "What would that be?"

He drew out the moment with a poetic pause. "Why . . . only a kiss."

Color flooded her cheeks. "You're joking."

"Not at all. Do you know, Miss Boyce, I dropped a hundred pounds last night trying to entertain myself. But I must say, the amusement you provide me, merely by enacting the role of righteous justice-seeker—well, I couldn't put a price on it."

Her chest heaved magnificently. He felt a pang of loss that she was not in evening wear. These horrendous redingotes buttoned right up to a woman's throat. "You are a—"

"Boor," he said, coming to his feet. "Wastrel, rapscallion, heathen, savage, consumer of rubbish, dandy. Yes, I know. I don't profess otherwise. But I think it's a fair trade. You may have your forgery, and my discretion, for two minutes of friendly fun."

"Minutes!" She was gawking at him so vigorously

that he could see the rims of white around her remarkable irises. She took a step back. "What on earth!"

Had no one ever kissed her for that long? It just got better and better. He gave her a deliberately dark smile. It sent her back another step. Did she realize what sort of power she gave him, with that simple little move? "Against the wall again," he observed. "Seems we're uncovering a deviant bent. I quite like that."

She looked around frantically, as if only now realizing that she'd come to the end of the room. "I . . . I cannot."

It was fabulous how seriously she took such a little thing as a kiss. One would think he'd asked Joan of Arc to barter her virginity to expedite the second coming of the Lord. "You must have been raised in a cave," he murmured. "I don't think even country girls have a leg up on your naiveté."

By sheer luck, he'd said exactly the right thing. Her chin came up. Her eyes narrowed. Apparently she did not like to consider herself naive. He tucked that piece of information away for future consultation.

"Very well," she said flatly. "But I will have your word: one kiss, and the stela is mine, free and clear. And you will cease slurring my father!"

"My word," he said. "For two minutes."

With the dignity of a rebel facing a firing squad for political principles, she lifted her face and shut her eyes. "Do it," she said between her teeth.

His breath caught. It was the most erotic thing he'd heard in recent memory. The words seemed to take hold of his groin and give a tug.

Oh yes, he had definitely grown perverse. About

time, really. "Brace yourself," he whispered, and fought a laugh as she took a tremendous breath, like a diver launching into deep waters.

Lydia expected an attack. What else might she anticipate, when he had issued such a warning? But all he did was set his mouth, very gently, to hers.

She held still and tried not to breathe on him. His lips were warm. She smelled mint again. Did he chew on the leaves? It was not, precisely, unpleasant. As the moment drew out and he did nothing alarming, the muscles in her neck began to unwind. She'd been expecting a kiss like George's—some rough, bruising contact, full of design. But the viscount seemed content to stand there. Well, it shouldn't surprise her; he seemed lazy by nature. How many seconds had passed now? Surely they were halfway through.

A puff of warm air hit her: his mouth had parted a little. He was laughing, a silent gust of humor.

Mocking her! When it had been *his* idea! In a fit of temper, she pulled away. His hand came up and wrapped around her bare nape. It startled her.

He took advantage. His tongue pushed *inside* her mouth. Just a little. And then his mouth gently closed around her upper lip, and softly, very softly, he shaped it with his own.

The sensation did something strange. Her knees went weak. Her stomach fell. She gripped his arms, and their unexpected density—the way the muscles flexed above his bent elbows—disconcerted her. An aristocrat built like a dockworker. His legs came into her skirts, pushing her back into the wall—she could go no farther; what was he *doing*?—and then she realized: it felt good. He was pressing into her, and the feel of his long body against hers—hard, surprisingly so—made something in her uncurl and stretch like a cat in the sun. A low throb moved through her abdomen. This was . . . different. A wild thought dashed through her brain: his mouth was not taking something from her; it was persuading her to take from *him*.

Alarmed, she started to slide out from beneath him. He pulled away just enough to settle his forehead against hers. "Two minutes," he said softly. His eyelashes tangled with hers. She shook her head, and he laughed again, a kinder sound, as if she had pleased him. "Two minutes," he said soothingly, but made no other move. His eyes remained on her face, watchful.

She battled down a sudden feeling of guilt. This was for her family. That was the only reason.

Slowly she nodded. His mouth came back. Now he took her lower lip between his teeth and lightly bit. His tongue stroked away the injury, and his lower body pushed forward, so they were touching from lips to knees. So close. Could he feel the outlines of her legs through her skirts? The possibility made her breath go. He made a soft noise—she hadn't known men made such noises when kissing, noises that did not sound angry— and his hand slid around to cup her head, while his other arm took her by the waist, pulling her away from the wall. The only support she had now was his body.

At that realization, something opened within her. And his mouth opened, too, so the kiss became complex, dizzying. It spilled through her like music, like the vibration of an orchestra. She could not follow it in her head, but she was kissing him back now. How? This was a part of her she had forgotten, given up on. *I will never kiss a man again*—so many times she had thought it, alone, in the dark of her bedroom, feeling angry and wrong even as she mourned. It wasn't as if her first experience had recommended itself. But she was kissing a man now and it was *something else entirely.* With dim astonishment, she observed that her skill seemed more than adequate to the task; he made a little sound of pleasure and used his lips to open her mouth wider.

Amazed, she let him. The way their mouths moved together filled her brain like a puzzle, a map whose outlines were hot and ever expanding, spilling routes of warmth down her breasts, her stomach, the backs of her knees. As they unfurled, they summoned unmentionable places into awareness. She opened her mouth to it; she marveled at it; she was allowed to do so, just this once. What a bizarre, amazing thing this was, that his mouth was teaching her! A *real* kiss. A first-rate one. Oh, she had not known!

He broke off suddenly. His chest moved in a deep, fast rhythm. There was a peculiar look on his face. "Well done," he said, as if she'd just taken a trick at cards. "Not at all naive. Tongue and all."

Tongue and all! What power, in three small words. The sound of them moved through her, as overwhelming as his touch.

His eyes narrowed on her face. He reached for her. He was going to kiss her again.

But—she had no excuse for it.

She jerked away. For a long moment they stared at

each other. Oh, he was beautiful—his face narrow and chiseled, his cheekbones and jaw so firmly defined. He would have modeled for icons had he lived in the Byzantine Empire. Silver for his irises, topaz for his hair. She felt drunk on his face. He was—

He was a bottomless, flashy butterfly, full of empty attractions. About as trustworthy as a snake. And this charm of his was like an unguent. She would slip on it into her doom if she did not step away *this moment*.

She retreated a pace. The larger room, the commonplace furnishings, invaded her awareness. A weird bewilderment filled her, that the world did not seem changed. To think that she would have gone to her grave with only that pathetic memory of George— "You will send the stela to me?" Her voice sounded breathless, like a debutante with her first *parti*. She felt dizzy. She felt overturned.

"Ah." He blinked. "Yes."

Against her will, she turned to go, realizing as she did that his arms had settled again to either side of her, caging her against the bookcase. He seemed to like this position, the way it held her immobile. She put a hand on his forearm, testing it. For a long moment she simply stood there, looking at her fingers against his sleeve, feeling the warmth of his skin beneath the cloth—until she realized that what was stopping her: she was *flattered* by this. Oh, dear God. Her pride had better things to fasten to, surely!

On a sharp breath, she ducked out to freedom. At the door, though, she could not prevent herself from peeking back. He was still standing in that peculiar way, as if he were the only thing holding the bookcase up. His expression was puzzled.

The sight settled her. How often had she seen similar expressions on the faces of her father's colleagues, or the men in her audiences? *Men are trained to discount women in any number of ways, Lydia.* Papa was right: they never knew what to do, when one exceeded their expectations. She was not flattered by his interest after all. She simply felt glad to have unsettled him—and, of course, to know now what kissing should properly be like.

Feeling better, she took a moment to smooth her gloves. When she looked up, he was watching her. His bemusement had disappeared; in its place was a sardonic smile. "All straightened out?" he asked.

"I believe so."

"Would never do to appear in public looking less than neat," he said solemnly.

"My thought exactly. Viscount, I told you at the dinner that I did not have enough information to classify you."

His brow cocked. "And?"

She nodded. "I think I have gathered it now. You are suffering from an acute case of boredom-induced paranoia. No one is out to cheat or swindle you. And as for your bizarre idea that Lord Moreland was somehow involved in this mix-up—well, I expect he has more important things to do than conspire with ladies to play tricks on his son."

His smile turned thoughtful. "Are you throwing down the gauntlet, Miss Boyce? I'll gladly take it."

Wrong, very wrong, that the prospect should send a thrill through her. "No," she said, with more force than perhaps was necessary. "I simply wish to express that—that these pranks of yours are the most *childish* things I can imagine."

"Then your imagination wants exercise, darling." More softly, he added, "Perhaps I'll be the one to provide it."

She had no doubt he could do an admirable job of it. The thought disconcerted her; she blew out a breath to dispel it. "Or perhaps I will simply take it on a stroll through the park." Dropping him a mocking curtsy, she exited into the hall.

# Five

$\mathcal{P}$ain, like music, had its own rhythms. *Piano:* the glancing tap of a fist off the jaw. *Stacatto:* knuckles, jabbing one-two-one-two into the flesh of a muscular gut. *Forte:* the blow that took James in the nose and sent him stumbling backward in a spray of blood.

Hands smacked into his back, halting his retreat. The support kept him from stepping over the chalk line. There were few rules in this dark, smoke-filled place, but crossing the chalk would disqualify him. The crowd did not want that. There was nothing more popular in this part of town than the chance to see an English lordling get beaten to pulp by a man from home.

James's ears were ringing. He shook his head, and his teeth seemed to rattle in his gums. His opponent was a strapping Irishman, fresh from Cork, renowned for his ability to lay men flat—occasionally snapping a neck in the process. As James had ducked down the stairs into the ginnery, the proprietor had taken his arm and pulled him aside. "Go home," he'd said. "Not tonight, m'lord. I can't have a nob beat to death in me place. I'd be transported faster'n you could spit."

News of a worthy opponent had cheered James. In the quiet, well-appointed clubs of Maiden-lane, Queensbury rules prevailed; one might as well be boxing puppies. Here in the East End, where the only law was to avoid murder, he generally had an unfair advantage: a lifetime of steady meals and good medicine put him hands and stones over the competition. But this Irishman, judged from across the room, looked tall and thick, able to crush rocks with his palms. At any rate, there were worse ways to die than by a broken neck. One could rot slowly, locked away in a sanitarium in the country—or be smothered to death by feudal obligations.

A fiver had soothed the proprietor's worries. The crowd had yelled its approval.

Two rounds gone by now, and no murder yet. James was growing bored. The Irishman relied too heavily on his size. He had no speed, and his right hook left his flank exposed. Perhaps he was a late bloomer? As the man pulled away from his cohorts, his meaty fist delivered a very promising smack into the palm of his other hand. "C'mon, your lordship," he sneered, and crooked a beckoning finger. "Taste a little Irish justice."

James smiled and shoved away from the helping hands. Every muscle in his body was warm, glowing. A feint to the left, a jab to the right. A paw caught him in the belly; the breath wheezed out of him. The Irishman took advantage. A crescendo of pain: the bones in his face might break under this sweet hammer of fists. *Fortissimo:* the singing of agony in his blood.

But it did not suffice. It never sufficed, did it? The pain was not loud enough; it could not envelop him and it did not silence his thoughts. The basic flaw remained apparent, even as he swallowed blood. He could come here and play all he liked. He could walk the meanest street at midnight, unarmed, inviting all comers. He could throw himself down the stairs, but the architecture of his body conspired against him. He had fists like hams, didn't he. He had height, and muscle, and training. It would never be the same. He had defenses, and she hadn't. He would never forget having seen that knowledge in her face—the fear created by her own helplessness—how small she had been in comparison to Boland—

Anger ripped through him. His fists felt now like meteors, swift and dense, afire. An uppercut knocked the Irishman back. "*Hit* me," he screamed. Four jabs took the man to his knees. "Is that all you have? Stand up, goddamn you!" Spittle, blood—the warmth of it dripping down his face did not faze him. He barely felt it. His skin had gone numb. One small aim realized.

Fingers hooked under his arms, clawed into his shirt. He was dragged up, off bended knee, away from his opponent.

The interior of the public house was thick and hot. The Irishman lay in a heap on the ground. James lifted his head to watch the smoke spiral upward in lazy blue plumes, joining the mass that roiled beneath the timbers. Old building, this. Here and there a pewter pint glass clinked against wood, or a customer whispered for a six of gin; but the crowd was largely silent. James drew a breath.

"*Erin go bragh,*" he said, and let out a gusty laugh.

"Jesus, James."

He glanced up. A form was paused on the stairs, his features obscured by the light streaming in from behind him. But the low, smooth voice was unmistakable. At university, when very drunk, Phin had liked to sing. In the interim, he'd found other callings for it. Two years ago, during one of his brief stays in town, they'd met for a drink. Phin had been on the edge of what doctors would later diagnose as a malarial relapse, though he hadn't realized it at the time. A few whiskeys into the conversation, he'd said, out of nowhere, *I am a crack hand at interrogation: you would not believe the power of a warm voice speaking to you through the dark.*

It had been James's first inkling of the places to which "cartography" had led his friend. *I'll keep the lights on,* he'd replied. "Kind of you to drop by," he said now.

His remark broke the spell of silence. At once, voices babbled up from every direction—victors crowing for their wagers, erstwhile adherents of the Irishman cursing his name. From the corner of his eye, James saw someone deliver the downed man a kick in the ribs.

"Julking time!" yelled the proprietor. He wrestled his way through the now-milling crowd, two steaming glasses of gin in his hands. James took them gratefully. They reeked more sharply than turpentine, but went down like water.

Phin fought through the mob. "Bloody well done," he said. "Literally. You look as if someone took a mallet to you."

A throb was setting up in James's jaw. He poked his tongue back. The inside of his cheek was torn, but all his teeth seemed intact. He'd live to be pretty another day. "You wish to nurse me to health?"

"Beyond my capabilities. It's your brain that's broken, I believe."

James would have lifted a brow, but the attempt

made him wince. "Don't be tiring. If I need lectures, I'll visit Moreland."

"You're lisping."

"Am I? I know just the cure for it." He waved to the proprietor. At the counter, the bird fanciers were lining up their wicker cages. Best to get in his next order before the match started. "Another glass of your best rotgut, sir. Phin, will you join? The birds tonight looked very promising. I spy a German canary in that lot."

"No, thank you. I prefer my liquor cold."

"Right. Or in a pipe, I suppose."

Phin's brow lifted. "What a clumsy way to drink liquor. Are you sure you're not concussed?"

"If not to drink or to fight, why are you here?"

"To ask for your help. But I see you're determined to be useless for the evening."

"No surprise there," James said mildly. "Although I have just finished laying out the pride of Ireland. Some would call that a national victory." It dawned on him that Phin was in full evening dress. "Coming from somewhere?"

"The Stromonds'."

Ah, yes, the annual ball. Every matchmaking mama's most prized invitation. "My condolences," he said. "They must be on you like flies to honey." He rolled his head, feeling the sinews in his neck unwind. Another drink was pressed into his hand. "Bless you, O'Malley." He sucked in a breath, then downed the mug.

When he lowered it, Phin was still standing there, his expression attentive but unreadable. "I'm concerned for Elizabeth," he said.

"Oh yes?"

"Yes. It's a nice arrangement Nelson's got, there."

James sighed. This prudish streak had first appeared at university: while his fellow students had been chasing every skirt in the county, Phineas had read poetry and sighed in chaste admiration over the wife of a local vicar. "She's a woman grown, and hurts no one but herself." On a sudden laugh, he added, "I thought the army would have cured you of this Puritanism."

The curve of Phin's lips was enigmatic: a man obscurely pleased with himself. "So did I," he said. "Thank God for small favors. But you've mistaken me, James. It's Nelson I'm judging here. Although I will admit—I don't recall Liz being quite so . . ."

"Unpredictable?"

"That's it."

"Thank the late Mr. Chudderley. You missed those years." And then, as the hordes began to retreat to the walls, he waved away Phin's next comment. "Talk over the julking and you'll be bloodier than I am."

A fancier stepped forward, wicker cage in his hand, to set the German bird on a table. He tapped on the cage and stepped back.

The crowd audibly inhaled, as if fueling the bird's lungs for him. And then, easy as that, the canary began to warble. No fifteen-minute wait tonight, thank God. As the bird sang on, several spectators cupped their hands to their mouths, looking, James thought, about as reverent as if they were hearing the word of God.

At length, the German fell silent. The room exploded into cheers.

"Nine full julks," he remarked to Phin. "A record, surely."

"Perhaps. Ended on a tug whizzy, too. Nice touch, that."

"No doubt. I caught a tollick in there as well."

"Yes, I heard it. Now," Phin continued mildly, "as I was about to say—Puritanism aside, Elizabeth is stumbling about the Stromonds' ballroom with all the grace of a baby elephant. Granted, she doesn't weigh much, but it may prove fatal to the Stromonds' porcelain."

"Christ. Nello?"

"Nowhere in sight. She came in alone, and says she drinks to forget him."

James rose off the stool and shoved his arms into his jacket. This was the third time this month he'd had to hare off to rescue her. "You couldn't deal with it?"

Phin shrugged. "I don't deal well with irrational women."

"That explains your bachelorhood."

"And what of yours?"

"Moreland wants a grandson." Really, he was half inclined to put a gun to Nello's head and force him to the altar. Perhaps he would have done, if he'd thought marriage would reform the swine. But one couldn't reform a man's sincere lack of affection for his bed partner. When sober, Lizzie understood this. "I tell her to stick to wine," he said, as they wended their way toward the exit. "But she will insist on experimenting. Not with your tonics, I hope?"

"God, no. To her? You know me better."

"Right. You have a vehicle?"

"I'm traveling in full state. A brougham would be quicker."

"I came by cab, myself."

"A cab! To this neighborhood? Christ, James, have you a death wish?"

James did not answer. He preferred not to speculate when the answer wasn't clear to him.

The Stromonds' ball was famous for its luxury, and this year looked to be no exception. Exotic, hothouse flowers spilled from every nook. The ballroom windows had been replaced with screens of ferns and roses, so the light breeze passing through them carried fragrance into the crowd. The great electric chandeliers had been turned off. French lamps glowed at regular intervals along the walls, shedding a soft light that glimmered over jewels and silks. They also afforded the Stromonds a pretext to display the vast manpower of their staff. Resplendently liveried footmen circulated through the guests, trimming the lamp wicks before they could so much as flicker.

As Lydia watched this operation from the sidelines, she found herself torn between cynicism and amusement. Every society had rules that governed the proper display of wealth. As for England, the new democratic mood had forced the beau monde to find subtler methods for flaunting their fortunes. No one's footmen rode postilion anymore. One thought twice before taking out a carriage with the family crest. But richly garbed servants and expensive flowers? So long as they remained costly, they would never go out of style.

From the periphery of her vision, she spotted Lady Stratton bearing down, Mrs. Upton in tow. A sigh moved through her. She had planned to lurk

unobtrusively at the sidelines. But tonight, fresh on
the announcement of Ana's engagement to Mr. Pagett,
anyone who knew her was obliged to extend their best
wishes. The task of presenting a cheerful face was exhausting her.

Regretting her rudeness, she turned for the exit.
Apart from Ana's happiness, everything seemed a mess.
A wire had arrived from Papa this afternoon. He had
interviewed each of his workers, but still had no idea
how the forgery had gotten into Mr. Hartnett's shipment. The mistrust generated by his investigation had
soured the excavation, and led to carelessness and resentment among the laborers; he therefore thought it
best to close the site for the season, and book the next
available ticket to England.

Only a day ago, she would have wired him back,
begging him to reconsider. Of course it would be lovely
to have him here as they planned Ana's wedding, but
an early return would cost him precious weeks of work
at a very crucial time. Now, however? This morning,
Carnelly had delivered Hartnett's items. She had broken
open the crate in her sitting room and gone through the
pieces one by one.

Five faked artifacts. *Five,* out of six total.

Her heart began to drum again, as it had on and off
all day. She stepped into the hall, where a crowd milled,
brilliant in silks and jewels, to exchange compliments
and gossip. Below, latecomers crushed into the foyer,
fighting for access to the cloakroom. Her temple stabbed
complaint. She was tired and anxious, and there was
nothing she would have liked better than to leave early.
But she could not abandon Ana to the sole custody of

Sophie. Sophie was in a terrible mood. She had dismissed
the stela as a fluke, but news of these other forgeries had
panicked her into all manner of wild fears. Papa would be
labeled a criminal for certain. Mr. Pagett would jilt Ana.
George's political career might suffer, Sophie's friends
would disown her, etcetera, etcetera.

Her fears were baseless, of course. How could the
news get out? Lydia had the forgeries, and she had settled with Sanburne. The only real concern was how five
frauds had gotten into the shipment. But when Sophie
was in one of her moods, logic found no purchase with
her. "Then why did you even tell me?" she had cried,
when Lydia tried to soothe her. "Why ruin my nerves
like this?"

To Lydia's disappointment, the refreshment room
was already overflowing. As she continued on by, the
high, sweet note of a cornet floated out from the ballroom. The floor trembled as scores of feet stamped in
unison. A reel was underway. She felt in no mood for
such gaiety. With a quick glance over her shoulder—no
one was looking—she ducked into a darkened corridor.

In the relative silence, she found a little bench and
sat down. She could imagine only one credible explanation for the forgeries. Papa reserved his nicest pieces for
Hartnett. If an unknown villain had intercepted the
shipment, and knew enough about antiquities to iden-
tify the finest specimens, it was not so surprising that
only Hartnett's lot was plundered. A knowledgeable
thief would only take the pieces worth stealing.

But to replace them with fakes? It suggested a concern that someone would remark the missing items.
The criminal must work closely with Papa, then. He

must have access to the shipments at a very early point in their travels, when someone might yet notice that part of the cargo had gone missing.

Maybe it was good that Papa was closing the site early. Otherwise, the idea that he was being preyed upon by someone who lived and worked with him would leave her mad with worry.

A sound impinged on her reverie. She tilted her head to listen. A woman was . . . weeping? The noise came from somewhere nearby.

Lydia came to her feet and moved tentatively down the hall.

"I can't!"

The objection stopped her in her tracks. She peered ahead. The next door stood slightly ajar. Creeping forward, she laid her ear to the crack.

"Let me alone," said the woman.

A scoff sounded.

Lydia jerked back. That had been someone else—a man.

A fresh sob now—louder. It ended on a wail, as if the woman were in pain.

Oh, very nice. Drag a woman into the darkness and abuse her. This was exactly why she took such a hard line with Ana. She looked right and left. Her gaze stopped on a small candelabrum that stood unlit on a low table across the hall. She stepped forward and plucked out the candles, then gave the fixture an exploratory heft. It was not heavy enough to do much damage, but a branch in the eye would stop anyone.

On a deep breath, she turned back to the door. Beneath the nudge of her shoulder, it swung silently open, revealing a dark Turkish carpet that unfurled across a long, book-lined room. The Stromonds' library. As she stepped inside, she held the candelabrum low. If this was a simple lover's quarrel, she did not want to look a fool.

It took a moment for her eyes to adjust to the dim lighting. And then her breath fell backward in her throat. A lady lay crumpled on the floor in a pool of turquoise silk. A man knelt over her, and his face—

*His face was bloodied.*

"Unhand her," she said. Neither of them appeared to hear. She hefted the candelabrum and strode forward. "I said, *unhand her*! Or I shall"—she couldn't hit him from this distance—"*throw* this at you!"

The man looked up. The swelling disguised the cast of his features. Had it not been for that tawny hair and those striking gray eyes, she would not have recognized him.

*Sanburne!*

The viscount's eyes remained on her as he spoke. "Oh, look, Lizzie." His tone was unexpectedly casual. "A heroine comes to save you from your brandy."

# Six

The candelabrum still in her hand, Lydia hesitated. Fresh cuts scored Sanburne's face. He looked piratical. Her first thought was to congratulate his assailant; her second was to wonder if she should be threatening the lady instead. It took a great deal of strength to deliver such a beating.

Sanburne noted her indecision, but misread it. "Be sure to put some weight behind it, Miss Boyce. I would hate to see you stub your toe."

Rustling silk drew her attention. The lady, formerly face-down on the rug, now shoved herself upright. Her arms and face looked unwounded, but a manhandling had knocked her coiffure askew, and chestnut locks were slipping down her shoulders.

As she shouldered a strand out of her face, Lydia gasped. It was Mrs. Chudderley, the professional beauty, and, rumor had it, Sanburne's fiancée. An unpleasant sensation twisted through her stomach. The woman was even more beautiful in person than in photographs. Had she any idea what her betrothed did when closeted with other women in his study?

"Damn it!" the woman burst out. "Bloody tournure. It's gotten twisted. James—give a hand!"

"Straighten it yourself." The viscount dropped onto

a sofa, stretched out his legs and crossed them at the ankles. "God knows you need some project to keep you busy."

"No one asked *you* to come," the woman shot back. Her speech was slurred, as though she'd just woken from deep sleep. "I was doing very . . . *well* on my *own*."

Lydia's fingers twitched around the candlestick. Something was odd, here. She felt terribly awkward, as though she'd stumbled onto a stage where a play was in progress, and the actors, being otherwise occupied, did her a kindness by ignoring her.

"Before or after you toppled into the water closet?" asked Sanburne.

"I didn't *topple*." Mrs. Chudderley slumped again to the carpet; her words became muffled. "Slipped."

What had he said as she'd entered? A sinking feeling overcame Lydia. *Come to save you from your brandy.*

Oh, heavens. Swallowing, she lowered her weapon to the ground. The viscount remarked the movement with a malicious smile. "Will you look at that," he told Mrs. Chudderley. "Even your savior despairs of you."

What a fool she was! Her cheeks felt afire from mortification. What was it about Sanburne that led her into these predicaments? "Forgive me for interrupting. I will—I'll just go now."

The viscount swiftly sat up. "Pardon me, Miss Boyce, were we ignoring you? I do apologize; one mustn't neglect one's nemeses." From his seated position, he sketched a low bow that took his chest to his knees.

"Miss Boyce?" Mrs. Chudderley rolled to one side for a look. A bejeweled pin slipped from her lolling head, dropping with a glitter to the rug. "The bluestocking?"

Lydia grimaced. She was no self-taught ninny, but people would insist on applying the label. "Good evening to you both." She pivoted on her heel for the door.

"Wait," the woman called irritably. Lydia looked over her shoulder. Mrs. Chudderley was making a desperate face, all large eyes and fluttering lashes. Alas for her, Lydia had been inured to such mugging shortly before Antonia's sixth birthday. "Help me with this," the lady pleaded.

Her waterfall skirts *were* tenting oddly to one side. One of those new bustles, no doubt. Served her right for helping to set such an absurd fashion. "Fix it yourself."

The woman let out a sob. "For God's sake," said Sanburne, and dropped out of view.

Where had he gone? She took a step back in his direction, and discovered that he had draped himself across the sofa, one arm pillowing his head, like some sort of male Odalisque. Meanwhile, on the carpet below, the professional beauty clambered onto hands and knees to give the act of standing another try.

Out of nowhere, Lydia felt the urge to laugh. What a perfect mess they were! "I'm not a bluestocking, you know. I'm a graduate of Girton College."

A brief silence ensued.

"I've already been lectured about her credentials," Sanburne said to his fiancée. "I believe she's talking to you."

"Yes, yes," Mrs. Chudderley said irritably. "Please— help!"

Lydia considered her. Shy young girls and moonstruck boys saved up their allowances to purchase photographs of this woman. Would they spend their money elsewhere, if they could see her as she was in this moment? For that matter, would Sophie still consider her glamorous?

With a sigh, Lydia decided that they probably would do. After all, even she could recognize a certain brash panache in the way Mrs. Chudderley clambered on all fours. Biting down on a thoroughly inappropriate smile, she marched back to the sofa. "Stand up, then."

"Can't."

Lydia looked to Sanburne, who heaved a dramatic sigh and sat up. Sliding his hands under his fiancée's arms, he hauled her upright. "Lizzie's a bit like a children's top," he offered over the lady's head. "Unbalanced, but very entertaining—at least for the first five minutes."

His manner was quite unexpected. He seemed exasperated, even a bit amused—but Lydia detected none of the reproach one might expect from a man whose future wife was behaving so outrageously. Alas that Mrs. Chudderley did not seem to recognize the rarity of his temperament. "Funny," she said, and scowled. "Hurry up, now, do. Reach under and straighten me out. Sanburne won't look!"

After a moment of hesitance, Lydia sank to her knees and reached under the woman's skirts. Her advance was obstructed by a shocking petticoat: crimson silk, with baby ribbons threaded into the hem!

"Oh, look," Sanburne drawled. "Miss Boyce disapproves. She is *blushing*."

"What do I care?" Mrs. Chudderley snapped.

"Perhaps you should," Lydia muttered. *Or I will leave you tangled like a fish in a net.* She fought up through the lace and finally located the problem: the disgraceful petticoat had gotten twisted. She could not imagine how that had happened. "This back-shelf style is ridiculous. You could support a tea-tray on it!"

Sanburne laughed. "Excellent. Ring for some Earl Grey; Lizzie can make herself useful for once."

"Stuff you," Mrs. Chudderley said rudely. "Anyway, I meant to have it sewn in with half-hoops, but the seamstress is an *idiot.*"

One good yank brought the petticoat around. The bustle settled into place. "There," said Lydia, and came to her feet just as a knock sounded.

A tall, dark gentleman poked his head through the doorway. These pretty men traveled in packs, it seemed. "I've had her carriage brought around." His sober manner relieved Lydia. At least someone in the group had his head screwed on straight. "Are you all right, Elizabeth?"

Mrs. Chudderley sniffed. "Sanburne is so *mean,*" she said, and launched herself across the room, staggering from bookshelves to chairs for balance.

When her hand came down precariously near to a priceless statue, Lydia took a quick step forward. "Careful," she said sharply. "That is the Lady of Winchester!"

The gentleman sprang forward from the threshold to grab Mrs. Chudderley's elbows. She submitted with a limp flop onto his chest, saying plaintively, "*You* will not be mean to me, will you?"

His free arm closed around her waist. "Never." He glanced over the lady's head to the viscount. "I'll drop her home, shall I?"

Sanburne had retreated to slouch against a bookshelf.

His hands hooked casually into his pockets, he seemed unmoved by the sight of his fiancée in another man's arms. "Good luck with that." His laughter sounded unkind. "She will want to go to the Trocadero."

Mrs. Chudderley turned in the man's arms. "I will *not*. Though . . . I shouldn't mind oysters from Rules'. May we, Phin?"

"Home," the man said gently. He drew her out the door. It closed, shutting them into an ominous silence.

The viscount stared at the space vacated by his fiancée. Lydia could not read his expression. If Mrs. Chudderley had not given him those bruises, what had happened to him? It looked as though he'd been hit by an omnibus.

The depth of her curiosity alarmed her. He was a simpleton with a taste for flash, that was all. If she could not keep her eyes from him, it was only for the same reason that terrible accidents drew a crowd. The fascination he exerted was entirely morbid.

His regard shifted to her. "That's not the Lady of Winchester."

Startled, she cast a glance toward the bust. "Yes, it is."

"As the Yanks like to say: nope, it ain't."

His arrogance needed a knock-down. She threw him an arch look, then walked to the item in question. It sat on a low table, its ancient surface lit by the steady glow of a gas lamp. "The Lady of Winchester is significant for its perfect blend of indigenous and Roman aesthetics," she said briskly. "You see here"—she laid a finger on the diadem in the Lady's hair—"a classically Celtic feature. But you see *here*—in the widened eyes, the long, flat nose, and the downturned mouth—touches more reminiscent of Greco-Roman theatrical masks. It is the lady," she concluded. "I've seen prints of her many times."

He pushed off the wall to stroll to the other side of the bust. "You see *here*"—he rapped his knuckles against its scalp—"a very lovely reproduction of the original, which I purchased and installed in my library two years ago." He looked up, giving her a playful smile—inviting her to laugh with him.

The temptation was so strong that she had to fold her lips together to contain herself. *Do not encourage him!* "Of course. For a moment I thought you might be more learned than I gave you credit for." She turned on her heel.

"Running away?" He sounded surprised. "I didn't mean to embarrass you."

Her hand paused on the door-latch. She stared at a knot in the grain. "You did not embarrass me, sir. We are alone, without chaperone. It would be improper."

"Improper? As opposed to what came before? That was a very heroic entry, by the way."

She snorted and gave him a look. As if she'd been instrumental in the making of that scene! *That* honor clearly went to brandy and bustle. "I thought you were assaulting her, Sanburne. But if you were feeding her liquor, it's no concern of mine."

"Feeding her liquor? Good God. And here I thought you'd met Lizzie before."

"No matter," she said with a shrug. "I won't breathe a word of it."

"In keeping with your role as the upright moralist."

She laughed, a short sound of disbelief. "A moralist

would no doubt preach to you, and then spread word as quickly as she was able. No, Sanburne: if I plan to be discreet, it is out of concern for the lady—and in keeping with my *character.* "

He crossed his arms and leaned against the back of a chair, looking for all the world as if he were preparing for a lengthy conversation. "So you mean to say that you pass no judgments? That gels poorly with my memory of our recent conversation."

"I pass many judgments," she said frankly. "But unless I'm asked for them, I do not assume that they are of interest, or concern, to anyone but me."

"And if I asked about my own character? Oh, I know you've decided I'm paranoid. But would the scientist share with me her other conclusions?"

The curiosity in his voice seemed genuine. But why would he care what she thought of him? She rubbed an anxious finger over the door latch. He had such a lovely mouth, she thought. Full and well developed. It might have overwhelmed another man's face. But the firm slant of his cheekbones, the straight blade of his nose and that uncompromising jaw, balanced it out very well.

Her fingers tightened. That was his problem, of course. A weaker chin, or muddier eyes, and perhaps he would have endured a few knocks as a child and learned some humility in the process. Clearly his assailant tonight hadn't achieved a thing. "You're a butterfly," she said. "Aimless by nature, useless by choice, and highly decorative. Annoying, when you flap into someone's face."

To her irritation, he laughed. Surely there was no

greater nuisance than a man who did not mind being insulted! What weapon could a woman employ against him? "A butterfly? All right, Miss Boyce, well done. Yes, I rather like that. A butterfly, pinned in a very nice glass cage."

Whatever had happened to give him those bruises, it had clearly made him maudlin. "Oh, yes, *Mayfair*," she said, and pulled a face. "What a *terrible* prison. Would you rather be in the factory with your workers?"

"Been asking after me, have you?"

"Would I need to? I cannot think of any place short of China where your reputation fails to precede you."

His smile was lazy. "I told you I was popular."

So he was. He behaved very stupidly, and people adored him for it. Ah, the wonders of a title! She pitied etiquette writers; what an onerous task, to convince people that social conventions had any basis in reason. "Indeed. Despite your best efforts, everyone bows and scrapes to you quite willingly."

He sighed. "Unfair, I know. The larger world is moving beyond such attitudes, but you'd never know it in Hyde Park." He looked moodily around the room. "Noblesse oblige. Just keeps on kicking, like a fallen horse that needs a bullet. Ah, well." He shrugged and pulled a flask from his jacket. "I find my freedom where and when I can."

"You will not find your freedom in a bottle," she said scornfully.

He looked up at her, his gray eyes sharp. "And you will not find yours in books, or rules, or books about rules. But that hasn't stopped you from being damned smug about the effort."

The words stung. Did he think it gratified her that the world demanded such punctilious behavior from her? Perhaps he forgot that not every woman could depend on a heroic rescue from the dangers of brandy and a badly sewn bustle. She drew herself upright. "Do you know, I believe my analogy was mistaken. You are not a butterfly, but a billiard ball. You crash about in the most aimless sort of way—"

"Yes, I've gathered you disapprove of me. When you're not kissing me, that is."

A flush warmed her face. Of all places, how dare he mention the kiss here, in the room his fiancée had just exited? "Disapprove of you?" She manufactured a laugh. "No, I'm not so energetic as *that*. Should I disapprove of you, I would have to disapprove of dozens of other gentlemen, all of them over-moneyed and over-privileged and—dare I say it—under-occupied. No, Sanburne, you mistake me entirely. I hate to admit it, for I know it will strike at the heart of your posturing, but I am *bored* by you. You, and your whole little circle I expect, are one of the more typical instantiations. You find them the whole world over. Privilege rarely produces a mind worthy of note, or a manner worthy of emulating—or, for that matter, a lifestyle deserving of interest."

"My." He cocked a brow. "What a mouthful. And yet you have lingered several minutes to engage with me. I suppose I should feel grateful: I would not have expected a scientist to risk her good name for the chance to be *bored*."

He was right. The intimacy of this whole exchange struck her suddenly. Why *had* she lingered?

"Do you know," he said more gently—she must look

overwrought to merit that tone—"I'm really not trying to provoke you. In certain circles, Miss Boyce, this approach is known as small talk."

"Small talk?" She could not figure out if he was making fun of her, now.

"Yes. Are ladies of science not familiar with the concept? Generally concerns the weather, cricket, the deserving poor. Well, you're right on one count—lovemaking generally isn't acceptable for discussion." His lips twitched. "Oh. I see by your charming blush that you *do* know the concept!"

She did not dare ask which concept he meant. "You are wicked, Sanburne."

He flashed a row of unusually straight, white teeth. "And you are a good judge of character. Also, of course, fraudulent antiquities. Not to mention that look you can deliver with your eyes: lethal! I say, what other talents are you hiding? At present, they seem potentially numberless."

"*Now* you are trying to provoke me."

He grinned. "Yes. Now I am."

The admission disarmed her. She looked at him in bewilderment. "Why?" she asked. "*Why* do you try to provoke me?"

"Hmm." He propped an elbow on the chair as he considered her. "I'm not sure. You amuse me? I enjoy these little chats."

And so did she. That was what kept her here. Against every better judgment in her brain, she enjoyed matching wits with him. Dear heavens! And here she'd assumed that he had none. Her bemusement grew as she studied him. Something about him didn't quite square. Unfortunately, this made him . . . interesting.

"Ah," he said suddenly. "One more thing comes to mind: I admire your mouth, and I'd like to kiss it again. Anything else? . . . No, I believe that covers it."

She swallowed. His inappropriate declaration meant that she had to leave now, which seemed strangely . . . disappointing. "Well," she said. *A little more indignation, Lydia!* "I also possess a talent for a memorable exit." She pulled open the door. "Watch: you will learn something."

"Scared away by talk of kissing? I suppose it is only to be expected, from a woman of your limited experience."

Scared away? That could not stand. She whirled back, the door slamming behind her. "Is it? How delightful to hear! Is it also to be expected that I should find you looking more colorful than a Christmas tree? I confess, if *I* drove an omnibus, I should not brake when you fell into my path."

He stared at her. With some satisfaction, she realized that she had managed to startle him. "Oh, you *are* entertaining," he said, and pushed off the chair to prowl toward her.

Alarm darted down her spine, settling, with a queer, pleasant shiver, in her stomach. "Don't get ideas."

"I can't help it," he said in a meditative tone. "You inspire them. May I say, this is a lovely coincidence. I'd been hoping to run into you."

"I can't imagine why. Good evening, Viscount."

A hand closed over her arm, pulling her back. "Can't you? I thought I'd just explained myself."

"Let go of me."

His light eyes moved down her arm, coming to rest on the bare patch between her glove and sleeve. His thumb settled into it, pressing gently, calling forth—with that one small touch—an acute awareness of how closely they stood. Her body came to life; her nerves lit: they remembered this, and more. They remembered how he had felt pressed against her. "That is what you are supposed to say," he murmured. "But tell me, Miss Boyce: do you really want me to let you go?"

There was her problem: she very much feared the answer was no.

His thumb made a slow stroke across her inner elbow. Her breath hitched. "I do not mean to ruin your exit," he went on, and his hand began to exert the lightest pressure—not enough to pull her forward, but enough to suggest the idea. "It looked very promising. You're very good in this role, aren't you?"

He was wearing a subtle cologne, the barest trace of scent, a cunning ruse that lured one to step closer and breathe more deeply. She fought the temptation by focusing on his mouth and instantly recognized that for a mistake. He had kissed her with that mouth. She wrestled her eyes down to his open shirt—scandalous to appear in shirtsleeves, to bare the length of his throat to any passerby—and then, finally, to his free hand. His knuckles were split. He lifted them to her waist, his long fingers settling, light and warm, at the crook where her hip began. "What role?" she whispered.

"The typical spinster. Righteous, stiff, bloodless. You don't quite convince me."

"That's not my failing." Her words emerged in hushed tones, and suddenly the conversation felt intimate, as if they were whispering secrets. "If you subscribe to such preconceptions, you've only yourself to blame."

"Educate me, then."

The invitation solicited a quick pulse between her thighs. She colored. There was no reason for his words to affect her like this. But the scene was rapidly assuming an unreal quality, as though her mind had detached from her flesh, rising to float somewhere above her, permitting her baser instincts to reign. *You should go. You should turn away.* So a little voice nattered from that space of remove. This was how women were ruined. This was why they *let* themselves be ruined.

But curiosity held her immobile. No one had ever tried to seduce her. She could not count that incident with George; it was too shameful, and he had been drunk. Besides, he had blamed her for it.

The thought darkened her mood. She would have pulled free, then, but he chose that moment to close the distance between them. The fit of their bodies startled her. It felt like an answer to some question she hadn't yet thought to ask. Her curiosity did not feel satisfied, though. It felt . . . whetted.

"You are far from bloodless," he said into her ear. "On the contrary. You stick your chin out and practically invite people to bash up against you." His thumb pressed harder into her arm as his voice lowered. "And I will admit it, Miss Boyce: I find the prospect of a bashing irresistible. I'm always looking for new ways to break my head open."

"You're raving again," she whispered.

"No. You take my meaning. That's the joy of seducing an intelligent woman: you follow me perfectly."

His lips settled against her temple, and his breath washed over her in time to the thud of her pulse.

Goosebumps rose along her arms. His face turned, the bristle on his jaw scraping her skin as his teeth trapped her lobe. Heat, dampness—his tongue ran delicately along the tender rim of her ear.

She swallowed against an animal urge: she wanted to press her face into his throat. Oh God she wanted to do it so badly she could imagine exactly how his skin would feel beneath her lips and nose. What was *wrong* with her? She should never have come in here; she should have left as soon as she realized Mrs. Chudderley was not in danger. Her mistakes were very clear to her now, and how strange to think he encouraged them! He praised her for doing exactly what she should not do, and the fit of his body against hers was causing something within her to unfold, to grow stronger and clearer as it developed. Like an anagram unriddling itself, or a maze slowly straightening. With her face against his neck, the darkness would be so complete. Her eyelids trapped shut by the warmth of his skin. No distractions to prevent her from focusing on this inward sensation.

Her hands moved of their own volition, sliding up along his back. In the hollow beneath his Adam's apple, a pulse throbbed, picking up strength as her lips touched it. His skin was hot, firm; it smelled of things she couldn't parse. Sweat, yes, but also something darker, thoroughly male. She had tasted him in his father's hallway, but he had smelled different then—more civilized and predictable. A wild impulse unraveled in her, spreading out to her fingertips, which curved and dug like claws into his back. She opened her mouth on his throat.

He made a guttural sound, but did not move. Did

not question her. She held still, waiting. He must be shocked. Pray God he *must* be. *Reprove me,* she silently begged him, with the taste of him on her tongue. He tasted like salt and cream, darkness and heat; and he made no remark. In the hush, even his breath seemed to halt. The texture of him was rich and carnal, spiced like a fine dessert from a sophisticated kitchen, where sugar was considered too simple a flavor. She was so hungry for something new, and he had put his teeth on her. It was fair play.

Her teeth closed on his throat.

He reacted instantly. His hands drove up her rib cage and caught her beneath her arms. He pushed her back against the bookcase and she caught one glimpse of his silver eyes before his mouth pressed against hers. This kiss was harsher, stronger, more delicious; she had more of his tongue now, and she was willing to take all of it. Surprising him no longer mattered; the taste of him fired her blood, lured her body forward, stiffened her fingers on his shoulders to pull him in, until he thrust as closely against her as physically possible. His fingers would bruise her, but she liked the pressure. *More, more, more:* the word beat through her as her hands moved up to knot in his hair, tightening until it must hurt him. But his kiss spoke only of pleasure. Hot, wet, coppery, rich—

She wrenched her face away. The taste remained on her lips. "Stop," she managed.

He leaned back. The split in his lip had come open. The trembling hand she wiped across her mouth came away dotted with blood. Dear God. The sight girded her impulses, snapped her wits back into place. Mauling each other as if they were savages!

Her eyes lifted. She beheld him now through a haze of better sense. His face was a stranger's, and she had more respect for herself than to settle for the cheap curiosities of a libertine's touch. She sidled away from him, along the bookshelf, her back thumping painfully over the leather-bound spines. When she was safely out of his reach, she said, "I hope you are entertained!"

A beat passed. He cleared his throat. He was still breathing heavily. "I do not think it one-sided," he said.

She could match that composure. "Of course it wasn't. I'm not the only one who plays my role well!"

His lips formed a smile that seemed more disbelieving than friendly. "Do you mean to call me a rake, Miss Boyce?"

"A cad, more like."

His eyes narrowed as he studied her. "I can only think of one caddish motive for touching you, and I will gladly admit it. My father thinks you very sensible. Disproving him, even privately, would delight me."

The taste in her mouth turned sour. "This is another episode in your silly game, then? You are shameless."

"I am honest," he corrected gently. "There are a dozen reasons to kiss you, and not all of them are good. They never are, I think. But rest assured, the most compelling reasons concern only you." His eyes dropped to her mouth, then, and all at once, she realized he wasn't joking. Whatever his motives, he felt this weird tumult as strongly as she.

The knowledge shook her as his taste, and the blood, had not. If he was baiting an ape-leader, she could dismiss him out of hand. But if he was genuinely interested in her . . . stars above, it seemed as nonsensical as the prospect of a zebra romancing a hen. Science did not support such mishaps! Like was drawn to like, and she was nothing like him at all. He belonged with a woman who looked like Mrs. Chudderley.

His *fiancée*.

Pain—humiliation?—spiked through her. *Mrs. Chudderley,* one of the most beautiful women in England. Oh, he was a rascal! "Your fiancée would not appreciate this."

He frowned. "My . . . do you mean Elizabeth?" What, did he have more than one tucked away somewhere? "On the contrary, darling. I expect she would be very entertained."

*High-flyers.* Perhaps it was the shock of this little tête-à-tête, but she had difficulty mustering her usual contempt. "That's very odd, and I can't approve of it."

"You don't have to," he said with a shrug. "At any rate, we aren't engaged. It's a rumor, one she finds convenient. Keeps the fortune hunters away."

"Ha!" He thought her born yesterday. "That's a very *convenient* story, indeed."

"Let me persuade you of my sincerity." His smile was meant to tempt. "You could make a study on it."

And he would manage to persuade her. She had no idea how he'd come to hold such a power over her, but every bit of her flesh responded to the prospect of an hour's distraction. She wrapped her arms around her waist, remembering now why she had been glad to be done with gentlemen. The nerves, the butterflies in the stomach—the sickness of uncertainty—it completely unbalanced her, and she could not afford such distractions right now. But no doubt that was her main appeal:

it must afford him real pleasure to set her on her ear, to watch a woman of good sense goggle and fluster despite herself. He would laugh about it with his friends later on. *Not bloodless,* he would tell them, *but a bit desperate, all the same.*

The thought acted like ice. She was too smart to repeat her mistakes. She would not become entertainment for another handsome sophisticate whose real interest was reserved for women of equal flash. Not that she thought Sophie flashy, of course. But if not flash, then beauty. She started for the door. "Don't come near me again," she called over her shoulder, realizing, only belatedly, that it had been she who'd come to him, both this time and the last.

Thankfully he did not remark on it. But when she had reached the threshold, he did call, in a taunting singsong like some brattish child, "Save me a dance, Miss Boyce."

"I do not dance," she said firmly, and pulled the door shut on his smile.

# Seven

It was a bad month that brought James to his father's home twice. As he entered, his body rebelled: throat closing, shoulders knotting. The place felt like a crypt. Stagnant, moist air, at least ten degrees cooler than the street outside. The scents of orchids and lemon wax were so thick that he felt dizzy as he made for the library.

The door stood open. As he paused to let his eyes adjust to the dim interior, his father's voice floated out, dark and noxious as tobacco smoke. "Late. What a surprise!"

Moreland sat in an easy chair flanking the low table by the hearth. He did not rise at James's approach, but the man beside him came to his feet. Dark, closely trimmed hair; a clean-shaven jaw; rigid posture. Military background? Contempt had James's lip curling. Yes, must have a soldier or two to keep order at the madhouse. God forbid the lunatics should forget discipline.

"This is Mr. Denbury," said his father. He had a cane propped by his chair—not something James had seen before. Doubtless the old loon was too proud to use it in public. "An attendant at Kenhurst."

"How do you do," said Denbury. His fingers were limp and damp, his handshake reluctant.

"Tolerably," James replied, and they took their seats. "Dwyer couldn't make it, eh?"

Denbury shifted. "No, sir. He is unwell at the moment."

"Right." Poor chap was probably curled up in a ball somewhere, trembling. "What a shame. I would have been very gentle with him, this time. Do tell him I said that."

"Sanburne," his father said warningly. He had lost more weight, and the spareness of his frame was turning his looks against him. His high cheekbones now emphasized the sunken hollows beneath. Those deep-set eyes—Stella's eyes, such a bright and unlikely blue— were sinking also. He looked more devilish by the day. James hoped he did not survive to reach the point where small children ran from him. No doubt their fear would gratify him intolerably.

With a yawn, James reached for the port. "Denbury! You have the look of the lock-step about you."

The man sat up a little. "Yes, sir. A fine eye you have." Moreland's snort made him hesitate only briefly. "I served with the Forty-third in Burma."

"Infantry, were you?" James uncapped the decanter and lifted it for a sniff. "Well. Explains the second-rate port we've been served."

Moreland thumped his cane. "The deuces! That is a Forty-six, you bufflehead!"

"Ha! Is that what Metcalfe told you? Dished once again by your butler. I always suspected he didn't care for you." To Denbury, James continued, "It must have been dreadfully tasking." The port gurgled out of the bottle. One—two—three fingers. He already had a headache; there was no reason for moderation. "Transitioning from the tropics to Hampshire, I mean."

Denbury cleared his throat. "Well, sir, I can't say I was sorry for it. It's certainly a sight more peaceful than the Orient."

"Oh, indeed, I expect the madhouse is *very* restful."

Denbury made a little hiccupping sound. "Ah—that isn't what I meant, sir. Not that I find it—unpleasant, like. I'd hoped to become a doctor, as a child."

Moreland made an irritated noise. "Enough small talk. Shall we begin?"

Denbury handed them each a sheaf of papers. Stella's name was printed neatly atop the uppermost sheet. "Lady Boland's quarterly report."

Quarterly report. As if Stella were some stock, whose progress might be charted and codified for the shareholders. James paged through it with increasing disgust. What she had eaten for breakfast each day. How long she had slept each night. Her attitude at evening services. The level of interest she exhibited in improving texts. *17 March: Lady B— refused copy of* Practical Piety. *Threw* The Invalid's Chapbook *at attendant's head.* "What is this? The boredom cure? Christ, *I* should go mad if you forced me to read Hannah More."

Denbury goggled at him. "Begging pardon, sir, but Kenhurst is not meant to provide entertainment. Our business is no less than a full rehabilitation of the morals."

*Morals.* Good God, if he could strike one word from the English language, that would be the one. "Of course. That was always my sister's problem. Had nothing to do with Boland beating her within an inch of her life. The problem was her *morals.*"

Moreland pounded his cane against the floor. "Your

presence is not required for this meeting, James. Mind yourself, or I will have you thrown out!"

"But it's so interesting," James said. "Don't you think? This is, after all, your daughter we're discussing. Tell me, Denbury, how does one evaluate morality? Does it have to do with"—he flipped to a random page—"how many bites it takes to chew a piece of bread?"

"Well, we might say it does, sir." Denbury slid an uncertain glance at Moreland, whose grunt made him hesitate briefly before continuing. "Mr. Dwyer holds that there's a proper way of doing every thing. And I expect he's right, sir. Why, one could choke on a piece of bread, if one did not chew it well enough. Or give offense to one's companions—"

"God forbid," James muttered.

"—which would demonstrate a lack of compassion that is un*christian*," Denbury said stubbornly. "At Kenhurst, rules and regular order are thought key to the health of body, spirit, and mind."

"My. That line sounds familiar. Does Dwyer make all his employees memorize it?"

"Thank you for delivering these," Moreland said curtly. "You may tell Dwyer that I appreciate it."

As Denbury rose, James gave vent to an incredulous laugh. "That's it? You're not going to ask about her parole?"

The startlement on Moreland's face hit him more sharply than a fist. "Come to reality, James. The court would never grant it."

"How many judges do you own, old man?"

"It is not so simple as that—"

"And parole is not uncommon."

Moreland made a scornful noise. "She's in no state to be released. Why, it's by her own insistence that we don't visit."

"I have yet to see proof that she made that request," James said flatly. "A letter, in her own hand—it would not be so difficult. But you're content to believe Dwyer's nonsense, aren't you? You're happy to leave her there rotting."

Moreland flushed an impressive shade of red. "By God, we will not have this argument again. Speak to Boland's family about whether she is rotting in the manner *they* might wish for."

Denbury cleared his throat. "In fact, Lady Boland has made significant progress. Mr. Dwyer expresses some reservations, but believes a full recovery might be possible by next year."

Moreland pushed himself upright. "You tell Dwyer that such announcements are not his to make."

A prickle of shock moved down James's spine. "Sweet God. You have no intention of getting her out, do you? You intend to keep her in there for the rest of her natural life."

Moreland cast him a furious glance. "Don't be a fool. We are speaking of the here and now."

Why was he surprised? If Moreland—hell, if *any* of them, her old friends, old lovers, cousins, aunts, and uncles—had their way, she *would* remain at Kenhurst. She was no longer a person, after all. She was merely a—blight. A blot, that threatened to spread in the manner that blots did, thereby staining the names of those who'd been associated with her. Even Elizabeth barely mentioned her, now. Better to keep her locked away, then, where she might do no harm to their precious reputations.

God *damn* them. He came off the chair. Denbury's abortive flinch provided him only a fleeting satisfaction. "I would wish you to the blackest hell," he said to Moreland, his voice low and rough; it was the best he could do to keep from screaming it. "But why bother? You're already halfway there."

The old bastard did not so much as blink, although his breathing grew audibly labored as he struggled to come to his feet. The sight should have stirred pity in a son's breast. The coldness with which James watched this effort no doubt appalled Denbury. It would appall anyone: objectively, he knew this. But it was *Stella* who had been closest to Moreland, *Stella* who had cosseted and petted him. If Moreland wanted compassion, he would have to find it from her. He would have to release her, God damn it.

His father finally attained his footing. "Denbury, you will excuse us."

"Yes, God forbid we should have witnesses," James said coldly.

Denbury walked quickly out. As the door closed, Moreland's lip twitched into a sneer. "Tell me," he said. "I am most interested to hear it, James. What use should I have for your opinion? A rash, good-for-nothing libertine, who is content to sit on his hands and whine—why should such a man merit my respect? My mistake was to invite you here in the first place. Stella's welfare is none of your concern."

"She is my *sister*, you black-hearted bastard."

"Quite right," Moreland snarled. "Your sister. My

*daughter. My* responsibility, not yours. And thank God for it! You would have her back on the streets, exposed to the scorn and derision of her peers—"

James's laughter felt wild, hot in his throat. "So dirty looks are a worse fate than imprisonment? Is that why you put her away?"

"Good God! She *killed* a man, James!"

"She defended herself against a brute twice her size! And you would lock her away for that? You should have applauded her!"

Moreland smacked the cane onto the tabletop. "Enough! By God, you are like a three-year-old—so damned stubborn about the way things *should* be that you cannot recognize the reality! She is sick! She cannot be set loose!"

He spoke of his daughter as though she were some rabid dog. "You are the biggest bloody hypocrite in London. *You* talk of helping her? That's rich. Where were you four years ago, when she actually needed you?" When she had run from Boland, and society had whispered and mocked and forced her back to that deathtrap on Park Lane. "You're lucky it was Boland they buried. Had Stella not picked up that knife, *she* would be the one in the grave."

Moreland's face grew stony. "I will not rehash this."

"You never *hashed* it in the first place. Is this to be her punishment for surviving that monster?" To be locked away for good, where her swallows might be counted, her every mutter frowned over and analyzed? Where she might be *improved* until the day she died? "What of *your* punishment? When she really needed your help, what the hell did you do? You sent her back to him. *You* sent her to her doom."

"Enough! *I will speak no more of it!*"

"Yes, set it from your mind! Clearly it does not trouble your goddamned sleep!"

"Sanburne." The voice, the soft touch on his arm, took a moment to register. His rage was like a cloud, holding him in a numb crimson thrall. But his stepmother's hand squeezed, very lightly, and he was forced to exhale and address her.

"Countess," he said. He cleared his throat. "How do you do."

"Better, if you will take a calm breath," she said gently. "You will not settle this argument now. And I think you have both given each other enough pain for today."

If she thought Moreland was capable of feeling anything, then she knew a different man than James did. He managed a slight smile for her, then turned on his heel for the door.

In the hallway, he surprised a footman lounging against a sideboard. The man jumped straight. "Sir. Are you leaving?"

"I don't require an escort." He'd grown up in this house, God help him.

The man swallowed audibly. "My apologies, sir. Orders from Lord Moreland."

"Ha! Very well." James cut a swift pace down the hall and into the anteroom. He wanted out. The very air here strangled him.

But by a stand of flowers, he found himself slowing. His stepmother had redecorated this room. A simple scheme of blue and white now prevailed. White orchids bent graceful throats over the lips of blue Bohemian vases; the carpets, drapes, and upholstery were cobalt.

She'd always nursed strange beliefs about colors, crediting them with any variety of abilities—white to calm the spirit; blue to inspire good will. Two very ambitious aims, when living with Moreland.

He reached out to touch the waxy petal of a fresh orchid. Stella had loved the countess like a mother. What did Lady Moreland think of this? Did she miss her stepdaughter? Did she care nothing for Stella's freedom?

James glanced toward the window. An unusually strong wind had set up; branches were whipping against the glass. He stepped forward to grip the casement. He could see the wind bowling toward him. It bent the tops of trees, so they curved at him like claws.

*Boom:* the gale hit the window. Glass rattled as bits of dead leaves and rain splattered against it. He laid his palm to the pane, and found it icy. "'Oh, to be in England,'" he said mockingly, "'now that April's here.'"

It would be sunny in Nice, right now. Alas that he could not go: his father would be too grateful to see him gone. The tedium of the season stretched out before him, longer and bleaker than the vista through the glass. *You think Stella mad,* he thought. *You think* she *would cause you problems, that* she *would disturb your comfortable little life.* Oh, yes. He would stay in London until hell froze over, so long as his father was here to witness him.

His fingers fell to the crank at the base of the casement. Let it all in, he thought. Wind, twigs, rain, sleet—the scent of a bleak, bloody, depressing London spring.

"Sir," the footman said nervously. "Please don't, sir. I think I saw lightning a moment ago."

"But don't you know?" James said. "I am rash and reckless."

The footman hesitated, then took a step back. "No, sir."

"A rash, reckless, good-for-nothing—that was the exact wording, I believe." He paused, struck by the way the comment echoed. Someone else had voiced a similar sentiment recently. The lovely Miss Boyce. *Over-privileged and under-occupied.* Dishonesty was not one of her failings. Perhaps that was why he'd felt moved to speak honestly in return. It was rather entertaining, hearing such clear verdicts issue from such a lush mouth. An *under-occupied* mouth, he decided. She really should thank him for the business he provided it.

He straightened and cast a grin at the bewildered footman. The season still had too many weeks remaining to it, but he knew how to occupy himself.

It was coming on one o'clock. Outside, in the galleries, the tourists were pushing for the best view of the Elgin Marbles. In the Reading Room, however, all was calm. The hundreds of desks, arranged in circular fashion around the great bank of blue-bound catalogues, were nearly full. Scores of hushed conversations blended into a low drone that made Lydia slightly sleepy. In the row before her, two ancient gentlemen, decked in the long frock coats and bow ties of an earlier generation, harrumphed at editorials. To their right, a young couple sighed over prints of Venice.

She watched the pair, feeling oddly bereft. When the gentleman, reaching out to turn the page, brushed the lady's arm, she blushed quite prettily. He smiled, and whispered something in her ear that made her turn her face into his sleeve.

Mr. Pagett had behaved similarly with Ana last night. Now that their marriage had been set, he felt free to take such liberties.

Sanburne took such liberties with no license at all.

Lydia swallowed and looked back to her book. Two hours now she'd been trying to read this essay on the bedouins, but her thoughts preferred to wander. It was purely humiliating to acknowledge how long she'd lain awake, these last few nights, reliving that incident at the Stromonds'. She would not blame herself for being attracted; she understood the facts of biology. But how *vexing* that she could not seem to forget him! This must be how gin addicts felt. One read of their plight in the papers. They could deny the drink for weeks, but the hunger never died. Given cause to reawaken, it killed them.

She had not accompanied Sophie and Ana to any events since the Stromonds'.

She came to her feet to walk to the catalogue. The scents of ink and aging paper gathered most strongly here, acting like a tonic on her nerves.

"I have a message for you."

Lydia looked up. A young man stood a couple paces off, perusing the bookshelf. The watery light of a rainy afternoon was falling through the great glass dome overhead; it gilded his silver-blond hair, and lent his skin a bluish cast. Next to him, a girl in a green polonaise was browsing. He must have spoken to her. Illicit lovebirds, no doubt, making a grand production of their secrecy. With a wry smile, Lydia took hold of a directory by its zinc-faced bottom.

"I said I have a *message* for you, Miss Boyce."

Her fingers spasmed. The volume slammed onto the floor. Lithograph entries, their paste loosened from age, fluttered out across the ground.

Murmurs rose behind her. She was dimly aware of readers looking up from their desks, frowning. An attendant, bent over a stack of books, straightened and stared in her direction.

The weight of the blond man's regard pressed against her cheek. After a cowardly hesitation, she squared her shoulders and turned to face him.

In his dark, modest attire, he looked like a scholarship student, come to the British Museum to do a little research. His youth—the flush on his cheeks, the rounded contours of his jaw—should have eased her. "Who are you?"

"A friend of a friend," he said. "Here—" He reached into his pocket, and she took a sharp step away. Her skirts brushed up against a desk—an occupied desk, judging by the protest behind her. She paid it no heed. Her eyes had only one focus: his hand, sliding into his waistcoat.

The note he produced was thin. Unaddressed.

She licked her dry lips. "That is not for me. My friends communicate with me directly."

"Some things cannot be sent through the post," he murmured. "Won't you take this letter, miss? I have been charged to deliver it to you."

A movement in the corner of her eye caught her attention: the attendant was approaching. He would scold her for abusing the catalogue. Worse yet, he might revoke her reader's ticket. It was too horrifying to countenance.

She straightened her spine. "I do not know you," she said stiffly. "I do not speak with strangers who accost me in public. Should you truly possess information for me, you may convey it through Baron Southerton."

His eyes, a steady, guileless blue, held to her own. "I think you know why this should best remain private."

Her heart, which had been doing a very steady job of it, began to knock. "No. I have absolutely no idea what you mean."

"I say, miss!" The attendant tapped her elbow, his bushy brows knotted in disapproval. "You must have a care with the catalogues! This one will have to be rebound with fresh guards, I fear!"

"I am sorry," she said breathlessly. "It was—I was startled. That gentleman said something very shocking, and the book slipped from my grasp."

"Hmph. Giving you trouble, was he?"

Trepidation lifting the hairs at her nape, she glanced behind her. The stranger was retreating, moving at a determined clip toward the exit.

"You must report such behavior to the attendants, miss. We are determined not to tolerate hooliganism."

"Yes," she said faintly.

"Oh—you've dropped something else." He started to bend down, but she beat him to it. The letter still held the warmth of the other man's body.

Back at her desk, she pulled out the little reading platform by its leathern handle and smoothed out the note.

> *I must speak with you about Mr. Hartnett. I should not like to trouble you, but I require my share.*
>
> —*Polly Marshall.*

An address in St. Giles followed.

She looked up. In a trick of the light shed by the dome, the room abruptly grew darker. What on earth was this about? Mr. Hartnett was dead. And how could such a gentleman have formed connections in London's most notorious slum? And even if he had done, how could it concern *her*?

Goose bumps rose on her arms. There was only one connection between them: the forgeries. But no one should know of those! It was impossible!

She stood. *I must tell Sophie.* And then, in the next second, she sat back down. Great ghosts. If the other news had troubled Sophie, this would give her fits.

"Looking lovely today."

She gasped and turned in her seat. Sanburne stood behind her. "You!" Was this one of his pranks? Lord knew he had already demonstrated a perverse taste in entertainments. Oh, *please* let it be a joke. "Did you send me this?"

His eyes flicked to the note in her hand, but his pleasant expression did not change. "That depends. Is it a love letter? If so, I'll gladly claim responsibility."

"No." Her spirits falling, she looked back to the note. *I require my share.* It made no sense.

"Wasn't it signed?" When she shook her head, he dropped into a crouch, so their eyes were level. "You look distressed." At her shrug, he said slowly, "I don't suppose this letter mentions anything about tears, or curses, or the whatnot."

"What? No, what rubbish. It— I beg your pardon!" For he had snatched the note out of her hand, and was straightening it. She came to her feet to grab it, but he held it out of reach.

"St. Giles, eh?" He gave a soft whistle of astonishment. "Not your usual haunt, I'd wager. Hartnett's the one who was to receive the forgery, yes?"

"Keep your voice down!" She made a rapid survey of the people around them. A sea of heads, bent industriously over books and newspapers. Generally the Reading Room was her refuge from the critical eyes of fashionable society. But if Sanburne of all people had taken to visiting, she could not say who might appear here.

He was studying her face. "So I'm right," he said. "How mysterious. And who's Polly?"

The temptation to confess caught her off guard. Had she lost her mind? She could not seriously think to share confidences with this man.

But to whom else might she turn? Not Sophie. Certainly not George. A wise woman would consult the police, but the mention of Hartnett made that course unthinkable. The inspectors would want to know his connection to Papa. And now that he was dead, the only connection was the five forgeries sitting in her dressing room. How would she explain *that*? She could not even explain it to herself.

The letter-writer might have explanations.

She eyed Sanburne. Her instincts, she discounted. They clamored like schoolgirls for her to step nearer; they were witless when it came to men. But logic agreed that she might rely on him. He already knew of one forgery. And by his own admission, he found her amusing. If she had formed any certainty with regard to the viscount, it was that he valued his little amusements. So long as she entertained him, he might prove amenable to keeping a confidence.

"All right," she said slowly. "Not here, though. If someone spies us together, it will raise talk."

Surprise crossed his face. He hadn't expected her to agree. As she fought down an irrational pleasure at having startled him, he leaned forward, his voice dropping to match hers. "That's right. Who knows what people would make of it?" His eyes widened. "Perhaps they'd assume I've taken an interest in you."

"Exactly," she said. "That would never do."

He laughed softly. "Are you stupid, Miss Boyce? Or only woefully naive?"

Oh, she took his meaning well enough. "I am neither," she said, her cheeks pinkening, and then turned on her heel, toward the exit.


Lydia led Sanburne out of the Reading Room, to the long hall where the Egyptian collection began. It was the best place she knew to conduct a discreet discussion: always crowded, but never crushed. Passing the cluster of visitors around the Rosetta Stone, she stopped at a bench facing a small statue of the goddess Isis and her spouse, Osiris.

Taking a seat, she briefly gave a summary of the events to date. "There is no way to tell when the forgeries might have been introduced," she concluded. "Port Said, where they're crated for a sea journey—the ports at Malta and Gibraltar—or even Southampton, where they're transferred to rail for London." Her eyes dropped to the note still clutched in her hand. Folding it, she slipped it into her reticule. "I can't imagine what this woman wants. But perhaps she knows something."

He sat beside her, his expression uncharacteristically thoughtful. "Why not take the matter to the police?"

She nodded. "For one thing, Southerton is a vocal critic of Scotland Yard. He's done nothing this month but rail in Parliament about their failure to stop that bomb attack. If the police learned that his father-in-law was connected, even tangentially, to art fraud—well, they would be glad to trumpet it from the rooftops, wouldn't they? No, it's out of the question. But perhaps . . ." She felt herself blushing, and averted her face. Her attention focused on the black granite statue. Visitors, dazzled by golden sarcophagi and famous hieroglyphs, rarely remarked it. She had a soft spot for it, though. Rarely did paganism appear so clearly as in this statue. The goddess was twice the size of her husband.

Sanburne had followed her look. "Very fierce, isn't she? Rather reminds me of your look at the Institute." He pulled a face—his lips turning down, his eyes narrowing to a squint.

Offense made her stiffen. "I beg your pardon, sir. I looked nothing of the sort. And that does not resemble her in the slightest. She is stern, yes, but not ugly."

"Ugly? You're right, then; I didn't do it properly.

More like this, perhaps." He glanced back to the statue, then wrinkled his nose.

"How childish you are. Everything is a game to you, isn't it?"

"Of course. If I took it seriously, I'd go mad." As she looked to him in startlement—his tone had sobered on that alarming statement—he went on, "But you're right. This is very serious research I undertake, here."

"Oh? And what is your research question?"

"Why, only this: was she carved from life, or is a human face unable to imitate her expression?"

She glanced back at Isis. It was actually an interesting problem; she could not recall any work that addressed whether ancient Egyptians had used human models for their art. "From life, I think," she said hesitantly. "If one's mouth can manage it—" She pressed her lips straight and scowled. "Like this."

He sat back in mock fear. "Dear God! That's it exactly! Miss Boyce, only show that face to your letter-writer, and you'll have an apology on the double."

She fought a laugh by frowning more deeply. "And when shall I have one from you?"

"That's right, I owe you one. Well, I do apologize, Miss Boyce. I should have kissed you longer, and insisted that you dance, whether you like it or no. I cannot think why I failed to do so."

No use in trying to disguise this blush: she was no doubt red as a postbox. "Congratulations, sir. You have squandered the opportunity to redeem yourself."

"As an admirer of Isis, you should have predicted that."

"You're familiar with the Egyptian pantheon?"

"I'm familiar with Cleopatra," he said amiably. "A Macedonian who wanted to be an Egyptian queen, and who claimed kinship with the goddess to legitimate her rule. Alas, she forgot what every true Egyptian knows: that Isis requires Osiris. And so, along came Antony, and she asked him a favor: play the obedient god, and share in her rewards. Unfortunately, like most men, Antony made a hash of the opportunity, and Cleopatra paid for it in snake venom. Make your requests carefully, is the moral of the story—particularly, I suppose, if you're a woman."

A dreadful suspicion knocked at her. This was not the layman's version of the story, which painted Cleopatra as a witless, malicious trollop. "You did not learn that from Miss Bernhardt's performance."

"Oh, there's a terrible rumor going the rounds. Apparently I *may* have taken a degree in Classics." As she sucked in a mortified breath, he added, "But very long ago, darling—and it was second-class at best. Not good enough to spot a forgery, at any rate."

The forgeries. Yes. Her ears burning, she turned back to the matter at hand. "As for that, I thought you might come along to St. Giles. Please don't mistake me," she continued hastily. "I'm not trying to . . . Well, I need an escort, and I thought it might entertain you, that's all. You *do* seem to have a taste for odd amusements."

He was grinning openly now. "Miss Boyce. Are you calling yourself an odd amusement?"

Heavens above, so she was. She gave a bashful shrug—and then they sat smiling at each other, as though she'd made a very good joke. Her smile widened. So did his. She put a hand to her mouth, as the oddest urge to laugh came over her. As if he knew it, he began to laugh himself. And then she suddenly was giggling. *Why, am I flirting?* But what a bizarre scene this was! Sitting side by side on a bench, like a pair of laborers, and speaking as if—oddest thought!—they were friends.

Impossible, of course. Men and women rarely managed such things. But what else to call his relationship with Mrs. Chudderley? Her laughter fading, she looked down to her lap. She had never wished to be anyone other than who she was. But for just a moment, the notion appealed: to wake up in Mrs. Chudderley's body. To be beautiful and admired, and to have the freedom to make as many reckless mistakes as she wished, because he would be there to lean on and to help her out of her blunders.

The wish sobered her. There was something so ignoble in it—as if she discounted all her abilities, and preferred a hero to come and save her, when in fact she could manage perfectly fine on her own. Besides, a moment of flirting did not make her into the sort of woman who could keep a man's attention on a regular basis. Her temperament was more serious than silly, and anyone drawn to her for longer than a few days would realize she was not as entertaining as he might have hoped. George certainly had.

Clearing her throat, she said, "I could take an armed footman. But servants talk. It's imperative that word of the forgeries not get out."

"Ah yes, God forbid the gossip should tarnish your father." She did not like the sarcasm inflecting those words; she would have protested, had he not pressed on. "Why, what a terrible tangle for you, Miss Boyce. To safeguard your father's name, you are faced with a threat to your own. Two threats, really: one from your escapades, and another from my attentions. You must feel quite desperate."

This answer, given in a tone of amused sympathy, was so far from what she'd expected that she did not know how to reply. Stupid to be hurt by the idea that he enjoyed her troubles. But coming so quick on the heels of their laughter, it was impossible to hide her bewilderment. "Do you dislike me so much, then?"

"Quite the opposite," he said immediately. "I like you immensely. I suspected I would, when you swept down from the lectern like Athena bringing justice. But I didn't realize it fully until you walked into my study to demand the stela. And now you plan to hare off to St. Giles—and all this, for the sake of dear Papa's career?"

"It is not simply his *career*, Sanburne. It is his calling."

"And what is your calling, then? Him?"

She bridled. "Of course I should not expect *you* to understand loyalty. You, who treat Lord Moreland with unmitigated contempt!"

"True enough," he said easily. "Sometimes it verges on outright hatred."

"For shame," she muttered. "You are speaking of your *father*."

"What of it? Kinship is the work of coincidence, sweetheart. The only thing it truly engenders is proximity. And sometimes not even that, as plenty of the world's bastards will be glad to tell you."

"What a cold sentiment! To whom do you owe loyalty, then, if not the man who fathered you?"

He shrugged. "To those who have earned it. Friends of long standing, etcetera."

"But you do not *earn* faith," she said heatedly. "In the same way you don't earn love. It is freely given, and asks nothing in return. Sanburne, I'm quite shocked by you!"

"And I by you," he said with a wink. "If love isn't earned, then by definition, it isn't deserved—which makes it quite dangerous. Why, just consult your *Aeneid.* Dido could have saved herself a suicide, if she'd only asked first whether Aeneas really merited the heartbreak. Myself, I always thought him a bounder."

She came to her feet. "You are the bounder, I think."

He rose as well. "No doubt," he said. "But at least I'm an honest one. And now, at least, you will know better than to fall in love with me, for certainly I'll never earn it."

She stared at him. "I had no such intention. But really, what an odd statement! If I didn't know you better, I would think you had a very low opinion of yourself."

He arched a flirtatious brow. "Do you know me very well, then? And here I'd hoped there was room to know me better."

Her stomach fluttered. Oh, she was being very foolish, here. "Forget I asked you anything."

"Oh, no. You asked, and I'll gladly agree. Foolishness may not sway me, but I've always had a terrible weakness for romantics. Do we go tomorrow, then?"

She hesitated only briefly. It wasn't as if she needed to approve of him in order to accept his help. "All right then, eleven o'clock tomorrow. We'll meet here." She thought to walk away, then, but she could not help herself. *"Romantic,* Sanburne?" It was the last word she would choose to describe herself. Perhaps once upon a time, but now?

He grinned. He'd been waiting for this, she realized: he knew she would not be able to resist the bait. "It's not an insult, darling. I'm a romantic myself. Why else would I have come looking for you at the library?"

She gave a laugh, to show that she did not take him seriously. But the sound emerged awkwardly, and as she started down the hall, butterflies fluttered through her stomach. Surely he hadn't *really* come looking for her?

How lowering to realize that no woman in St. Giles posed any threat so grave as she did to herself.

# Eight

For the journey to Seven Dials, Sanburne had hired a clarence, one of those huge vehicles that the wits called "growlers," for the clatter their wheels made over stone. The interior smelled of mold and old sweat. At odd times (particularly when rounding corners), she also caught a sudden note of manure. This last caused her to look with great suspicion at the muddy straw on the floor.

Sanburne found her squirming funny. "Pretend you are in the country, Miss Boyce." But as she pointed out, the countryside was not furnished in indeterminately stained velour. This amused him anew; he launched into an absurd exercise about the proper furnishings and decorations for various natural landscapes. Somehow she got caught up in it, so by the time the carriage stopped it made perfect sense to her that a man-made lake would required chintz and tasseled pillows, but for a small spring (so she proposed, to his fervent agreement) only raw silk and bolsters would do.

The court was too narrow for the carriage, so they entered on foot. On either side of the lane hunched decaying brick buildings, their shattered windowpanes stuffed with rags and newspapers. Disembodied voices floated through the air: a baby wailed; a man yelled for his tea; a woman sang the scales in a surprisingly sweet soprano. The band of grubby children playing knucklebone in the mud seemed unconcerned by their appearance, but when the contents of a chamber pot splattered directly behind Lydia, causing her to spring forward a step, they burst into riotous laughter. "This is appalling," she snapped, when Sanburne joined in with them. "Have you no sympathy for these people?"

"Immense amounts."

"Do not be flip! These conditions—"

"I'm not being flip. Indeed, from time to time, I've been known to call myself a radical."

The statement was so absurd that *she* laughed. "A radical who owns factories?"

"Why, Miss Boyce, you would be surprised. I am"— here his hand lifted, and he began to enumerate on his fingers—"for Home Rule. Friendly to labor unions. Impatient with the shenanigans in Sudan, bored by our impositions on Egypt. I admit, India is a bit of a puzzle to me, and Australia is too far away to care. But I think Russia may have a point when it comes to Kabul, and— well, did I say I simply adore lady suffragists? They look so lovely when their preconceptions are disturbed."

He thought her a suffragist? Perhaps he meant to tease her, but the idea gave her an obscure pleasure. "I would not know. That is—I support suffrage, but I don't spend my days yelling in the park about it."

"Of course you don't," he said. "Too obvious for you. You'll be the lady who writes scathing letters to the editor under a male pseudonym. Am I right?"

She gritted her teeth. It sounded rather cowardly, when he put it thus. "And if I did, it would be out of necessity, wouldn't it? My brother-in-law is political. And not everyone can afford to openly cross their relatives."

"More's the pity." When she gave him a sharp look, he said, "Where was I? Ah, yes. I've a mind to let Canada go, when I'm feeling generous. No opinion on the Transvaal. Oh! This may shock you: on rainy days, I incline toward vegetarianism. Sheep look so unappetizing when their coats are muddied."

His smile, bared in full splendor, revealed a row of strikingly white teeth. The boisterous good health, the telltale privilege inscribed in that smile, gelled poorly with her ideas about men of the people. "Well, if I have misjudged you—that is, I had no idea that you were a man of such principles—"

"Ah—no." As he waved this idea away, the rings on his fingers glittered. She had asked him at the Museum if he should not remove them. In smiling reply, he had pulled back his jacket to show her his gun. He took vanity to the far extreme, if he was willing to shoot to protect it. "I am not a man of *principles*," he said. "Not in the plural, at any rate. I am a man of one principle, Miss Boyce—or rather, of one position. Luckily, it is very easy to remember. If my father opposes something, I support it heartily. And vice-versa, of course."

It took a moment for her defeat to register. She grimaced. Her fault for taking him seriously, when by now she should have learned better. "What a remarkably simple philosophy. A shame you do not show similar restraint with your jewelry. You sparkle more brightly than a dowager duchess, Sanburne. It makes my eyes sore."

"O!" He clutched his chest. "Coldhearted woman,

to disparage me when I take such pains to look pretty for you."

She ignored this nonsense. "I would say that I pity your father, but I will save all my sympathy for you and your juvenile *principle*. Languishing in a prolonged childhood must prove remarkably taxing."

"But what can I do?" he asked. "It's the wonder of primogeniture that keeps me young. Pity us poor heirs, Miss Boyce. All the outdated trappings hang over our heads like an anvil—the properties, the tenants, the staff; the hundreds if not thousands of people who will one day rely on us for a living. But not yet! Oh, no. Until the anvil drops, we are frozen in its shadow— sometimes for decades, if the old sods live that long."

She rolled her eyes. "Some might use the time to imple- ment their fortunes in more useful ways—to help people like these, for instance, instead of buying factories that do nothing but produce a whole lot of smoke and misery."

"And soap," said Sanburne cheerfully. "Don't forget the soap. *Elston's Cure-all,* only a penny a bar at your local chemist's. Ah, here we are."

The building was five stories, and seemed to be slumping over on itself. As they went up the narrow staircase, the groaning occasioned by their steps did nothing to soothe Lydia's nerves. People died every day from building collapses. It was not an end she fancied.

Five floors up, the staircase ended at a small door. As she rapped on it, Sanburne's hand slipped quite casu- ally into his jacket. She hoped he would not shoot the woman before they had a chance to speak with her.

A brisk voice came from within: "Who's there?"

"Miss Boyce," Lydia called.

The door cracked open to reveal a plump, middle-aged lady in a threadbare gray gown. Her eyes were shadowed with exhaustion, and the sallow cast to her face contrasted unhealthily with hair dyed carmine. "What's your business?" she asked, sounding puzzled. And then, as her eyes ran down Lydia, she stiffened. "If you're from the church, you can go on your way. We've no call for hand-outs here."

"No," Lydia said quickly, "we're not connected. Are you Mrs. Marshall?"

The woman's brows lifted. "Miss Marshall would be my sister. She's not here, so you'll have to find your money elsewhere." The door began to close.

Lydia stepped forward to prevent it from shutting. "Forgive me, madam, we don't want any money. A young man gave me a most mysterious note that claims to be from your sister. It instructed me to come here."

A look of disgust crossed the woman's face. "Of course it did! Thinks me place is some sort of zoo; you're the fourth to come by for a look at her. Well, at least you're a woman. That's some improvement."

Sanburne gave a muffled laugh. Lydia repressed the urge to elbow him. "We don't wish to disturb you, but if you have any idea where she might be—"

"No, and you're a day late anyway. I kicked her out last night; she won't show her face here again." A frown bent the woman's brow. "I didn't want to do it. But she left me no choice, the way she carries on." She lapsed into silence, but seemed to have abandoned the urge to shut them out. Her eyes traveled curiously over Lydia. "Can't imagine what she'd want with you. Sure and certain you're not from the church?"

Now Sanburne laughed openly. This caught the woman's attention; she craned her head around the door to have a look at him. When her attention lit on his rings, she made a little *tsk* of surprise. "What's Polly to do with *you*, then?"

"I don't know," Lydia said. "It seems she knew a business associate of my father's—a Mr. Hartnett."

"Oh, I'd say she knew him."

"Perhaps you will explain it to us," Sanburne suggested with a charming smile. "But the stairwell doesn't offer near as lovely a view as your flat, Mrs. . . ."

The woman snorted. "Mrs. Ogilvie, and the flat's more trouble than it's worth—seven pound a month for less room than you'd give a mouse. You're more than welcome to it."

A bank note flashed in his hand. Lydia took a mortified breath; Mrs. Ogilvie scowled at the note as though he'd offered a glowing coal. "I don't want your money," she said. "I'm not like me sister."

"Consider it a fair exchange," Sanburne suggested. "We're quite puzzled by why your sister would contact Miss Boyce. As she says, her father was acquainted with Mr. Hartnett, but we don't understand his connection with your sister."

"Well. I can't tell you what she wanted of you, but I know a thing or two of what she had from *him*." Mrs. Ogilvie glanced back to the note. "And she did eat me out of house and home."

Lydia peered over her shoulder into the small, dark room. The roof sloped, so there was barely space to crouch at either end of the room. But the place was neat, and tried to be cheerful. A pretty chintz sheet draped a small table by the stove; another lay across the cot shoved under the eaves. A fern sat on the windowsill, soaking up what sun it could get. And the walls were decorated with framed prints, some of them professional beauties. Making a quick decision, she said, "Why, you have a picture of Mrs. Chudderley! Viscount, look—she has a picture of Elizabeth on her wall! The viscount is a great friend of hers," she confided to the matron.

"*Viscount*, you say?" Now the door swung fully open. "La dee da! What's Polly about, poking around in *your* affairs? Don't tell me she's crossed you."

"Indeed not," Sanburne said.

"Well, then. I expect you can afford *this*." She took the money. "Don't pay to be proud, they say. Though you might count it a poor trade, for the story's quite simple. Come in, then, but the tea's run out and I've only got the one chair."

Inside, Lydia tried to resist the seat, but Mrs. Ogilvie insisted on it, clearing away a newspaper and a very fine sketch. Lydia commented on the picture.

"My youngest did it," the woman said, and handed it over for inspection. "Quite a hand with the drawings. And she adores her aunt Polly. That's Polly, there."

Smiling eyes, and a gentle quirk to her mouth. "She's very lovely," Lydia said, and felt unaccountably displeased by the discovery.

Mrs. Ogilvie shrugged. "Flash, is what she is. More's the trouble—Mary looks up to her for it. Worries me. Bright as a button, Mary, but with her auntie's eye for trouble." She gave Sanburne's money a little shake. "Don't think it's for me. 'Twill go to Mary, all of it.

Now, as for me sister. I'm not sure what I can tell you. She's never been one to confide in me."

Lydia waited for Sanburne to reply, but he seemed content to let her speak. She cleared her throat, treading tentatively into murky waters. "You recognized Mr. Hartnett's name. Was Miss Marshall . . . close with him?"

Mrs. Ogilvie's mouth took on a wry twist. "Now, there's one way to put it. Are we going to speak plainly, or do you fancy ladies like to dance around the matter?"

"Plainly," Sanburne said, with a wink in Lydia's direction. "Miss Boyce does not enjoy dancing."

Mrs. Ogilvie looked at her as though reconsidering her decision to let them inside. "There's a shame. Whyever not?"

Lydia felt herself turning red. "Um—"

"She thinks she isn't good at it," Sanburne said

"I never said so," she shot back—although he was right, of course.

"La, lass! I could think of worse partners," Mrs. Ogilvie said, with a brief but encompassing look over Sanburne's form. "Make merry in May, I say. December comes all too quickly. At any rate, we'll speak plain, then. Polly was in Hartnett's keeping." She gave a philosophic shrug. "Some eleven years now. Took up before the wife died, and kept on ever after. He had set her up over in St. John's Wood—good as married, she said; what's the use of a ring? But when he passed, it left her in a fix. Not a penny for her in the will. There's the use of a ring, says I. Landlord had her out within two days. I took her in, fed her, gave her a floor to sleep on. But it came to enough when the men started coming by to harass her. A rotten lot, they are: bunch of petty swindlers and thieves. I've Mary to think of, don't I? And she took a dislike to Reggie—caused trouble between us, last night. Couldn't have that, even if she is me sister."

Lydia had latched on to a single word. Everything else paled in comparison to its significance. "Thieves," she said softly. Could Miss Marshall or her friends have gotten to the shipment? But how?

"Oh, aye. Had that look to them, at any rate."

"Did Mr. Hartnett know she kept such company?"

Mrs. Ogilvie gave a sour smile. "I've no idea, miss. Although I heard them mention him a few times—did sound like he was right cozy with them. Called him Johnny."

She sat back, shocked. This did not square. Surely her father's old friend from university was not familiar with petty criminals!

"Don't mean to upset you," Mrs. Ogilvie added. "I'm sure your father has nothing to do with it."

To Lydia's discomfort, the reassurance sounded patently insincere. "Of course he doesn't," she said forcefully. "Do you have any idea where we might find your sister, then?"

The woman sighed. "Wish I did. I told her Molly Malloy might take her in. They're friends from back in the day. But Molly hasn't seen her. Maybe ask at the gin palace down the lane. I smelled it on her, a couple of times. Couldn't rightly blame her, what with the troubles she's been through of late. Say." This was for Sanburne, as she nodded toward Mrs. Chudderley's photo. "Tell me about that one. I like to look at her, I do. But tell me she's a mean, wicked thing, won't you. For I don't believe in justice, if her heart's as kind as her face."

*I could tell you a thing or two,* Lydia thought.

"Alas," said the Viscount, "I can tell you no such thing." Lydia gave him a disbelieving look. "Elizabeth is all sweetness and light."

"La! *Elizabeth,* is it? That's right friendly. Around here, it's not till an engagement that a man gets so forward." Her brows waggled suggestively.

Rolling her eyes, Lydia came to her feet. But if Sanburne took notice of her intention to depart, he ignored it. "We're very old friends," he said. "She was raised on the neighboring estate."

"Estate," Mrs. Ogilvie cooed, looking about as reverent as if he'd shared the secret to immortality. "Well, isn't that something. I expect she has a big fancy carriage, and a wardrobe full of dresses, all velvet and sateen."

The floor began to vibrate. Lydia looked with alarm to her feet. It felt as if her wild thoughts were coming to fruition, and the building was about to come down. But as the shaking continued, she realized that an audible thumping accompanied it: someone was climbing the stairs to the garret.

As Sanburne and Mrs. Ogilvie nattered on about the magnificent Elizabeth, a whistle began to penetrate the walls. At this sound, Mrs. Ogilvie's pleasant disposition faltered. "Why, that's Reggie! He's supposed to be at the workshop!"

"Oh, yes?" Sanburne put his hat back on. "We'll bid you good day, then."

"You can't go out—he'll pass you on the stairs. I'm the only one in, this time of day." Mrs. Ogilvie was turning white. "God in heaven! One look at you and he'll think I'm whoring again, he will. He'll take one look at your fancy clothes and try to kill you. Out the window," she concluded abruptly.

Lydia, still shocked by the main admission, did not catch the significance of this last bit. But she did notice Sanburne frown toward window. *"Really?"* he asked.

"There's a little ladder to the roof. You can wait it out there."

Sanburne shrugged and began to cross toward it. Catching on, Lydia grabbed his arm. "I beg your pardon! I will not be scrambling on roofs!"

Sanburne stopped. "No?"

The matron was clearly in a panic—she had clawed back the mattress and was stuffing Sanburne's cash beneath it. "It's perfectly safe out there," she said distractedly. "Why, on a fine night, Mary and I like to go out and see if we can spot any stars."

"I could always shoot him," Sanburne offered.

"No!" Lydia and Mrs. Ogilvie said at the same time.

"Then let's go for a climb." He began to wind open the window. "Oh yes," he said as he looked over the sill. "Come, Miss Boyce, there's a nice little balcony for you to jump to."

The whistling was growing louder with each passing second. She was badly tempted to tell Sanburne to go ahead: surely Reggie wouldn't kill a woman?

A rough shove at her back had her stumbling forward. "Hurry up," Mrs. Ogilvie puffed in her ear. "Bless you, miss, *hurry.*" And then Sanburne was taking her by the waist and lifting her out into the soft spring air.

She looked down—and jerked backward, right into his arms. The children playing knucklebone looked very tiny from this height.

"Don't do that," he said mildly, and stepped out after her.

"Don't do what?"

"Look over here instead." He took her hand and planted it firmly on the windowframe. "Simply step around to your right. I'll be right behind you. Come, Miss Boyce—it's an adventure."

Her knees were shaking so badly that she wondered whether they would support her. She sidled along the narrow ledge—one could not, in fairness, call it anything so dignified as a *balcony*—to the point where the dormer ended and the flat roof began. On a deep breath, she stepped onto it—and promptly fell to hands and knees, scrambling forward to a spot sufficiently removed from the eave. She turned in time to see Sanburne step onto the slate. Beyond his head was a sea of rooftops: dormers filled with cracked windowpanes; chimneys balancing at odd angles against a vast and empty sky.

She scooted back against the side of the dormer. *An adventure, indeed.* Humans weren't meant to have such views. "It will collapse beneath our weight."

Sanburne lowered himself to sit beside her. "It's sturdy enough for an elephant, Miss Boyce. And what a view!"

She did not agree. The skyline raised a queer feeling in her. It brought to mind a game she had once seen for sale in the Strand, a moveable model of the West End, with little bridges and palaces and houses, a miniature Buckingham Palace, tiny carriages to push along the finely painted paths of Hyde Park. But the game had glossed over this slum. So many buildings, huddled and cracking. She had no idea what the names of the streets were, here. The thousands of people they housed might as well have not existed, either, for all they were meant to matter to her. They were in the heart of London, but it could as easily have been Egypt to her. "Mrs. Ogilvie does not come up here to look for stars," she muttered. The sight of this dark, tangled sprawl must make her garret feel like a palace—a bulwark against the tide of poverty stretching out before them.

"No," Sanburne said quietly. "I imagine not."

"It's not fair," she began—and then stopped. It was a childish observation, and he would no doubt laugh at her for it.

His hair brushed her cheek as his head turned toward her. His breath warmed her neck as he spoke. "You look angry," he observed. "Not with me, I hope."

"I am not angry," she said stiffly. She felt embarrassed, although she didn't understand why. "I simply don't understand why we had to climb out the window."

"Hostess's rules, darling. Bad form to brawl with her husband."

Her gaze settled on a pigeon. She had never expected to feel envy for such a creature, but its confident hop across the shingles made her covet, rather urgently, the luxury of wings. "I do not like heights."

"I would tell you I won't let you fall," he said. "But perhaps I shouldn't."

"I hope that doesn't mean you intend to push me!"

"It means fear has its own pleasures."

She gave him a sidelong look, but could muster no answer to that piece of rubbish.

"Behold its miraculous effects," he said. "I have my hand around your waist and you haven't taken note."

She looked down in startlement. He was right. But there was nowhere else for his arm to go. "That's no pleasure. That's necessity."

He laughed. "How lowering. But when my hand lifts . . ." He slid it slowly upward.

She caught her breath, her eyes widening. The scoundrel was going to—

"*Et voilà,*" he said. "Not necessary in the least."

His fingers rested on a part of her anatomy that had no business being touched by him.

"Now," he murmured in her ear, "you can say I am taking shameless advantage of this situation, or . . ." His fingers tightened slightly, cupping her. "You can praise my creativity. Either way, you're no longer thinking about falling."

# Nine

Lydia sat frozen for a moment: not from the shock, precisely, but more because the sudden throb within her seemed dangerous to her balance. Only two layers separated his hand from her breast. The sun spilled a mild warmth over the roof; the pigeon made a low warble and fluttered suddenly away. And his fingers rippled over her, causing a very inappropriate part of her to tighten and become conspicuous.

"You seem to like it," he said.

His tone was so mild that he might have been commenting on her reaction to a flower arrangement. But as the meaning registered, a flush swept her. She cleared her throat. In a low voice, she said, "A cold bath does the same."

His delighted laugh ghosted along her neck. "You are *so* amusing," he purred. "Let me put my lips there, and I will convince you of the difference."

She did not need convincing. She felt the difference well enough. A cold bath cleared her thoughts. His touch muddied them and made her warm all over. *I could lean into him,* she thought. Even on a rooftop, he seemed strong and stable. How had he acquired such confidence? His birth had given him privileges, of course, and so had his sex. But there was more to it than that. Eyes were always on him. The newspapers dissected his smallest shenanigan. Yet he bore such attentions as though they hardly concerned him. She could not imagine him hesitating on the threshold of a room for fear he'd be judged and found wanting. If someone tried to cut him, he would only laugh. To live a life of such bold assurance, never caring what others thought . . . why, it must be another species of living, entirely. No uncertainty. Invulnerable to jibes and slanders. What could one not do, when so free?

She would lean on him, she thought. Just for a moment, up here, where no one would be looking. His shoulder was warm beneath her cheek; he smelled like bergamot and soap. It didn't count, somehow, to touch him like this. He did not move a millimeter; as her cheek came to rest on him, he barely breathed, that she could detect.

At length, he said softly, "Still afraid?"

She focused on a pair of tattered curtains in the distance. Someone had chosen the yellow fabric with hopeful intentions, but coal smoke had dulled it, and it unfurled now in ragged strips.

She sighed. One pretended these places did not exist. But one did so only in order to convince oneself of the vast distance that separated one's own life from this one. "Of course I'm afraid," she said softly. "I'm always afraid of something." Wasn't that her duty, as a woman? If it wasn't her reputation, it was her sisters'. If it wasn't Papa's project, it was Ana's future. Or the eyes that pressed on her everywhere she went. There was always something to watch out for.

But what safer and more invisible place to be, than

a roof? She found herself relaxing against him. His silences were comfortable. The sunlight was mellow, dimmed by clouds; and the air felt very mild, stirring around her in long, lazy breezes. Up here, bereft of any option but to wait, she might cease—just a moment— to worry about anything.

His hand still rested on her breast, but his fingers had stilled. The touch that had been so agitating now felt comforting. As though he soothed her by it. A languorous feeling spread through her limbs. She let the full weight of her head fall onto his sleeve. "What do you mean?" he asked. "What are you afraid of?"

She could not answer him. She did not want to talk anymore. It was peaceful up here, in the late light of spring. The irony struck her dimly. "Never mind that."

Minutes passed. A question stirred in her mind, random, distracting. "How did you get those bruises you wore, that night at the Stromonds'?"

His fingers tightened very briefly—a reflex, she thought; she had surprised him somehow. "Had you asked me on solid ground, I would no doubt have told you that clumsiness runs in the family. Always falling up stairs, over curbs, into doorknobs." He paused. "But the truth is, I box. At a place very near here, actually."

"It must hurt."

"Yes," he said. "That's rather the point of it."

He was not speaking of the sport in general. She understood that. "You go to excesses," she said. "In all things. You are the most outré gentleman I've ever met."

"A gentleman? And here I thought I was a scoundrel."

"You shouldn't sound so proud of it."

"I'm not," he said quietly. "But of course I must

sound like I am. You, of all people, should know that. I have a role to play, just as you do."

Yes. He was right. She should not be sitting here, taking solace from his touch. The proper reaction was anger. Indignation. And later, perhaps, reprehension, for placing herself in this situation to begin with. "It is very tiring," she whispered.

"Tremendously." And then, after a moment: "Why are you afraid, Lydia?"

Strange to hear her name from his lips—and to realize there was no urge in her to object. How could she? His body had tensed as he'd spoken of pain, and even if it made no sense to her, she knew that he had given her a piece of honesty, one that clearly cost him something.

It would have been nice to be able to repay him with a truth of her own. But what could she say? Her worries were pedestrian. Any unwed woman of advancing years would share them. Her articles brought only pittances. Papa spared her what money he could, but most of his profits went back into his project. He would leave no settlement for her after he was gone. What would happen then? *My whole future,* she thought darkly: poor relative, unwanted burden, the face peering through the banisters at night, while the lovely guests laughed and danced below. Spinster aunt to Ana's future brood. Or worse yet, to Sophie and George's. Wouldn't that be splendid. Nanny and governess in one, sustained through the unwilling largess of the man she'd once thought to love. Unpaid servant in the home she'd hoped to call her own.

Of course she worried. Who wouldn't, in her position? But the idea of voicing such thoughts repelled her.

They would only serve to classify her as one more example of that pitiable type: the well-bred but penniless spinster. Every sensibility within her balked at the notion of counting herself so typical. *I am vain,* she thought. But she could not help it. As a child—dazed by a sense of wonder about the world, fed by Papa's encouragement of her learning—she had dreamed of a special life. Being lauded and loved, respected and admired. But the world had very little use for a woman with nothing but wits. When people took note of her now, it was not for her mind (*the competence with which you mastered this strenuous roll*—oh, how pityingly George had said it!) but for the apt example she offered to debutantes. *Don't get above yourself,* mamas whispered to their daughters when passing her in a ballroom. *Don't count your chickens before they're hatched. You don't want to end up like her.*

How could she speak of these things to him? What would *he* understand of it? It would only bore him. Besides, sitting here—beholding the vast, impersonal cruelty of London—her complaints seemed embarrassing. Look at these hovels! No special regard would keep her safe from them. Yearning for something more seemed childish in the extreme. She should be grateful. She was lucky to have an assured place in her sisters' homes. This anger, this sharpening desperation—she did not know what to do with them. The sullen skyline warned her where ambitions might lead her.

If she could have told him the truth, what would she have said? It would have made no sense. *Sanburne, I am afraid of myself.*

"I can feel your heart racing," he murmured.

"Yes," she said unsteadily. It was so easy for *him* to talk honestly—a man whose options seemed infinite, whose absence would always be remarked. Who did not see possible repercussions everywhere he looked. "What of it? You are toying with me." Offering her chances she could not, must not take.

"There are other words for what I'm doing. Perhaps you're not worldly enough to know them."

There it was again: an assumption that her reluctance was owed to naivete, rather than its opposite. "I am not so sheltered," she said quietly. "I have been to Egypt, you know. My sisters haven't been, but I went. My father invited me a few years ago, just before the bombardment of Alexandria." And she had gone, gladly, to escape her humiliation. She had missed her sister's wedding, left it to Aunt Augusta to organize, simply because she could not bear to look the groom in the eye. Sophie had never forgiven her for it.

"Have you?" She could tell from his neutral tone that her segue puzzled him. "I've been myself, just this winter."

"For tourism."

"Yes, of course. And you?"

"No," she said. "I never saw Cairo, the Second Cataract, anything like that. Just Alexandria, really. My father was working nearby. I stayed in the Hotel de l'Europe for two months." And cried, mostly. She'd wallowed in the most terrible, disgusting pity for herself. It had chagrined her for a long time afterward, to think on it.

"That's a shame." His fingers resumed a rhythmic motion—the slightest stroke across her nipple. She tried to brace against it, but there was no leverage save the long, warm surface of his body against her side. "Not much to see in Alexandria," he mused, "at least in comparison with the rest of the country. Pompey's Pillar, of course." His fingernail scratched across the cloth. "Cleopatra's Needles."

"And the city." Her voice had gone husky. She would not acknowledge his fondling in any other way. If she spoke of it, she would have to come to some decision about it.

"The city?" His hand halted. "Don't recall it very clearly. We landed there; I was tired from the journey. Ugly—that's all I remember."

"You don't even remember the smell?"

"A swamp." His fingers recommenced, and a little sigh escaped her. He rewarded her with a firmer stroke, a growing aggression. "There's a swamp on the outskirts of town. It stank."

She produced a little laugh. "No, it didn't. It smelled of saltwater, and spices, and acacia trees. Somehow I hadn't realized that acacia blossoms smelled. Had you? But of course they smell: they smell sweet." She turned her face into his shoulder again, breathed in the scent of him. He was not for her, that much was clear. But he smelled delicious, and his mind was on her, just as his hand was. He was not thinking of anyone else. "I expect you also didn't bother to spend time at the harbor."

He drew back, just enough to provoke her into looking up. At this proximity, his eyes were purely extraordinary. The silver irises melted into a ring of gold around his pupils. "The harbor," he repeated softly, his lips a breath from hers.

"You were tired, of course." She whispered it. "And the harbor is considered very ugly. But most of our sugar is trafficked through it. Did you know that?"

A line appeared between his brows. "I suppose."

"And probably some of the cotton you and I are wearing. You wouldn't have thought of it, at the time. You were probably thinking of Giza—or arranging your houseboat for the Nile trip. But now that I've told you . . ." She looked away from him, staring at the smudged horizon. "Well, you will wonder about the harbor. And next time you pass an acacia tree, you might stop and sniff it, for curiosity's sake."

His free hand took hold of her chin, turning her face toward him. "You are telling me something," he said steadily. "That much is clear. But I'm afraid you'll have to take pity on a less complex brain."

She gave her shoulders an impatient little roll to dislodge him. "There is nothing complex about it. I'm merely pointing out that it's easy to ignore what seems mundane, until the mundane becomes . . . elusive. And then it suddenly seems very interesting—for a short while, at least."

His mouth quirked. "Wait a moment. You think I take an interest in you because I find you . . . mundane?"

"I think you find it puzzling that a woman like me might be able to resist you." This was her pièce de résistance, the key, she thought, to driving him off: to let him know how clearly she understood him. No man liked to be obvious. "You wish to crack the riddle. It's a very tedious motive. And my disinterest is not mysterious either. I am not the sort of woman who is flattered by the attentions of a vain, shiftless dilettante."

He surprised her with a smile. "A woman like you. What sort of woman is that, I wonder?"

"A learned one," she said. "Sober. Focused. Set aside my resistance, and you will not find me so interesting. Call me bookish, if you like. Someone who values her dignity and pride, and will not be swayed by a pretty face."

"Oh, I think you're swayed, Lydia. I think you're so swayed that you can't bring yourself to push my hand away."

He liked her given name. This was the second time he'd spoken it. *I will not count.* "But I should," she said, more to herself than him.

"And there is a large part of your charm," he murmured. "You know the rules very well. But you don't believe in them very much, do you? After all, why else would you be here right now? And do not tell me you came to St. Giles for your father's sake."

The faint curve on his lips struck her. His smile seemed terribly intimate. As if he saw the thoughts passing in her head, and he commiserated with them. *Him!* This light-heeled, beautiful, maniacal creature. "I *am* here for Papa." That was certainly part of it.

But not all of it, maybe.

He stared at her for a long moment, as if waiting for her to continue. And then, when she didn't, he gave a little shrug and said, "I know how that goes, believe it or not. Being boxed in."

She attempted a laugh. "You? What can't you do, Sanburne? You act on your whim all the time."

"And you fight yours," he said. "But not happily, I think."

Panic fluttered in her breast. The strength of it

seemed out of step, illogical. He was turning her own trick back upon her, and getting better results for it than she had. She could not stand to be laid bare. Not by him. Not like this. There was no way to escape him—she didn't even have the room to lift her hands to cover her ears. "You don't know me. Don't presume to think you do. I am *not* a romantic, Sanburne. Unlike you, I face consequences if I'm caught."

He leaned very close, and his words came out like a dare. "*What* consequences? Here, on the rooftop? What are you so afraid of, Lydia?" He paused. "Are you afraid that I'm right? Or are you simply afraid of me?"

*I am afraid of what I will do with you, if you keep encouraging me.*

She turned her face back to the skyline. Enough of this. Enough of it!

"Nothing to say? Very well." He rose to his feet.

"Where are you going?"

He reached down for her hands. She let him draw her up, simply for fear that his pull would send her lurching over the edge if she resisted it and he then let go. "Words are all very nice," he said, "but I agree with you: there are more powerful ways to make a statement. Close your eyes."

"What? Why?"

"Close them," he repeated calmly.

"I will fall!"

His hand slid down to her waist. "Have a little faith in your body for once. Your brain will forgive you for it."

"Faith? You don't believe in faith."

"Not true. I said it had to be earned. And I will earn yours, Lydia. Close your eyes."

Oh, she knew what he was about. And she would not do it. She would be the woman she had described to him: a woman of dignity and restraint. Dignity was a cold word, perhaps. She had liked once to think of herself as passionate, in love with her books, drunk on history, enamored of the wide world, of all the peoples within it. To be studious was to be the opposite of boring, she had believed; it was to be so interested, so madly curious, that one simply could not wait for the answers to arrive on their own: one had to go chase them in the only manner available.

But her eyes had closed. Just once, then. On the roof. It was easier like this—as if she were dreaming. He was right: no one watched, so far from the ground. No responsibility for her actions, here, only this submission to imagination. She could believe this was a fantasy, his lips on her throat, his tongue tracing the curve of her jaw. It had been so long since she'd done something rash and selfish. If she did it once now, it did not mean she would do so again. The nip at her jaw made her gasp and tighten her hold on his shoulders. She could not imagine why cold baths might be more appealing than his touch on her breast. She wanted to admit that to him. She knew what his reaction would be: he would laugh, and praise her. He was a mad creature, who no doubt said *up* when everyone else said *down*, just to be contrary. But he liked this side of her—he *liked* it, this side she tried to put away, which produced words she should not think, much less speak. *Could* not speak, except in the company of someone like him. George had asked her to speak freely, but he had not really wanted to listen to her. Sanburne did. And that was what made him such a danger.

That was what made him so attractive.

His hand pressed against her thigh. He was pulling her skirts up, his fingers looping into material, inching it upward bit by bit. Through her stockings, she felt a cool breeze wash over her calves. "You really *must* let me seduce you, Miss Boyce." He spoke against her lips, in a voice that had gone hoarse. "We would have such a good time of it, you and I."

She knew a brief puzzlement. "What is this, if not seduction?"

"A very pleasant overture."

Her lips curved. "Are all rakes so punctilious with their classifications?"

"I expect they lack the scientific inspiration for it." His mouth settled over hers, his tongue playing at the seam of her lips. She let him coax them open. His tongue tasted sweet, not at all like a mistake. His body shifted, to pin her bunched-up skirts against the wall, and his fingers skated past her garter along her thigh, a hot, delicate pressure through the thin fabric of her drawers. She had never felt another person's touch in these places; she had barely touched herself there. Such parts were allegedly inviolable. But her body did not object. It was greeting his strokes with a more than friendly clamor.

His fingers found her where she felt most liquid: they cupped her between her legs and gave her another source of balance. With the roof at her back and his hand between her thighs, she felt firm, grounded, free. Her hips pushed forward; his palm pushed back harder. *Wanton,* she thought distantly, clinically. And then, as he found the slit in her drawers, and his fingers touched her bare flesh, an ache moved through her that redefined her idea of wantonness: he had found the source of it, there. In another moment—if he kept rubbing her like that, his finger so insistent, prodding at a part of her whose name she could not even bring herself to speak, but which he *touched,* which he apparently knew even better than she did— "Ah," she gasped.

"Good," he whispered against her mouth. "Louder."

His fingers pushed *into* her now—a slight burning, the smallest discomfort, which somehow lent the stroking of his thumb, higher up, a delicious edge. Her body bucked once, as a great rush of feeling came over her, pure feeling, untainted by any thought that could be framed by language. And then everything in her, caution, concern, it all splintered, and her hips were lifting in a contraction that made her knees go. He caught her on his hand, his other arm wrapping around the back of her hips, holding her as she bit into his shoulder.

*I am undone.*

After a long minute, in which her breathing began to steady, it came to her that she would have to pull away eventually. The prospect of meeting his eyes loomed before her, horrifying, humiliating. But . . . was it? To learn a secret about oneself—a secret like this, so basic and elemental, but powerful enough to knock her sideways and leave her shaking—and at her age. Had she played the coward any longer, had she decided to turn away from him, she never would have known it. Strangers, men behind pulpits, scowling grand dames, the whole proper, polite world would agree: her body should remain a stranger to her. But his body had been responsible for introducing them. He was not proper, and thank God for it.

Tears pricked her eyes, and she drew a shuddering breath. No, she would not regret this.

He nudged her, a soft suggestion. His hand detached itself from that tender place—drawing an unwilling gasp from her—and then came to her shoulder to push her gently back. "Lydia," he said. "You're going to believe me now, when I tell you you're beautiful."

She sucked in a sharp breath. She would look him in the eye, she thought. She would ask him to tell her again, as she watched his eyes. And then, maybe—

A scream came from below.

She jumped. "Was that Mrs. Ogilvie?"

Sanburne turned, his face in profile to her, his focus on the direction they had come. "I think so."

Another scream came. Now the sound of something breaking in the garret. What did Mrs. Ogilvie have to break? So little.

"Stay here," Sanburne said. In one long stride, he crossed to the ledge, put his hands to the dormer frame, and swung out of sight.

She started after him, only to abruptly remember that she was far above the ground, with no wings to catch her. On a shuddering exhalation, she stepped back against the dormer. Her limbs hummed and quivered, as if she were some wind-up toy slowly dwindling to a stop.

Well.

With shaking hands, she smoothed down her skirts. She would have thought a rake might understand there were better ways to woo a lady than to seduce her, then strand her on top of a building.

She focused on the curtains across the way and

counted her breaths. Quick, shallow. The sky was darkening now, the light dimming as clouds moved in. He had touched her *there*. She had let him. It had been— glorious.

When wet, the roof would probably make for very tenuous footing.

She had reached the count of twenty when another yell came, shrill and feminine. "You'll kill him!"

She bit down on her knuckle. Her future flashed before her: a skeleton scattered across the eaves, dead because the viscount had been foolish enough to get himself killed in the garret, while she remained stuck here in fear. A very fitting end to seduction; no doubt the moralists would approve.

*"Stop it!"*

All right, that did it. She forced herself to take one step forward. At the next, her joints congealed. She'd had so many nightmares in which she was falling, falling, with nothing to stop her, hands reaching out from darkness but curling shut as she grabbed for them. She could not walk toward the edge. Trying to fly would have been easier.

*Coward.*

A gust of air escaped her. Very well. She could crawl, then. She lowered herself to the warm slate and inched forward, little by little. It seemed to take an eon to reach the edge. *If I die in St. Giles, Sophie will never forgive me. George will be horrified.* She startled herself by laughing. What an optimist she was, finding cause for cheer in the prospect of her own death.

Once at the roof's end, she turned herself around, struggled to her feet, took hold of the edge of the dormer, and stepped onto the narrow ledge. Five steps to the window, if she could take them. Her fingers felt rigid where they clutched the wood frame.

A pigeon landed near the space she'd only recently occupied. Its beady eyes fixed on her as it strutted about. She wanted to flap her hand at it, but her hand would not loosen its grip. So what if the bird jumped about like an acrobat? It should not feel superior. She was bigger, and well equipped to give it a scare.

The thought was so ridiculous that it loosened her limbs. She sidled very quickly along the ledge, but the sight through the open window stopped her dead: Sanburne had Reggie up against the wall—one hand at his throat, the other pushed over his nose. Reggie was making wheezing noises, and Mrs. Ogilvie was clawing at Sanburne's arm to no apparent effect.

The woman spotted her and came hurtling across the room to yank her inside. Lydia landed on her hands and knees; Mrs. Ogilvie grasped her by the waist and pulled her up. "Stop him," she said hysterically. Her face was bloodied and her eye was swelling from the impact of a fist. "He's killing Reggie!"

Lydia cleared her throat. Sanburne's face was perfectly expressionless, but his outstretched arm trembled with the force he was exerting to crush the other man's throat. "Sanburne," she called sharply.

He did not seem to hear. His silent, flat focus made a chilling contrast with Reggie's dwindling gasps. Mrs. Ogilvie moaned and shoved her forward. She stumbled on the hem of her skirts, her eyes on the viscount. He had a fresh cut on his cheekbone, but the other man's shirt was covered in blood, and his nose sat oddly askew—broken, no doubt. "Sanburne, stop it." Her throat felt very tight. "Let him go!" She lifted her hand to his arm.

At her touch, his elbow bent quite suddenly, like a snapped wire. The other man thudded to the floor. Mrs. Ogilvie knocked past her, falling to her knees by her husband's side. As a retching gasp burst from his throat, she said to Lydia, "He's mad! *Mad!* I told him I didn't need any help!"

"He hit you." The viscount spoke the words with no intonation.

"It's not your concern, is it?" the woman cried. "Oh, get out of my place!" She wrapped her arms around Reggie's torso and pulled his back to her chest.

The corner of Sanburne's mouth quirked, like a man confronted with proof of his most cynical predictions. He drew a long breath, his nostrils flaring with the force of his exhalation. Lydia felt numb. How had she ever thought him shallow? No man with two faces could be counted a simpleton. If anything, it was the classic mark of a villain.

His attention turned to her. Whatever he saw caused that peculiar smile to shift. The curve of his lips assumed a spiteful edge. "Speechless," he said. "That's a first. Feeling a bit of sympathy for Moreland now, are you?"

The tone of his voice intended no kindness. He spoke as though *she* were to blame. A sick feeling rose in her throat. He had touched her so gently. He had spoken as though he understood her, appreciated her. She had been so sure, for a few minutes, that her instincts were right about him—

Sanburne turned on his heel. "Come," he said over his shoulder, as if calling a dog to heel. A springer spaniel, in fact. She followed him slowly out the door, battling a mounting sense of humiliation. *I did not reveal myself to him.* Had she? No. She had not admitted herself enamored of his attentions. And if he had been able to tell—as surely he had—then what of it? Her flesh was only that: dumb matter. She could not control its response.

He started down the stairs. The balustrade was rough beneath her palm; a splinter speared her finger, and she lifted her hand to her mouth, sucking absently. Such wild ideas were flooding her mind. He was not a butterfly after all, but something more predatory. His bright colors, his laughter, and his flirtation were empty facades. She had been fooled again, but by an even more nefarious sort of man. And she had gone waltzing around town with him, as if she had no cause to know better!

They passed the fourth landing, and then the third. One of the floorboards was broken away, yielding a God's eye view of the flat below. A pot of soup boiled on the stove and the smell of onions brought bile into her mouth. She could not have been so badly mistaken.

"Sanburne." His name burst from her. "Wait."

He pivoted on his heel. *"What?"*

The snapped word had her retreating a step. All at once, his face transformed. Sanity returned to it. He raised his hand to span his temples, his eyes closing briefly. "I'm sorry. Christ, I—" He slid his hand up through his hair. His knuckles were raw; one was bleeding. That man's nose. Dear God. "Lydia," he said quietly. "Don't look at me like that. I wouldn't hurt you. You must know that."

She had seen him battered before. He'd claimed pain was the point of it. What sort of man desired pain? "Of course not," she said. But her tone was not convincing.

His hand fell, and he drew a long breath. "No," he said. "You would be right to mistrust me. Especially after that. Of course you would. I cannot blame you."

She was an idiot. For at his admission, her instincts rose up in protest; they clamored to make excuses for him. "You lost your head," she said tentatively.

"No. I fully meant to strangle him."

"But not to death!"

His laughter was not pleasant. She didn't know what had birthed it, but she recognized its proper clime: a darkened room, solitude, winter. "Do you really want me to answer that?"

"Yes," she whispered.

He slouched against the wall, tipping up his chin to study the ceiling. "Perhaps," he said at length. "I don't know." His head rolled toward her. "I should have killed him," he said conversationally.

She was listening to a man speak casually of murder. Of his desire to commit it. Why was she not running? Why was everything in her inclining toward him, in sympathy, in the desire to *comfort* him? "Don't say that," she murmured. "You don't mean it."

"Don't I?" He shrugged. "It's his life, or hers. If she stays with him—and she will—he will kill her. She will leave in a coffin, long before her rightful time."

"You can't know that!"

"Yes," he said flatly. "I can."

"But—" She swallowed. "She did not want your help."

His face shuttered. "No. They never do."

"Perhaps she *will* leave on her own."

"She was groveling at his feet. After he blackened her eye. Did you miss that bit, Miss Boyce?"

His incredulous tone was intended to mock her and perhaps, too, the woman upstairs. The latter possibility infuriated her. He had seen that garret. He knew as well as she did that there was no fancy coach waiting to carry Mrs. Ogilvie to safety. "Everyone is brave in his own way. You can't blame others if they don't fit your mold."

For a few heartbeats, he simply looked at her. "You are so incredibly naive," he said softly.

A memory awoke in her, then. There had been rumors, during Lady Boland's trial, of misbehavior on her husband's part. "Is it your sister?" she asked slowly. "Is that why?"

The question acted like a tonic: he blinked, looked away, and when his face turned back, he had reacquired the way of it, that regular mask of smiling amusement. "What a clever girl. Why, you're a regular Athena, aren't you?"

She stiffened. He was striking out, as Sophie sometimes did when confronted with a difficult truth. It was childish, but that did not make it less hurtful. She watched helplessly as he started again down the stairs. "Wait," she called, and followed after him. He stopped three steps below her, his posture uncharacteristically rigid. She screwed up her courage. "You are right to be concerned," she said to his back. "It is noble. But there are other ways to help. You cannot simply go around attacking men—"

He turned on her so suddenly that she flinched. "I know," he said in a rough voice, "*exactly* what I can and cannot do. I live with it every day, Miss Boyce. I do not suffer from it, if you have noticed. Under-employed, under-occupied, and thoroughly useless: it is a glorious way to live, if you have the bank account. So why don't you save your goddamned preaching for someone who needs it. I know I will thank you for it."

She stood there, blinking blindly at the wall. After a moment, the sound of his bootsteps came again, but they sounded very dim, lost as they were beneath the mortified pounding of her heart. He was walking away. He was finished with her. *My God, I will never learn.*

She had to continue down after him. There was no other choice. She knew that, but her feet would not obey her. A deep breath, a nod of her head. *Straighten your shoulders, and now you will move.* Her feet went down the steps, out into the cooling air and dim light. A thin rain started to fall as she walked up to him, announcing itself by a drop on her nose, and then another on her wrist, startlingly cold. "I did not mean to offend you," she said quietly.

"You didn't." He sounded exhausted. "But you are right; I am thoroughly useless. You should find someone else to help you."

The words disquieted her. She had not called him useless. But no doubt he was right: it had been foolish in the extreme to ask him to accompany her. She hugged her arms to herself and walked past him, keeping her eyes to the ground. Water began to freckle the cobblestones. By the time they reached the hack, it was raining steadily enough to churn mud between the stones.

As the driver came round to open the door, she threw Sanburne a quick glance. His expression was aloof, his posture formal; he had detached himself from the scene. And only a quarter-hour ago—it seemed like a lifetime, now—she had been on the roof with him, and the sun had still shone, and she had felt so carefree.

An impulse seized her. It was not quite so wild as to be called recklessness. She recognized the logic of it: she did not want those earlier moments to have led only to this. It would diminish them so terribly. She heard herself ask, "Do we go to the gin palace, then?"

This won his attention. She could not read his face, but after a beat, he shrugged and said, "Why not. God knows I could use a drink."

# Ten

Lydia did not know what she was doing. She felt breathless and unsure of how to look at him. This urge to mend things seemed to have taken her into new territory. It had led her to a gin palace, hadn't it? She had never laid eyes on such a place before, but as she gawked up at its exterior, this fact seemed less a consequence of righteous living than a stupendous fluke. There was no way she could have missed such a building, had she passed one. Three stories of ornately molded and gilded plaster hovered over her, like a fairy tale castle placed directly into the weary surroundings of the slum. But surely no castle had ever emitted such a tremendous reek: the sourness of alcohol mixed with the rich aroma of fried food. She inhaled deeply. Oysters, or perhaps whilks.

Inside, the heat and noise hit her first. The long saloon was crowded; a variety of customers yelled, laughed, slapped each other, banged mugs, thumped the bar, stamped their feet. Laborers in rough-spun woollens rubbed shoulders with clerkish lads in sober suits. The lady in the drooping boa, her face painted with lacquer and blush, did not surprise Lydia, but the middle-aged matron in the modest dress, sharing a glass with her husband, seemed less likely. A few paces away, two girls in patched gowns flirted with a young man; none of them looked a day above seventeen, and their pallor suggested that their money would be better put to food. But they were laughing so merrily that Lydia's lips moved in automatic response.

She cupped her mouth, surprised by herself. "The addiction knows no class."

Sanburne's laughter was brief. "So *all* of them are addicts?"

"Why else would one be consuming deleterious spirits at this hour?"

"Boredom? A happy way to pass an hour?"

"Happy! To rot one's brain on poison?"

"Spoken like a woman who's never been drunk."

"You speak as though that's a failing."

He cocked a brow. "And if I say it is?"

She arched a brow back at him. "Then I will remind you that I've never needed a stranger to fix my bustle."

He looked at her in surprise, and then, after a moment, smiled. A simple and commonplace thing, but she saw the appreciation in it. Her heart gave a sudden, sharp thud.

*Stop it*, she told herself. *You don't know the rules to this game. It is beyond foolish to try to court his favor.* She started to move past him, in the direction of the bar, but her path was blocked by a man carrying a basket of boiled shellfish. Mussels—she'd been wrong all around. The two girls bounded forward, handing over a coin in return for a bounty packaged in greasy cones made of newsprint. She was glad to see them eating.

A hand took her elbow. She let Sanburne steer her through the crowd, craning her head this way and that to absorb the place. She knew gin palaces as pits of doom, where poor people met their ruin, but this room was as gaudily resplendent as the lobby of an opera house. Gas lamps bloomed from the walls like exotic flowers of gold and glass. The ceiling was gilt laid over sculpted plaster. Cherubs peeked from the four corners, and mirrors polished to high clarity covered the wall behind the pewter-topped bar.

Oh, and there was the gin! Opposite the bar, behind a brass rail, sat row upon row of barrels, each painted in cheerful shades of gold and green. Handpainted signs announced their contents. THE SUPERIOR CREAM. THE REGULAR FLARE-UP. THE DEW OFF BEN NEVIS. "What are the numbers written on them in chalk?" she asked, gesturing.

"The number of gallons remaining. There are pipes embedded into the walls, leading over to the bar. The tapsters need only depress the right lever to fill a tankard."

At the bar, she meant to watch this process, but was distracted by the smooth gray countertop, which bore hundreds of tiny holes that formed a decorative pattern of flowers and vines. "To catch the spilled liquid," Sanburne said, tapping on one. "They sell it very cheaply— 'all sorts,' it's called. Care to try it?"

She grimaced. "No, thank you."

"What'll it be?" This from a giant man in a fur cap, who glanced casually toward them from his position behind a spigot. He was chewing on a piece of straw and had a paper flower tucked behind his ear.

"Sixpence of Old Tom for me," said Sanburne, "and a Cream of the Valley for the lady."

"I won't drink it," she muttered to him, but thought

it best not to protest more publicly. When the tapster returned with their drinks—giving a bite to Sanburne's coin before handing the tankards over—she said, "We're looking for someone. Miss Polly Marshall."

The man shrugged. "I don't ask their names before I serve 'em. Good luck to you."

They passed down the bar, through an arched passage that bore the sign To THE WHOLESALE DEPARTMENT. The next room held an equally dense crowd (in the middle of the day! she could not comprehend it), but there was no sign of the woman from the drawing. The final room was smaller, the bar lined with plush red benches, the walls covered in vibrant murals drawn from Greek mythology. The quality of the artistry surprised her. How many people came here not only for gin, but also for respite from the bleak surroundings in which they lived? She felt quite overturned.

After they had taken a seat, Sanburne lifted his glass for a long swallow. She waited for him to speak, but he seemed content to look moodily about. The silence that opened between them was not comfortable. She realized, with faint embarrassment, what bothered her: in all their interactions to date, he had watched her very closely, and with keen interest—as though nothing else existed. She'd rather grown to like it.

He caught her looking at him. She cast about for some remark, but he spoke first.

"I owe you an apology."

Did he refer to the scene on the roof, or in the hallway? The ambiguity left her balancing between chagrin and an equally discomfiting curiosity. "Please, let's don't speak of it."

"No. You were right, earlier. When you asked about my sister." She glanced up in time to see his mouth curve briefly. She would not have called it a smile. "I'm sure you've heard the story."

She hesitated. "Some of it," she said.

"The papers left out the most important part. Namely, that Boland was a goddamned pig."

She flushed. The language was shocking.

"He beat her, and I couldn't do a damned thing about it," he continued, running a finger around the rim of his mug. "Prying her out of that house was impossible. Until the end, of course. At the end, she wanted to run. But I had nothing to offer. No factories yet, no inheritance. My allowance from Moreland would have gotten her to the continent, but it would not have kept her in style. And she could not face poverty, though I offered to share it with her." The surface of his gin rippled beneath his soft laugh. "Stella was always a great hand for spending money."

She sat uncertainly for a moment. "And your father . . . ?"

"What of him?"

"He would not help her?"

Instead of answering, he drained his glass, then dug out a coin for another round, flipping it over to the tapster.

"You will get drunk," she said warily.

"Unfortunately, no. Pleasantly numb is about all I can achieve, these days."

"Then perhaps you should stop drinking."

The tapster brought the glass over, but Sanburne made no move to pick it up. "Perhaps," he said. "And no, my father would not help. The gossip about her marriage was affecting his political alliances. He told her to return to Boland's home. He told me to keep out of it. Between a husband and wife, he said. Boland was a gentleman, and Stella had always inclined to melodrama." He picked up the cup. "I did offer to kill him for her. My mistake was to listen when she told me no. Harder to put away an heir than to lock up a woman."

His face was so dark. All the possible replies running through her mind felt flimsy, useless. "You tried to help," she said finally. "You mustn't blame yourself."

"Oh, I don't," he said lightly. "I blame him. I blame Moreland."

Her throat tightened. What a terrible thing it must be, to have such loathing for one's own father. "But he did not realize," she said. "He thought her safe. And think of how terrible it must have been for him, once he realized the truth."

"He has *never* realized."

"Sanburne, surely—"

"No." He gave her a grim smile. The blazing light of the ginnery suited his looks, picking out the bright strands in his hair, emphasizing the high, sharp bones of his face. But his beauty did not seem appropriate to this moment. The look in his eyes belonged to someone much older. "He truly thinks Stella mad. I have tried every available means to get her out of that damned asylum. But he keeps her in there. I rather think he believes Boland never did lift a hand against her, till that last time. And so she rots. She rots in there."

She heard something else in his voice now. The contempt was not solely for his father. "That is not your fault."

He glanced up at her. "That's rich, coming from the woman who braves a gin palace to atone for her father's mistakes."

"And even if the forgeries were owed to his mistake, I would not blame *myself* for it," she said. "But you do. Why else whould you do these idiotic things? Why else would you go to the East End to let yourself get thrashed?" When he gave her a cutting look, she said more sharply, "Don't tell me these things if you don't want to hear my opinion. You said you liked pain, didn't you? You behave like a child to spite him and to punish yourself. I must say, Sanburne, it confirms my earlier opinion of you. It is unoriginal, and transparent, and *beyond* stupid."

He blew out a breath. "Well." The large swallow he took left his glass half-empty. "Here I thought I'd come for a drink in the company of a friend. Instead I'm delivered a sermon."

"I do like you," she said slowly, wondering over the wisdom of it even as she made the admission. "I will admit, though, that I find it very difficult to respect you. You have great potential, you know. But you waste it, despite all your opportunities."

"Potential," he said flatly. "Yes, I suppose I do have a great lot of that. Why, I'll be coming into two hundred thousand acres some time before I'm fifty. Think how many sheep I could raise."

"I find self-pity very distasteful as well."

"And yet you're so good at it. What else to call it, Lydia, when a fascinating woman considers herself a bookish drab?"

"Do not flirt. We're being serious."

"I can't help it. Your idiocy provokes me."

She looked down to hide the little smile that wanted to form. Strange, that she could listen to his accusations without taking offense. With one finger, she traced over the looping grain of the tabletop. Someone had carved his initials into the wood: *DSR Aug 81*. It had been etched very deeply. Not the work of one sitting, then, but of several nights. Yet the table would be sanded down at some point. The carver must have realized that, even as he labored.

The thought touched off a sadness too large for the provocation. Everyone wanted to leave a mark, even the patrons of a gin palace. But for most men, a tombstone would provide the only lasting record of their names. "You do have so many opportunities," she said quietly. "Sheep are the least of them."

"Oh, I'm not entirely useless. My factories are not . . ." When he trailed off, she looked up, her brows lifting in question. He shook his head. "I wouldn't mind having your respect, Lydia. But to be honest with you, I don't think I have it in me to bother earning it. It would ruin my whole routine, you see."

The remark was probably not meant to be cruel. But even as self-deprecation, it struck her like a lash. "Fair enough," she said briskly. "And I certainly have no intention of trying to entertain you." And then—forgetting the nature of the liquid that she held in her hand, and in an attempt to behave casually, as if inwardly she were not smarting from some obscure hurt—she lifted the mug for a sip.

It burned. Gasping and choking, she set down the cup. Her fingers dug into the carving, anchoring her as she tried not to retch.

He did an admirable job of restraining his laughter. "So," he said. "Cream of the Valley. Creamy, or no?"

The liquid trailed a path of fire down her throat and into her stomach. Once it hit bottom, it became a not-unpleasant sensation. Was that why people drank it? "*Not* creamy." He was smirking now. If he did not want her respect, she hardly needed to earn his. But now she was intrigued. She took another sip of the gin. This mouthful went down more easily. The bitterness seemed to complement her mood. "More like a lit coal," she decided.

"Ah, well. 'Embers from the Fire' does lack a certain ring."

A giggle escaped her. Shocked at herself, she touched her lips. Yes, the sound had come from her. "Am I drunk so soon?"

He grinned. "Highly doubtful. Why? Do you intend to become so?"

She had opened her mouth to answer when she spied, through the open archway, the woman from the sketch—a slim brunette of middling height, with a foxy cast to her eyes. "That's her," she said, and came to her feet. "That's Miss Marshall."

Nothing in Polly Marshall's manner bespoke cramped garrets and bad company. She smiled when she greeted them, and showed polite surprise upon learning of Sanburne's station. "What pleasant company for a chat," she said, and waved them to a bench that could accommodate all of them more comfortably. When she sat again, a casual twist of her wrist lent her brown

skirts a smart drape. "Amazing you found me here."
Her vowels were long, more refined than the company
she'd been raised with; Lydia fancied that the voice
of Mr. Hartnett echoed in them. "What good luck
for me. It's a hard road I've walked to meet you, Miss
Boyce."

This did not sound like an overture to blackmail.
Very cautiously, Lydia let the woman tap their tankards
together. "I hope you will tell me why, Miss Marshall."

Miss Marshall took a generous sip, then set the mug
down with a clank. "Sorry," she murmured, her eyes
on her hand. Her fingers, Lydia saw, were trembling.
"I would ask my share from you." She looked up, her
mouth firm. "I deserve it."

Lydia hesitated. "I don't understand."

The woman's fingernail made a sharp tattoo against
the mug. "Let's be frank, Miss Boyce. It was a fine deal,
while it lasted. And I wouldn't be so forward if he'd
made some provision for me. But eleven years, good
as married, and what does he leave me? Spit. I deserve
something, don't you think?"

She had no idea how to reply. Sanburne stepped in,
speaking quietly. "Be more specific, madam. *What* do
you deserve?"

"Just one of them." Miss Marshall glanced beyond
them, then leaned in confidentially. "I'll sell it for a
ticket to the country. A nice plot of land. It's a good
bargain for you, miss—and I'm owed it. Would you
have found a fencer without me?"

The woman made no sense. Lydia found herself
shaking her head, an expression of simple disbelief.

Miss Marshall frowned and sat back. "Don't refuse,"

she said. "You'd leave me no choice. I've a friend work-ing at Fleet Street who'd put out the word."

*The word?*

Sanburne's hand closed over her wrist, exerting steady pressure. "You mean that you want one of the forgeries?"

"Forgeries? Oh, I see. Is that what they used? Clever. But no, I've no use for it—won't be shipping it onward, will I? I just want one of the gems."

The paralysis that had gripped Lydia now snapped. "Are you insinuating that my father is a *smuggler*?"

Miss Marshall went still. "Dear God." She gave a short, strangled laugh. "Never say you didn't know?"

Lydia came to her feet. *Laugh*, would she? "I don't know what you think to gain from these lies." She spoke very calmly. She would not exert herself to yell at this trollop. "If you contact me again, I'll set the police on you for extortion."

Sanburne caught up as she crossed into the front room. "Lydia. Perhaps we should hear her out."

"Hear her out?" She turned on him. "She accused my father of thievery!"

"She knows of the forgeries," he said quietly. "How could she know of them, if Hartnett had not planned to receive them?"

Yes. How could Hartnett's mistress know of that? She drew a sharp breath. "Did Hartnett arrange for the substitutions, then? But why? He was Papa's dearest friend!"

"Lydia." He sounded weary, of a sudden. "You're an intelligent woman. You mentioned before that your father requires a good deal of money for his projects.

Have you really not considered the possibility that he plays a part in this?"

She opened her mouth to rebuke him, but the impulse faltered. An hour ago, she would not have understood him. But then he had told her of his sister.

She found herself reaching out to touch his arm. Maybe he did not need to earn her respect to have her friendship. After all, she could think of nothing more intimate than this: a knowledge of someone that stripped his harsh words of their power to sting. "Not all fathers are like yours, Sanburne."

A muscle ticked in his jaw. "This has nothing to do with Moreland. It's a matter of facts and logic. The simplest explanation points to your father."

She studied him for a moment, then smiled. This could be a lesson for him, one that he needed. "The simplest explanation is not always correct. But you're right, there's no point to wondering when we can test the facts ourselves. You think there are diamonds in those forgeries? Then come." She took his wrist. "Come with me now."

"Where?"

"Why, to shatter my naivete, or your cynicism. We will have to see which."

The houses lining Wilton Crescent were quiet as tombs in the yellow dusk. All the doors along the street stood closed, stern green mouths beneath the twin eyes of the gas lamps flanking them. Like fairy lights on the moors that lured wanderers into bogs, these lamps shone a false welcome. They suggested that one need only take hold of the knocker to be invited in for tea. Lydia knew better, of course. What invitations she received were extended in deference to George and Sophie, and always on the tacit understanding that she would occupy a seat unremarkably. She was taking a large risk, then, asking Sanburne to her home. But one took risks for friends.

In the front hall, she startled the butler with a request. "I need a hammer, Trenton. And have the crate in my dressing room brought into the garden."

She led Sanburne down the hall and out through glass doors into the little plot of terraced greenery. Her stomach was only jumping because of him; it had nothing to do with that woman's lies. *Never say you didn't know?* It was a morbid coincidence that Sophie had said the same four years ago, after George had left the drawing room and she'd come in to find Lydia crying. *That* had been naivete; *that* had been foolishness. But she was not a fool to trust her father.

"You don't need to do this," Sanburne said.

*Yes, I do.* An uneasy feeling came over her. She was doing this for Sanburne. Wasn't she? She looked away. The sky was the color of a dusty yellow dog, smudged here and there by long, thin clouds that looked like streaks of mud: sunset, seen through a haze of coal smoke. In the strange light, the garden looked artificially illuminated. The emptiness of the stone benches and graveled path seemed oddly conspicuous, as if they were set pieces on a stage where the players would soon arrive.

A footman stepped out with the linen-covered crate; Trenton followed with a hammer. She waved them back into the house, then knelt to withdraw the stela. Placing it carefully on the ground, she tapped the rough edge with her fingernail. "Note that the surface of the stone is seamless. I don't see how anything could have been placed inside it."

Sanburne crouched down by her side. "It seems unlikely." And then, once more, he said, "You don't need to do this. Not for my sake."

The careful neutrality of his manner inadvertently betrayed him. He had no doubt; he fully believed Polly Marshall. "You think faith requires proof," she said. "That it must be earned. So, I will produce the proof for you."

His light eyes touched hers. "Is it so important for you to have my faith, then?"

Her heart skipped a beat. "If we are to be friends," she said steadily, "faith is a requirement."

He smiled a little. "Hammer away, then. But do recall whose skull was broken the first time Athena swung her mallet."

"I also recall that her father was a great rogue," she said dryly, "and no doubt deserving of the bashing." She raised the hammer. But her grip faltered, and she was forced to lower it hastily, lest she drop it.

Ridiculous to feel a stir of nerves. It was crucial to show a confident face to him.

"Do you want me to do this?" he asked.

"No," she said firmly. "I will do it."

As he settled back, she lifted the hammer again. "Shield your face." Then, screwing her eyes shut, she brought down the tool.

A small piece of the forgery flew off, smacking against the railing. Nothing. Only stone. She felt herself smile. "Do you see?"

"I see," he murmured.

More confident now of the technique, she slammed the tool down, so the crack of steel against stone echoed off the garden walls like a gunshot. When she opened her eyes, relief swept through her, and immediately on its footsteps, a sense of shock at herself. "Only stone," she said, but shame made her voice unsteady, and she did not try to smile again.

"No jewels," he agreed, but his voice sounded thoughtful, and he was studying her face, not the stela. She did not like that.

"Don't look at me," she said sharply. "Look at the stela."

Another blow now. The rock was stubborn, jealous of its integrity; at this rate it would take an hour to destroy. At her third strike, he caught her wrist, saying, "Enough." She shook her head. She could not stop until she had destroyed the thing, and proved her point very clearly—not to him, God forgive her, but to herself, and the little doubting demon in her brain that she would also like to pound to bits; she wanted no truck with it, she did not recognize it as part of who she was.

Her anger gave her strength: again and again she hammered, until tiny splinters and chunks of rock lay scattered about them, and her arms were aching. She sat back, breathing heavily. "Another minute," she managed. It was not Sanburne's fault, any of this; but the patient way he watched her was infuriating. How dare he look so uninterested in the outcome of this task. She had started it for him, would not have done it otherwise, would never have had to experience this horrible revelation. "Another minute," she repeated in withering tones, "and then you'll see for sure, won't you."

He rose to his knees and moved behind her. She gave her shoulders an angry jerk as his chest pressed into her back, but he made a low, soothing noise—*springer spaniel, calm the puppy*—and his hands slid slowly down her arms, until his long, tanned fingers braided through her own. The sight silenced something in her, like the sudden muffling of sound upon a dive into deep water. His rings felt cold against her skin. Such gaudy glitter he used to disguise himself. "We'll do it together," he murmured. He spoke low into her ear, the way he would to a child trembling from nightmares in the dark. "That makes sense, doesn't it? Doing it together, in the manner of friends." He laughed softly; for a brief, deliberate moment, his cheek, rough with stubble, pressed against hers.

"Yes," she whispered. That laughter confused her a little. She did not know what to make of it. No matter. It made things inside her go liquid. Had it only been a few hours ago that they'd stood on the roof? How had she forgotten that, even for a second?

She pulled back the hammer. His fingers tightened and his arms banded around hers, so the hammer plummeted with great force. The force of the explosion made her flinch.

"Done," he said. A kiss pressed into her neck. "And not a diamond to be seen. You are quite avenged, Miss Boyce."

She opened her eyes. Rubble covered the small patio. Her triumph lay in this detritus. How strange. Stranger yet to feel a weird sympathy with the broken bits of stone. She had imagined herself as Papa's rock, unwaveringly loyal. To discover otherwise left her feeling shaken and unwholesome. Less than whole, certainly.

She shivered, and Sanburne's arms tightened around her. He knew. Somehow he knew. Thank God he didn't say anything.

*I could blame him,* she thought. For putting bugs in her brain. But—*you don't need to do this,* he'd said. And perhaps what he'd meant, but could not say (for she would not have understood or believed him) was, *You shouldn't do this.* After all, he knew a few things about love that she didn't. He knew what it felt like to fail someone precious to you. Maybe he'd wanted to spare her that.

A weird feeling swarmed up in her—melancholy and gratitude and elation, all in one. She had not been wrong to trust him, had she? On impulse, she turned on her knees to face him. She laid her hand to his cheek, her thumb to his lovely mouth, her index finger pressing the corner of his clear gray eyes. A stranger would never guess at the darkness behind them. But she was not a stranger to him now. *I could love him,* she thought. But what she said was, "Thank you," and then she kissed him.

He was startled. It took him a moment to kiss her back. Then he made a murmur of approval and slid his hand around her nape. His mouth still tasted faintly of gin, but through some strange alchemy, it now seemed delicious. She rubbed her tongue against his, making a little noise as he broke away to kiss her chin, her throat, the crook of her shoulder. *The servants,* she thought dimly, and permitted herself one last moment of pleasure before pulling away. When he reached for her, she said, "We'll be seen."

She half-expected him to dismiss this worry. But

he hesitated, and then nodded, casting a concerned glance toward the door as he rose. This sudden care for propriety unsettled her. Well. It seemed Southerton's house warranted more care than a rooftop. And why not? If caught kissing her here, he might be pressured to offer for her.

As she ushered him into the hall, disturbed by her own displeasure, it occurred to her for the first time to wonder why he wasn't married. She had looked him up in Debrett's (ridiculing herself all the while); he was already thirty, and the earldom would need an heir—

But that was precisely the reason, she had no doubt of it. With his bachelorhood, he'd found another way to strike at his father. As they passed the long mirror at the foot of the stairs, she spied a bitter smile on her lips. Building castles in the air, indeed. Sanburne had been very honest with her. He not only lacked a steady foundation, he'd taken pains to smash his cornerstones. Like the task of earning her respect, they, too, would ruin his whole routine. The rumors of his engagement to Mrs. Chudderley must prove as convenient for him as they did for the lady.

At the door, as he put on his hat and gloves, she thanked him again for his help. He opened his mouth to reply, and then, with a look toward the butler, appeared to change his mind. With a bow and some empty, mannerly phrase, he took his leave.

As she watched him retreat, she remembered his behavior in the hallway of his father's house. He had not cared then who might see them. Why, he must like her very much, now, to want to avoid being put into a position where he would be forced to reject her publicly.

For there could be no other choice for him. *My father thinks you very sensible.* Perhaps if she'd been a common trollop, she would have had a chance.

As she started up the stairs, she marveled at the oddness of it. A month ago, she could not have imagined that learning to understand and like a man would be her best defense against letting herself fall in love with him.

# Eleven

The crowd at the Empire was not feeling very patriotic. When a pretty young blonde took the stage to sing "Hats off to Empire," a wave of hissing drowned her out. Someone's mug spattered against the crimson draperies behind her. Blushing and bowing, she backed toward the curtains, then ducked inside. The orchestra, belatedly realizing that it had no one to accompany, sputtered to a stop.

Muttering rose from the pit. The electric lights glared down on a mass of milling patrons. James was seated in one of the private boxes that ran, in a horseshoe shape, along the fourth story. From his perch, he spotted a young man vomiting behind a marble column. Others were clambering onto friends' shoulders to yell for the next act. The cream and gold seats would bear more than a few shoeprints before the night was over.

He glanced to the far end of his box, where Phin, not an hour ago, had been knocking back whiskey like a man bound for battle. Now he was lounging low in his seat, chin collapsed to chest. "Is he dead?" Dalton asked.

James reached over and shook Phin's shoulder. "Here's fun," he said, to no response. "Phin. We're about to have a riot."

Dalton's soft gut pressed into his shoulder. He leaned over James to bellow, "Look lively, man!"

"By God!" Wincing, James elbowed him back a pace. "That's my ear, Dalton, not a speaking trumpet!"

"Well, why the deuce did he come, if all he wanted was a nap?" Dalton sat down with a huff. "Poor show. What did I ask for? A celebration, that's all. Not every day a man comes into money." He leaned past James again. "It's a party, Ashmore!"

Phin yawned. Dalton turned to complain to Tilney. One of Phin's eyes cracked open; he offered James a slight smile before lapsing back into the appearance of sleep.

Right, James thought. It should be amusing to see Dalton fussing like a schoolgirl, but he did not feel like laughing. What the hell was Phin on about? The role of the hapless ne'er-do-well did not suit him. And if he'd decided to reinvent himself, he could at least show some ingenuity, come up with an original part. James was already too sick of himself to take on an understudy.

He leaned toward Phin, intending to speak quietly. But from this new proximity, he detected something else: a faint, sickly sweet odor. Opium again. Christ. Was the man in thrall to this poison? "Even gin would prove a kinder master," he murmured. "Arsenic would be gentler on your brain."

For a brief moment, it seemed Phin would not reply. And then he said, "True enough. You needn't worry for me."

"The hell I don't. This needs to stop."

"I can't discuss it right now."

"I can. Since you've come into the title—"

Phin's eyes opened. "Have you a mirror, James?"

*Touché.*

He sat back. Once, he might have pushed on. He might have said, *Yes, come to think of it, I've made a jolly good hash of it myself.* He might have pressed for answers of his own. Once, they had been closer than brothers. Then their paths had diverged, and necessity had forced Phin into reticence. So James had assumed. But now it seemed damned clear that Phin *chose* to maintain this remoteness. Rather than speak around the requisite silences, he built on them. His unknown reasons. His bloody choice. And James was not going to give trust where he no longer received it. He was done with attempts to close this distance.

On stage, the curtains flew back to reveal Mr. Campbell. A fat man with a jolly air, he scanned the pit with a vague smile, nodding once to acknowledge the hoots of his admirers. Then, with little ado, he launched into a rousing song about the depredations of the aristocracy.

Behind James, Dalton let out a curse. Four floors did not provide enough distance for his comfort; he began to strip his wrists of his diamond-studded cuff links. "Should never have come straight from that dinner," he muttered. "Uncomfortable night to show up in tails."

"Ha! Scared of a few Irishmen?" This from Tilney, who was stretched out in the seat beyond Dalton, his boots propped on the balcony railing. A redheaded ballet dancer he'd found wandering the promenade during intermission was tucked under his arm. Her large brown eyes fastened on the diamonds.

James shouldered Dalton and lifted his chin toward the girl.

"How they glitter," she said softly.

"You like them, darling?" Dalton dumped them into her cupped palms. To James, he said, "Where is that waiter? I could use another glass."

"I'll go," James replied. He'd been drinking steadily since dinner, but his spirits felt flat and uncreative, and his vision had not yet blurred. Might as well try harder, then.

"There's making yourself useful," said Dalton approvingly. "Take note, Ashmore."

James ducked out, past Phin's immobile form, into the stuffy little corridor that led around the dress circle. The walls here were lined in maroon velvet, and lanterns, set every few paces along the wall, offered small pools of illumination. The owners had boasted that the new building was fireproof. But in the cloistered space, the air smelled burnt, as if the electrical wires had gotten crossed.

He intended to make a quick trip down to the foyer, where holders of the cheaper tickets purchased their gin. But he found himself standing stock still, his palms pressed to the soft nap of the walls on either side of him, his eyes fixed on the spot where the corridor curved into darkness. In contrast to the gaudy Moorish architecture of the theater proper, in which every available space glittered with gilt and mirrors to draw the eye, there was something appealing about this space. Its lack of options, its silence, pulled something from him. A calmness—a sort of *blankness,* he supposed. Here was a proper spot for boredom. And God, he was bored.

Lydia Boyce came to mind. She was like a chorus he could not get out of his head. As he focused on her consciously, he became aware that his mind had been straying toward the thought of her all night. A week had passed since he'd seen her last. Not at the Spencers' garden party, not at Elmore's rout, not even at the Mowbrays' musicale. Why the hell had he attended such idiotic events? To run into her? The possibility should not trouble him. He was in the mood for some righteous condemnation, a lecture in a darkened hallway, another kiss, more besides. He'd lounged about quite vigorously, waiting for her to appear. He would amuse her sufficiently; he had no doubt of it. But it seemed she did not want for amusement. She'd hared off to the Pateshalls' home in the Chilterns, and he knew this only because Elizabeth had traveled there for the weekend. In the letter she'd sent this morning, she mentioned how quietly his "nemesis" sat at a table.

Quiet? The description left him uneasy. It did not fit with what he knew of Lydia. He might have thought she'd mention him, even if only by way of a dry, cutting remark.

But perhaps not. What cause had he given her to speak his name? *We are to be friends,* she'd told him. But she could not respect him. Christ, how could he blame her for that? He'd thrashed a man near to death in her presence. And her face when he'd looked up from the bastard—it had nearly snapped his mind. She'd been staring at him as if he were a brute, the sort of man who left women battered at the bottom of staircases. It had been wrong, bloody wrong of her to look at him as if he would *ever* raise a hand to her. The expression on her face could have been Stella's, during those last few weeks at Boland's.

And then afterward, for no reason whatsoever, she had forgiven him. It had thrown him for a loop. He flaunted the worst of himself to her. Why? Did he want her to be repelled? Had he grown so sick now that he taunted women for fun? Lovely women, who tasted like spun sugar, and melted sweetly beneath his touch. She had stolen his breath, on the roof. And later, over the remnants of the smashed stela—she had looked at him and there had been more wonder in her eyes than a newborn's. He could have done anything to her, then. She should not issue such invitations with her eyes. Someone should warn her. One might skip from lust to fear and back; he knew several women who favored that recipe. But one did not go from fear to friendship in the space of a day. One exercised caution and demanded demonstrations. If her goddamned father were the hero she thought him, then he would have taught her these things. But no. She was even more naive than Stella had been. Terrifying thought.

Dalton wanted a drink.

He continued onward. The foyer was buzzing with patrons lined up for refreshment. He fought forward to the bar, where a girl in wilting feathers was dishing out gin in sixpence measures. Two giggling girls clasped onto his elbows and begged for a dram. He bought their rounds first, but declined when they offered to accompany him upstairs. He could not say what ailed him, but he felt curiously removed from himself, as if watching from above. Overdressed, with an elegantly amused sneer on his mouth: how stylishly he did a whole lot of nothing. *I find it very difficult to respect you.* Well, good for her. He hoped Lydia parceled out her respect in very stingy doses, since having it seemed to give one the ability to command anything of her. *Write my papers. Find me money. Brave a slum to protect me. Risk your safety for help from a fickle ne'er-do-well who fantasizes about pinning your wrists and bending you over a chair.*

He had just mounted the third flight of stairs when the man slipped from the shadows. Barely a man, really: not yet twenty, with dark fuzz where his beard would one day grow in. But the knife in his hand was real enough, especially when he stepped forward and pressed it against James's throat.

Caught off guard, James stepped back. The boy followed, his arm outstretched over the three glasses of gin James held. A curious sort of ballet, this: not a single drop spilled onto his fingers as he stared into the boy's face. His assailant had skin the color of teak and eyes that bespoke darker things than unlit hallways.

"Give it back," the lad hissed.

James glanced past him. It was a very bad place to do murder. There were people below and footsteps approaching on the stairs. "Give what back?" he asked.

The boy's fingers tightened. The blade bit at his throat. Killed in a music hall, no doubt soaked by gin during the course of his collapse: he would give his father apoplexy yet. "You know well enough." The pup's looks were swarthy, but his accent was purely Whitechapel. "Don't pretend you don't have it. I can read a paper well as you. The Tears belong to Egypt!"

Those bloody notes again. They had increased in the last few days. This bit about Egypt was new, though. Generally the letter-writer just whined on about curses.

*Egypt.* Something clicked in his mind. It seemed a

very unlikely coincidence. He might have asked, had the act of speaking not seemed likely to do the boy's work for him, and drive the blade in further.

"What— I say! Is that a *knife?*"

This from a fellow in a top hat, who paused to goggle through his monocle at the scene. The boy took one look over his shoulder, snatched back his hand, then bowled past the man and down the stairs.

James lowered the glasses to the carpet. Straightening he touched his neck. Blood stained his fingers. Right, then. He sprang forward, past the gabbling top hat, to take the stairs three by three. On the first landing, he caught sight of the boy a flight below. As he rounded the last stair and jumped to the lobby, the crowd was already closing around his trail.

Out into the warm night air. Leicester Square swarmed with noise and light. A thousand blazing lamps lit the cream and gilt exteriors of the music halls and public houses. Throngs of shrieking women and boisterous young mashers pushed and shoved by. The boy was gone. James struggled to calm his breathing. The air smelled of burnt sugar and fried fish and vomit.

A lunatic. That was how he'd dismissed the letter-writer, but the word no longer seemed to fit. The boy had mentioned Egypt. And when had his notes begun to arrive? James did not think he misremembered: the first had come the day after the debacle at the Institute.

Hell. Someone clearly thought he'd gotten more from Hartnett's shipment than he had. And if they'd connected it to him, they'd certainly connect it to Lydia—if they hadn't already. She had better open her eyes, and quickly. He didn't care what she saw when she looked into his face; he would rather not be forced to imagine *her* with her throat sliced open.

He quickly made his way back to his box. "Outside," he said to Phin, and ignored Dalton's complaint about the drink he was owed. In the dark little corridor, he said, "I need your help. Are you sober enough to give it?"

Phin hesitated only briefly before replying, "Just about."

"Good. I need you to put out an ear. To be brief: some boy has been writing me about curses, tears, and my imminent decline. Cornered me just now and tried to slit my throat. I lost him, and I want him found. He's delivering the notes somehow; perhaps a watch on my house would work. Can you do that?"

Phin arched a brow. "No question. Tears, you say? And a curse. Is that all he writes?"

"I have cause to think it connected to a smuggling operation, run out of Egypt." For Lydia's sake, he did not want to mention the Boyces. What a stupid impulse. Failing to share all the facts was not the best way to protect her. "It has something to do with that forged stela I bought." *Protecting* her? Was that his aim, now? How ludicrous. "Turns out it came from Henry Boyce's shipment." Ridiculous to feel a stir of guilt. "But it was placed in there by someone else, perhaps." Thoroughly irritated with himself, he shrugged and added, "You must have friends who play in that part of the world. If you consulted them, I'd appreciate it."

Phin was staring into the distance, an abstracted look on his face. "I can do you one better," he said slowly. "A rumor recently came to me." He glanced back to James.

"I cannot think how you might have gotten involved—I hope to God you aren't. But to dismiss it as a coincidence seems . . . unwise."

"I'd be glad to hear it," James said. "But we'll have to talk on the way to the train station. I'm spending the night in the country."

Most estates were deserted during the spring. But Bagley End was only two hours from London, and the Pateshalls liked to use it as a retreat from the tiresome formalities of the season. When Sophie received their invitation, Lydia's uncharacteristic enthusiasm had startled her into accepting. "Perhaps it will do you good," she'd remarked thoughtfully. "You've been very blue of late." They had looked at each other then in equal surprise, and Ana had clapped and told them to hug, which they did, although of course they were quarreling again before dinner.

The Pateshalls catered to an athletic crowd. Croquet, tennis, bicycling, and archery consumed most of Ana's day, while Sophie preferred to laze in the drawing room, gossiping with friends and reading novels. Lydia, who'd explained her "blueness" as a slight ague, was left to her own devices. She spent her time reading in the turreted towers that topped the manor's grand hall, and hunting through the public rooms for treasure. Already she'd found a mummy mask behind a tapestry in the morning room, and an Assyrian obelisk serving as an extra leg for the snooker table. She regretted peeking into the smoking room. To her horror, a Roman urn was serving there as an ashtray.

The first few nights, she retired early. She had an ague, didn't she? Certainly her melancholy had nothing to do with her revelations about Sanburne. But as she lay in bed, listening to the dim shouts of revelry below, she could not budge her thoughts from him. Her distress seemed obscure to her. Even if some bizarre alignment of stars had led Sanburne to fall in love with her, she would not have wanted to marry him. Oh, he had some cause for his anger at Moreland; she didn't doubt that. But he deliberately sacrificed his own happiness to torment the man. His rage mattered more to him than love ever would.

On the fifth evening, sick of her own thoughts, she decided to linger downstairs. Several new guests had arrived for the weekend, and in some chemical reaction, they had transformed the bent of the entire crowd, causing everyone to incline toward rowdiness. At dinner, Mrs. Chudderley's teasing remark about Mr. Ensley's figure triggered a round of risqué comments that showed no sign of abating as the party transferred to the drawing room. She tried to send Ana to bed, but Ana protested that she was grown and should not have to go, especially since Mr. Pagett was there. Lydia pulled her into the hall for a lecture on the different licenses allowed to women who were engaged versus those who were married, at the conclusion of which Ana yanked away and said, "What would *you* know of it?" And then, clearly shocked by herself, she burst into tears, sobbed an apology, and ran for the stairs.

Lydia was not in a festive mood when she returned to the party. Mr. Ensley stood by the mantel, speechifying to a rapt audience. "Hide-and-seek," he was proposing.

Lydia took a seat next to Sophie. "But let's give it a real twist. Close your eyes and pretend it's August. Epsom, Henley, behind us. The Bisley Meeting and Speech Day, over. You're knackered. Sick of cutlet for cutlet. Pretend this is a *real* country party—somewhere north, where it rains endlessly."

"The Hebrides!" Mrs. Chudderley cried out. Lydia glanced at her. She was sitting on a loveseat with Mr. Nelson, her hand resting quite casually on his knee. To Lydia's knowledge, they were neither family nor formally contracted. Of course *Sanburne* would not be surprised by such behavior. It was the sort of licentiousness he no doubt *required* of his friends.

"The Hebrides," Mr. Ensley said, miming a tip of an invisible hat. "Excellent. Stranded in the Hebrides, we must provide our own entertainment. And so I propose: kiss-in-the-closet." A gasp moved through the room, followed by nervous titters. "Oh yes," he confirmed with a grin. "You've heard of it: hide-and-go-seek with a difference. If a gentleman should catch a lady, he earns the right to kiss her. A lady is only safe if she manages to make it to the conservatory undetected!"

Mr. Pagett slipped from the room. Lydia thought better of him for his departure. Country weekends were famous for such juvenile entertainments, but usually they tended to break out during the late hours. She blamed this trend on the Marlborough House Set, with whom such games were rumored to be popular.

She made to rise, but Sophie caught her wrist. There was a feverish look in her eye. "You *must* stay," she said. "It will be so much fun, Lyd—but I can't play if you don't."

"And you shouldn't. It's not proper. George would—"

"Oh, *George* would not care. George cares only for his career."

"Put out the lights!" Mr. Ensley cried to a footman, startling them both. "The whole ground floor must be darkened." He glanced sidelong at Sophie, very briefly. But when he noticed Lydia's regard on him, color came into his cheeks, and he turned to speak officiously to the servant.

His reaction discomfited Lydia extremely. "Sophie, this is unwise. I do not trust Mr. Ensley to behave himself."

Sophie rose. The stubborn look on her face was all too familiar. "Mr. Ensley is a gentleman, and George *specifically* told me to be friendly to him. His father has great influence."

"But—"

"And who are you to advise me, anyway? You are hardly in society. Play the killjoy if you like, but what I do is none of your concern." With a toss of her head, she crossed to the other women, who had gathered to giggle and dart nervous glances at the men. And there went Ensley again, staring at Sophie—and by gad if Sophie did not blush prettily and give a little laugh at his regard.

Oh, this was very bad.

Lydia marched up to Sophie. "I shan't move from your side," she said grimly.

"Then you'll have to follow me."

"Then I will."

Someone turned down the jets on the chandelier. As

darkness fell, a cry of excitement broke from the ladies. Lydia grabbed her sister's arm. "I won't let go of you."

"Ninety seconds, ladies! You have ninety seconds to run."

"You're not my mother," Sophie whispered, and wrenched away so forcibly that Lydia stumbled. She knocked into someone—Mrs. Ellis, by the sound of the whispered protest. And then that woman, too, was gone. A pattering of footsteps, a fit of smothered giggles, and then silence.

No. Not quite silence. She could hear the rustling of clothes, and the soft squeak of shoe leather. Hushed breathing came from very near her.

"Forty-five seconds," Ensley called softly. "On your marks, sirs. The ladies are impatient to be caught."

A chill moved down her spine. She was surrounded by gentlemen waiting to give chase. In less than forty-five seconds, she would not want to be in this room.

Holding her breath, she moved toward the door, her hands groping before her, her shoulder tensed in anticipation of brushing against a male body. It was the longest walk of her life, those twelve halting steps. And then her hand hit something. The wall. She felt desperately to the right and left. Her fingers closed on the doorframe. She pulled herself into the antechamber and turned right, picking up her skirts to run toward the hall where the main staircase began.

Her hand had closed on the balustrade when someone grabbed her wrist. A finger scratched down her knuckle. "Got you," Ensley said, and yanked her around to thrust his mouth against hers.

She pushed him away so violently that he stumbled

off the stairs, landing in a beam of moonlight that fell from the window high above the front door. "Blast it!" He scrambled onto his knees. "Sophie, what the deuce—"

"Lydia," she said icily. *Her sister.*

He made a disgusted sound, as if he'd swallowed something foul. "Good God," he muttered. "I thought you were Sophie."

It should not have stung. "Who is married!"

The scowl on his face smoothed into a nasty smile. "Bitter, are you?" He came to his feet. "What are you doing on the stairs, anyway? The conservatory was the safe place for you." As he came toward her, she noticed the halting quality of his steps. The gentlemen must have drunk a great deal of port when they'd withdrawn after dinner. "One might think you wanted to be caught," he went on. "Poor, dried-up little—"

"Not so little," she said. "And I would rather kiss a frog. Now stop this, or you will regret it in the morning."

He took another step toward her. What a sly, self-satisfied slug he was. She was going to have to slap him.

A bright light startled both. They turned as one to the window. Thunder rumbled dimly through the walls.

The lightning seemed to call him to his senses. He dug a hand through his hair, muttered something profane, and turned on his heel.

She stood stock-still in the darkness, listening to the sound of his retreating footsteps. *Dried-up,* was she? She had looked in the mirror this morning. Perhaps there were lines around her eyes that hadn't been there four years ago. But if she was no longer a debutante, she was hardly old, either. Although . . . it was true that by twenty-six, most women had two children, and another on the way. That was not to be her fate. What of it? She had more important things to do than feel ashamed of herself.

Still. That sound he'd made when he'd realized her identity—retching, almost. He was a cad, a snake. It should not hurt her feelings. She'd been kissed by a far handsomer man than *he*. And Sanburne had seemed to like the experience. *Don't think of him,* she reminded herself.

Mr. Ensley had called her Sophie. *Sophie, what the deuce?* Why had he seemed surprised that her sister might reject his attentions? Why did he feel entitled to address her so familiarly? It was almost as if—as if they'd planned to meet, in the darkness.

No. She must be mistaken. Sophie would never do such a thing.

But the possibility of walking down that hall and finding out differently—she could not face it. The *hypocrisy* would infuriate her. Woo George beneath her nose, and then dally with Mr. Ensley?

"I am sick of it," she muttered. Sick of playing Sophie's keeper. Let her make her own mistakes. Let her pay for them, too. *Pretty is as pretty does, and it does a great deal.* Let Sophie test that hypothesis.

The thunder rumbled again. She found herself at the front door. She pulled it open to look into the sudden spate of rain. As a child, she'd liked to go out in such weather, to let herself be drenched and buffeted by the elements. "My little Bacchae," Papa had called her. But lightning scared Sophie. She hid in Mama's skirts, never seeing the beauty of it. Had Papa's life depended on it, she would never have gone to St. Giles. She liked pretty things, and pretty people, and dispatched her underlings to do any unpleasant work for her. *I cannot fathom how you deal in trade.* As if she'd never worn a pair of gloves paid for by Papa's artifacts!

Lydia stepped onto the portico. The lawn sloped downward to a little lake that tossed in the wind. When the door blew shut behind her, it seemed like an instruction. She would not go back inside until the game was over.

The house was a Gothic monstrosity, sprawled in the rain like some arrogant gargoyle. As the carriage began to slow, James opened the door and leaped out. He landed unsteadily. The gravel needed combing; the drive was turning to mud in the wet.

As he strode toward the entrance, he noticed something odd. The ground floor was dark. His impatient rap on the front door caused it to shudder and creak open.

The hairs lifted on the back of his neck.

He drew a steadying breath. His mind was racing with all manner of wild possibilities. Phin's fault. Quite a theory he'd proposed about the Tears. But even if a gang of thugs had managed to divine James's destination, there was no way they could have subdued the whole staff, not in such a short time. Something else was afoot, then. He stepped inside the lobby and spotted the dim, wavering halo of a lamp, retreating down the hall. "Ho," he called.

"What's that?" The halo did a little dance, then reversed course, heading back toward him. It shrank suddenly, as the lamp rose: he found himself looking into the startled face of a maid. "Oh, sir! Have you just come? We weren't expecting any more guests for the night!"

"Has the gas gone out?"

"No, sir, 'twas the guests that did it. They're having a game of chase—or they was. Now they're in the conservatory. Would you like the lamp, sir? I'll fetch another."

He shook his head. "Keep it. And—" It wasn't his house, but what the hell. After the scare he'd been given, he'd rather not be in the dark. "Turn the lights back on."

"Yes, sir."

He started down the hall. He'd been to Bagley End before, although not in a good while. Someone was playing a piano; he followed the sound of it. Find Lydia, explain the situation, and discover where she'd stashed the other forgeries. Smash them, hand them over to the goon, or give them to Phin, whichever seemed more expedient. *Voilà*: his duty discharged, his sainthood attained.

As he reached the southernmost antechamber, the music grew louder. He slid open the pocket doors and found himself at the dining-room. One mystery solved: the bulk of the staff stood around the glass doors that opened onto the conservatory, watching the guests dance and drink among the trees. He spotted Lydia's sister by a potted palm, gesticulating broadly as she smiled up into a man's face. The chase had roughed her up: her chignon had collapsed, and one of her lace gloves was ripped to the wrist.

As he passed the servants, they jumped and scattered like startled doves. Mrs. Joyner was here, and Lady Bulmer, and Michael Hancock—nasty piece of work, that boy, but a fine poet. The Pateshalls did enjoy the arts.

Lydia was not to be seen. "Lady Southerton," he called, but the lady was in some sort of grinning daze and did not hear him. He came up and touched her shoulder. "Madam."

She spun around. "Viscount!" She darted a feverish look to her companion. The man was built on slender lines, a delicate blond masher in tight trousers and monocle. He appeared to be one of those unfortunates who turned scarlet after a few drinks. "Mr. Ensley has just finished leading us through a very peculiar variation of hide-and-seek. Oh—do you know Mr. Ensley?"

Ensley. Yes, that was right. "We've met," he said. "Banking heir, yes?"

Ensley flashed a toothy grin. "Can't blame me for it."

"Also a womanizer and a card cheat," James said. "Not that I blame you for that, either. Lady Southerton, where's your sister?"

She looked uncertainly between them. Ensley had gone pale. It was a much better look for him, really. "Ah . . . I can't say. I thought she—but no, I haven't seen her since the lights went out. Perhaps she retired for the evening?"

Ensley sniffed. "She went outside."

Lydia's sister glanced toward the glass walls of the conservatory. "Rain," she murmured, as if only now noticing the water that sluiced down the windows. "Yes, then. Perhaps."

A curious reaction. "You say she went into the storm? But why?"

Ensley snorted. "Who can say?" He did not sound impressed with Lydia. "God knows, she's probably lost in the bushes somewhere. I'm sorry, Sophie, but you must admit, your sister is a very wet blanket."

"Is she?" Lady Southerton laughed uncertainly. "I suppose. Very serious, our Lydia."

A bolt of lightning lit the world outside the glass. Cries broke from the guests. James turned away with a snort. He was all for a bit of fun, but if they were exclaiming at lightning, they weren't trying hard enough.

He retraced his steps back toward the front hall. On his way, he ran into Elizabeth, who was patting down her hair and calling flirtatiously into the room she'd just left, "You will have to catch me again, then. Oh—James! What are you doing here?"

"Looking for someone," he said. "If you will excuse me."

A frown pulled at her brow, but she made no objection as he strode onward.

Outside, the rain was coming down hard enough to hurt. To make matters worse, a mist had settled onto the grass, making forward progress treacherous. When a tree root caught his foot, it was a second's near call as he scrambled to avoid the mud. This was ridiculous. What the hell was she doing out here? And why was *he* bothering to fetch some dimwit bluestocking who should know better than to wander off during storms?

A flash of lightning lit the parkland. It emblazoned the scene on his brain: a wave-stippled lake, two boats rocking on their ties—and the lone figure of a woman in a white dress, standing at the edge of the pier. Good God. He quickened his steps. Was she trying to take ill? Shelter waited a few paces behind her, but she stood with her face lifted to the open sky. The rain was coming down hard enough to sting his scalp; he could not imagine that she liked it slapping into her face, or what might possess her to linger there unprotected. Fright had paralyzed her, perhaps. Lizzie occasionally succumbed to such stupors—spiders, mice, dust motes, a slew of natural horrors that could make her freeze, or flinch and scurry like a spooked colt.

But as he drew near enough to see Lydia's face, his anticipation of hysteria—and the building anger with which he would meet it—faltered. For her lips were parted. Her hands were loose at her sides, palms up, fingers curling as if to beckon the rain onward. And as lightning once again licked the sky, he spied something like . . . euphoria . . . on her face.

The thunder cracked so loudly that his glance darted in momentary concern to the boathouse behind her. When he looked back, her eyes were open, resting on his. Slowly, she smiled.

A spider danced down his nape. The hairs on his neck lifted. Such a peculiar smile—knowing, aloof, removed. He could not tell what it produced within him, whether the sensation purling down his spine was revulsion (such a fey, curious expression she wore) or some novel variation on lust. He drew a breath and wiped wet hair off his forehead. "What are you doing out here?"

She laughed. It was a wild sort of sound. He wondered briefly if she'd been drinking, although the notion didn't square. "Hello, James." The serenity of her tone jarred him. It did not match that laugh. "When did you arrive?"

The staid greeting knocked him off-kilter. "Just now," he said through his teeth. Suddenly he felt foolish. Here he'd gone charging into a storm to rescue a damsel in distress, and instead he found—a jeremiad. A nymph. Some elemental creature who had no need of him.

All right, he was angry. But what else had he missed in her? Would she sprout wings when his back was turned? *I don't like heights,* she'd told him, and *we have no chaperone, it would be improper,* and of course the protestation that in retrospect should have given away her game: *I won't drink the gin.* She deployed these lines like bits of bait, tricking him into uncreative assumptions about her. How ungrateful of her—how very small in nature—to pretend to be so commonplace. The world had need of better things from her. *He* had need of them. "What a toll it must take," he said, not bothering to disguise his temper. "How it must wear on you, to constantly manufacture the appearance of a staid, bookish miss."

The smile dimmed into something more human. "You came to find me," she said.

"They thought you lost, up at the house."

"Oh, dear. I hope no one was worried."

Something else clicked in his head. Her sister had not been worried. She hadn't even expressed surprise. "Not at all. That is—you like it, don't you? You were not caught out here in the storm; you came out after it."

Her lips quirked. "Perhaps I felt in need of a bath." Then she shrugged. "I didn't think I'd be missed."

It was an odd little statement, but her expression was tranquil, accepting. As he stared at her, his embarrassment ebbed. A dozen discomforts dimly registered: his clothes were damp and clammy, his shirtsleeves sticking to his skin, and the rain pricked his cheeks like needles. But—it came to him suddenly—she had a point. There were things to be admired here.

He exhaled and looked around. Nothing to be seen for more than a few feet; the mist had thickened. But the smell of the startled earth was sharp and heady, as if everything were rising under the slap of the rain: rich loam, raw young green things, sap and grass, broken flower stems. A faint note of ozone overlay it all. Lightning lingered invisibly around them.

Lydia stepped past him, off the pier. After a moment's surprise, he slowly followed. As she trailed to a stop, her hands reached into the mist and pulled back into visibility, as if from the ether, the soft crimson nap of a rosehead. "They thrive in the rain," she said softly. "See how they open to it?"

The words registered low in his gut. Everything in him tightened. It was the remark of a voluptuary—of the woman she could be, if she only let herself. If only she were able.

A strange feeling moved through him, then. It was something like affection, but softer, more harmful to his balance. Of course she ran into storms. Like rooftops, they were safe for her. No one around to see her break the rules. She knew that no one had missed her at the house, she had counted on no one bothering to chase her. They were idiots, all of them.

He breathed deeply. He could smell the roses, now.

But she was wrong; they didn't like the rain at all. The rain forced the petals open; the roses merely submitted to it.

She glanced at him from the corner of her eye. He met the regard squarely. He'd expected her appeal to be a passing fancy, a temporary madness—that the next time he saw her, or a few weeks from now at the latest, the novelty would pall. How odd. How astonishing. "Is it some game by which you amuse yourself," he began to ask—*letting everyone think you standoffish, cold, disinterested*—but his throat closed over the rest of it. His curiosity was swamped by a strange fear that she would not answer honestly.

She frowned. She had no idea what he meant. Or perhaps she did, for now she looked away and shifted on her feet, uncomfortable. It was occurring to her that she had revealed too much of herself. He studied her long nose. Perfectly straight—it was a wonder her spectacles were not always slipping. Her mouth was plump in repose, carefully expressionless. *Too late,* he thought with sudden, fierce pleasure. *Too late, Lydia. I have seen you now.*

The mist flashed a bright white. She gave a small smile, quickly quashed. Well, then. She was still enjoying herself, but did not like his audience. She did not need to uphold this pretense. Not with *him,* for God's sake. That she continued to do it felt, bizarrely, like a betrayal. He remembered out of nowhere the day he'd discovered what Boland was doing, the helpless sick anger it had roused in him. And the hurt, as if his feelings were at all important in it. He'd put the wrong words to Stella, that day. What he wouldn't give to be able to take them back. *My God,* he'd said. *I'm going to kill that son of a bitch.* And then: *Why the hell didn't you tell me?*

He was not going to ruin this moment, or speak truths that would only give her cause to run. He took her arm and pulled her toward the boathouse.

For a moment, she resisted. It provided him an opportunity to channel his frustration. Beneath his tightening fingers, her muscles and flesh were firm. Here was the most elemental hypocrisy imaginable: to be younger than one wanted to be. She had decided herself too ancient for the more limber emotions, but she could not change her flesh. She could not change the way it spoke to him, or the fact that he could care for it, could tend its needs, better than she knew.

They stepped together into the small shed. A line of paddles hung along one wall and the air smelled of wood varnish and wax. She pulled away, her sodden skirts hissing across the planks. He shook his head vigorously, taking a childish pleasure from the knowledge that the droplets spattered over her. Inexplicable, this need to provoke some, any, reaction from her. It writhed inside him with a life of its own. It wanted to reach out and grab her, to shake her and make her pay attention.

She refused to grant him satisfaction. Her concentration was all for the straightening of her skirts. Long moments she spent fussing with them, until, in the silence, it perhaps became apparent to her that they no longer offered a credible pretext for her interest. She looked up, and her eyes widened as she found him watching her.

She was not playing a game. She had no idea of the effect she had.

The realization should have assuaged his annoyance. It did not. Christ, he had made a fool of himself over her how many times now? And still she remained naive. How could a grown woman be so fundamentally ignorant of her own appeal?

Apropos of nothing, she said, "I miss the country. We are always in town now, it seems." From the note of apology coloring her words, he gathered that she was offering this tidbit—aggravatingly impersonal, as if they were strangers—by way of explanation.

But he listened more deeply than she assumed. There was something about her voice, he thought. Surely he had noticed it before. At their first meeting, surely, he had remarked the huskiness beneath those carefully gauged tones. A bit of savagery there, no? As though she were biting down on the things she had really rather say.

She would say them to him. Again and again, for as long as she liked, until she no longer feared to speak honestly of herself. The decision crystallized in his mind, bringing with it a deep satisfaction, as though some long-pondered question had finally been resolved.

For the moment, though, he merely smiled. "You might try gardening, then. Running out into storms is decidedly de trop."

One brow winged upward. "Viscount," she said, as staidly as a chiding nursemaid. "Do you now offer etiquette lessons? And here I thought you were an *original*."

Poor girl. She hadn't realized it yet, but her game was up. The starch could no longer fool him. "Miss Boyce," he replied, in a fair imitation of her tone. "I know you take pleasure from disparaging the manner in which I live, but let us recall that *you* are the one who chose to go haring into a storm."

She calmly regarded him. "I did not ask you to come after me. I expect it was Sophie who requested it?"

His smile grew into a taunt. "Correction. You wonder if she even knows that you're out here. Alone with me. Whether anyone knows, for that matter."

"I have been alone with you before."

"Oh yes," he said softly. "Some of my fondest memories concern those times."

She was not easily flustered, in this mood. "How fearsome you are!" Humor flickered at the corner of her mouth. "I suppose I should run back into the storm to escape you."

He considered it. "You could try." No time like the present to begin a project. "It might be amusing."

Her smile faltered. She looked away. Knowledge unfurled in his brain: the idea of being chased excited her.

His own breath was suddenly not quite steady. He could picture it. Her hair coming unbound, streaming behind her as she crossed the lawn. "Has no one ever done it?"

"I beg your pardon?"

It was all coming together in his mind. A picture had been assembling, and now he had a sense of the outlines. In a few more moments, it would emerge in high clarity. He'd have her figured out. Pinned. Nailed to the wall. As a scientist, she would appreciate his thoroughness. "Has no one ever chased you, Lydia?"

She laughed, and the look she gave him was so frank, so direct, that his breath caught. "Yes," she said, "it seems someone has done. The question is why. Why are you here, Sanburne?"

"James," he murmured. She had decided to go toe-to-toe with him. Good for her. "Is it so odd that I should be here?"

"This isn't your sort of crowd, *Sanburne*."

"Perhaps I long for country company."

"Ha! I don't believe it. Far too pedestrian for a man of your sort."

"Smart girl," he said. "Why do you think I'm here?"

"Boredom, maybe."

"You know I'm not bored in the slightest."

"Oh," she said, drawing out the word, making it mock him. "I'm meant to be flattered by that."

"Are you?"

"Let me think on it."

The nastiness of her tone took him off guard. And then, just as quickly, delighted him. The sarcastic, prickly little thing.

Another crack of lightning split the sky. She mistook his movement toward her for alarm. Amusement crossed her face. "Frightened? Think we'll be struck?"

"Oh, most definitely," he said, and took her hand to pull her to him.

# Twelve

She did not let him draw her forward. The storm had activated some electric impulse that moved her to take the step willingly. His jacket felt cold and sodden. She didn't like it. It had to go. She pushed her hands beneath his lapels to force it off. It hit the floor with a wet, thick, slapping noise that pleased her. Her aggression pleased her. It dizzied her, made her drunk. She squeezed his bicep more tightly than could feel pleasant to him, but he made no complaint. Did he like it? Oh, she did not care. This restless, breathless feeling knocking through her might have been desire, but it could as easily be anger. The only thing clear to her was that she'd had it wrong, worrying about what she revealed of herself, of what he or anyone else might think about her. It was not *their* opinions that mattered. "I do not do this for you," she said. *I do it for myself.*

The barest hesitation. And then, very low, he said, "Fair enough."

Her mouth twisted. Of course he would not mind. What matter to him if her motives were selfish? The man could not be hurt; he had an immunity to others' opinions. *Hers* would not deserve more import than any passing stranger's. For all he knew, she would have lain down with any man to wander across her tonight. She was in a mood; he was there; it was convenient. He did not question this. And it should not matter to her that he failed to care.

His lips touched hers. Their heat threw her off. She had been cold without realizing it. She leaned into him. His tongue teased her lips too gently for her mood. She was not some frightened girl in need of solicitude. She started to pull back to make a nasty remark but his hand fisted in her hair to hold her still. She gasped as pins popped free, tinkling onto the floor. His fist tightened, holding her to him as his kiss became forceful. *Yes,* she thought, *this*—he was ravishing her mouth as though he'd done it a thousand times, as though there were no longer room for any fear or uncertainty, only an ambition to uncover new ground, to produce something that would surprise them both. He was always turning out to be cleverer than she'd imagined.

Dimly she became aware of his free hand pressing on her waist, turning her as though to dance. She had told the truth: she did not like to dance. Men assumed that a spinster wanted for excitement. *Dried-up.* They made a point of spinning her wildly across the floor. Once she had fallen, and thereafter she'd declined all invitations. The humiliation echoed through her now like a premonition. She would embarrass herself, here. She would make some mistake.

But he did not kiss her as though she were a spinster. He never had done. And the deuces with it! Even if she fell, she did not care! *She* would lead. She pulled out of his arms, her feet skipping backward soundlessly, light and fleet. Rain muttered dimly against the roof, but the air within this little shed felt hushed and full, heavy with expectation. She had been amazed, sitting by his side in the museum, to realize she was flirting; but only now, when she had left flirtation behind, did she realize its true nature. It was light and easy and aimless. Her backward retreat was too deliberate for flirtation, his steady advance too focused and silent. Both of them shared a goal now, and they pursued it with primal intent. His expression, in the dim light, looked grave, almost grim. She had no urge to smile as the wall touched her shoulder blades.

His palms struck the wall on either side of her head. Over his shoulder, the line of windows flooded white, and the sky beyond them blanched, revealing, for a second, a bank of moving clouds. And then his mouth was addressing hers. She groped with one hand to find the point of his elbow, letting it fill her palm as his tongue filled her mouth. Her other hand cupped the hollow at the base of his skull. It was unexpectedly soft, and an odd tenderness rose in her, quite at odds with the fierceness of this kiss. Every person was his own country, she thought, governed by a private language, a personal reason and custom. She was still discovering herself, but she thought she might use him as a guide; he was not the least complicated of her acquaintances. Whatever passed through his mind, whatever drove him to kiss her like this—he kissed her as earnestly as a prayer—it was right and good. And all of it, all the complex curious intricacies of James Durham, were here, bound by muscle and warm flesh, in the span of her hands.

Impatient suddenly, she unfastened the buttons on his waistcoat. The musculature of his torso, the patterns of his rib cage, entranced her fingertips. She wanted to unriddle him like a hieroglyph. Once she knew him, she would not find the looks he gave her so interesting; he would no longer keep her awake at night. This, all of it, was only for her. His body pushed against hers and she realized anew how much bigger he was. And how young. In the daylight hours, his sardonic manner disguised the smoothness of his skin, the plushness of his lips. He was not much older than she. Her fingers wound around to the small of his back, and he arched under the pressure like a cat. Muscles flexed beneath her palms as he moved, and she felt another part of him come against her. *Penis* was the name. Sophie had described this act once. There was pain for her ahead.

Doubt intruded, a cold wisp twining through the heat. She wasn't meant to do this. It would ruin her. But for what and for whom? *She* would not count herself ruined.

"You are thinking," he murmured against her lips. "Please stop."

Her laughter was soft and brief. "I always think. There's no way to stop it."

"Throwing down the gauntlet? All right." He undid the buttons at her throat. Her own hand coasted down to the spot where his back yielded to the swell of his buttocks. This caused a breath to burst from him, intruding between their lips. His laughter, nearly inaudible, stirred goose bumps on her arms. "A woman of good sense," he whispered. "Reach lower, and so will I."

*A woman of good sense.* The chill grew stronger, separating her from the scene. Objectively, it was odd: here in a shed with Sanburne, her sisters not three hundred feet away, the rain drumming down, a skiff to her right, draped in a white canvas sheet. That sheet was so blindingly bright that it glowed even in the darkness. Some servant, a woman no doubt, labored hard to keep it clean; in her sleep, her arm must ache from scrubbing it. No one would thank her. The perimeters of Sanburne's world, of Sophie's world, were full of such people—invisible, unmissed if they vanished. The only women less visible than spinsters were maids.

His lips pulled away. "Lydia."

"What?" The word sounded strangely defiant.

"Look at me."

She did not want to. "Just go on."

"Look at me," he repeated quietly.

The darkness cast him in grayscale, drawing gunmetal shadows beneath his angular cheekbones, glossing his lips, damp from kisses, with silver. His eyes fixed firmly on her, a resolute pewter, the shade of dim moonlight on dark water. He reminded her of a photograph, a postcard. "The handsome bachelor at play," she muttered.

Her resentment was not well hidden; she felt him stiffen. "I left my role outside," he said.

She did not know if that made it better, or worse. "Then why are you doing this?"

His hand cupped her cheek, his thumb stroking over her mouth. "Because you're with me. Because you're lovely."

"Lovely."

"That's what I said."

Her doubt infuriated her. She had wanted to abandon it tonight. "I'm not some fragile flower," she whispered. "Name another reason. One I can believe."

"True enough," he said readily. "You aren't fragile. That's another reason, a very good one. Or do you think me the sort of man who would find a woman's frailty attractive?"

No. She knew he wasn't. The conviction reverberated through her, loosening all her ingrained objections. His waistcoat was flapping open—a missed opportunity, really, begging for redress. She brushed it off his shoulders, and he straightened his arms, so it dropped to the floor. "All right," she said, "together then," and after a moment in which they stared at each other, he nodded once and she drew a deep breath and he sank to his knees, where he undid the rest of the buttons on her bodice.

His mouth brushed the top of her breast, and then he lifted it out, closing his lips over her nipple. Here was a new meaning for *delicious*. The sensation, the small noise he made, the strokes of his tongue, sent heat flushing through her. A whimsical notion strayed through her mind, that perhaps the truly fine delicacies, the chocolates and truffles, enjoyed being devoured. His hands under her skirts stroked up her calves as he sucked her, first one breast and then the other. His hair felt soft and damp beneath her fingers, and she squeezed it as his mouth grew demanding, stroked it when his lips did the same.

The sodden weight of her skirts grew lighter. Her belly contracted beneath the movements of his hand: he was untying her drawers. The rain-soaked material fell to her ankles with a thump. He scooped up her chemise, and her thighs contracted beneath his lips. Fingers brushed up the backs of her knees, tracing slow circles, spirals that climbed as his kisses did. And then—and *then*—

She looked down. The shed might have fallen but she would not have made a sound. Her astonishment was so complete that physical sensation faded; nothing registered but the sight of his head between her thighs. She articulated to herself, in a coherent grammar of nouns and verbs, what he was doing. He was licking her. He was using his tongue to open and stroke her. Still she could not comprehend it. His hand was outstretched to hold her skirts away, to pin them against the wall; his forearm corded with the effort of maintaining this awkward angle. He gave her the view deliberately. He wanted her to look.

That realization re-embodied her. Back in her flesh, her awareness ran south like a broken yolk, to where his tongue flicked and teased. A whimper came out of her. This was awful. It was ecstasy. It was making her come out of her skin. There were no words for the feelings rising within her, except a sudden, overpowering need to have him back up against her, pressed to her as he had been, but harder, more deeply—

"Please." She pushed at his shoulders, urging him down to the bare floor, and then sinking onto her knees beside him. She was going to do this. He started to speak, and she clapped her palm to his lips. He licked it, and she pushed harder. "Please," she said again, and then she realized her mistake: if this was for the both of them, she had no need to ask.

Releasing his mouth, she put trembling hands to the hem of his shirt. He lifted his arms to help her slide it off, and this triggered a queer elation. She could do as she liked, and he would submit to her. She tossed the shirt away and stared at him. She had never looked at any person so boldly before. She studied him as closely and unabashedly as if he were an artifact, and he held still for the inspection, save of course for the rapid rise and fall of his chest. His belly was flat and sectioned with muscles; they contracted beneath her touch, foreign, enticing. Not a dockworker, as she had once thought, but a boxer. He used this body to fight. And he gave it to her now for a sweeter use, if not for a more peaceful one.

She leaned forward and pressed a kiss against his bare shoulder, so so large and solid beneath her mouth. He lay back, and she followed him down, the loosened locks of her hair dropping around her, framing the expanse of his lean torso. His nipple hardened beneath the brush of her thumb. She curled her toes so her slippers fell away, and then stroked her bare foot down the wet, hard length of his clothed calf. Even there he was muscled. She straightened her legs over his, wrapping her feet behind his ankles and curling her arms around his back, wanting to sink into him, like rain into earth.

He turned beneath her, laid her against the ground, and rose over her. Her hands ran down the length of his back, and around to the fly of his trousers. This was what she wanted now. She fumbled with the fastening, and his hands guided her, until her fingers molded to his length—hard, hot, unexpectedly smooth. The strength of her hunger shocked her. She trembled in it, suspended on a fine, agonizing edge that was not merely physical desire, but something else, something purely jubilant. It fed on the remnants of her fear; it turned the risk into an aphrodisiac. *This is the woman I will be.* There was nothing of dignity in this moment, in her wet skirts bunched at her waist, holding their bellies apart. From the small details to the largest facts, her actions now were utterly foreign to the expectations others had for her. She might have been a country maid, a scarlet woman—anyone but Lydia Boyce. Except that she *was* Lydia Boyce. And she would do this, gladly, with a willing and joyful heart.

She kissed him with new ferocity. His penis nudged against her, a blunt, unyielding pressure. The aggression of the act stole her breath; she felt herself grow more pliant as everything in her loosened to the force of him. She had wanted wings, and now she was drifting, held together only by the pulsing perimeters of her skin. Even the floor that dug into her shoulder blades seemed welcome to her, a hard, pleasurable contrast to her laxity, to the melting in her limbs; it mistranslated in her mind as yet another dimension of his touch.

Not pain so much as burning, then—slowly being opened to a sensation she could not have imagined. And then he made a sharp, forceful push, and pain did bolt through her. She whimpered and he froze. She was full in a way she had never been, abruptly conscious of spaces within her that had not been accessible to her awareness before. Some word, he whispered then—she could not make sense of it—but she nodded, and this was all he required. His hips drew away, then pressed back. He was moving inside her. Her fists knotted in his hair, on his shoulders, at the small of his back—to take him in, with her mouth, with her body; the idea made her aches dull, made hunger untwist inside of her. She lifted herself to him, and felt the beginnings of it again, everything coming unknotted, untangled. She urged him on; he remained with her, focused, his lips now on her shoulder, now on her jaw; a courtship above, a steady invasion below—she could make any noise, do anything she liked, he would never go—

He pulled back so his hand could slide between them, reaching down to touch her—only two quick, firm strokes. But it was enough. The muscles within her clenched and seized. With a groan, he slid his fingers back into her hair and thrust against her rapidly—once, twice, again—and then stilled. His head fell onto her shoulder. She lay there, hot, trembling, gasping from the weird wonder of it.

After a few moments, he rolled away, pulling her with him, so they lay side by side, with her face tucked into the crook of his shoulder. His pulse still drummed a rapid beat, and a fine tension ran through his arms, lending stiffness to the fingers that cupped her back and hip. She felt an urge to say something. But if there were words that suited such a moment, she did not know them.

As the physical sensations ebbed, the enormity of her actions seemed to grow. She remembered the couple in the library. Watching them, she had thought of Sanburne, and deplored herself for it. But now he was stroking her back, it seemed to her that his touch was not without emotion. And certainly, as she gently teased his hair, her touch was not without care.

God above, had she been arrogant to think she could do this without regret? She lay curled against him like a child, no desire to move, to so much as blink. She had not lain so closely with another person since she was nine or ten—yes, that summer when she'd been taken with a bad fever, and hallucinations, ghouls, had danced before her eyes. Crying with fear, she'd only calmed once Mama had come to her bed. How cool Mama's throat had been. Only with her face pressed against it had Lydia felt safe enough to sleep. Safe: that was how she felt now, his warmth all around her, his arms tightening at her every inadvertent twitch. But this was not safety. He offered her nothing of the sort. And she had not done this in order to *have* anything from him. Had she?

Uneasy with herself, she began to sit up. "Wait," he murmured, his hand pressing into the small of her back. "A minute longer. Whatever's going through your mind—whatever you're telling yourself—just ignore it for now."

"This was reckless."

"Extremely. The best decisions generally are."

Her eyes fastened on the window. Rain no longer tapped at the pane, and the clouds looked to be clearing. "It's very unlikely this will result in a child, though. I know biology, and my . . . courses."

"Is that what concerns you?" He paused, and his next words emerged in an awkward rhythm, as if he no longer knew properly how to speak to her. "I told you I was no libertine. I would not abandon you."

From a man so immune to natural sentiment, the reassurance seemed out of character. But she kept forgetting that there was another side to him. To balance his horrid attitude toward Moreland, there was his love for Lady Boland. The two aspects meshed poorly in her mind. She felt oddly off balance, although she had not moved an inch. How could he not understand her unflinching devotion to Papa? It was so similar to his own feelings for his sister. Why, to have that sort of devotion from one's lover . . . the idea made her breath come short again.

The next second, she was angry with herself. He said he gave his loyalty to those who earned it. Was she seriously entertaining the hope that she'd earned it by lying on her back? How incredibly lowering.

She rolled away from him. Her fingers felt stiff and bloated, clumsy on the buttons of her bodice. When he sat up and reached to help, she twisted away. "I can do it."

"Let me," he said.

"No."

He knocked her hands away, and she smacked his in return. He caught her wrists and caged them at her side, as if she were nothing, as if she were the weakling he'd claimed she wasn't. She sat back on her knees and gave a hard jerk, but his grip did not break. It aggravated her. With a grunt, she tried again—managing to pull him off the ground onto his knees, but not to yank free. She gave it another go, and then another—her irritation turning quickly to anger. But his grip did not waver as she thrashed. His fingers remained hot and firm around her bones, his eyes fixed on her face. The steady quality of his regard began to bother her. He looked so calm and composed, whereas this fury—whence its source? It made her eyes sting. It felt all out of proportion to the moment; it felt as though he had betrayed her, when of course he had not.

On a long, jerky breath she subsided. Sanburne's

hands smoothed down from her wrists to her fingertips, then moved to the buttons of her bodice. Very quietly, his eyes on the task at hand, he said, "Listen. Are you listening?"

"Yes," she muttered at length.

"I want you to trust me, Lydia."

What quick work he made of the buttons. He had done this a thousand times, clearly. "Why?" She tried for a laugh, but it sounded unconvincing. "You want to give me counsel?"

"I'm not so generous as that," he said. "No, I want your trust because I want your honesty. You must have gathered by now that I value that. Plainspeaking is rare, and I believe . . . I believe I could come to depend on it, given time."

It was a strange answer. And it brought something strange out of her in return. Her wariness collapsed. It twisted into a weird wistfulness that clogged her voice as she spoke again. "Then be honest with *me*."

Finished with the buttons, he helped her up, then withdrew a pace, linking his hands behind his back in a movement that struck her as oddly formal. "What do you wish to know?"

Her first impulse was born out of an old reflex: almost, she asked, *What do you really want of me?* But even as the question came to her, its purchase faltered. She could no longer doubt that he saw something in her that attracted him. He thought her . . . lovely. And she believed him. Otherwise she'd never have come with him into the boathouse. Her conviction in his sincerity had been the aphrodisiac that prompted this episode.

But she also remembered their exchange in the

hallway outside Mrs. Ogilvie's flat. He had not wanted
plainspeaking, then. "Why should my honesty appeal
to you? What do you really want to hear me say?"

"Anything you like."

The answer left her dissatisfied. It struck her as
evasive, and too easy. She'd asked the wrong question.
"What are you afraid to hear me say?"

He gave her a wry little smile. "I think you've already
said it, Lydia. You have a talent for that."

"So I am like your boxing club, then. Another way
for you to hurt yourself." She laughed unhappily. "And
another way to humiliate your father, no doubt?"

"God, no." He came toward her, but she retreated
a quick pace—she did not trust herself when he was
touching her—and he stopped immediately. "All right,"
he said, and raked a hand through his hair. "*No.* This
isn't about my father at all. You see very clearly, Lydia.
And sometimes I can't. I—you endure these things
with grace. I don't." He exhaled. "And it is so easy *not*
to endure. To simply let yourself get . . . lost in it, in all
these feudal trappings. And to start to believe in them.
Give me another year like this, I'll become another one
of these mindless cuckoo birds, bowing and primping
for lack of anything better to do." He laughed, and it
was not a happy sound. "I'll become my goddamned
father, won't I? And if I don't? If I broke out? Why, then
I might find myself as—as *useless* as you call me."

He was not a man meant to stammer. It hurt her ears
to hear it. "No," she said, and moved forward to press
her lips to his. When she withdrew, his expression had
changed. He looked . . . arrested. "I can't help you with
that," she said softly. "Your fate is your own making,

James. You have no idea how lucky you are, in that regard."

His voice dropped to match hers. "Fine. Forget that. You want freedom, don't you? I understand that, too. I know better than most how the rules of good society can imprison a woman. Perhaps I can help you."

*I am not your sister,* she almost said. But instinct stopped her. He danced around these issues for a reason. And God save her, but she knew, all at once, that she did not wish to drive him away. "It's not your job to rescue me."

"Certainly not. But life isn't fair. If you require an opportunity, I could give you that."

She no longer knew exactly what they were talking about. Nor did he, she suspected. They stared at each other in the gathering silence. One of them was going to have to break it, and ask the questions that needed asking. But she had learned her lesson. It would not be she who spoke first.

A knock sounded at the door. With a gasp, she dove behind the skiff.

Now came the squeak of hinges, and a feminine voice: "They have decided to go boating in the moonlight," said Mrs. Chudderley. "If Miss Boyce is here, I suggest she walk with me to the house."

The wet lawn sparkled with trapped rain. Lydia's skirts gathered mud and weight, forcing her to kick up her skirts before each squelching step. Mrs. Chudderley, apparently too lithe to be affected by such mundane things as dirt and gravity, floated ahead, her pretty head lifted high, her skin smooth as porcelain in the cold light. Occasionally she directed a thoughtful glance over her shoulder, and made a little humming noise beneath her breath—a sound of amused curiosity, perhaps. It made Lydia's face burn.

At the portico, where they paused to shake out their skirts, Mrs. Chudderley said, "You will call me Elizabeth. And I will call you Lydia, which is a lovely name, by the way."

As the silence drew on, the woman's brows lifted expectantly. Lydia had no choice but to clear her throat and say, "Thank you."

"You're welcome. Now we're on informal terms, Lydia, I will ask you: what are your intentions toward James?"

Her skirts fell out of her nerveless fingers. "I—is that not a question more often addressed to the gentleman?"

Elizabeth laughed. "And here I'd fancied you a New Woman. Darling, James is like a brother to me. I would have to be blind to miss his interest in you. And don't mistake me; I'm not opposed to it. Since that whole sad business with Stella, he hasn't taken an interest in much of anything. Well"—she shrugged—"except his factories, of course. But that's to do with her, anyway."

The offhanded tone did not fool Lydia. Something in the lady's manner—the quirk of her head, or that quick, sideways glance—betrayed her. She wanted to be asked to elaborate, and Lydia saw no reason to resist. "What do you mean?"

"Hasn't he told you?" Elizabeth glanced off across the lawn. A party of guests was winding down toward the lake, encircled by a handful of servants whose torches cast writhing shadows along the grass. "Perhaps I am wrong, then. You know about his sister, of course."

"A little," Lydia said uneasily. "Who doesn't?"

"Well, his factories are meant for women like her. Women of lower birth, of course—who are trapped in a bad situation with no means to get out. He gives them employment, and for a small fee, their children can go to a crèche on the site or attend the school they run there. It keeps him entertained, at any rate." She smiled. "You look flabbergasted, darling. Did you think him a total waste?"

She searched herself for the answer. *I could come to rely on your honesty.* "No," she said slowly. "Despite his best efforts."

"Indeed," said Elizabeth.

They stepped into the front hall. It felt like eons since she had run out into the rain. She had left this house on a wild impulse, and with every step she took, the ache between her thighs reminded her that she returned a different woman. Her emotions were veering wildly, between glumness and numbness and something that felt curiously like excitement. Was this what they called hysteria? As if to prove it, she blurted out, "What do you think you are wrong about?"

Elizabeth had mounted the stairs. She turned back, one lily-white hand draped over the balustrade. "Why, that he is in love with you. I hope you won't get ideas—it's quite possible that I'm wrong. Certainly you're not at all the sort I would expect to pull him from this melancholy. But if it's only a dalliance, I shan't oppose it, either. Anything to bestir him from this *endlessly* bleak mood. It's grown so tedious." With a little shrug, she turned and continued on her way.

Lydia stood in astonished silence. Only an acknowledged beauty could make such a leisurely exit: the straight, slim line of Elizabeth's back, and her failure to so much as glance again over her shoulder, announced her utter unconcern at the turmoil her comments had occasioned.

A maid scuttled through the hall, a bottle of port clutched in her hand. Her curious look prompted Lydia to take a deep breath and start up the stairs herself.

As she reached the first landing, the sight of her face in the long mirror startled her: pale and red-eyed, as if she were about to cry. As if her body knew something her brain had yet to recognize. She stared at herself for a long moment.

*Lydia Boyce, fallen woman.*

*Lydia Durham, Viscountess Sanburne.*

Her cheeks warmed. Oh, lovely. She, who had never believed herself a typical sort, now blushed at the fantasy of marrying a recreant. And wouldn't that be a great joke, anyway. The ton's resident darling, forced to pluck his plain brown bride from the shelf. For all his apparent disregard of others' opinions, she could not imagine he would handle mockery so well. He liked being adored. He'd all but bragged about it. And as for Mrs. Chudderley's bizarre speculation—it deserved no thought. Sanburne had not spoken of love, much less matrimony. He had simply promised not to *abandon* her. Even a high-priced whore might have expected a better offer: carte blanche, a lodging of her own.

A breath shuddered from her. She turned away from

her spiteful reflection, heading down the hallway to Sophie's door. When her light rapping won no response, she tried the handle. Sophie's maid was sleeping on a cot in the corner. The bed itself was empty, the sheets pressed crisp and smooth.

So Sophie had gone boating with the others. That was all.

But as she turned away for her own room, a sick feeling touched her stomach. Perhaps there was something to Sanburne's philosophy of love. Sophie had barely traded fifty private words with George before accepting his suit. All the things which had led her to declare her love for him—his fine manners, his face, the luxuries he could provide—had nothing to do with how he'd treated her. And now she complained of him constantly, and ungracefully labored beneath the weight of all her fulfilled expectations. She should have made him prove himself, Lydia thought.

For that matter, Sophie should have proved herself to him.

In her room, she found Ana already asleep. A telegram was propped by the lamp. Papa had wired from Gibraltar with a theory: he had run into an acquaintance on board the ship, a mutual friend of his and Hartnett's. To his grave dismay, this man suggested that Hartnett had struck up a friendship with Overton shortly before his death. Papa did not like to think that an old friend might have conspired with his bitter competitor to undermine his reputation, but the possibility could not be discounted.

She lowered the telegram. It made sense. Carnelly had mentioned that Overton's stuff had also gone awry.

It was shocking, but not inconceivable, that Overton had arranged the mix-up of deliveries in order to replace Hartnett's real antiques with frauds. A nasty scheme, but a sound way to discredit a competitor.

She knew what she should feel: relief at a credible explanation, and a fine rage at Overton. But her emotions felt oddly blunted. *I would not abandon you.* What had he meant by that? She wished she could believe him, but Moreland would no doubt tell a different story. There lay James's real error—and Sophie's as well. Once love was declared and loyalty given, one could not go back on one's word, not if one expected to be believed ever again.

With a sigh, she folded the telegram and tucked it into her valise. Time to visit Carnelly again, she supposed.

# Thirteen

The express to London bore only a few passengers at this hour of the morning. A university student with a cowlick, mooning over a letter whose margins were covered in hearts. A mother with a boisterous little girl, who gave James a toothy grin as he passed. A grizzled don scowling at the latest translation of Herodotus. And finally, the woman on the green mohair bench across from him. She'd not spoken a word since he sat down. Buttoned to the throat, one hand braced against the wall to resist the rocking of the carriage, Lydia Boyce looked the last thing from friendly.

In other times, other moods, he might have teased her for it. But amicability was eluding him. He'd not slept more than an hour. Shortly after dawn, he'd finally abandoned bed for a stroll. He'd found her in the front hall, directing a footman to ready the coach. This woman whom he'd lain down with last night, whose thighs had trembled beneath his kisses, intended to leave without a fare-thee-well. It enraged him. "Running away unchaperoned," he'd said sarcastically. "Not only cowardly, but also, dare I say it, a bit *unwise.*"

She'd looked at him a long moment, during which her brow tightened slightly, as if she were trying to bring him into clearer focus. Concern had touched him. "Did you misplace your spectacles?" The question had sounded mocking, but only in order to disguise a worry so large as to seem ludicrous. She could hardly take the train alone if she couldn't see properly. "Don't do this," he'd continued. "Stay and talk to me." And to his astonishment, a blush had warmed his face. At that, his mouth clamped shut more tightly than an oyster. Idiotic schoolboy babble.

"I'm sorry," she'd said pensively. "I must return to town. A pressing matter, I'm afraid. We'll speak some other time, when I'm thinking more clearly."

So she got to flounce off and postpone the discussion until it suited her? "We'll talk now. I agree, you aren't thinking clearly. You're in no state to travel unescorted."

Out of nowhere, she'd smiled. "Do you think me some hothouse flower? After all of this? I manage my father's business, Sanburne. I daresay I can take a train on my own as well." And then, with a cool nod, she had turned on her heel and walked out.

For a good minute he'd stood there gawping after her. She had warned him, once: *I possess a talent for a memorable exit*. But he hadn't listened. His opinion of her was much like a sand castle: it stood in constant need of repair. Oh, vanity. Whatever her motives for sleeping with him, he'd certainly assumed himself to rank among them. But in the sound of the closing door, he heard a truth he hadn't bothered to consider through the long hours of the night. Aside from an hour's fun, and an occasional escort to unsavory parts of town, she didn't want a thing from him.

Disbelief sent him after her. He was handsome,

wealthy, well-liked. Heir to a title and a superfluous fortune. As a result, women came to him with concrete ambitions. Why, the last time he'd lain down with someone who wanted nothing more than his company, he'd been sixteen, and she thirty, the bored widow of a family friend. A delightful interlude, yes; but he was not sure, suddenly, that its advantages still appealed to him.

He'd followed her to the train station and booked a ticket back to town.

He looked at her now, sitting so rigidly across from him. The rain was a dim, distant hiss beneath the louder thump of the wheels passing over ties in the track. It made him feel contemplative. What was she afraid of? She liked him so much more than she was willing to admit. She had liked him enough to sleep with him. He suspected that she liked him enough to dream about him. But she was far better at being honest with him than she was at being honest with herself.

At least she seemed as cross as he did. From beneath the high gable point of her bonnet, she directed a furrowed brow toward the wet fields streaming by the window. Even the little bird trimming her hat seemed caught in some complex dilemma; it quivered as though on the verge of revelations.

Maybe he knew what ailed her. His remarks last night had surprised her; they had confounded her worst expectations of him. If he was not a villainous seducer, but a man with a genuine interest in her person, then her little attempt to play the scarlet woman had failed. In short, she had fucked him for nothing.

God, it was ridiculous to feel this sense of—hurt? Like a kicked puppy, wanting a quiet place to brood and lick his own wounds. The pleasures of sex did not guarantee deeper emotion. He should know that better than she. How many women had he bedded, in his time? And she'd been a virgin.

But it seemed as if everything had gotten muddled in his head. He could place the exact moment it had happened: he'd been trying to speak of Stella, of this damned prison he lived in, of the time he dreaded was coming very soon, when he would wake up and find himself another mindless cog in the social routine, as hopeless as the rest of them. And she had kissed him, so sweetly. As if the words were already known to her, and she wanted to prevent him the hurt of speaking them. That kiss had held understanding and compassion. Or so he'd thought.

In fact, she'd been trying to silence him. She had not wanted confessions. Intimacy was not her aim. A short laugh escaped him. *I am a bloody idiot.* He wished he could work out how she managed to unsettle him. Perhaps if he did, he could also cure this ridiculous need to lay his hands on her. He suspected it was a case of sublimated violence: unable to imagine abusing a woman, he mistook the urge to shake her for the urge to screw her.

The thought of provoking her cheered him a little. He sprawled in his seat, so his knees touched her skirts. She gave them a pointed glance, but made no comment. She was becoming increasingly difficult to ruffle. Good God, he'd had her virginity. The least she could do was blush. Perhaps there was a hole in her brain, and everything to do with men slipped right out of it, leaving her clearheaded for the more important things, like dusty rocks and distant lands. He had to give her credit:

she'd reoccupied her body for a brief time, but she had a million strategies to guarantee that her mind remained elsewhere.

He cleared his throat. "I'm convinced that the notes I've been receiving are related to Hartnett's shipment." His generous pause yielded no response. "It was a sudden insight, of course. But assassination attempts do get you thinking."

This comment antagonized the dimple into an appearance. "Speak plainly, sir."

"*Sir?* I say, Lyd. Are you always so formal with men you've made love with?"

The whip of her head caused the bird to saw wildly, like a famished woodpecker in range of a tree. "Am I meant to be embarrassed by that remark?"

"Not at all. If you weren't moved by the act, I can't see why a reference to it would faze you."

Again came the knitted brow and that strange, peering look, as if she were trying to catch of glimpse of his brain. "If you want to know something," he said slowly, "you only need to ask."

Her chest rose on a deep breath. "Very well. What assassination attempt?"

"Coward."

Her blush deepened. "Go on."

"Very well." He shrugged. "A boy approached me at the Empire. Rambled on about tears. You remember those notes I've been getting. This time, he mentioned something new. *Egypt.* Isn't that fascinating?"

Alarm flashed over her face. And then, just as quickly, her face settled into a mutinous cast. "Egypt is a very large country—and one of our major trading partners to boot. I expect a lot of people mention it on regular occasions."

"True, but something else occurred to me. These notes began arriving shortly after the newspapers covered our tête-à-tête at the Institute."

She held silent a moment. "It is troubling," she finally admitted. "But why would someone want them enough to threaten you? The forgeries are worthless."

"Perhaps there's something about them that isn't so worthless. These tears he keeps mentioning." He paused. Phin had come up with a very provocative theory, which reverberated all too neatly with Miss Marshall's claim. "Have you ever heard of the Tears of Idihet? Fabulous set of diamonds, went missing a few years back?"

She visibly stiffened. "Yes. They were part of the Egyptian royal treasury. What are you implying? Don't be daft, Sanburne."

"Hear me out. The khedive accused British spies of the theft—said we were trying to undermine his authority. My father was quite cheerful about it," he added dryly. "He's always been a loud advocate of greater involvement in Egyptian affairs. At any rate, we claimed we'd nothing to do with their disappearance, and perhaps we hadn't." Phin had been unable to say; it seemed his concerns centered on Oriental matters. "The jewels never resurfaced, though, and the khedive was right; their loss made him look weak. His army general mounted a mutiny, which gave us all the excuse we needed to bombard Alexandria, and assume unofficial control of the country."

She had gone very pale. "I don't need a history lesson. Had it happened two days earlier, my father would have been in Alexandria for it. What's your point?"

"Perhaps these are the jewels Miss Marshall was told about."

He expected a snide remark. But she appeared, however briefly, to consider the possibility. "Then where are they?" she asked. "You saw me smash that stela. And I've examined the others a dozen times now. They're solid stone."

"And that in itself has always puzzled me, Lyd. Why would anyone pay to ship worthless pieces of stone?"

She turned toward the window. "I do not like your tone," she said, but again, the expected vigor was curiously absent. "I have told you the switch must have been made after the items were crated."

"And that's even more curious," he said carefully. "Why bother to put faked antiquities into the shipment? Lydia, have you gotten any more answers from your father?"

"In fact, I have. He put forward a new theory concerning one of his rivals—"

"Rivals?" He laughed. "I had no idea academe was so dramatic."

Now she looked back to him. "It is a business rival," she said soberly. "A man named Mr. Overton, who could not tell you the difference between archaeology and ditch digging. He has been bitter ever since certain of his clients defected to my father. At any rate, I'm going to town to investigate."

Christ. "Did you not hear what I said before? A man with a *knife* assaulted me. You do not need to be investigating this. If your father's on his way, let *him* handle it. It's *his* business, isn't it?"

"His business, which *I* manage."

"Bully for you."

"What does that mean?" Her eyes narrowed. "What should I rather be doing, Sanburne? Needlepoint and piano?"

He held his tongue. But oh, he saw the way of it now. She handled Boyce's affairs for him. Cleaned up his messes. An amanuensis-cum-manager, at the cheapest rate going. Wasn't Papa the clever one.

She was still eyeing him. "Come to think of it, you were in Egypt this winter, weren't you? Perhaps someone thinks *you* brought back a surprise."

No quicker way to put her on the offensive than to criticize Papa. The ludicrous idea came to him that he was in competition with a sixty-year-old. "It's possible. Alas, all I brought back were fleas." He shrugged again. "Well, it was a wild theory. But right or wrong, we agree on one thing: the forgeries are worthless to us. Since they're worth killing for to the lad, I say we hand them over. Spare my postbox the abuse—not to mention my throat."

"Indeed no," she said coolly. "If this madman wants them so badly, then he must be the key to it. Once we catch him, we can find out whose pay he's in—Overton's, or someone else's."

"Good God," he said softly. Starchy, he'd once thought her. But it was not coldness that animated her. It was grim, delusional resolve. "Lydia. You would knowingly endanger yourself for this?"

She looked at him as if he were the greatest idiot alive. "Sanburne, what don't you understand? If this is a deliberate conspiracy to stain my father's good name, I have no choice."

"The man had a knife," he said. "What part of that don't *you* understand?"

Her lips thinned into a grim line. She looked away.

*What fun,* he thought blackly. What had started as an innocent little caper to embarrass his father had brought him to this—an inadvertent role in the most hackneyed melodrama imaginable: the redemption of her father's honor.

Stupid to feel a shiver. But it was eerie, downright uncanny really, how much she put him in mind of Stella. His sister had been so stubbornly determined, so blockheadedly focused on her own aim, that giant explosions would not have knocked her off her course. Boland had upbraided her in public for looking at another man, and she'd apologized for it. He'd pushed her off the dance floor when she laughed at his misstep, and she'd excused him by blaming a cut-rate orchestra for his crankiness. He carried on an open affair with the Duchess of Farley, and when Stella confronted him, he slapped her for her temerity. She predicted that the walk down the aisle would reform him. Wrong. Slaps were useful warnings. Slaps and knives: only martyrs and future victims ignored them. "You are in for a hard road," he said grimly.

She did not pretend to misunderstand him. "Stop slurring my father, please. I forgave you for it once—or no, twice now, counting your antics at Lord Moreland's dinner. But I cannot allow it again. Not in good conscience."

"Do not fool yourself," he said. "If you proceed with this, you're not playing the dutiful daughter. You're gambling with your life."

She laughed. "And would I be so different from you, in that regard? How many gallons of gin do you drink each day to spite Moreland? Can that be any healthier?"

Perhaps she had gone too far. His eyes narrowed and his mouth tightened; she did not like or recognize the look on his face. Seeking a new view, she glanced down the aisle. The other passengers were seated some distance away; no one seemed to have remarked their sparring. Of course they hadn't. They must assume that he was her husband. For these moments, at least, she had false license to sit alone with him. To touch him very discreetly, even.

Her heart tripped, as it had on and off since he'd popped up at Bishops Stortford Station. She could not believe that he'd followed her, that he was shameless enough to sit across from her, and flirt and taunt her as though last night had never occurred. She wished she might match his panache, but it was hard going to maintain her composure. Meeting his eyes was enough to raise a blush. His smile made her pulse dance like a drunkard.

*What did you do to me?* Her body seemed a catalogue of foreign sensations, opaque to interpretation, resistant to attempts at governance. As he removed his hat, her lips remembered the softness of his hair. He crossed his legs, and her fingertips twitched at the recollection of his thighs, the muscled density and textures. His hand—*oh, stop it! Do not think of where it has been!*—delved into his jacket now, and extracted a flask.

She scoffed. "Lord Moreland is not here to see you, you know. You might at least wait until we're at St. Pancras." His reply was to unscrew the cap and lift it to his mouth. The depth of her concern rattled her. "You drink too much, Sanburne." As his throat rippled—once; twice; three times—she lost her temper. "Stop it! Good Lord—it's barely eight in the morning. You will become insensible!"

"One can only hope." He dragged a hand across his mouth. Outside, the sun emerged from behind a cloud, and the light coming through the window warmed his face, illuminating the fine-grained contours of his skin. Stubble showed on his jaw; he had not shaved this morning. The liquor left his lips wet. She found herself staring at them. His lips did amazing and dreadful things. His tongue—

She looked away. But a glitter at the corner of her eye drew her attention back. He had raised the flask again. "You are a lush," she snapped.

He lowered the flask and looked at her. "Of course. A remarkably devoted lush. Also a useless butterfly. Had you not heard? You should ask my sister; she'll tell you all about it."

She felt like slamming her fist into the seat. "You want my honesty? Very well: I cannot trust a man who does not respect himself. What chance he would respect *me*?"

Sanburne laughed. "Oh, excellent. That's the best temperance speech I've ever heard."

The floor beneath her feet shuddered as the train began to brake. They were pulling into the concourse. A cloud of steam billowed up past the window, blotting out the view. "End of line," called the porter.

"May I offer you a ride home?" asked Sanburne.

"I think not. No doubt you'd drive us into the Thames." She grabbed her umbrella, shot to her feet, and strode down the carriage. This was ridiculous. She did not understand her anger. He was right about himself. He could not disappoint her; it was her own description that he had used to explain himself. He was only behaving to type.

She stepped down from train into chaos. At this hour, every track in the Brighton concourse was occupied with bright yellow passenger carriages. A tide of bankers in sober black suits moved in lockstep toward the terminal, each with his chin tucked into his muffler, a morning paper crammed beneath his arm. She fell in behind one such man, trusting him to forge a quick path through the various vendors (hot cross buns; potatoes; tea, piping hot), newspaper boys, and mothers who balanced crying children and picnic baskets.

Near the end of the train, a gentleman lounging in the doorway to a second-class compartment tipped his bowler hat to her. The rogue, making advances at a stranger! She threw a look over her shoulder as she passed, and spied Sanburne a few paces behind her. The man with the bowler hat leaped down to walk behind him, and as her eyes brushed his once again, she recognized his face. Where had she seen him before? She had been thinking of Sanburne at the time—

The library. He was one of the lovebirds who had been sitting near her, that day she'd received Polly Marshall's note. Perhaps he'd recognized her. It was still very wrong of him to acknowledge her, of course.

As she passed under the great clock, she reached into

her reticule to hunt for cab fare. She would go straight-away to Carnelly's; it was her responsibility to do so, and she did not trust herself to put it off, not when she'd felt a moment of temptation at Sanburne's suggestion that the matter be left to Papa. *Assassination attempt,* she thought tartly. If it really had seemed so serious, he would have mentioned it last night. No doubt he'd been drunk as a fox, and stumbled into someone who'd taken offense. At worst, these notes came from Overton's man. What better way to ruin Papa than to have a prominent figure accuse him of dispatching thugs?

A hand brushed her arm. She glanced back, a sharp word on her lips. But all that met her eyes were dozens of retreating backs—and the man in the bowler hat. He was directly behind her, now. A tremor shot down the backs of her knees. Silly. Still, she adopted a brisker pace. Where had Sanburne gone, then? The sudden, high-pitched shriek of a train had her flinching. She forced out a small laugh. This panic was irrational. But she looked back anyway. The bowler hat was gaining ground. In another few steps he'd be able to touch her. But he was not following her; he was only heading toward the southern exit.

Her body did not accept this logic. Her heart hammered a warning. She peered around and ahead, searching the crowd for the viscount's bright head.

A stranger stepped into her path. "Miss Boyce," he said. He was tall and thin, with a bony nose and deep-set eyes that fastened upon her confidently. "We must talk." His eyes flicked beyond her and she knew, knew instinctively, that he was looking to the man in the bowler hat. They were together.

His hand reached into his jacket. It would not produce anything good for her. She looked into his face. In nightmares, too, events sometimes transpired thus—very slowly, so that her thoughts outstripped her actions. "Leave me alone," she said, and on a great heave, tossed her umbrella at his face and broke into a run.

A hand closed over her elbow. Her voice came blasting out of her, loud as any suffragist's. *"James!"* But her voice could not cut through the din. Yanked around, now. The bowler hat had pockmarked cheeks and a tiny mouth. His hand came up, only it was not his fist that he slapped against her mouth. The cloth held a cloying, sickly sweet perfume. It spread up her nose and cast tendrils into her lungs.

Her nails clawed into his knuckles. *Don't breathe; don't.* A cough seized her; she tasted fumes. She tried to back away but collided with a body that pinned her in place. She was choking. The sounds around her began to slow. She thrust back an elbow but her muscles were loosening, unraveling into strings. Falling now. The ground met her. For a moment it hurt; and then all at once it felt like sponge beneath her cheek. Feet passed by in a long blur. She shut her eyes. There was fear here but she felt too tired to manage it.

Now the world shook around her. It dissolved into violent streaks of color that lengthened like melting rubber as she was lifted. Her limbs dangled, annoying, heavy and numb, nothing to do with her torso. Sanburne's face rippled, a reflection in wind-tossed water. He was speaking, but she could make no sense of it. His voice jumped and narrowed like a poor phonograph recording.

She was in his arms: the realization made its way
through her brain. He was carrying her. She put her
cheek to his shoulder and let the darkness bloom like a
night-dark rose. One could not read much into flowers,
anyway . . .

Lydia felt as light as a child in his arms. He had no
patience with the bobbies' questions; he wanted to get
her home. For once, being a paper lord suited him: he
dropped his title and borrowed his father's sneer, and
within ten minutes, the police were bowing and scraping. They agreed to interview him later, at his house.

In the hack, she barely stirred. Occasionally she
would whimper something. Once, he caught his name.
*James,* she whispered. He did not think he was imagin-
ing it.

He stroked her cheek until he was assured that it
was not growing colder. And then, on a long, steadying
breath, he looked out the window. The day had dawned
wet but now the sun had broken through the clouds.
Its light reflected off the slanting rain, which streamed
like a shower of diamonds onto black branches studded
with pink blossoms. Finally, spring had remembered
London.

He'd said that liquor did not affect him but he lied.
He'd not been steady on his feet as he walked down the
platform. Or was it the early hour, and the exhaustion he
felt, deep in his bones? Either way, he could not excuse
himself. The disgust burning in his chest made his breath
come short. If he'd had one more swallow, it was possible
he would not have been able to subdue those men.

She stirred in his arms. His fingers tightened in her hair. *This cannot happen again.* A better man would drop her at Wilton Crescent, knowing the scandal he courted by taking her elsewhere. He was not a good man. But by God, he was also not going to be the sort of useless goddamned swine that sat by and watched another woman stumble merrily toward her doom on some blind and misplaced faith.

And he was not going to be sitting there drunk again when he received news of her fate.

Her eyes fluttered open. She stared at him, her pupils abnormally small. He wondered what she saw. He did not know if he would recognize his own face, in this moment. He felt strange to himself. "I'm here," he murmured. "You're all right."

It was a simple enough equation. He thought he could make it work.

Her lashes fluttered shut again, and she sighed.

# Fourteen

She woke slowly, to a sound that at first seemed like distant thunder, and then, as awareness sharpened her senses, like a piano. Someone was attacking the lowest keys. It made her head hurt. On a deep breath, she discovered that her stomach was sore. Her eyes opened to a view of an old-fashioned bed canopy that did not look familiar. She pushed herself upright.

The room was spacious and well-appointed. Curtains striped in cherry and white stood open to the late afternoon sun. Paintings of country scenes covered the walls. She had no idea where she was. She pressed a hand to her chest, feeling the frantic trip of her heart. Her wool bodice felt faintly damp. She lowered her head and sniffed lilac water and the faintest trace of vomit. Had she gotten sick on herself? Was that why her stomach—

*Stop. Don't think about it.*

She slipped to her feet. Her bonnet rested on a nearby chair; her boots sat waiting on the carpet. As she laced them up, she surveyed the room. Surely ruffians would not provide their prisoners with silk wallpaper and French linen sheets. But something about the room made her uneasy all the same. The enameled French toilet table was very fine, and utterly bare. The walnut writing desk sat empty of paper and pen. The mantel held candles that had never been lit, and in the fireplace, no ash had ever touched the gleaming blue tiles. A more generic and sterile room, she could not imagine. It might have been anywhere in Mayfair. She very much doubted it was Sanburne's.

With her tongue lying like a slab of dust in her mouth, thirst proved stronger than fear. A silver pitcher stood atop the toilet table. The cold water tasted more delicious than ambrosia, and she drank it all, sip by eager sip, as the distant piano thundered onward. Once satisfied, she set down the pitcher to consider the door. It stood ajar. A ruffian would have locked her in. She retrieved her bonnet and followed the music out through an anteroom, into a dark hallway that smelled disconcertingly like Alexandria. Incense, she belatedly realized: in the Arab quarter, they had burned it continually.

She found the piano after a short walk down the hall, in a high-ceilinged salon whose curtains stood open to the light. This furious music was being produced by a child— a young girl in a white lace dress, with a blue sash tied at her waist and a matching ribbon in her long blond braid. Lydia's step across the threshold was met by a discordant crash: the pianist planted her elbow on the lowest keys for leverage and spun herself around on the stool. "Finally awake!" she cried. "Was it the music that did it?"

It took Lydia a moment to recover her manners. "No indeed," she said. "I——" And then the girl bounced off the stool, and she was surprised once more into silence. Why, the girl was startlingly beautiful—and her dress was not from the schoolroom, after all. It was one of those new Aesthetic gowns, the loose folds of which revealed a figure more womanly than childish. How old was she, then? Her face was heart-shaped, her hair that impossible platinum that tended to darken with age, her eyes as huge and blue as a newborn's. Sixteen, perhaps? "Forgive me," she said. "Is . . . is your father about?"

The girl laughed. "Wouldn't that be nice?" As she stepped forward, the irony in that laugh still rode her face, causing Lydia, quite abruptly, to revise her estimate upward. The woman was twenty at the least.

She cleared her throat. "My apologies. My head is still muddied, I fear."

"I don't doubt it." The woman had a peculiar accent—one moment flat and American, and the next, purely English. "Chloroform can knock you out for hours. Or was it ether? We couldn't decide."

"Ah . . . I have no idea."

"Well, were the dreams delicious? Or terrifying?"

"Terrifying."

The woman made a face. "Chloroform, then. Poor you. Had to breathe that stuff once in Hong Kong." She shuddered. "Made me dream of Phin, in fact."

Waking up from an attempted kidnapping, one could want for more balanced company than this woman. "Do you know where I might find the Viscount Sanburne?"

"Depends. Phin's had two visitors today. Is he tall and pretty, or short and fearsome?"

"Tall," Lydia managed.

"The library." The woman brushed past her, trailing a curious, foreign-smelling perfume. As they turned down the corridor toward the stairs, she added, "I would advise you not to ask him for help. It gets sticky very quickly."

"I beg your pardon?"

She flicked a measuring look over Lydia's figure. Her eyes paused on the bonnet, which seemed to amuse her. "Or perhaps you wouldn't mind it," she said obscurely. "What a *lovely* stuffed bird. Phin will adore it."

The lady seemed to think she had a connection to this Phin. Lydia cast her thoughts about, until she recollected a tidbit she'd heard about Sanburne's circle. "Do you mean the Earl of Ashmore?"

The woman's voice veered again toward American. "Yes, whatever he told you to call him. Monroe serves, too."

Her brain felt too muzzy for such nonsensical talk. She took a good grip on the railing as they descended the staircase. "Is this the earl's residence, then?"

"Residence, prison, boarding house, you name it. Also, occasionally"—the woman's voice dropped, and her spectacular eyes widened—*"pleasure palace."* At normal volume, she continued, "I take it you're not friends, then."

"No, we are not acquainted."

She paused on the bottom step. "How lucky for you. Here, maybe some of it will rub off on me." Out came her hand for a brisk, thoroughly American shake. "I'm Mina Masters. You may have heard of my hair tonics. No? Ah, well. Only five shillings for spectacular shine. Phin's in there." She nodded toward a door off the hall. "Do tell him you met me: it will give him fits." With a wink, she lifted her skirts and turned back for the upper floor.

Lydia had not expected this desertion. Glad for it, she paused to smooth her skirts. Given the circumstances, she thought her composure impressive—until the moment she entered the library and spotted Sanburne.

The relief that washed through her then brought with it a slew of detritus—fear, panic, a still-echoing sense of shock. She pitched herself at him. She had no care what the other man might think of her; all that mattered was how deeply she could push her face into his chest. His arms closed around her and his hand cupped her skull, stroking her hair. "James," she whispered, choking back tears that came from nowhere.

"Shh." His voice was so blessedly familiar and calm. "It's all right, Lyd. You're perfectly safe."

With her nose crushed against him, she drew a great breath. She was hardly a five-year-old who required shushing, but as he rubbed her head, her heart began to slow. He was not a steady man; that much she had decided. But he seemed steady as he embraced her. His arms banded about her so tightly that she felt nothing could break his hold. It calmed something in her that had been trembling since—since she knew not when.

When she felt composed enough to pull away, she saw a nasty new bruise purpling his cheek. She touched it in concern. He caught her hand, gave a small shake of his head, and smiled. She smiled back. She felt almost giddy, of a sudden. "I ran into the most peculiar woman upstairs," she told him. "I think I may have imagined her."

"Oh, I met her, too," he said lightly. "It seems Phin has acquired a cousin." He slid a glance to the other man that she could not interpret.

The earl took this as a signal to approach. She recognized him at once: he was the man who had fetched Mrs. Chudderley home from the Stromonds' ball. He was lean and tall, and everything about him was brown: his eyes, his hair, his sun-bronzed skin.

He bowed over her hand as James introduced them. "Lyd, the Earl of Ashmore. Phin, Miss Boyce. Be nice to each other, and don't quarrel. You're both too stubborn to lose gracefully."

Lord Ashmore gave her a dry smile as he straightened. "Never fear, Miss Boyce. We may be old friends, but I learned my manners elsewhere."

She smiled back, but could not prevent a questioning glance for James. Reading it correctly, he shrugged. "Since Phin is unconnected with the forgeries, it seemed safer to bring you here. And there's something else besides. But will you sit first, Lyd? You must have a terrible headache."

She let him guide her to one of the chairs at the fireplace. As they settled, she found herself the object of two sober stares. The mood seemed to have shifted on her. Or perhaps she had missed some remark; she still felt disoriented. She scrubbed a hand over her face. "I have no idea how I got here," she confessed.

James shifted in his chair so his knee came into her skirts. "Simple enough. No easier way to skip the queue for a cab than to show up flanked by two inspectors, with a woman passed out in your arms."

"The police came?" Something inside her relaxed. "They caught the men, then. Who were they? Thieves? Slave traders?"

He gave her a peculiar smile. "Oh, they caught them, all right. But not for long. By the time I installed you here and made it to Scotland Yard, they'd been released."

"Released!" She stared at him. "But—what on earth? They tried to *kidnap* me!"

"Indeed." He glanced again toward the earl. "Here is

where Phin comes in. Before the title fell upon him like a black plague, he actually made himself useful."

"That is one way to put it," said the earl.

Her head ached too sharply for this obscurity. "Please," she said. "Speak plainly." And then, all at once, she noticed the sympathy gathering in James's expression. Her throat closed. "Oh," she whispered. "Do *not* say this is about my father."

James held her eyes. His expression was calm, but the scar bisecting his brow betrayed him: it was flushing red. "Phin made some inquiries. To make a long story short, the men who attacked you are in the pay of the government."

She could not have heard him right. She looked to the earl, who showed no sign of surprise at James's claim. Finally, she considered her lap. Her fingers were more flexible than she had guessed: they knotted together so tightly that her knuckles looked bloodless.

Sanburne's hand touched her knee. Long, strong hands. Ridiculous rings. He was showing her kindness, but she did not want it. So often, in her experience, it was motivated by pity. "Tell me," she said flatly.

The earl cleared his throat. "I have great faith in James. When he says you can be trusted, I believe him. So I will tell you, in confidence, that I have worked with one of the men who assaulted you today. I did not enjoy the experience. He is generally employed to handle messes too nasty to be dealt with through official channels." His tone gentled. "His involvement is not good news for you, Miss Boyce. You are lucky he thought you were traveling alone. James took him by surprise, I think."

What a rare voice he had—so low and warm that it forced her to attend to it, even though the words themselves were horrible. She folded her arms around her torso. She knew what came next. "You are about to pass accusations against my father." Her voice sounded very dull. "Go ahead. Let's be done with it."

The earl traded a glance with James. No doubt they feared her on the verge of hysteria. "I know nothing of your father," he said. "I know only what I've been told. A woman named Polly Marshall—"

"Is a liar," she finished softly. In this curious, colorless mood, she could not work up her usual outrage; all she felt was fatigue, and a strange sense of inevitability. Again and again she recited this defense, but it did not seem to convince anyone. "It now seems that her lover was conspiring with a business rival to ruin my father."

"Anything is possible," the earl said mildly. "But I understand there are sources in Egypt, as well."

This was new. It suggested a vast investigation. A brief panic pierced her daze. Papa had no idea of any of this. "What do you mean?"

"Alas, I don't know the details. Suffice it to say that the government believes your father to be in possession of the Tears of Idihet."

So. Someone had said it aloud, now. The words ricocheted through her mind like cannonshot. She had a sense of things collapsing inside her: possibilities, hopes, everything good, all the fantasies she'd entertained to coax herself to sleep at night. "The government believes this," she said, and was amazed by her calm.

"Yes. And retrieving the jewels has become a matter of utmost importance. If the jewels were to surface in

England, the political ramifications would be disastrous. Renewed unrest in Egypt, certainly. It would also provide damaging ammunition for our critics. France already protests our control over the Suez Canal. The embarrassment would not leave us a leg to stand on." He paused. "You see now why the government has decided to handle the matter through unusual channels. But the need for secrecy does not to work to your advantage. Far nastier things can happen when there is no need to explain them to the public."

She shook her head dumbly. But she understood what Ashmore meant. "They are going to kill him."

"No," James said sharply. "Lydia, that's not it at all. Phin has an offer for you."

She looked up.

"It seems your father is scheduled to land at Southampton tomorrow," said the earl. Was he? She hadn't known that. And had she thought Ashmore handsome? She hated his face. How distant and unimpressed he looked by the tidings he delivered. "Contingent on this discussion, he will be permitted to proceed to London. And he will remain unimpeded, on one condition: that within the next seven days, the jewels are handed over to the government."

A fine deal. There was only one problem in it. "And if he doesn't have them?"

"Ironically, you must hope he does." The kindness in his voice seemed grotesque. "No matter your own convictions, Miss Boyce, they believe he had a hand in the theft. If the jewels remain missing, he will be arrested and interrogated. However, any party responsible for their return will find that no blame attaches to him, publicly or privately." He hesitated. "Of course, the same offer goes for a woman."

She was too dazed to remark the implication of that. James's curse alerted her. "Yes, she looks like a thief, doesn't she? Sod off, Phin. I'm taking her home now."

The earl gave an apologetic shrug. "It had to be said. I'm sorry for it."

With great effort, she came to her feet. The air seemed thick and viscous, as though she were moving through water. "So his innocence will condemn him," she said softly. "For he has no diamonds."

In the carriage, James's arm came around her to draw her to his chest. She had no urge to protest. Why should she? She was nearly resigned now to the fact that he could provide a measure of comfort when her own efforts failed her. "I don't know what to do," she whispered. "How can one prove that one *doesn't* have something?"

"I don't know," he said quietly. "Just rest for a bit, Lydia. You can't solve it all right now."

His answer depressed her. She wanted optimism, a course of action. She turned her face into his sleeve and inhaled his familiar scent, bergamot and mandarin and that particular element she could never put a name to, except to call it his own. "You must be honest with me." She closed her eyes. "Do you think me a fool, for believing in him?"

As they turned off the macadam onto cobblestones, the windows began to rattle. The noise swallowed the sound of his sigh, but she felt his chest rise and fall beneath her cheek. "No," he said. "You've been shown no proof. And I understand that you would believe your father over a stranger."

The generosity of his remark made her throat close. It had taken him a great leap to acknowledge her logic. Such a leap, she thought gratefully, might as well be an act of faith in itself.

"May I ask you something?" He spoke with a strange formality. "What would you do if you found out that he *was* involved?"

She could not respond immediately. That question sank to the core of her. It found purchase in a dark, cold space that had opened when she'd smashed the stela, and had widened in the days since. Every time she had refused to ask herself this question, it had widened. And now she must look into it. "I can hardly bear to think ill of him," she said haltingly. "You must understand how wrong, what a betrayal it seems to even contemplate the possibility of his guilt. But I suppose—if he were guilty—there would no other choice than to proceed as I am. Until—unless someone were able to prove beyond doubt that he had done this, I would still be bound, by my honor and my love, to do my duty as his daughter."

She waited in pained silence for his response. But when he spoke again, it was on a different matter entirely, and in a voice that strained to be neutral. "Phin and I have arranged for men to watch your house. You will be followed when you go out, but only for your protection. Is that acceptable to you?"

She had not thought of such necessities, but after this morning, she would be mad to refuse them. She pulled back in sudden anxiety. "My sisters—are they in danger, do you think?"

He smiled a little, and reached out to brush a strand of hair from her neck. "I'd have a care for myself, Lyd. If there's one thing everyone knows about you, it's that *you* are your father's man in England."

Hesitantly she smiled back. He meant no insult by the remark; she understood that now, as once she would not have. And there was *her* leap of faith, she thought. It was not difficult at all.

She lowered her face to his chest. In less than ten minutes, she would be back at Wilton Crescent. After such a day, she should be grateful for the prospect of home. Her sisters had been scheduled to arrive on the afternoon train; the expectation of their company should gladden her. But she wanted only to stay like this, warm in the curve of his arm.

In the darkness created by their bodies touching, she could admit it to herself. She had fallen in love with him.

The truth brought her no comfort. This touch of his had become her most precious possession, but it did not belong to her. When they arrived at her house, they would part. And in public, at a ball or a dinner, if their glances met, she would have to look away, because they had promised nothing to each other that might give her the right to gaze at him boldly.

The carriage slowed. She glanced out the window. They were in Piccadilly yet. James sat up. "Stay here," he said. His tone jarred her. He sounded very distant, of a sudden.

He went out to investigate. She waited, alone, for what seemed like a very long time. But perhaps it was only minutes, for the church bells in the distance chimed only once, announcing the half-hour. And then the door opened again, and he was climbing inside.

This time, he sat on the bench opposite. "Over-turned dray," he said.

As the vehicle rumbled forward once more, she opened her mouth, then closed it again. She did not know how to call him back to her side.

He spoke first. "So you will continue with this, then."

"With—with trying to figure out the truth, you mean?"

"If that's what you call it."

"What else am I to do?"

"Leave town," he said. "Spend the week in the country. Let your father handle his own mess."

Had her earlier words not registered? "I have told you I cannot abandon him."

"No," he said. "I suppose not." And then, with a strange laugh, he added, "Of course not. Nothing will make you back down."

She was relieved. It was not in her to have this argument again. "You understand me, then."

He nodded once. "I do. I am done with you, Lydia."

The words fell into the space between them. She could not have heard them correctly. They were not for her. "What?"

He spoke coldly and slowly. "I have already been down this road. I have watched one blind, obstinate, forceful woman kick and fight her way to ruin. I have not had the pleasure of watching her die, but it seems you are determined to provide me that chance. I will not take it, Lydia. You walk alone from this moment onward."

"No," she whispered.

"*Yes.* This is not a game. Those men this morning meant to harm you. Had I been carrying a gun, there would be bullets between their eyes right now, and a great deal of blood on the ground. Do you understand that? We have moved beyond dumb rocks, now. We are dealing in death. You are playing with it. The boy at the Empire held a knife to my throat. He will do no less for you. If you do not step away from this—if you do not let your father solve his own problems, as any grown man should—then you will end up in the ground. And I will not stand by your grave and weep for you."

She tried to swallow. Her throat fought against it. The image formed in her mind: a stormy day. A crowd of mourners, crows flocking around the kill. Fresh roses, bloody blots on the upturned soil. And him standing in the distance, his coat flapping about him. Refusing to cry.

A chill trembled through her. It was so vivid, it felt like a premonition.

"I do not *want* to do this," she burst out. "I do not want to endanger myself! But what are my choices? James—"

"Your choices are very clear," he said flatly. "A great many people think your father guilty. Right or wrong, you must accept that, and let *him* be the one to manage it. Or you can go it alone. Gamble your life on your belief in him. And lose."

She blinked back tears. Anger? Devastation? She did not know. Nothing was clear to her at this moment. It was all an illogical muddle, fueled by the most irrational thought of all: the wish to move to his side. That he would hold her hand as he said these horrible things.

Ridiculous! Anger, yes, that was what she felt; most of all, for herself. "What do you care if I land myself in a mess? You would not cry even if you had your way, even if I abandoned my father and threw myself at you. Have you ever claimed to love me? And what would my feelings for you be worth, if I proved capable of doing such a thing? Would you want the love of someone like that?" Her voice broke into desperation. "You blame your father for claiming to love Lady Boland, but not fighting for her. How would I be any different? To abandon my father because it was *convenient*? Tell me, James—you want nothing more than to see your sister free. Would you give up on that? If the whole world told you she was mad, would you accept that she belonged in an asylum? I think not!"

He took a long time to respond. Minutes passed before he spoke again. "You have already made your choice." He sounded weary. "I am not going to try to convince you otherwise. I know how well that works. They say history repeats itself, but it will not with me."

She sat frozen until the coach slowed. Already home? Her startled glance alit on Sophie's house, then shot back to him as he leaned past her to open the door. A footman was waiting. She had no choice but to exit.

As she set foot on the stair, he spoke again. "It was not a game, though." His face was lost in the darkness of the interior, but she thought she saw him shrug. "You should know that. It stopped being a game some time ago." And then he said, "Good evening, Miss Boyce."

# Fifteen

As she entered the front hall, she heard Ana's laughter floating down from the floor above. She leaned against the wall to listen. Such an ebullient sound, uncomplicated by anything but joy. She wished James might have heard it. He might have understood, then. Ana had been born with her face to the sun, and if that sun tried to set, all of them would gladly burn themselves to hold it up for her. Even Sophie would do so. One did not surrender love when it became painful.

She dashed tears from her eyes and took up her correspondence from the silver salver. Ashmore was right about one thing: a wire was waiting for her. Papa would be home by tomorrow night.

The print wavered before her eyes. Her whole body ached as though she'd been slammed into a wall. She could have put it down to the chloroform, but she was not an idiot.

"You're back!" Ana spoke gaily from the top of the stairs. "Goodness, Lydia—did you go straight from the train station to the library?"

"Yes." As she spoke the lie, a cold finger touched her spine. She shook it off and started up the stairs.

"Well, I have the most—" Ana broke off on a sudden frown. "Are you all right? You look unwell."

"A headache," Lydia said, and took Ana's arm to steer her down the hallway. "What were you saying?"

"Only that I have the most exciting news. But are you certain you're all right? Yes? Really? Very well, then." She darted ahead to open the door to Lydia's sitting room. "Lady Farlow has managed to get St. George's for the wedding!"

"Oh, that's lovely." Lydia pulled her into a hug. How sweet her sister smelled, like violets and sunshine and wide-eyed naivete. She would know suffering, in time. All people did. But it would not be for a mistake her family had made. "I'm so happy for you, dear. And *you* are happy, yes?"

"Terribly," Ana said. "I have always dreamed of being married there." Her cheeks pinkened. "I must confess something else, Lyddie. I haven't told anyone else, but—he kissed me! Out on the tennis court this morning, at Bagley End. We were behind the shrubbery; no one saw. Oh, it was *so* dashing of him! You aren't shocked, are you?"

Far more shocking was the idea that Lydia should be the first to hear of it. She knew how prim Ana thought her. "You didn't tell this to Sophie?"

Ana made a face. "She's been in a terrible mood all day. I don't know what ails her."

Lydia feared she knew the cause. "I'll go speak with her," she said grimly.

She found Sophie draped across her bed, a compress tied over her eyes. The curtains were drawn, and a package of willow bark powder sat open on the washstand. As the mattress sank beneath Lydia's weight, Sophie rolled away and muttered, "I don't want company."

Lydia sat silently for a moment. They were not confidantes, in affairs of love. Of course they weren't. Until recently, she'd had nothing to tell that didn't concern Sophie's husband. She hoped that the same was true of Sophie. And if it was otherwise—God above, she didn't want to know.

But her sister's misery was so plain that it compelled her to brave the silence. "Is it Mr. Ensley?"

Sophie ripped off the compress and sat up. "Do not mention him. He is a rude, uncivilized rakehell!"

Lydia digested this for a moment. "You seemed to be enjoying his attentions at one point last night."

"And what of it? That did not give him the right to—*expect* things of me. He said I was teasing him!"

She sucked in a breath. George had cast a similar accusation at her, once. It had made her feel low and ashamed, but now she saw more clearly. Men could restrain themselves better than he'd claimed. She had not deserved such behavior. "Sophie, did he manhandle you?"

A queer look crossed her sister's face. "Not much."

Alarm and the first spark of rage had her inching closer. She would kill this man. "*How* much, dearest?"

"Oh, just stop it! I don't need *your* guidance on the matter."

She shot to her feet. "Fine, but we must tell George directly. This cad can't be allowed to—"

Sophie grabbed her wrist and yanked her back down. "No. Do you hear me? He's not to know. *Ever.*"

Lydia had never seen her look so shaken. "God above, Sophie. It wasn't *your* fault that he—"

Sophie's nails dug into her wrist. "I mean it. Lydia!

If you so much as breathe a word to him, I will—I will throw you into the street!"

Astonishment silenced her. Never, even in their nastiest quarrels, had Sophie voiced such a threat.

Sophie's eyes dropped, and her hand fell away. As a flush began to stain her cheeks, everything clarified. "Dear God," Lydia whispered. "You encouraged him to kiss you."

"I do not wish to speak of it."

"*More* than that? God in heaven, Sophie!"

"I said it *wasn't much.*" Sophie's shoulders squared. "But if it had been, what of it?" She flopped back onto the pillows. "*George* wouldn't care. If he cared, he would come along with me, wouldn't he? But does he ever? Of course not." She gave a bitter laugh. "*Parliament* is in session. Never mind that half the House is away to the Henley! I might as well be a spinster, too, for all I see of my husband."

A sharpness rose in Lydia's throat, bursting out as a scoff. "Oh, there's a fine justification. You knew what he was when you married him."

"And when I married him he promised to love me, didn't he? Not lecture and scold me as if I were a scullery maid. You've seen him! He barely pays me a word of attention, unless it's to rebuke me for not taking more of an *interest* in his political wrangling. As if I care about the divisions! I told him he married the wrong sister if he wants *that.*" At Lydia's muffled gasp, Sophie made an impatient noise. "Well, I don't care. It's true, isn't it? And you needn't look at me as though I'm a monster. I married him for *us,* didn't I?"

A queer laugh slithered out of Lydia. "For us?"

"Yes, and now *I'm* the one who suffers for it," Sophie said stubbornly. "*I'm* the one who must go to these boring dinners and tedious speeches and behave like some dead-dull buttoned-up stick in the mud, all because George's friends might *disapprove* if I show an inch of spine. And meanwhile, you and Ana get to gallivant about doing whatever you please, because George's money will pay for it!"

Lydia stared at her. "Let us be clear," she said slowly. "You misled me. You lied to me. You mocked me behind my back to save *us*?"

Sophie waved an exasperated hand. "Oh, for heaven's sake! Don't let's start on *that* again. Where would we be right now, if I hadn't accepted his suit? You're very smart, no doubt, but you couldn't keep the three of us in tea with the money you make from Papa's sales!"

Lydia laughed. "You mean I could not keep us in *style*."

"What is that supposed to mean? Am I meant to be ashamed, because I prefer to live decently?"

"No." Lydia's voice felt like venom; it burned in her throat. "I know how much your comfort means to you. I know very well the sacrifices you made to get it! You knew I loved him, but you took him from me anyway. You *took* him and now you complain that he doesn't suit? And better yet, you expect my *sympathy* for it? My God! It is beyond selfish, it is *beyond* childish—"

"Amazing! You're *still* telling yourself that he fancied you first?"

"*He did!*"

"You were nothing to him!"

"All London knew he was courting me!"

"Great ghosts, Lydia, he never gave two *glances* at you! He befriended you to meet me—that was all!"

They were both on their feet, screaming. Anyone in the hallway would be able to hear. The knowledge throttled Lydia's next words. Sophie, glaring, felt no such constraints. "Just say it, then! Tell me something else I've done wrong! I know how you *adore* playing the martyr!"

Martyr? The accusation momentarily threw her. Early on, she *had* given vent to a righteous sense of injury. But Sophie had never seemed to remark her jabs. "It's been years now," she said with open bewilderment. Years since the anger and heartbreak had shaken her awake at night. That period and those feelings no longer made any sense to her. She saw now, lucidly, that her love for George had been premised on fantasies. The man himself had never made her feel a hundredth of the things that Sanburne did. Their conversations had been superficial, his attentions scripted by etiquette. Oh, she did not want to waste another thought on him. "It really doesn't matter anymore which of us he wanted first. What matters is that you got him. And thank God for it! I mean that, Sophie. I wouldn't want him anyway."

"Ha!" Sophie pointed at her, wearing the same triumphant expression with which she took points at tennis. "And yet you are the one who continues to bring up the matter!"

Lydia goggled at her. "Sophie, *no*. Don't you see? The matter has nothing to do with George at all. It has to do with us." She sank back onto the bed. "You *betrayed* me. You knew that I fancied him, but you let me

blunder on. And then you laughed with him over it."
She paused. That bit still had the power to astonish her.
"How could you do that to me? To your own sister?"

Sophie lowered herself to the opposite side of the
mattress. "It sounds very cruel," she admitted. "But it
was not meant to be so! I was young, and afraid to tell
you. And who was there to ask for advice? Aunt Augusta was dotty. Ana was in pigtails. It was too private
to put to my friends."

It was the soundest explanation she'd ever offered.
Lydia appreciated the effort. If only she could believe it.
"We talked about him all the time. If you had screwed
up your courage, I would have forgiven you. It would
have hurt me terribly, but it would not have been *your*
fault that George's affections had shifted."

Sophie had gone very white. "*You* might have forgiven me," she said faintly. "But Papa would not have
done. He never would have allowed it, Lydia."

She shook her head, her befuddlement slowly shifting to shocked comprehension. "You can't *seriously*
mean that Papa would have stopped your marriage?"

Sophie gave her a disbelieving smile. "To the man his
darling little Lydia had fallen in love with? Of course. I
have no doubt whatsoever."

"My God." Lydia put her knuckles to her mouth.
"How . . . horrible for you. He loves you. You're his
*daughter.* You—"

"Oh, do not condescend to me!" Sophie leaped to
her feet and strode around the bed. "What of *you*? Running off the way you did before the wedding? Did Papa
ever console me for the scandal *you* created? The stares
and the snickers we received?"

"Who do you think endured the brunt of those stares? *I* did!"

"*You?* No one cared enough about you to bother looking! *I* was the one who suffered. It overshadowed the wedding entirely! Everyone asking where you were, where Papa was, and all the time with the most horrible, knowing smirks! Imagine that: having to explain your own father's absence, having to lie when everyone already knows the real story. Perhaps I *should* have told the truth: that as far as Papa's concerned, he only has one daughter—Ana and I are orphans!"

There were advantages to height. As Lydia rose, Sophie had to look up to meet her eyes. "Is *that* the real reason you did it? You wanted revenge against me for being his favorite?" As Sophie rolled her eyes, another intuition struck. "Or you wanted his whole attention," she said more slowly. "*That's* it, isn't it? You'd be the first to marry, which makes you special. Better yet, you'd marry the man Papa knew *I* had hopes for. What better way to win his attention, than to show him that another man had judged you worthier? Oh," she said softly. "But it didn't turned out as you planned, did it? Papa was with me. He never witnessed your triumph."

Sophie's eyes shifted beyond her, fixing on nothing as she sank back down to the bed. "No," she said, but she sounded uncertain.

There was little charity left in Lydia. But this was only the truth. "Papa very much wanted to be at your wedding. He talked of nothing but you, that day." He had recounted endless stories of her and Sophie's childhood, of the time when Sophie had been her greatest friend and admirer.

"*One* day?" Sophie gave a curt laugh. "My. How generous of him." And then she gave a small shake of her head, and her shoulders slumped. "Lydia—really. All of it was—it was not to *hurt* you, precisely. That is— sometimes I feel angry with you, but I know that makes no sense. What reason have I to envy you? None, really. I would hate to be alone—although I know you do not mind it," she added quickly, as Lydia bit down on an incredulous smile. "But I am different than you. I could never be content with books and studies. And I would care very much if gentlemen found me plain. I do not think myself shallow for it. It's not wrong to enjoy being well-liked." She hesitated, then shrugged. "So what care should I have for Papa? I have so much that you don't. Perhaps it's only fair that you have him."

Lydia rose and walked to the door. One hand on the knob, she spoke calmly. "Papa is not yours to give, Sophie. And if you feel that I'm in need of charity from *you,* then you have made a mistake in tallying our accounts. You do have a great deal, but like all spoiled children, you criticize and abuse every gift you receive. Only here's the rub: you aren't a child, and the gift you abused this weekend isn't a toy. It's your marriage. If you break it, it can't be replaced."

She let herself out. In the hallway she took a deep, cleansing breath. The air in the little bedroom was stuffy, choked with perfume. How could Sophie stand to lie in there for hours at a time? No wonder she had headaches. Of her own accord, she made a prison for herself, and a punishment. She was blinding herself to any real possibilities; if she continued like this, she would never be happy.

*I am so much luckier.*

The thought seemed foreign and startling. But it was true: as she started for the stairs, she felt lucky. It seemed she was not done with dreaming, after all. The fears that had embarrassed her on Mrs. Ogilvie's rooftop seemed very dim to her now. And she did not feel too old or wizened to gamble with her heart. After all, what was dignity compared to the chance for happiness? It was only another sort of prison—respectable, sterile, and cowardly.

A smile came over her. She laughed out loud. So *this* was what it felt like when logic and instinct accorded. Ana was well set. There was nothing she could do for Papa at present. But with unshakable certainty, she knew what she must do for herself.

Dusk fell over London like cool, soft hands, cupping the city in blue darkness. He blinked up at the sky through the glass walls of his conservatory. The flowers were in bud on the acacia trees. *Did you know they smell sweet?* The clarity of their edges fascinated him. A drink would solve that, he supposed. He liked to be drunk by twilight. The evening they had come to tell him, it had been dusk. A sky the shade of drowned, deadened lips. Elizabeth had been at the piano, playing some tinny tune—a sharp tinkling of notes, a cold melody on the high end of the scale. All the carpets taken up for beating. Beneath his feet the floorboards had squeaked, thick with new wax.

His father had not bothered to come. A piece of paper from the gloved hand of a man whose name he'd never learned: that was how he'd found out.

It had been unusually cold that spring, the branches still bare. They'd scratched at the glass, a complaining counterpoint to Elizabeth's tune. Black ink against cream linen, the seal not even fully dry yet. It split open beneath his fingers like rotten fruit, disgorging a stark, brief message. He'd read it four times, five. Still the essence eluded him. Printed, inarguable, baffling.

Stella's husband was dead by her hand. Stella herself was badly wounded—insensate—not expected to survive the night.

Amazing to think such horrors might occur so casually, on such a tedious evening. From one moment to the next, as he'd sat in the window and sipped his drink and watched the sun set over St. James's Park and all the black spiderlike trees blur and condense into a thicker line of darkness, she'd faced a horror. Lonely and terrified. Blood everywhere. Stairs rushing up, her own screams filling her ears.

Had she thought of him, in those moments? She had asked him to save her. Not a week before, in this very room.

And after the fall? As she lay in insensibility, had her spirit wandered past him? He'd been bored, sitting in the window, and a little fretful at Elizabeth's single-minded pursuit of the melody. *Pedestrian,* he'd thought. *Will you never learn to play with both hands?* Such selfish, petty, smug, arrogant thoughts.

For four years, he'd spent a great deal of time hoping she hadn't been aware. She had fallen down the stairs into soft black tranquillity, a holiday from life. She had not tried to cry out for him, only to find herself imprisoned in dumb, agonized flesh. So he told himself.

But he'd never dared ask. Not by letter, not during their one brief meeting at that hellhole she'd been in before Kenhurst. Regardless, he did not like to be sober at twilight.

He glanced down at the glass of water in his hand. Why should he be sober at such a time? There was nothing kind about the passing of the sun. A cold that leached the land of color. The immense, haunting sadness of twilight was not (he thought) only a product of his personal experience. It was simply an elemental truth—one that he had grown sensitized enough to perceive. Twilight was the hand of night, pressing onto earth a darkness that would eventually consume them all.

"You look unwell."

The flinch was full-bodied, but he did not turn. After all, *damn her,* there was no need for him to always look *well.* This was his home. He could do as he liked. "How did you slip past Gudge?"

"Your butler? He let me in."

"Remind me to fire him."

Lydia sighed. It was an unhappy sound, and a dim, silenced part of him stirred in discomfort. *A host is always gracious. A guest is always honored. Be kind to the ones you love.*

But—old lessons, old manners, which he'd shelved along with all the rest. The lies he'd liked to believe; the memories that no longer made sense: Stella's happy laughter, her hand curving trustingly over his arm. Or the scent of his father's chest, pressed to his nose so long ago: cigar smoke, starch, vetiver water. Astonishing to think that those smells had once comforted him.

She still stood there. Her silence was like the hand of

twilight: it pressed on him more loudly than her words had done. "Be gone," he said.

"No. I must speak with you."

"Must you?" Something ugly and malicious entered his voice. "I wonder. Do you actually know how to speak your thoughts?"

After a moment, she said, "I don't follow you."

Yes, of course she didn't. She required logic, rules, huge crimson arrows. Feeling had no part in her brain's operation. She had no ability to chart the wide spaces that might open between two people who shared a history—or, for that matter, the dark terrains inside herself. He took a sip of the water. Thin, dull stuff. Well, he would spell it out for her. "You're angry," he said. "You're starting to realize I'm right. Your father had a hand in this. But you still can't bring yourself to believe it."

"I'm not angry at all, James." But her voice trembled. "I am . . . hopeful."

"Oh? So then you've come in the hopes that I'll retract my decision." He made his voice hard. She would hear the words: he could make her do that much. "You see that I was a help to you. So you *hope* I might help you again. Of course, you know I probably won't. You've realized, for all my faults, that I say what I mean. So you've come prepared to bargain. With your body, I assume? What a sacrifice, Miss Boyce. This time your gamble might bear consequences."

"You have it wrong."

"Then damn me to hell for accusing you. Curse me to Hades—that is the way you would phrase it, I expect. Or tell me I'm a sodding bastard, if you've got the vocabulary. But I beg you, do not scrape and bow to me. If you put your head down by my feet, I'm as likely to kick it as thank you for the courtesy."

Her inhalation was audible. "What a low opinion you have—"

"On the contrary," he said, and his laughter stirred the water as he lifted it again. "I consider you the epitome of good *ton*. Posturing and all."

"A low opinion of *yourself*," she finished. "And to imagine I would let you kick me! Really, James—and you call *me* foolish."

He considered again the glass in his hand. A very fine piece of crystal, straight from Waterford—the product of England's finest cruelties against the Irish. This was the sort of thing his father fought for, in his endless crusade to crush Home Rule. But its beveled edges were not so fine. They grated, suddenly, against the oversensitized pads of his fingers, as if all the blood in his body were pooling in his hands, stretching the skin out past the flesh's endurance. He had felt this as a boy, in the north country. It had snowed, and he and Stella had raced about, tunneling into their very own igloos, building snowmen to keep the devil away. How cold they had been. How rosy, how deliciously amused by themselves.

That little girl lived now in a prison, behind locks whose keys she did not possess, watched and fed and tended to like a pet mouse.

"I need you," she said. "Not for him. For—myself."

"How unfortunate," he said quietly.

Now there was the rustling of skirts, and it kicked up her smell, that distinctive blend of vanilla and violets, lavender and roses—an entire moving garden with a kitchen thrown in for good measure, and God save the allergic. "I am willing to bargain," she said.

The liquid sloshed onto his knuckles. "Large of you. But I advise you to trade elsewhere."

"Oh." The soft word held a queer hitch. He looked up. And saw, in the next moment, that she had been crying.

Her face arrested him. An invisible fist punched between his ribs to take hold of his heart. It held him in place as he stared at her. Her dark hair a nimbus around her pale face, the violet sky behind her a flag that signaled every horrid memory he sought to disown. "God," he said, and only became aware when the word reached his ear that his lips had moved at all. "Lydia— for God's sake. Cry elsewhere. Cry for someone who wants to be swayed."

"I can't help it." Her head lowered. And there was the part of her hair, straight and fine and white and bold against the dark waves, cutting through them like a flag of truce. His breath went from him as her fore-head settled against his knee. "I can't let either of you go," she said, her voice low and miserable. "And I don't know how to help you."

For a moment, he thought he'd misunderstood her. Help him? The sentiment was so astonishing that he laughed. "It's you who's the trouble," he said. "You who's determined to get yourself killed. Since I have no interest in sainthood, you'll forgive me if I turn away from the spectacle."

She held silent. He felt her breath, warm against the cloth, calling his consciousness back to the flesh, to the surface that he sometimes forgot, when he was lucky. To the part of him that felt such things—warmth, and dampness, and also the cold. He opened his mouth. But what else was there to say? *You don't mean it.* Or, *You'll help me? It's you who needs the help.* Dried-out, bloodless bluestocking.

Or even this: *You are all that I need.*

His lips weren't willing. He reached out—to touch her hair? To trace the parting? Such certain progress it cut across her crown. In his hand, the water was all a-tremble, like the legs of a green girl during her first waltz. He drew a long breath and set the drink on the wicker table beside him. His hand, now freed, hovered uncertainly over her head. Still her face pressed into him, a steady pressure, no trace of hesitation or doubt. "You should take care," he murmured. "Don't put such advantages in my hands."

"I trust you." She inhaled a breath that audibly shook. "I have faith in *you,* James."

His fingers settled on her hair. The purest, softest shade of black. The shade one saw when one closed one's eyes, in a warm, comfortable place, to rest. "You're an idiot," he said gently. "How have you made it this far through life? I've done nothing to merit your faith." Difficult to dredge the words up from his gut. They felt sharp at the edges, awkward. The cost of voicing them was a bitter burning in his throat. "*Anyone's* faith."

Her head lifted. Two shining lines traced the path of her tears. "I've told you time and again. It is nothing to be earned. It is simply *given.* And why shouldn't I give it?" She paused, and said very softly, "What happened with your sister was not your fault."

What did she know of it? "She came to me for help. All I could give her—"

Her fingers clenched on his trousers. "It wasn't in your power to stop Boland. You gave her *everything you could*. You offered to help her get away from him. If she refused to go, then that was *her* decision, not yours. Good God! Why can't you see that?"

He let the words settle between them. Considered them, turned them over in his head. She opened her mouth to say something, then seemed to think better of it.

"Let it go," he said. "That is what you were going to say."

"What? No!" Something tender and amused moved across her face. "Good lord, that's the last thing I'd tell you. Me, of all people! Why, your love for your sister, your loyalty to her, is . . . ." She exhaled. "Admirable? Moving." She shook her head. "I don't have the words to express it. It is deep and fierce and has made you do terrible things, and perhaps to think some very twisted and wrong thoughts, which I can't approve of. But it is a part of you that . . . that calls to me." Her lips curved a little—a smile that spoke more of sadness than joy. "It calls to me so strongly. And anyway, I should hate to see it go. It's the only thing holding you to the ground."

Something moved through him. Strange. Like the chills preceding a fever, the first sign of sickness. "It is not the only thing," he said slowly.

Her lips parted. She licked them. Swallowed, as if nervous. "Kiss me."

He thought again of Stella—of the horror of watching her stumble straight into tragedy. Of her refusal to heed him. How damned helpless he had felt. The pain of it, the humiliation of his own failure, still lived so strongly within him.

He looked back at her. Her face was upturned, her eyes closed: waiting for him to touch her.

If he did this, he was committed. Chained and bound to the path she was walking. He could not be a bystander to it. Not again.

But he could not deny her, either. Not when she waited so trustingly.

He took a deep breath, then sat forward to lay his lips on hers. Her mouth was soft against his—as soft as her trust, as easy to break. It was an unbalancing thing, this knowledge of her delicacy. He'd told her she was not fragile, but his hands easily spanned the curve from her collarbones to her nape, and he could trace the sharpness of her bones with his fingertips. And yet the woman housed in this flesh denied its weakness—defied it and risked herself recklessly. He kissed her, harder than he should have done. She would be made to see sense. To acknowledge her vulnerability, so she might reckon her actions more wisely.

Her arms came around him. She pulled him fearlessly off the bench. He slid down onto his knees, but she kept pulling, until he reclined full-length against her body. His weight, atop her, should have made her gasp. It must crush her. But there was resilience to her as well; the muscles of her arms and torso were firm. She made a soft sigh; her lips slipped down to his throat. She bit him softly, where his neck smoothed into his shoulder. She had no idea of her own limitations, even if she understood too clearly what they were supposed to be.

He caught her wrists and placed them above her head, pinning them when she would have jerked free. Her eyes came open, gold now, like harvest moons. They rounded in question.

He stared down at her, his breath coming harder. There was some dark impulse that lived within every man, perhaps—the urge to be brutal, when subtlety failed. But it was a poor excuse for action, fit only for cowards. He would give her a choice. "If we do this, I am not letting you go. Do you understand?"

"I don't want to go," she whispered. "James, I've already made the choice. I came to *you*."

He wanted to accept that. But his nature was not as generous as hers: he would always wish to test what others claimed to be truth. He rose, ignoring her protest. And then he took her by the waist and lifted her into his arms. As he started for the door, her struggle grew pronounced. "Where are you going?"

He stopped. "Past all the servants," he said. "Past everyone in this household who talks. And then, up the stairs to my rooms." He waited a moment, to see what she would do.

Her deep breath brought her breasts into his chest. His fingers reflexively tightened, digging into her thigh. He forced himself to relax, to count his breaths. He would not leave bruises on her. She was pale, and would mark so easily.

"All right," she said, and put her face into the crook of his shoulder.

He meant to make a point, but as he crossed out into the hall, he found his patience was not strong enough for it. There was a chambermaid, lurking in the door to the drawing room; her witness would have to serve. The stairs fell away beneath his feet, two by two; he was on the first story now, and shouldering his way into his apartments. Too many bloody anterooms until he reached his bedchamber. He laid her on the bed and avoided her grasping hands. This was not going to be a reprise of the boathouse. There would be no darkness between them. Or clothes.

He expected protests, but she took his guidance, lying quietly as he untied her boots, slid off the garters and peeled away her stockings. Her legs were paler than he had expected, like cream. The possibility that there might be other secrets her body was keeping lent his movements urgency. Another time, he would pause to lick these dimples behind her knees. For now, he would lay her bare, methodically, deliberately. She had fought so hard to keep herself hidden. She would not turn back, after this.

Off came her petticoats and chemise; her bodice and this godawful plague upon mankind, the corset. She submitted to his manipulations with closed eyes. Occasionally a soft humming broke from her throat. That little noise would drive him mad. His hands began to shake. Her drawers he pulled off last, over hips that curved as gently and gracefully as the Chiltern Hills where he'd first had her. Now she was naked before him. Athena and Venus in one. He withdrew to the foot of the bed. "Open your eyes," he said hoarsely.

Her breasts moved on a long breath. A flush stained her cheeks as she looked him over. He was still dressed, and this seemed to fluster her; her head rolled away. He crawled back over her, and cupped her face to force her eyes back to him. "I see you," he whispered. He slid his hands down to cup her shoulders. She wet her lips. Now to the exquisite softness of her breasts, which filled his palms so perfectly. Beneath the brush of his thumbs, her nipples beaded. He laid his mouth to one, sucking softly, and then harder, until she arched up beneath him. How could any woman's skin be so soft? It was as if the world had never touched her. His fingers skimmed onward, along the gentle inward dip of her waist, and these miraculous hips, beyond any expectation or hope. Her inner thighs yielded beneath his hand, falling away like obstacles to a revelation. He bent to lick her once, simply so her flesh might tremble again, as he'd remembered. And then his palms traveled down past her knees, to the tensile length of her calves, the tender arch of her feet. He lifted one ankle to his mouth for a kiss. "I see every part of you," he said softly. "Your body was only the last bit, Lyd."

Her throat moved in a swallow. She began to sit up and reach for him, but he withdrew. Falling back against the pillows, she murmured, "Take off your own clothes then. Let me be able to say the same."

He kept his eyes on her as he undressed. Her gaze dipped once as he removed his trousers, and her flush deepened. As he came back over her, he slid an arm under her to turn her over, so the long slope of her back was exposed to him. He laid kisses down her spine, and his fingers skated up the back of her leg, pausing in the hollow behind her knee, cupping the luscious expanse of one buttock. He pressed himself over her, so he covered her from head to toe. She made little twitches beneath the bites he pressed along her shoulder. "Nothing to hide now," he whispered into her ear.

"No," she said, "nothing." She twisted back around beneath him. His cock brushed against her wetness, and a groan slipped out of him. He slid lower, to avoid that temptation.

But her hands followed. She caught and stroked him, at first clumsy, and then, as his hand covered hers and showed her the way, with increasing boldness. He met her eyes, and a little smile moved her mouth. "You will educate me also," she said, and looked down, to watch him guide her.

Only a glance. But it nearly undid him. He removed her hand, licking from the base of her palm to the tip of her index finger before setting it aside. Then he turned his knuckles to charting the soft slope of her belly. He delved through the soft hair between her thighs, until he found her slit. His thumb traced upward and pressed; her gasp was sweet, sweeter even when he pushed his finger inside her, and her hips jerked.

He needed to be inside her then. It was not a matter of mere flesh. As he moved over her and positioned himself, and her eyes met his and her arms came around him, he felt a tension that was beyond lust. Like the vibration that moved through the floor as an orchestra reached its crescendo. Pain was not like music at all. *This* was what his sinews vibrated to: her body, as he pushed into her, as she gasped and her head fell back. For the oddest moment, he did not know if he would be able to withdraw in order to thrust again. The hot, wet clasp of her and the fleshly weight of her body beneath him and her arms around him made something settle in him definitively; it pulled him down like a weight, grounding him deeply within her. And then she smiled up at him, and it traveled like a shock from his brain to his groin, and he began to move.

Everything: soft, hot, giving, carnal, their tongues tangling, her nails in his back. *You are not weak at all,* he thought wondrously. How had he forgotten? She was a Valkyrie. His fears were useless to her. He would never let them trap her. Her fingers pulled at his hair now, and he rolled over so she pressed down on him, and her movements, so inspired, *She will educate me, native genius;* he had known this from the first moment he saw her, somehow. He took hold of her waist and thrust faster now, feeling the moment that she learned to find her own pleasure, the sudden certainty of her hips, her increasing aggression. It was coming to her. She stiffened and bit down on his lip, and he turned her over again, once, twice, climaxing with a power that had him gasping as he collapsed onto her.

They lay there for a long moment, and her shudders were not less marked than his. Her hands slipped from his shoulders, a gentle stroke down to his buttocks, and she kissed him long and deeply. A woman like her— who would fight for her father so fiercely—her kisses were their own commitment. "You won't let me go," he murmured.

"No," she said. "I won't."

A long pause opened between them. He brushed her hair from her shoulders. Her blushes came and went; her lashes fluttered down beneath the barest brush of his fingernail across her brow.

And then her dimple popped out.

"What?" he murmured.

"Nothing."

He kissed the indentation. "Too late."

"What does that mean?"

"You've got a tell, Lydia. At the card table, we'd call you an easy mark."

The dimple faded as her lips curved into a smile. Her eyes came open. As she looked at him, wistfulness sketched across her face, and she sighed.

"Your father," he said softly. "We'll figure something out. I promise you."

"That's not the only thing." Her glance shifted beyond him now. He followed it to the decanter sitting across the room. "It's you I'm worried about," she said. "I would not ask you to let go of your sister. But this trouble between you and Moreland—you must make peace with it. Or it will stand between us, too."

What rubbish was this? He frowned. "He has nothing to do with us."

Her regard was too steady to be comfortable. "My honesty is no good to you if you won't listen to it." She slid out from beneath his touch, leaning over the edge of the bed to grab her corset. "Help me dress."

"To hell with that."

Impatience touched her voice now. "I have to go, James."

His anger came from nowhere. "You shouldn't have come in the first place. But you did. And now you are here, by God, you will stay."

"Don't be childish," she said calmly. "It's one thing to risk rumors. It's another to ask for them."

"That's not what you said downstairs. You knew very well what you were committing to by coming up here."

"True enough." She shrugged. "I took a gamble. A

great leap. I still don't know how it will turn out. But I see how far you are willing to go for it, and that doesn't reassure me."

He caught her by the elbow. "We are in this *together,* Lydia."

She looked him in the eye. "I thought we were. But you are being cowardly now. Oh yes, I saw that you were drinking water. But as long as you nurse this hatred, there's no reason to believe you won't go back to the whiskey."

He took the strings of the corset, forcing himself not to vent his frustration on her ribs. "This is not fair," he said, punctuating his words with a sound yank. "You will not let go of your father, but you ask me to let go of her?"

The look she gave him over her shoulder was full of surprise. "Never. James, the two have nothing to do with one another."

"You know nothing of it."

Her smile, now, struck a chill in his heart. It looked so strangely resigned. "Nor do you, it seems."

# Sixteen

She did not want to go back to the house on Wilton Crescent. It felt wrong to her now, nothing like home. But James's house would not be a home, either, so long as it remained a fortress erected for the sole purpose of antagonizing his father.

Sophie and Ana were out; they had gone to a dinner, the butler informed her. She dressed for bed early, not because she was tired, but because she wanted the day to be over. And also, perhaps, because an expectation hummed inside her, steady and immune to reason: he would come for her. It was foolish, perhaps, but one could not repress such hopes. He would not come in the night, but that did not stop her from lying awake to count the chimes of the grandfather clock in the hall.

Sophie and Ana returned at half past two. Wide-eyed, she listened to their murmured good nights. The house quieted again, and after some immeasurable time, the old clock in the hall wound down and the chimes ceased to ring. The steady sound of her heartbeat finally lulled her eyes shut.

When she woke again, the room was flooded with light and Ana stood over her, smiling. "Come downstairs quickly! You will not believe who is here."

As she descended the stairs minutes later, she could

hear the happy noise spilling from the drawing room. Her feet wanted to fly to him. It was angering, to realize that this reunion had been tarnished by the news she must share.

But when the sound of his voice—as familiar and comforting as lullabies—reached her in the hallway, her cares fell away for the moment. She burst into the room, and his dear face appeared to her like an answer: the same graying mustache and sun-browned skin, the rounded shoulders, the little paunch that no amount of abstention would ever mitigate. He had not changed a bit. "Papa."

He broke instantly from some remark he was making to Sophie. His face lit, and his arms opened to her. "Lydia! My darling, where have you been?"

His embrace smelled of his journey, of coal smoke and sweat. But beneath it was the intangible essence that she had once associated with everything safe and loving and wonderful. She realized all at once that she had never needed him more than she did now. "Papa," she whispered into his lapel. "Thank God you are home."

She lifted her head, looking past Ana's beaming face and Sophie's fading smile, to where George glared like a gargoyle at the edge of the room. Papa followed her glance, and murmured into her ear, "We must speak privately, Lydia. Very soon."

And that quickly, her spirits deflated.


Later, after a long luncheon in which Papa regaled them with tales of his journey and the antics of his workers, she withdrew with him to the guest bedroom where his luggage had been stowed. "I do not know how to tell you this," she said, and he drew her to his side and laid an arm over her shoulders as he might have done with a son.

"Simply tell me," he said. "You can tell me anything, dearest."

But as she recited the tale—the lies of Miss Marshall, and the strange boy with the knife, the men at the station and (haltingly, and with a creeping sense of mortification) Ashmore's offer—he withdrew from her. First his cheek, which had been pressed against hers, and then his stiffening arm, which fell away to lie inert on the arm of his chair. His face grew red, so red she feared for him. She lapsed into silence.

He came to his feet with such force that the chair legs thumped against the carpet. "But this is *preposterous*!" he burst out. "Who is this Ashmore? How do you know him? How dare he feed you such lies?"

"He is a friend of—of a friend," she said awkwardly. *A friend of the man I love.* She had hoped to confide in him about that as well, but the violence of his pacing served to focus her on the matter at hand.

"Who does he think he is? Passing judgment on such flimsy happenstance?"

"I don't know." She moved her hands under her thighs, clenching the seat to channel her nervous energy. "He—he gave the impression of being involved in government work."

Papa wheeled to stare at her. "Aligned with such scum? Who would attack you in plain sight?" Spittle beaded his mustache. "It is *outrageous*! Is this what our government has come to? I can think of better pastimes for them—Egypt overrun by the French, Russia preying on our Indian borders. And they will harass girls over some paranoid fantasy about a khedive's paste gems?"

His fury was so out of character that she hardly knew what to say. "I am sorry," she whispered. "I told him of your innocence. I told him it was all lies. I swear it!"

His face changed, the craggy line between his brows smoothing. "Of course you did," he said, and came to her, pulling her up into a hug. "Lydia, my girl, don't look so distraught. We will straighten this out. We always do, don't we? There is no trouble we can't face together."

It was all she'd wanted to hear, for so long now. But as she closed her eyes in his embrace, her fear did not subside. "How?" she managed. "What will we do?"

He pulled away. "I will go see this Ashmore."

"I will go with you," she said instantly.

"No. Absolutely not! I will not have you exposed to him again." He rubbed his knuckles across her cheek. "So much like your mother," he murmured. "Lydia, you mustn't worry about this. I will take care of it, now."


James caught the train from Victoria Station shortly after dawn. It was a direct shot to Kedston, where he hired a coach for the five-mile journey to the asylum. The asylum was set back from the main road, behind ornate black gates that opened onto a long drive winding through low, rolling hills. For several minutes, his only view was of grazing sheep and a blue sky as mild as a baby's eyes. A row of trees cropped up for a brief stretch, and then fell away, revealing a circular drive. The carriage pulled to a halt by a short flight of steps.

He stepped out of the carriage and looked up. Stella's prison was a grand stone mansion, sprawling some sixty rooms across and three storys high. At the west end rose a high tower. Judging by the stained glass windows, that would be the chapel, the centerpiece of her improvement. A short flight of steps rose to the entrance; an inscription had been chiseled into the tympanum: "Except the Lord buildeth the house they labour in vain that build it." With a snort, James passed under it into the lobby.

He had wired ahead to expect his arrival. Predictably, Dwyer had absented himself. A young woman named Miss Leadsom came out of the office to receive him. She was as small-boned and brown as a wren, and the overburdened key ring at her waist lent her an air of housekeeperish authority. She tried, at first, to turn him away. She reminded him that Stella did not want visitors.

"As I said in my note, I am resolved to see her. I'll wait in the lobby until she changes her mind."

He took a seat in a soft chair. Morning tea came and went. "Please, sir," said Miss Leadsom. "She says she will not be swayed."

"Pity," he said. "Nor will I."

Around lunchtime, the attendants began to give him nervous glances as they passed through the entry hall. Miss Leadsom appeared again. "My lord, she begs you to go."

"After I see her," he said grimly.

There were no clocks in the lobby. Was that deliberate? Did the passage of time wear on madmen's nerves? Generally he would have counted that a bad sign for himself, but today he felt infinitely untroubled by waiting. Eventually the stained-glass windows began to yield shadows. He watched them creep across the floor. His stepmother's old words whispered to him: Blue, to calm the spirit. Green, to animate the will. Red for passion, yellow for joy. Lydia had no need for any of these colors. Well, perhaps a bit of yellow, but he would help with that. He had no need of any of them, when he was with her.

High tea, now. His stomach was rumbling. He focused on the green bars of light, which had almost reached the main staircase.

A clearing of the throat drew his attention. Miss Leadsom stood a little way off. "Please come with me," she said.

He rose. She led him down a richly furnished corridor, to a wing she referred to as the "ladies' department." They passed a maid once, carrying a tray of half-eaten food, but no one else seemed to be about. The place was immensely silent. A thick Persian leader muffled their footsteps and the heavy tapestries on the walls further dampened noise. It unnerved him, though perhaps it was preferable to the screams and cries he'd assumed were endemic to places like these.

"Lady Boland has her own set of rooms," Miss Leadsom told him. She came to a stop before an unmarked door. He took note of the peephole and the lock on the handle. "She enjoys the gardens, when the weather permits it, so we placed her on the ground story. I believe you will find she has no complaints."

He braced himself for the moment when she would reach for her keys. *Caged and studied like an animal.* But when she lifted her hand, it was to knock at the door.

"I will speak with her in private," James said sharply.

The wren gave him a startled look. "But of course. I would not dream of intruding."

A voice called for them to enter. Miss Leadsom stepped back and bobbed a curtsy. "I will wait in the hall."

He entered into a little sitting room, sparsely furnished, with a Venetian carpet and a writing table, and a bookshelf against the wall. The curtains were drawn, the atmosphere heavy. With a visceral shock, he realized that it smelled like their father's house. Orchids and lemon-wax. He drew a testing breath. Stella had always favored rosewater, but there was no sign of it in the air. Did they not allow her such luxuries?

"James." The voice came from the next room, startling him. "Give me a moment, please."

That he hadn't recognized her voice unnerved him. He prowled the perimeter, letting his fingers trail across various knickknacks. An embroidery frame, empty. A volume by Mrs. Gaskell. A small portrait of a kitten. She'd always liked her pets.

A rustling announced her entrance. He turned, and his chest clenched. In the dim light, she looked unchanged. Tall and slim. Her skin mercifully unmarked, save the scar on her chin, where the stairs had knocked it. She was dressed simply, in a dark woolen gown. It took him a moment to realize why the outfit looked so old-fashioned: she wore no bustle.

"Darling," she said, and came forward. They embraced, but not as long as he would have liked. She pulled back immediately.

He opened his mouth, and realized he had no

idea what to say. Her little smile suggested that she understood. It jarred him. He had forgotten how completely she took after Moreland. He was unused to seeing that smile without feeling a lick of resentment and rage.

"I am sorry to have kept you waiting," she said, and gestured toward an easy chair. After he'd sat, she took the other chair. "You should not have come, of course. But I am pleased the weather held so pleasant for your trip. You came by train, I think?"

Of all the things he had expected her to say to him, he'd never imagined she might begin this way. These were the sort of mundane pleasantries that had once driven her mad with boredom. "Yes," he said slowly, "by train. And you? Are you well?"

Her lashes swept down. "I am well," she said. "Very comfortable. They take splendid care of me here."

He stared at her. "Do they really?"

"Oh, yes. Not a moment of uneasiness. At first, of course, it was frightening—I had only the other place to compare it to. But it's very different, as you see. A bit like a hotel. Well—" She laughed. "A hotel with some very queer guests. But I may pick and choose where I socialize. And I've made some lovely friends. You would not believe what counts as madness, these days."

He felt off-balance, as if he were dreaming. "A hotel. Right. With a slot in the door so they can look in on you whenever they please."

Her brow knitted. She did not like the remark. "I know it must be hard for you. Father has written of your distress. I wish you would not let it bother you."

His unease sharpened. "Good God, how can it not

bother me? You deserve better than this. You deserve to be *free*."

She sighed. "And this is why I agreed to see you, finally. I wanted to say this in person." She drew a breath. "I know it will be hard for you to hear." Another breath, and then: "I don't wish to leave. Darling, I am happy here. I *want* to stay here—for a little while, at least."

"No." It sprang out from his throat so violently, he had to stop and regroup. "Moreland has gotten to you."

"*Father,* James. I have never called him anything but *Father.*" Her eyes were large and trusting—the eyes of a puppy. Easily kicked, more easily cowed.

The thought startled him. "So," he said. He was shaken. He had never felt venom for her. Never. "I find myself confronted by yet another woman who refuses to think badly of her father—no matter how much he might deserve it."

She made a face. "Oh, he's no saint. You mistake me if you think I have no complaints for him. But he is not responsible for what happened to me." The corner of her mouth curled upward, in an odd little grimace. "That was mostly Boland."

"Mostly!"

"Mostly," she said firmly. "He was a brute, and deserved what he got. But . . ." Her face turned to the window, and he saw her swallow. She was not as calm as she appeared, but for some reason, it was important for her to seem so. He drew a breath and remembered the advice another woman had given him: *Everyone is brave in his own way. You must not blame others if they don't fit your mold.* "I was very young," she said. "Flighty, headstrong. So many things I regret."

"That is no damned excuse—"

"Of course not. But you warned me, didn't you? Oh, I know you introduced us, but you quickly realized how badly we suited. You warned me all the way to the church. But I refused to listen."

"It was the talk that stopped you. Those gossiping harpies—"

"You are so determined to place blame elsewhere," she murmured. "Can you not spare a little for me?"

The old rage was stirring. "It had nothing to do with you. Boland and Moreland—"

"It had *everything* to do with me." The words held the beginnings of temper. "I am not sorry I killed him—and I *did* kill him, James. I was glad to do it. I still am. I had no choice; I will not regret it. But *God* knows why I stayed with him in the first place. You are right—you may scream it from the rooftops if it makes you feel better—you offered me an escape. But did I take it? God in heaven, *why* didn't I take it? All of this could have been averted . . ." She pressed a hand to her mouth, shaking her head when he would have moved to embrace her. "No," she said finally, and her hand fell, a dead curling weight, to her lap. "I failed *myself.* I betrayed *myself.* I chose to stay with him, and until I know why, how can I possibly leave? How can I possibly forgive myself, if I don't understand why I chose to hurt myself so? How can I live in the world, if I don't feel certain I won't betray myself again?"

All he could do was stare. The emotions raging within him were too complex and fierce to be parsed into coherent thought. "You will stay here," he said numbly. "To—*understand yourself*?"

She looked directly at him. "Yes. That's it exactly. And in the meantime, you can be angry at Father all you like. But do not be angry with him for *my* sake." She came to her feet, and he realized, with a shock, that he was being dismissed. He rose clumsily, and as she noted it, she smiled. "There is something I should like to show you before you go. I should let you keep it—I think you have as much need of it as I do—but I'm too selfish to give it up." She crossed to her writing table and slid open a drawer, extracting a sheaf of letters bound in a yellow ribbon. As she pulled the end of the silk, the envelopes spilled to the floor. "Silly me!" she exclaimed, and fell into a crouch to gather them.

How freely women could move, when not corseted and trussed up like game-hens. He sank to her side. But as he reached for the first letter, disbelief had his hand closing. "What is this? These are all—"

"From Father, yes," she finished gently. "He writes me every day. Did you think he had forgotten me?"

He sat back on his haunches. He could not keep his eyes off the letters, but the thought of touching them did something queer. Made him feel light-headed and panicky. Like the prospect of touching a dragon, or reaching into a closet and brushing up against a monster. Something rare and unbelievable, the tactile proof of which might very well destroy the foundations of everything one believed. Everything one told oneself, to get to sleep at night.

"This one," she said, and picked up a piece of paper. "Read this one, please."

When his hand still hesitated, she reached out for his fingers, closing them one by one around the letter.

Then, pulling him by his wrist to his feet, she went up on tiptoes to kiss his chin.

"Please read it," she said somberly. She sat back down and picked up her knitting needles. The quiet clicking of the sticks was the only sound in the room.

He stared at the letter. Slowly he lowered himself to the seat.

*My darling daughter,*

*Another dinner party. These seasonal obligations never end. Ah, well. Such is the price of politics, I'm afraid. I could have used you tonight, my dear. Your stepmother is gracious and charming, but she lacks the joie-de-vivre that you bring to a table. When an awkward moment arises, she smoothes over it, but cannot erase it. You always have had that gift. I cannot count the times your laughter made us forget our cares.*

*I hope you have not forgotten to laugh, at Kenhurst. Mr. Dwyer tells me you are doing better, well enough to entertain visitors. I do not understand your reluctance to meet us. Your stepmother and I should love to see you, if you will change your mind.*

*I have little to write. The dinner was dull, apart from a brief interruption by your brother. He appeared with an opera dancer. She quite enjoyed the croquettes. I feared Gladstone would take offense. I should have known better. I sometimes think James could convince the Devil to take communion. God save my fellow conservatives when he comes into the title.*

*If you seek a reason to get well, Stella, please
think on him. There is no reasoning with him, and
I have all but given up the attempt. He will not
forgive me for failing you, or hear a word from me
without skepticism. I think he will never be whole,
until you are home with us again.*

*Your loving father,*
*Moreland*

The paper was trembling in his hand. Bizarre. He
found himself shaking his head.

"He knows I wish to stay here," she murmured.
"Until I have come to peace with all of it, I am safer
away from the world."

"I can't accept that."

"No, of course not. Unlike you, Father is able to *respect* my wishes."

It stung like a slap. "Well, you've certainly chosen the
sweetest letter of the bunch. I suppose the others sing a
different tune."

"Oh, James." She put down the needles and held out
her hand. "Give it to me. I don't even know which one
it is. I chose it at random."

The paper crumpled in his fist, an ugly sound. "He
will write epic poems to you, I am sure, so long as you
are safely locked away. It's me he has to deal with in the
flesh." He tossed the paper onto the floor "And unfortunately for him, I won't be going away."

"Stop bedeviling him," she said sharply. "You will let
me fight my own battle, now."

"Oh yes, a grand battle you will wage, locked up here
in the madhouse!"

She shot to her feet. "By God, it is none of your affair how I choose to live my life!"

"Your life? You call this a *life?*" The anger that had seared him for four long years—that he had fought and endured and managed occasionally to ignore, but never, ever to extinguish—raged up within him so suddenly that he could not manage it. "*None of my affair,* is it? What the hell do you think I've been doing, these last years? Do you have any idea what I've done? The things I've done—the nights I've lain awake, the visions I saw of you—while you sat here and *searched your soul* and did not bother to so much as *write* me? Do you know how I—" His voice broke as she came toward him; to his astonishment, his eyes were welling. "Stella, have you no idea how I've suffered for you?"

She took his face in her hands, gripping hard. "It is *not about you,* James. My God—yes, I am sorry that you have mourned! But what must I say to convince you to let it go? Yes, I should have listened to you! Yes, I should have gone with you when you offered to take me away!" She blinked, and a tear slipped from her eye. "But the price for my failure is not yours to discharge. It is *mine*! You will *let me have it*!"

"I can't accept—"

Her nails dug into his face. "This is the last time I will say this. I love you. I love you for trying to rescue me. I love you for what you have done with your factories. But I will no longer be your excuse. And on the day I do see you again, it will be because *I* am ready for it—not because you wish it."

Her blue eyes held fiercely to his a moment, and then she let go his face. Her arms came around him, and her forehead pressed into his shoulder.

He drew a shuddering breath. Haltingly his own hands lifted to her back. She was shaking. He felt a brief moment of desolation, and then the faintest, most tentative stirring of something lighter and miraculous. His arms closed tightly around her. "I love you," he said hoarsely.

"I have never doubted it," she whispered into his chest.

It came to Lydia, after her father had left for Ashmore's, that she had made an awful mistake. Ashmore knew something of her dalliance with James. What if he made mention of it? She was not sure how Papa would react. His anger, earlier, had been so unlike him. Would he think Ashmore lied to taunt him? Would he be moved to do something rash?

She found herself back in the drawing room. Sophie and Ana had gone shopping; they were assembling Ana's bridal trousseau with great earnestness, now. She paced around a cast-iron pot of aspidistras and tried to calm herself. Ashmore would be discreet. He would say nothing, surely.

*I should have gone,* she thought. *It was too important, not to go.*

Her sisters had taken the brougham. There was no choice but to walk. She snatched up a cloak and set out by foot, startling as a man emerged from a nearby vehicle. Dread rose in her throat.

"Miss Boyce," he said. "Lord Sanburne has set me to accompany you wherever you wish to go."

Well. He would not come himself, but he would spare her a servant. "Very well," she said. "Follow, if you like."

She set a quick pace along the winding lanes of Belgravia. It took no more than half an hour to reach Ashmore's house. Sanburne's man fell back as she approached the entrance. She rang the bell with trepidation, and the door opened immediately. "I am here to see the earl," she said.

The porter ran a skeptical eye down her form. She realized that in her haste, she had not donned a bonnet or gloves. To prove herself, she unbuttoned the cloak and shrugged it off. At the sight of her fine gown, his manner changed.

"He is occupied. Perhaps you could come back later, miss."

"I believe he is with Mr. Boyce, my father."

"Oh. I was not informed to expect you, miss. Please wait."

She stood there a moment as he moved off, and then, on a sudden decision, followed him.

Around the corner and a few steps down the hallway, a noise caught her attention: muffled shouting. She recognized her father's voice. "—don't know *where* it is, but if someone rips it apart, we'll all be in a load of trouble. And if my daughter comes to one bit of harm—"

The butler came to a stop. So did she. Something about her movement drew his attention, for he looked over his shoulder and gasped. "Miss! Please let me go ahead to announce you."

"No," she said softly. "No. I have changed my mind." And turning on her heels, she quickly retraced her steps to the front door.

Outside, she turned in the direction of Oxford Street and the omnibuses. *Don't know where it is. If someone rips it apart.* There was only one explanation she could draw from those ominous statements. Surely she was wrong.

There was only one way to find out.


Mr. Carnelly looked surprised to see her. "Hullo there, Miss Boyce." His voice seemed to come from a great distance. "Been a while."

"Yes," she said. "Mr. Carnelly, you repackaged Hartnett's things before sending them to me. Do you still have the original materials in which they were shipped?"

He frowned. "The crate, do you mean? Aye, it'll be back there somewhere. What do you want with it?"

"Only to inspect it. I fear some correspondence attached to the shipment may have gotten separated and is somewhere stuck inside it." When he made no response, she added, "The crate properly belongs to my father. I expect it will not be a problem."

"No," he said slowly.

"I will need a tool of some sort, as well."

He rummaged under the counter for a hammer, then nodded for her to follow. Back they went, through aisles stacked with the detritus of a hundred shipments. "Thank you," she said, when he drew up. "I require privacy now."

Looking mystified, he withdrew.

It was not easy labor. As she pried up the top, the wood splintered, and scraped her knuckles raw. To cushion valuable items during shipment, two layers of roughspun canvas were stapled to the interior boards. It took all her strength to pry away the tacking; each time one of the heavy staples gave way, she went stumbling backward from the force of her exertion. Slowly the bare boards of the crate bottom began to appear. Nothing, she thought.

And then, with the next staple, she was able to pull the canvas up far enough to spy the corner of a small roll of cloth. She watched her fingers close around it. Her hands were quicker than her brain: they untied the knot holding the cotton together, so the roll split open, disgorging a soft velveteen bag.

She upended it.

Five glittering jewels, and the fragments of a sixth, thumped onto the floor. Red, blue, green, yellow, violet, and clearest white—they seemed to consume all the light in the room. As their radiance brightened, the shadows around her deepened and grew colder.

She had found the Tears of Idihet.

As she stared, they began to blur. Distantly she marveled at this: the wisdom of her body, which already understood the consequences of this discovery—the conclusions which her mind revolved and revolved around, but refused to grasp.

As her eyes closed, the tears began to fall.


"You did it, didn't you? You helped to steal the jewels."

Papa looked up from the page in front of him. Then his attention went to George's valet, who was laying out his evening clothes.

It told her everything, that one glance. That his first reaction should not be confusion, or shocked denial—but concern for who might overhear. "Give us a moment," he said to Harkness. Then, when the door had closed behind the man, he looked directly at her. "You spoke to Ashmore?"

"Better than that," she said. "I found the jewels."

He stiffened so abruptly that the chair legs squeaked against the floorboards. "Where are they?"

"Safe," she said. "Unlike the rest of us."

"Lydia . . ." He pulled his hand across his mouth. "You must believe me: I had no choice."

"Oh?" She gave a scornful laugh. It seemed to bruise the lining of her throat, so that her next swallow ached. "Permit me to ask for specifics. Did someone put a gun to your head?"

He sighed heavily and came to his feet. "When it came to the Tears? Very nearly, yes."

"I see. Were there a great many guns, over the years? Because Polly Marshall seemed to think you and Hartnett long-standing partners in this business. And it seems to me that guns are not so dependable. Had one been pressed against your head so often, you'd surely be dead by now."

"Lydia." He hesitated. "You know how difficult it is to fund one's work. And you understand the significance of what I am undertaking here. To provide physical evidence of the biblical tales! Surely you can understand—"

"No! I don't understand in the slightest." God, when she thought back to her endless protestations of his innocence, the lengths she had gone to defend him—and for what? "My God," she whispered. "I feel a *fool*. So wholly taken in by these high-flying vows of yours. Your project? *What of it?* You are *robbing* them, Papa—you are helping thieves make away with their bounty! You very well may have helped to destabilize the khedive's government. Do you know how many people died in the bombardment of Alexandria? *I know you do!* You could speak of nothing else, for *months* afterward!"

He flushed. "And do you know how much better off Egypt is with Urabi Pasha gone? Lydia, the man was an anarchist! I will not apologize if I had a hand in his exile. By God, I would like to shout it from the rooftops!"

"Oh," she said softly. "So it's Egypt for the Egyptians—so long as they're the *right* Egyptians. The ones *you* think are proper."

"This is irrelevant," he snapped. "How do you think this fine roof came to be over your head? Could Sophie have managed this on her own? Do you really think those pathetic pieces you sell are enough to have supported your debuts? Or did you assume the rest of the money was coming from my *funding*?"

So long ago, then? This had been going on for that long? "Then why?" she cried. "Why even pretend that it was important? Why involve me at all?"

"I had to," he said flatly. "The authorities began to grow suspicious. There had to be a legitimate traffic, to cover for the illegal one."

Of course, she thought dully. She'd always believed that he relied on her, that he trusted and depended on her as no one else had. But that, too, had been for convenience's sake. Very convenient, to have a spinster daughter to arrange his alibis for him.

God, what an idiot she was! Even with George, she had not played the fool so thoroughly.

"Daughter." He reached for her hand. She let him take it. She could barely feel his touch anyway. "You know how much I love you. It's *because* I love you that I did this. I did it for *us.*"

Sophie had said the same. And like Papa, she'd said it with regret. False sacrifices, Lydia thought. True sacrifice required no victim but oneself. It did not leave the recipients of its beneficence bleeding.

She exhaled. He was right, the roof over her head was very fine. Richly furnished—Kedderminster carpets, priceless oils on the walls. George was no vulnerable young man. He stood at the center of powerful alliances that could not afford to cut him if it were discovered that his father-in-law had misbehaved. Mr. Pagett was also publicly committed; Ana was probably safe. "You did it for yourself," she said. "There are no ends that justify these means." Her voice had turned ugly: tears clogged her throat. She would not shed them for him. She would not give him the satisfaction. "And *none* of this around you is owed to your theft. George did not love Sophie for the fine gowns she wore, or the ill-gotten funds you used to buy her combs. He fell in love with her for *her* sake. God help him, but it had *nothing* to do with you. Your excuses sicken me."

"No," he whispered. "Lydia, you are wrong. I *did* do it for you. And for Ana. I could not count on your marriages. I could not leave you unprovided for. There is an account set up for you—I never told you of it, but it troubled me greatly, the idea of what might happen to you after my death—"

"And for Egypt?" She drew a hiccupping breath. "I suppose you did it for Egypt, too."

He frowned. "Yes, I suppose."

"And for the papers you can publish. The *money* you can earn, so you can continue to make a name for yourself."

He drew back. "You think I do all this for fame? You think I spend years away from you, from your sisters, simply to purchase a little immortality? My project is above all that, Lydia. It is about the origins of *humanity*!"

She had no use anymore for such rhetoric. The details were what enraged her. "Years? *Years*, you spent away? Our whole lives, you've had no time for us! It was always Egypt that came first with you! When Mama was *dying*—" She caught herself. She heard how young she sounded, like a five-year-old in a tantrum. "Ana barely knows you," she said more quietly. "Do you know how often she asks whether you've written to her? And every time, I explain to her: His work is important. He's very busy. His cause is noble. But this?" Her voice rose again. "*This* is what you abandoned us for? Smuggling and thievery and profit?"

"Don't talk nonsense," he said sharply. "How can you doubt my dedication? *You* of all people! My God, have you lost all faith in me?"

Faith. She knew better than anyone what it was. More durable than any substance science had discovered—and when it shattered, more violent and cutting than glass. She would walk across its shards for the rest of her life. At every step, the pain would be with her.

She forced herself to look into his face. The brackets around his mouth had deepened in the past year. His brow had begun to sag over his eyes. Still, it was him.

Papa. She could not reconcile it, this dear, dear face, and the stranger within it. It seemed morbid to look upon him, like staring at a corpse that talked and walked just like the man she had adored. "Well, you can have your Tears," she said. "You can deliver them to Ashmore, and buy your freedom."

The surprise on his face—and then the dawning revelation, like a man hearing himself excused from the noose—nauseated her. His fingers tightened around hers, making her flinch: she had forgotten he had hold of her. "Bless you," he said hoarsely.

"Yes," she said bitterly, "what a good daughter I am. What a loyal little girl."

"You have saved us," he muttered. His eyes unfocused; he looked into the distance, dazed.

"Certainly angels are singing somewhere," she said. "But not over Egypt."

# Seventeen

At Wilton Crescent, the butler informed James that Lydia was not at home. He was deliberating whether to hand over his card or wait in the drawing room when Lydia appeared at the top of the stairs. "Wait," she called. At her first step toward him, he knew something was wrong. She moved stiffly, like an old woman, or a girl attempting cold, formal dignity. "I am glad you have come," she said when she reached him. "Unfortunately, you missed my father. He is gone to Whitehall. Otherwise I would have introduced you to the greatest thief in the empire."

Something in him turned over. He saw now that grief had etched lines around her mouth, and between her eyes. This was how she might look, thirty years from now. But not for this reason, pray God. "Lydia," he said, and reached out to her.

She let him hold her for a brief moment, and then pulled back, lifting her chin in an attempt to smile. "I don't want your pity. It's hard enough to know I deserve it."

"It's not pity you see in me." It was rage for Henry Boyce. "I could not pity you if I tried."

She swallowed. "I wish I could say the same of myself. I actually found the jewels, you see. They were in

Hartnett's shipment all along. But in the original shipping materials, not the crate Carnelly sent me."

He wanted to grab hold of her and carry her out of this goddamned house. But his instincts warned him to proceed cautiously. "I'm so sorry." Christ, but words were useless. The emotion sweltering within him was too large for syllables to contain.

She drew an unsteady breath. "I must figure out what to do now." Her eyes looked wet, and she turned away suddenly, making for the stairs. After a baffled moment, he followed. The first story was quiet; down the hall a door stood open. Her sitting room. At the threshold, it became clear that she had wrecked the place. Dozens of books lay scattered across the floor. A valise stood open on the carpet; she had been stuffing papers into it. Beyond, in the bedroom, a mess of clothes spilled off the bed.

She sank to her knees by the luggage and recommenced crushing the papers. "These are my articles," she said, and gave a strange laugh. "The last ones I will write, perhaps."

"Don't talk nonsense," he said evenly. "This was your father's sin. Not yours."

Her hands paused. "Sin. That's the right word for it. But is it really his alone? All I can think is what an *idiot* I am." Her face lifted. "It's a grand irony, isn't it? I fancied myself so smart. But he never meant any of it. And then I grow angry with *myself*, for surely—" She busied herself again with the papers. "Surely it is very selfish to feel so poorly when so many people are dead over the matter," she said rapidly. "Do you know how many people died at Alexandria? No, don't come closer"—he had stepped toward her; she gave her head a violent shake. "I am . . . too embarrassed, right now, for that. I have wronged you, too, you know. I preached at you like the most self-righteous, blind, *idiotic*—"

He did not think he could obey her. Everything in him was inclining toward her, like a sail caught by a breeze. "Lydia," he whispered. "It doesn't matter."

"Ha!" She came to her feet. "It *matters*," she said fiercely. "You called me naive, and you were right. Why, *you* nearly died for it. Had that boy in the music hall killed you—"

To hell with this. He stepped forward, ignoring her denial, her stumbling retreat. The spines of books cracked under his boots; pages ripped. It did not matter. He would buy her new ones. As he folded her against his chest, she whispered, "You have been good to me, James. So good." Her breath was warm against his neck. "But I feel as if—my skin is crawling. Shame, I suppose. I don't know what to think anymore. Of myself, as much as him. I don't know if I can . . . do this."

He pressed a smile into her hair. "When you came to me, I said much the same thing. You told me then that you had enough faith for both of us. I'll say the same to you, now."

"Perhaps I was wrong." He opened his eyes, and found her stubbornly staring at one of the battered books. "Maybe there is nothing so enduring as I'd hoped."

The words cut into him. His hands tightened around her arms. "You were not wrong."

"You have no idea—"

He set her away to peer into her face. "Remember whom you speak to. I have *every* idea what it is like to feel betrayed—fundamentally betrayed—by the man you love most in the world. I have lived with that feeling every day for the last four years. *Yes,* it burned me. And I thought it had destroyed my faith. My hope." He waited for her eyes to return to his. "You brought me awake. When you came to me, you made a promise. Whether you recognized it or not, it was *binding,* goddamnit. You are not going to turn away from me now."

A struggle played out in the small twitches of her mouth. "I will not," she whispered. "I keep my promises. But . . ."

"But you are afraid," he said flatly. "If your father could betray you, what hope I would not? You forget one thing, though: I am in love with you, Lydia. And whether or not the knowledge has managed to percolate up from your heart to your brain, you love me back."

For a moment she looked gratifyingly startled. And then, on her next breath, she frowned and said, "What of it?"

"What of it?" He laughed in disbelief. "I will tell you *what of it:* I would like to marry you. Good God! I should not be surprised that this is the way it happens. I want to share the rest of my life with you, Lydia. My bed, my thoughts, my properties—Christ, my bloody antiquities collections. You like the Lady of Winchester? You may have her. You may have all of it, if you please. Or if you like, you may smash a statue nightly, as the spirit moves you. I don't care; so long as you're down the hall, I'll be content."

As she stared at him, he could not, for his life, guess what moved through her brain. But when she spoke, her tone was despondent. "I have nothing to give you."

"Excellent, because I don't want anything from you but yourself. That is what love means, Lydia." He laughed again. "And now I sound like you. There's fun."

The volte-face did not amuse her. She turned away from him, and her head drooped, baring the graceful slope of her nape. "I did not tell you the worst part."

He put a hand to her shoulder to turn her back to him. Looking down into her face, into those sad, sloping eyes, made his own ache. "Say it, then."

She wiped her nose with the back of her hand. "I gave them to him. I gave him the Tears."

"Of course you did. What else were you to do?"

She squirmed out of his grip. "Don't you understand? He will get off scot-free. No harm to his name. I reckon I should be grateful. It will make my sisters' lives much easier." Her eyes were welling. "But there will be no justice for him. None!"

"Lydia, you had no choice."

"Of course I did! I claim to be a woman of principle? I could have returned them myself." She grimaced. "Let *him* see what it feels like to be betrayed."

"No," he said. "I *know* you. You cannot be the architect of his downfall—no matter how fitting it might seem to you right now."

"*You* are the one who is constantly raging on about hypocrisy." She gave a broken laugh. "Here was a chance to break the trend. How can you ever look at me with respect?"

"Easily. Did you not hear a word I just said? The bit about love, and all that?"

Her expression turned distant. "But perhaps love is

not worth your trust. Just look at my sister. It goes off, like milk."

"Ours would not."

"How can you know?"

"Because of you," he said. "Because when you believe in something, you fight for it. At any cost, you fight."

"And I have been made a fool for it," she muttered.

He considered her, frustrated. The right thing to say eluded him. She was in a black place, that much was clear. "I know you feel very dark right now, but the hurt will dull."

"It eats at me," she whispered.

"But not forever, Lyd. Eventually you will find it in yourself to forgive him—to love him for what he was to you, what he did for *you,* even if you loathe what he did to others. And I will be there the whole time. I'll help you through it."

He could not read the look she gave him. "I had never thought to hear such a thing from you," she said. "You, who have made your whole life into a vendetta against Moreland."

"I was wrong to do it," he said slowly. The odd smile she gave him in answer made him very uneasy. He did not know how to convince her. True, his words did not match his past actions, but—

Realization broke over him. He laughed softly. Brought low by his own terms. No wonder she could not have faith in him. "You're thinking me a terrible hypocrite, aren't you?"

"No," she said, but there was no conviction in her denial.

He came to a decision. "There are a few things I have to

do." He grinned at her alarmed expression. "But this discussion is hardly finished. I will call on you tomorrow."

"My father will be here," she said glumly, and turned away, back to her valise.

It was the hardest thing James had ever had to do. But he would do it for her. It was the only thing he could give her that she did not yet have of him.

His father sat behind the great desk in his study. Lemon wax and ink—that peculiar blend of smells conjured so many associations in his mind, all of them dark. As a child, he'd only been summoned here to receive punishment. Great thwapping cracks of a cane. The flat of his father's hand. Little infractions, James thought, the smallest things had won him beatings. A broken vase, knocked over during a game of chase. A spot on his suit. Failure to finish his supper.

Stella had been luckier. She had often crept in, against Moreland's orders, to tease and pet him. He had grumbled, but tolerated it. "The study is what separates us, James," she'd said once. "It was where I learned about love, and where you discovered resentment."

He watched Moreland struggle to his feet, reddening from the effort. And suddenly it came to him: the anvil would drop sooner than he'd imagined. Soon enough, this study would be his, and he would wipe it clean of the scent of lemon wax.

The thought should have gladdened him. But instead it dropped like a knife into some place deep within him, sealed until now, and released an overpowering wave of regret.

Things could not have been different between them. He saw his father—and himself—too clearly to indulge in that fantasy. They were too similar, both too stubborn, determined to cling to their principles, and, less honorably, to hold on to the wrongs done to them. God, he had nursed this hatred too long. At one time, it had powered him through life; he'd deceived himself into thinking it a noble cause, which lent his world a piquant edge. Now it had become a burden. He'd grown sick of it. It was tedious. If Stella did not require it, neither did he.

"Well?" Moreland barked the word. He was braced, his hands flat on his desk, expecting some harshness, some new hostility to battle. He was already mustering his own weapons: his knuckles were white with the force of his preparations.

James cleared his throat. He expected the words to be difficult to speak. But they emerged as though he had practiced them a hundred times. "I regret this," he said. "I regret that we cannot look at each other with anything save suspicion. I don't think we'll ever get past it. But you should know it does not gratify me any longer."

Moreland's brows drew together. Suspicion stamped every line of his face. "What nonsense is this?"

"The best kind. A little bit of honesty, unvarnished by courtesy. Dwyer will have told you that I went to see Stella."

"Of course he did. Against her express wishes, and my own, you would insist on having your way." With sudden heat, he added, "Damn you, James. You will leave her alone!"

"I will do," James said. "Now I have seen her." He sat down at the desk. The movement seemed to surprise Moreland; he gave a little snort and settled back into his own chair. When he stopped shifting and grew still—determined to stare James down; it was an old trick of his, best practiced on frightened eight-year-olds—James continued. "I understand a little better now why you are so content to wash your hands of her. It's a nice arrangement she has at Kenhurst. Quite a far cry from the other place. Of course, you knew that. And you knew I didn't. Pity, that you never bothered to reassure *me* of it."

Moreland cleared his throat. After a long moment, he said, "I don't need to make explanations to you."

It always came to this, didn't it? He guarded his sense of entitlement with such inflexible devotion. "I never asked you for anything," James said grimly. "But you could have told me all the same. Instead you let me wallow in my own imaginings." And he must have known exactly what visions James entertained of Kenhurst. They had gone together, after all, to visit Stella at the first place. Only by James's insistence had she been transferred at all. "But of course you wouldn't tell me. Not because it is *beneath* you to reassure your own son, but because it *pleased* you to have the upper hand over me—even in this. Christ, Moreland—even in my fears for my sister. And *that* is what makes you a proper bastard!"

Moreland's nostrils were flaring. "You are a fool," he said. "Do you think I've entertained a moment's concern for your fears? You, who make a willing wreck of your life—"

"Yes," James cut in. "I have made a willing wreck of

my life. You are right on that count. I have devoted my-self to the task, and told myself it was for her sake. That I would force you to regret your actions. To admit you had wronged us both with your bloody-mindedness, and ruined her life for the sake of your pride. But even after I realized it was hopeless—that you are too damned full of your own import to ever admit to a fail-ing—I continued. I continued in it solely to spite you." He laughed softly. "Such perverse bloody devotion, all dedicated to *you:* has any child ever been more faithful? Even Stella has forgiven you, but her expectations were always lower. She disregards your faults because she loves you. Myself, I consider the greatest fault here to be my own: I loathe your faults but love you despite them. I would not hate you so much, were it otherwise."

Moreland sat very still. "What game do you have in your brain now?"

"None." James studied him a long moment. "I am tired of this standoff. It *is* childish. I am willing to let go of it. We're never going to like each other. Certainly I will never understand why you encouraged Stella to go back to Boland. But I can believe that she wants to stay in that place now, and that you knew this, and that it has dictated your more recent actions." He shrugged. "That's a start, at least."

Moreland released a breath. "If I could go back in time," he said hoarsely, "I would refuse Boland's suit. But what came after? I could change nothing, James. Neither you nor I could do anything. She was stubborn and reckless and bent on trouble. She was a danger to herself. She must stay there, for now. You must not try to convince her otherwise."

"I have said I won't. But I want something from you."

"In exchange," Moreland said sourly. "I should have known it."

"No," James said. "Regardless, I will let her be. As to this—I suppose I am asking a favor."

Moreland grunted. "This will be good. What do you want?"

"A matter has come up. I need—" God, every ingrained reflex within him shrieked at using that word in his father's presence. He drew a hard breath. "I need you to act as a father to me."

In the ensuing silence, he wondered what went through Moreland's head. "What matter?" the earl asked. His voice was gruff. "I will make no agreement until I know specifics."

"Just what I said," James said. "I want you to play the part of a father. I want you to help me win the hand of the woman I would like to marry. In exchange, I can do no less than play the part of a son."

Lydia had never realized that deceit could be a noble aspect of love. As her family sat down to the dinner table—George and Sophie; Ana and Mr. Pagett; Papa, who could not meet her eyes, but who had come to her rooms this morning to tell her, haltingly, that Ashmore had made good on his promise—she held her tongue and smiled as if she meant it. Ana was full of light, radiant under the gaze of her beau. George was on his best behavior for Pagett, full of the wit that had once charmed her into foolishness. Sophie, for once, was enjoying Papa's full attentions. Her quick smiles and

flushing cheeks, her teasing remarks to him, made Lydia
a little sad. It seemed that Sophie *had* longed to walk
into storms to catch his attention. She simply hadn't
been able to bring herself to do so. *And it never occurred
to me to teach her.* Lydia regretted that, very much.

The realization was enough to keep her quiet, when
Papa lied so boldly about his day. He made no mention
of the interrogation he'd endured, and no sign of shame
marked his demeanor as he spoke of the khedive's affairs
and his chummy relationship with his colleagues in Cairo.

James claimed she would learn to love him even if
she could not respect him. But she doubted she would
ever manage to bring herself to do it, if this was how he
meant to go on.

Talk turned to honeymoon plans. Mr. Pagett had
proposed Greece as well as Italy, and Ana was by no
means averse. "And afterward," she said, laughing, "I
shall be so spoiled by the climate that I will refuse to
return to gloomy old England!"

"Indeed no," said Mr. Pagett, as he laid his hand atop
hers. "For your sister shall be waiting for our return."
His eyes turned to Lydia. "You will come live with us,
won't you, Miss Boyce? I think Lady Southerton would
be selfish to insist on keeping you to herself."

Ana smiled, and put her free hand atop his. "There
was a promise between us," she reminded Lydia. "I have
not broken it, so you mustn't either."

There was no resisting Ana's smile. No doubting it,
even now. Amidst its radiance, something within Lydia
began to thaw—just a little, just enough, to remind her
soul of the suggestion of warmth. "We'll see," she said
gently. "But I thank you for it."

"I should have some say in it," said Sophie. "Why was *I* not informed of this arrangement? Suppose"—here she paused briefly, as the butler entered the room and bent to whisper in George's ear—"suppose *I* should not like to live without a sister's company?"

George looked up. "Lydia," he said. "You have a visitor."

"At this hour?" Sophie frowned. "How odd. Tell them we are not receiving."

George hesitated. "Well, I would do, but it's Lord Moreland."

"Moreland? What on earth?"

The fear that filled her was of an order she'd never known. Had something happened to James? She bolted to her feet. "If you will excuse me," she said, and ran out.

In the doorway to the drawing room, trepidation brought her to a stop. "My lord," she said. "I—is he all right?"

The earl gave a grim little smile as he turned to face her. "Your astonishment matches mine," he said dryly. "Had someone told me ten days ago that I would be playing emissary for James, I should have called him God's greatest fool, and tossed him out on his ear."

Emissary. That did not sound as ominous as her fears. Bewildered, she stepped inside. But the other chairs were empty. "He did not come with you?" she asked hesitantly.

Moreland snorted. "That would have made sense, wouldn't it. So, no, of course he didn't. He directed me to speak to you on his behalf. I understand that he has addressed neither your father nor Lord Southerton, so I will admit I find the request somewhat harebrained. If it discomforts you, I will gladly ignore it."

Harebrained was one word for it. She could barely believe this. He had sent his father? *James* had sent *Moreland*?

And then realization swept through her, so rapid and momentous that she could barely keep track of her emotions. Amazement. Disbelief. The beginning of real hope—the first genuine moment of hope in what felt like a very long time. It took a long moment to recover her voice. She felt warm and giddy, as if she'd drunk a gallon of gin. "No," she said, and her voice broke on the syllable. "The viscount understands me quite well."

"Don't be so sure," Moreland said irritably. "He had another outlandish request for me." He reached into his jacket and extracted a bundle of papers, which he held out to her with a hand that shook a little.

Her own were similarly unsteady. She took the papers, and then, at his nod, untied the twine binding them together.

The first sheet held details of a journey: a steamer to New York. A train to Toronto, Canada. Beside the name of this city, written in a firm scrawl, was the annotation, *From there, God knows how we get across the continent to the Indians. But what do you say? A honeymoon in the land of rubbish.*

She folded her lips together, whether to keep from laughing or sobbing, she did not know. With fumbling hands, she flipped to the next piece of paper.

It was a special license.

Moreland had fastened her with an uncomfortably close regard. "Yes," he murmured. "Perhaps he does know you, then. Well, at any rate, I will have your answer, and then do the proper thing, and consult your father. I reckon it's James's place to do it, but so long as he's hiding like a green boy, I might as well see the thing through for him."

*Don't,* she almost said. *This is no concern of my father's.*

But instinct stopped her. The earl did not look at all at ease in his role. His shoulders were set in a stiff, fierce line, and his fingers twitched over the handle of his cane. No doubt James was equally uneasy, wherever he was lurking. He must feel he'd taken a great gamble, putting this task in his father's hands.

*My God.* The magnitude of his action fully dawned on her. He had gone to Moreland for her. He had forged some sort of reconciliation. *For her.* Had she asked for proof of love, he could not have done better.

She wanted him here, now, all at once, with a need that nearly crushed her. Her breath jerked in her throat. But she would not cry in front of the earl. From the look of him, the rapprochement had been fragile at best, and she did not think James would appreciate it if she gave Moreland unnecessary advantages.

The thought caused a wisp of sadness to intrude upon her wonder. *We will be rather alone,* she thought. She would not want her father at their wedding. And they would not be spending holidays at Moreland's house. Not for some time yet, at least.

But there was Ana. In a few years, perhaps Stella would be with them as well. And their own children, eventually. A new cycle, a new chance to make things right.

*Our children.*

She had stopped dreaming of it long ago. She

had known such things were not meant for her. But now she could not doubt it. Had he pulled down the moon for her, James could not have proven himself more effectively.

She put a hand over her mouth. It was necessary: her lips were useless in this state. She pressed on them, forcing the blood back into them, so they could firm enough to hold and shape words. "Where is he?"

Moreland snorted. "Cowering in his coach, no doubt."

"And *where is the coach*?"

His eyes widened. "Good God, Miss Boyce. Control yourself. Where else would it be, but on the curb?"

She flew out of the room. Down the hallway. Past the astonished porter, who was too slow for her. The doorlatch was ancient and stubborn; it wrestled against her slippery palms, but she would not let such trifling things stop her. Down the steps now, her skirts tripping her once; she grabbed them up in great handfuls as she raced past the gate.

He had been watching for her. He knew her better than she did. The door of the carriage began to open. But she knew him as well. He was not useless, in or outside this little world of Mayfair. And if he wanted to prove it, why, there was no better place than Canada to start doing so.

His arms caught her, and he pulled her up inside. "Cheers," he said with a grin. "Did you like my surprise?"

She clasped his cheeks. "You are impossible," she muttered, and pressed kisses over his face. "Sending your enemy to court me. Another lady might have taken offense."

His fingers hooked behind her ears, to direct her mouth to his. After a long, delicious moment of tangling tongues and clinging lips, he murmured, "We've made a truce of sorts. Did he not tell you? Old bastard."

She pulled back a little. "You must not expect me to do the same," she whispered. "Not yet, at least. It will take time."

His smile softened. "We have time," he said. "The rest of our lives. What do you say?"

She paused. Caution was such a hard habit to shake. "I did not know you had an interest in Canada."

He cleared his throat and spoke soberly. "I have always known exactly what awaits me here, Lyd. I saw my future very clearly—and I realized I did not like it. I saw *myself* clearly enough to fear that there was nowhere else with a use for me." His hand slid down her arm; his fingers found hers, twining through them and tightening. He smiled at her. "I can't say Canada was ever on my list. But when I factor you into my visions of the future, nothing seems clear to me but *you*. Darling, I hesitate to say that—I know you're a creature given to plans and objectives. But you must believe me when I tell you what it means to me. It means that possibilities have returned to my life." He lifted their linked hands to his mouth, pressing a kiss to her knuckle. "It means that *you* are my freedom, love."

"Yes," she whispered. That was it exactly. "And you are mine."

"I should hope so. I rise to meet your expectations, and you . . ." His smile turned devilish. "You sink to my level most beautifully. So—yes. I have a deep and passionate and *abiding* interest in Canada." His brow lifted. "So long as you do, of course."

"Yes!" She leaned forward to press her mouth to his. "Canada is lovely," she breathed against his lips. "And you are lovely."

His laughter ghosted into her mouth. "That's my line, Lyd. You are supposed to think me *handsome*."

"Yes, well," she said happily, "I'm not so conventional as I seem."

"Never say!" He reached up to rap the roof of the carriage.

As the vehicle abruptly started forward, she clutched onto him. Her balance required no aid, but she thought it only polite, when one's lover was regarding one with such intimate admiration, to behave like a lash-batting coquette. "And where are we going, sir?"

His grin was purely lascivious. "To anticipate the honeymoon, mademoiselle—unconventionally, and somewhere far outside Mayfair."

"Praise Canada," she murmured, and lay back along the bench, grabbing him by the shirtfront to pull him with her.

Please turn the page for an exciting excerpt
from Meredith Duran's next novel

*Written on Your Skin*

Coming soon from Pocket Books

Trouble walked in around midnight. She was swaying on her feet from too much champagne, and had a man on each arm, though neither seemed to interest her much. Phin was leaning against the wall, nursing a glass of brandy and the beginning of a headache. He watched as her eyes skimmed the crowd. The line of red paper lanterns strung across the threshold shed a bloody light over her white-blond hair. When she spotted him, she smiled.

*Loose ends,* he thought blackly. A man could hang himself with them.

He handed off the brandy to a passing servant, a Chinese girl with a face as round as the moon. She balanced the tray high on her fingertips as she moved toward the exit, and he found his eyes following the glass, envying the way it coasted over the heads of the guests. A neat escape. Christ, he wanted out of Hong Kong. Every society luminary was in attendance tonight, save the governor and the American consul. As soon as he'd remarked their absence, he'd known the arrest was imminent. His job here was done, no reason to linger. But Ridland had forbidden him to sail until tomorrow evening. The man was out to prove something to him. *What matters is the results, Granville. Take some pride in your work: you've a goddamned talent.*

Pride, Phin mused. He wondered if a dog took pride in heeling to his master. The chain at his throat was tight enough that he saw no need to learn to like it; it would tighten or loosen at Ridland's direction, whether or not he saw fit to lick the man's hand. And if results were all that mattered, he should be gone by now. It was not his business to watch the consequences unfold.

He glanced across the room. Miss Masters was coming straight for him, maneuvering boldly through couples who twirled like puppets to the musicians' bidding. His brief flirtation with her had turned into a grave mistake. In the end, he hadn't required her. Limit complications: that was his policy. Alas, he had started to realize that his policy was the problem. Miss Masters was not accustomed to being abandoned by her erstwhile suitors, and the novelty seemed to intrigue her.

As he watched, the girl's advance overwhelmed her companions. First one, and then the other, was knocked away by collisions with waltzing pairs. She seemed to take no notice of their loss. That obliviousness had probably served her well, till now. With Gerard Collins for a stepfather, she would not benefit from too much insight. The things she might learn would have troubled her beauty sleep.

But the clueless featherbrain was about to awaken into a strange new world. Once Collins was in custody, her admirers would scatter like rats from a corpse. Her mother would probably try to throw herself out a window. Both women would learn, very quickly, what it felt like to have one's choices stripped away. He saw no good outcome for them; the mother's family did not speak to her, and neither of them had a marketable skill. Their beauty would sell, of course, but it would not survive a few rough handlings.

The thoughts darkened Phin's mood beyond repair. A veal calf in yoke, worrying for two lambs led to slaughter: it made for little more than a very bad joke. The women were not his concern, and flogging himself for what he could not prevent would profit neither them nor him. He turned and walked out.

Laughter and squeals swarmed the front hall; he shouldered without caution through careless elbows and dark-suited shoulders, making for a darkened corridor where lamps flickered dimly in windows left open to the humid breeze. Hong Kong was glossy and green, fragrant with flowers after the evening storm; the whole damned city smelled like a debutante. The Europeans and Americans lived very comfortably here. Collins's downfall was going to set them all on their ears.

"Mr. Monroe!"

She had followed him? Phin turned. She paused a few feet away, beneath an archway of red and black tiles; how she'd moved so quickly in that gown, he had no idea. It was tight and narrow, deeply bustled at the back, a sky blue silk that was probably meant to match her eyes. A mistake, in his opinion. Her eyes were such an unlikely hue that they really needed no complement. Paired with the silk, they took on a brilliance that seemed almost outré. He could see why Hong Kong disagreed on the question of her beauty; her coloring did border on the freakish.

"Good evening," he said to her.

"Mr. Monroe," she repeated, stepping forward. Her voice was breathless and distinctly triumphant, as if his name were the answer to a puzzle that had vexed her for some time. A drop of sweat curled down the delicate line of her collarbone; its progress riveted him. He had no idea why his body had the bad taste to be fascinated by hers. She looked breakable, and he was not a small man. "How does the evening treat you?" she asked. "Surely you don't mean to retire so soon?"

He mustered a smile. She played to her looks, no doubt of it. In private, when she thought no one was about, she spoke to that maid of hers, the sly-looking brunette with the skinny elbows and big ears, in a much lower register. He rather liked the maid; she did not bother to laugh when her mistress did, which either demonstrated character or rapidly thinning patience. "It treats me very well," he said. "And no, I was only going to fetch something from my rooms." He paused, giving her an opportunity to excuse herself. Of course, she did not take it. "And you, Miss Masters?" He very much hoped the maid stayed with her, when the time came that she required good counsel. "You looked to be enjoying yourself."

"Oh, thank you very much! I *was* enjoying myself. Happy as a clam at high water. But as I was telling my English friends . . . " She glanced over her shoulder, as if only now realizing that she'd left them behind in the ballroom. In the process of facing him again, she somehow managed to trip. The little hop she made in recovery brought her stumbling into his chest.

He caught her by the forearms. She smelled like a distillery, and as her eyes widened, they caught him like a fist in the gut. Such an odd shade. He would not argue with her beauty, but he preferred a woman to look like one. With her white-blond hair and huge eyes and petite figure, Miss Masters more closely resembled a porcelain doll. Alas that she could not behave like one. Dolls were mute; she chattered incessantly. He knew a way to silence that mouth.

*Christ.* The girl made his brain misfire. He set her away from him more forcefully than the instance required. "Have a care," he said.

She arched a silvery brow. "A care for what?"

*For falling on men in darkened hallways.* "For your balance. Trip in front of company, and people might decide you're intoxicated."

"Oh, dear." Her lashes batted. "Is that not allowed?"

He sighed. Even had circumstances not conspired against her, she would have managed to ruin herself eventually. Her little society world was perfumed and creamy, but it had its rules, and she grew increasingly rash in breaking them. "I don't think there's a law against it, no." His mouth had gone very dry; he paused to clear his throat. Good God, this headache was unwanted. Her glance flickered up, and he realized he was rubbing his temple. Come to think of it, the headache had something in common with her: they both grew more irksome by the moment. What had he been saying? Ah, yes. "But you wouldn't want others to think you intemperate by nature."

The officiousness of his tone belatedly struck him. She had a knack for inciting such asinine behavior. She was artless in the way of children or puppies; watching her, one found oneself braced for an accident. Puppies got stepped on; children fell from windowsills; Miss Masters was dancing at the edge of a cliff, and no one—not her wan, withdrawn mother nor even her tyrannical bastard of a stepfather—cared to leash her.

She was protesting. "But that is so unfair, Mr. Monroe! I drink nothing but champagne, which is very respectable indeed. And if I've had a bit too much—why, then it's only to anesthetize my boredom with the company!"

He laughed despite himself. Occasionally he came very near to convinced that she was having everyone on with this featherbrained routine. Certainly from another woman, the remark would have served a masterful set-down to his pomposity.

But no, she smiled along with him, sunny and vacant, ignorant of her own success as a wit. "Unless you propose to entertain me?" she added. As her eyes dropped to his mouth, his laughter died. She had better watch out. "Oh," she said softly, "Mr. Monroe—you have such lovely lips."

And then she launched herself at him.

He was too surprised to resist, at first. She was forward, yes, but he hadn't expected a seduction. Not that this *was* seduction, precisely—she grabbed his hair and pulled his head down with all the subtlety of a crank, and her lips banged into his so forcefully that he anticipated the taste of blood. He pulled back in simple self-preservation and she followed him, her breasts pressing hot and soft into his chest. The small, breathless noise that burst from her lips bypassed his brain and went straight to his balls.

*No, no, no.* He was not going to kiss her back. She was a reckless, scatterbrained child, and if he dreamed of her, it was only from boredom.

She opened her mouth and he felt the wetness of her tongue. He took her by the elbows, intending to push her away, but her skin, so astonishingly soft, scattered his intentions. He stroked his thumb down her arm, just to make sure that he wasn't mistaken, that it really was as smooth as his midnight thoughts had suggested. She moaned encouragement into his lips. God save him, but no doll had ever made such a noise. And she was twenty, not a girl.

*To hell with it.* His mouth opened on hers. She tasted of champagne and strawberries. Her small body, so sweetly curved, pressed against his. The top of his head seemed to lift off. Sweeter, so much sweeter than he had even expected; she was sinuous as a flame, writhing against him. Her hands pressed into his shoulders, persuading him to step back, against the wall. She needed a lesson in subtlety; she needed to be taught some truths about the world, quickly, before the morrow came. He would be glad to teach them. It would be a favor to her . . .

*What the hell was he doing?*

He thrust her away, breathing hard.

She stumbled backward, and his idiotic hands reached out to catch her; he balled them into fists and made himself watch. But she caught her balance against the opposite wall, her breasts rising and falling rapidly, her eyes wide. "Dance with me, Mr. Monroe?"

Good God. He ran a hand over his face, up into his hair. She had no sense whatsoever. That, or rejection was simply unfathomable to her. He wanted to reach for some remark that would recall her to propriety, assuming she even knew the meaning of the word. But his body mocked him and his brain felt like sludge. He settled for, "I beg your pardon?"

"My friends from England were complaining of how poorly Americans dance." She reached up to finger one of the diamond teardrops dangling from her ear. She had recovered herself now; her manner was perfectly casual, as if she hadn't just given him a taste of her tongue. "I simply cannot agree with them. *I* dance very well, and I feel sure you do, too. Shan't we prove it? For America, Mr. Monroe!"

Perhaps he *was* wrong to underestimate her. Certainly, to his continued astonishment, he was a damned fool to overestimate himself. "I don't think that would be wise."

She frowned. "Why not? Because I kissed you?"

He glanced down the hallway. "Precisely, Miss Masters." At this rate, someone was going to catch them sequestered together in the darkness. That was the last thing he needed. Maybe a bit of plain speaking would serve where manners had not. "Unless you have a burning desire to be fucked against a wall."

The image those words conjured made his own voice hoarsen, but the language did not even seem to register on her. "Well, I would never wish to do such a thing in a *ballroom*," she said, and took his arm.

He should have used some more genteel word; it was clear that she hadn't taken his meaning. Or maybe she'd taken his meaning all too well, for her grip was strong, as though the last shred of maidenly decorum had abandoned her. Either way, she was a force of chaos, and her insanity, as he'd been learning for three weeks now, was contagious; he was letting her tow him down the corridor toward the ballroom. He felt thoroughly light-headed.

A dance, then. Simple enough. He could keep his hands to himself for one dance, even if he had to bite off his tongue to distract himself. And it wasn't as if he actually had anything to fetch from his rooms. God knew if he tried to act on the pretense, she'd probably follow him into his bed.

The music came spilling out to greet them, much louder than it had been before. Aggressively loud, in fact. He found himself flinching from the clamor as she drew him inside. The current set was concluding. She said something, but he could not make it out. Why was he humoring her? His head ached. She was needless temptation, pretty flesh wrapped around a brain filled with air; there was nothing in her for him but a whole lot of trouble.

The dancers were parting ways. The next set was soon to begin. She turned to him expectantly. When he did not immediately extend his hand, she reached for it. He realized something was wrong when he couldn't feel her fingers.

He drew a breath, and the floor rocked beneath his feet.

He staggered backward, dimly registering a collision. A cry. The world disassembled, then swam back together. Miss Masters was mouthing something. It felt like twin screws were being forced into his temples. God in heaven. Was this some new variation on malaria?

The girl's face grew very large. Leaning toward him, that was all. He struggled to focus. Her visage faded in and out. God, he was cold. "Are you all right?" That was what she was asking.

As the darkness washed over him again, he realized the answer. Malaria did not strike so suddenly. The image of the brandy flashed through his mind, gliding away from him, its contents sloshing. Half-full. Only half. "No," he managed. He was not all right.

He'd been poisoned.

# *True love*
## is timeless with
## historical romances from
## Pocket Books!

A Malory novel

**Johanna Lindsey**

# NO CHOICE BUT SEDUCTION

He'd stop at nothing to make her love him.
But should she surrender to his bold charms?

**Liz Carlyle**

# *Tempted All Night*

When deception meets desire, even the most
careful lady can be swayed by a scoundrel....

**Julia London**

# HIGHLAND SCANDAL

Which is a London rakehell more likely to survive—
a hanging, or a handfasting to a spirited Highland lass?

**Jane Feather**

# A HUSBAND'S WICKED WAYS

When a spymaster proposes marriage as a cover,
a lovely young woman discovers the danger—and
delight—of risking everything for love.

Available wherever books are sold or at www.simonandschuster.com

POCKET BOOKS
A Division of Simon & Schuster
A CBS COMPANY

POCKET STAR BOOKS
A Division of Simon & Schuster
A CBS COMPANY

20472